PRAISE FOR TONY HILLERMAN AND HIS MOST RECENT NOVEL, *SACRED CLOWNS*

"This is Hillerman at his best, mixing human nature, ethnicity and the overpowering physical presence of the Southwest." —*Newsweek*

"There has never been anything ordinary about Hillerman's crisply plotted, magically evocative tales. . . . Mingling taut, deceptively simple prose with shrewd psychological insight and a scholar's understanding of Navajo culture and religion."
—*Entertainment Weekly*

"The long wait for Tony Hillerman's new novel was worth it. . . . Rich in understanding of the hard life on Indian reservations and taut with murder-mystery suspense . . . Penetrating insight that shines well above most of the detective genre."
—*San Antonio Express*

"[Hillerman's] clowns are . . . every bit as raucous, profane and funny as Shakespeare's."
—*The New York Times Book Review*

"How long can Tony Hillerman keep it up? *Sacred Clowns* is as good as anything he's done—as flavorful as beef jerky, so evocative of the land around the Four Corners area of New Mexico that even if you've never been there, you'll think you have." —*Chicago Tribune*

"Steeped in Navajo lore and traditions . . .The resolutions—personal and professional—ring true with gratifying inevitability."   —*Publishers Weekly*

"[Hillerman's] affection for his characters—and for the real world in which they live and work—has never been more appealingly demonstrated."
                              —*Los Angeles Times Book Review*

"A well-braided, spell-binding yarn . . . Mr. Hillerman's novels inject fresh urgency to the age-old question about good and evil. . . . [Hillerman] is at the top of his form."   —*Baltimore Morning Sun*

"Hillerman's writing is like the landscape he describes, unadorned yet profound, sparse yet beautiful."   —*Houston Chronicle*

"Another good Hillerman read."
                              —*The Independent* (Gallup, NM)

"*Sacred Clowns* continues Hillerman's unbroken string of excellent characters and plots. . . . Delve[s] into the complexities of the human soul . . . Prepare yourself for a thoroughly satisfying read."
                              —*Oklahoman*

"Not only a masterful novel in its own right, but an object lesson in how to develop an outstanding series."   —*Kirkus Reviews*

THE TONY HILLERMAN COMPANION

A COMPREHENSIVE GUIDE TO HIS LIFE AND WORK

Edited by Martin Greenberg

HarperPaperbacks
A Division of HarperCollins*Publishers*

"The Detective Fiction of Tony Hillerman" © 1994 by
    Jon L. Breen.
"Interview with Tony Hillerman" © 1994 by Jon L. Breen.
"Navajo Nation" by George Hardeen. Copyright © 1991 by
    APA Publications. Reprinted from *Insight Guide: Native
    America* by permission of APA Publications.
"Native American Clans in Tony Hillerman's Fiction: A
    Guide" © 1994 by Elizabeth A. Gaines and Diane Hammer.
"Characters in Tony Hillerman's Fiction: A Concordance"
    © 1994 by Elizabeth A. Gaines and Diane Hammer.
"The Witch, Yazzie, and the Nine of Clubs" © 1981
    by The Swedish Academy of Detection.
"First Lead Gasser" © 1993 by Tony Hillerman.
"Chee's Witch" © 1986 by Tony Hillerman.
Map is reprinted by permission of Weldon Owen Pty Limited.

HarperPaperbacks   *A Division of* HarperCollins*Publishers*
              10 East 53rd Street, New York, N.Y. 10022

A hardcover edition of this book was published in 1994
by HarperCollins*Publishers*

Cover illustration by Peter Thorpe

First HarperPaperbacks printing: May 1995

Printed in the United States of America

HarperPaperbacks and colophon are trademarks of
HarperCollins*Publishers*

❖ 10 9 8 7 6 5 4 3 2 1

CONTENTS

A HILLERMAN CHRONOLOGY

1925   Born in Sacred Heart, Oklahoma, a village near a Benedictine mission to the Citizen Band Potawatomie Tribe in Indian Territory. Son of Lucy Grove and August A. Hillerman, storekeeper/farmer.

1930–38   With older brother and sister, attended St. Mary's Academy, one of several farm boys enrolled in boarding school for Indian girls at Sacred Heart.

1939–42   School bus to Konawa High School.

1941   Father dies after lengthy illness.

1942   Enrolls in Oklahoma A&M College, works as dishwasher, dentist's housekeeper, irrigation project ditchdigger. Survives semester. Brother joins Army. He returns to farming.

1943   Enlists in U.S. Army. C Company, 410th Infantry. Twice gains rank of Private First Class. Receives Silver Star and Bronze Star with Oak Leaf Cluster.

1945   Wounded, gaining Purple Heart, broken legs, foot, ankle, facial burns, temporary blindness and a trip back to the U.S. Makes his first telephone call.

1945   On convalescent furlough, hauls oil field equipment to the Navajo Reservation. Observes part of a curing ceremonial for Navajo Marines.

1946–48   Attends Oklahoma University, marries Marie Unzner.

1948–62   Police reporter, political writer, editor in Texas, Oklahoma, and New Mexico. He and Marie accumulate five children.

1963   Enrolls as graduate student, University of New Mexico, with part-time job as handyman for the President's office. Sixth child attained.

1966–87   On UNM journalism faculty. Begins writing fiction in the late '60s.

1987   "Special Friend of the Dineh" status awarded by the Navajo Nation. Wins Golden Spur of the Western Writers of America for the Best Novel set in the West for *Skinwalkers*.

1990   Receives National Media Award of the American Anthropological Association and the Public Service Award of the U. S. Department of the Interior.

1991   Receives Mystery Writers of America Grandmaster Award.

Please see "The Detective Fiction of Tony Hillerman" on pp. 1–62 for publication dates of Hillerman's novels.

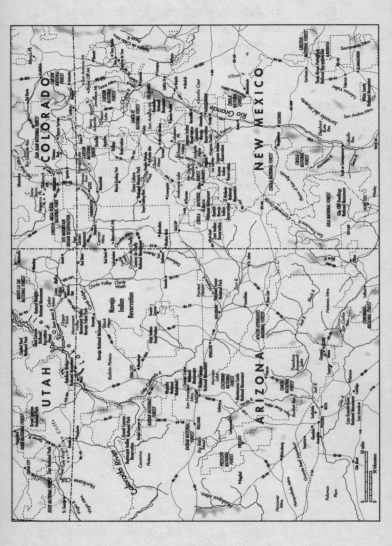

1

THE DETECTIVE FICTION OF TONY HILLERMAN

A BOOK-BY-BOOK GUIDE

Jon L. Breen

Jon L. Breen is one of the world's leading mystery critics. He has won two Edgar Allan Poe awards from the Mystery Writers of America, for What About Murder? *(1981) and for his excellent study of legal novels,* Novel Verdicts *(1984). In addition, his coedited* Synod of Sleuths, *a collection of essays on clerical detectives, won the Anthony Boucher award as the best critical/ biographical work in 1990. Hundreds of thousands of mystery readers rely on his reviews in* Ellery Queen's Mystery Magazine *each month, small gems that represent literary criticism at its finest. And if all this isn't enough to keep three people busy, he is also the author of six notable mystery novels, most recently* Hot Air *(1991).*

Long an admirer of Tony Hillerman's books, he jumped at the chance to write a detailed overview of Hillerman's work and conduct the interview that follows it.

The real innovators in mystery and detective fiction—and probably in literature generally—are seldom recognized as such immediately. There is no evidence to suggest Edgar Allan Poe, for example, was greeted with instant acclaim when he invented the whole genre in "The Murders in the Rue Morgue" or that Arthur Conan Doyle's cheaply sold novella *A Study in Scarlet* turned the literary world of 1887 on its ear with the debut of fiction's most famous consulting detective. Today, Marcia Muller is widely regarded as the pioneer of the realistic female private eye novel, yet when her first Sharon McCone case, *Edwin of the Iron Shoes*, was published in 1977, introducing such a character seemed a natural progression and created no great splash—indeed, it was five years before the second McCone novel was published. (The catch was that previous attempts at the female private eye, at least in book length, had almost all been made by well-meaning but underqualified men.) Ed McBain (Evan Hunter) has so defined the police procedural in his 87th Precinct novels, he is sometimes mistakenly credited with inventing the genre. But when *Cop Hater* appeared in 1956, the genre trappings were already familiar: the form was merely waiting for its Shakespeare.

Similarly, the first novel by Tony Hillerman, *The Blessing Way* (1970), for all its favorable reception by the critics, seems a much larger achievement in retrospect than it did at the time. Casting an American Indian (or, in current parlance, Native American) in the role of sleuth seemed such an obvious idea, surely it had been done many times before. But had it?

The results of *Ellery Queen's Mystery Magazine*'s first annual short-story contest were announced in its April 1946 issue. The list of second-, third-, and fourth-prize winners includes some prestigious names, among them William Faulkner, T. S. Stribling, Ngaio Marsh, Michael Innes, and Kenneth Millar (later to be better known as Ross Macdonald). The winner of the $2,000 first prize (five decades later still a handsome price for a short story) was Manly Wade Wellman with "A Star for a Warrior," for which editor Ellery Queen (Frederic Dannay) made heavy claims:

> It introduces not only a new detective character but a new *type* of detective character; and it places this new type of detective against a background hitherto unexplored in the field of crime fiction. . . . David Return . . . is a full-blooded American Indian—a young brave of the Tsichah, an imaginary tribe based mostly on the Cheyennes and partly on the Pawnees. Don't misunderstand: Mr. Wellman has not created another Leatherstocking; his David Return is not a J. Fenimore Cooper character detecting only by footprints and broken twigs in the forest primeval. "A Star for a Warrior" is a story of today—of modern American Indians; young David is government-trained, an agency policeman whose beat is the Indian reservation. . . . Faced with a murder case, David Return investigates not as a white man but as an Indian steeped in Red Man lore; and his deductions arise out of deep understanding of Indian char-

> acter, tradition, and ceremonials. David Return
> is the first *truly American* detective to appear in
> print—even more authentically American than
> Melville Davisson Post's Uncle Abner.[1]

Politically incorrect language aside, editor
Queen's description of David Return could apply
just as well to Joe Leaphorn and Jim Chee. But
David Return never was given a book-length case,
his only other appearance coming in the short story
"A Knife Between Brothers" (*EQMM*, February 1947).
His creator went on to a distinguished writing
career, mostly associated with fantasy, science fiction, and true crime.

If the encyclopedic Queen thought David
Return was unique to that point in the history of
detective fiction, I am prepared to take his word for it.
But what about the years since? Surely some writer
would have taken up the mantle of David Return and
created an authentic Native American sleuth. If so, I
can't find him or her. Undoubtedly knowledgeable
students of the form can dredge up any number of fictional detectives with some kind of Native American
blood in their veins, but finding ones who operated in
a distinctively Native American milieu and served as
a window into that culture is much more difficult, if
not impossible.

Thus it fell to Anthony Grove Hillerman, born
in 1925 in Sacred Heart, Oklahoma, a man who
grew up poor with Indians as close boyhood
friends, who was a decorated and wounded veteran
of World War II, who pursued a successful career as
journalist and academic before turning to the writing of novels, to realize the full potential of Manly
Wade Wellman's innovation, and the mystery genre

1. Ellery Queen, "The Prize Winners in *EQMM*'s First Contest,"
Ellery Queen's Mystery Magazine, April 1946, 6–7.

and millions of readers (including many who are not otherwise mystery buffs) have been enriched by his achievement. His direct influence was not Wellman but Arthur W. Upfield, whose tales of the Australian outback brought the same kind of sympathetic view of Aborigine culture that Hillerman would focus on the world of the Navajo.

The following survey will provide an idea of the plots, characters, and themes of Hillerman's novels—while refraining as much as possible from giving away any of their secrets—and will quote portions to give the flavor of Hillerman's approach and sample his philosophical and cultural observations.[2]

The Blessing Way (1970)

From the first chapter, *The Blessing Way* plunges the reader into the background Hillerman was to make his own. Luis Horseman, a young Navajo hiding from the police, stands on a plateau overlooking the Kam Bimghi Valley and sings traditional chants to attract game—kangaroo rats and prairie dogs—while using a porcupine's flesh for food, its blood and fat for bait, and its stomach sac for a canteen. As the chapter ends, Horseman encounters a Navajo Wolf—a man in an animal skin—and we last see him at the beginning of the second chapter praying for protection and wishing "he had listened when his uncle had taught him to talk to the Holy People" (page 11).

2. Page references for quotations from *The Blessing Way, Dance Hall of the Dead*, and *Listening Woman* are to the omnibus *The Joe Leaphorn Mysteries* (Harper & Row, 1989). References for *The Ghostway* are to the first trade edition (Harper & Row, 1985). Page references to all other novels are to the first editions, all published by Harper & Row or, in the case of *Sacred Clowns*, its successor, HarperCollins.

THE DETECTIVE FICTION OF TONY HILLERMAN

We next meet two old school friends: Navajo Tribal Police Lieutenant Joe Leaphorn, plowing through his paperwork in the Law and Order Building at Window Rock, and University of New Mexico anthropology professor Bergen McKee, drinking and neglecting final exam papers in Albuquerque while contemplating a return to the reservation to continue his studies of Navajo witchcraft. McKee receives a letter from Leaphorn, his former classmate at Arizona State, commenting on the quality of witchcraft rumors that summer. The two friends differ on the Wolf superstition: to McKee, it is a "simple scapegoat procedure, giving a primitive people a necessary outlet for blame in times of trouble and frustration," while according to Leaphorn "there was a basis of truth in the Navajo Origin Myth, that some people did deliberately turn antisocial, away from the golden mean of nature, deliberately choose the unnatural and therefore, in Navajo belief, the evil way" (page 17).

Jeremy Canfield, a colleague of McKee who plans to accompany him, introduces another reason to visit: the daughter of a friend, Ellen Leon, wants to locate her fiancé, Jimmy W. Hall, a Ph.D. in electrical engineering who is driving a light green van and testing equipment somewhere on the reservation.

Leaphorn, who is after Luis Horseman for a knife attack on a Mexican in a Gallup bar, visits Shoemaker's Trading Post with McKee. While the professor gathers witchcraft rumors, Leaphorn is trying to get word to Horseman that the victim has recovered, in the hope Horseman will either turn himself in or get careless enough to be caught. But Horseman's body is found near Teastah Wash by Joseph Begay, whose discovery is preceded by an owl's nearly running into the windshield of his pickup truck. The owl is a form frequently taken

7

by ghosts in Navajo legend, and the reference will recur throughout Hillerman's work.

Leaphorn and McKee go to look at Horseman's body with coroner Rudolph Bitsi. The fact that no tracks lead to the body except for those of Begay's pickup indicates the man died before the start of the recent rains. Other physical evidence tells Leaphorn the body was placed where it was found when already dead. But why was it left where it would obviously be found instead of in the wash where it would be buried forever? The autopsy report shows the cause of death was suffocation, as if Horseman had been caught in a cave-in or buried in sand, but there is no sand in his cuffs or pockets.

"Why kill somebody like Horseman?" Leaphorn muses. "Just another poor soul who didn't quite know how to be a Navajo and couldn't learn to act like a white. No good for anything" (page 46). One possible motive is suggested: a $10,000 reward offered to anyone who finds a misfired rocket on its way from the Tonepah test site in Utah to White Sands Proving Grounds in New Mexico. Could Horseman have found the rocket and fought with someone over the potential reward?

For most of the rest of the book, Leaphorn and McKee go their separate ways. Leaphorn questions Sandoval, a Singer doing an Enemy Way to cast out witches from Charlie Tsosie, a ceremony described in effective detail in chapter 10. McKee finds his partner Canfield has left their camp, leaving behind a note signed with the wrong first name. Following this discovery, McKee has his own visitation from a man in a wolfskin.

Ellen Leon turns up in McKee's camp, and the pair of them are stalked and finally captured by the character known for most of the book as the Big Navajo. He is Leaphorn's main witchcraft suspect, his hat having been used in the Enemy Way ceremony as an object of exorcism. The Big Navajo wants to force McKee to write a letter to his department head before killing him. Only McKee's injured right hand delays his execution.

Meanwhile, Leaphorn, convinced the Big Navajo killed Luis Horseman, follows the tracks of his Land Rover to trace his movements. His abilities as a tracker are in the tradition of James Fenimore Cooper's characters as well as Arthur W. Upfield's half-Aboriginal inspector, Napoleon Bonaparte. Leaphorn's thoughts on the killing of one Navajo by another say much about his culture:

> Why did Navajos kill? Not as lightly as white men, because the Navajo Way made life the ultimate value and death unrelieved terror. Usually the motive for homicide on the Reservation was simple. Anger, or fear, or a mixture of both. Or a mixture of one with alcohol. Navajos did not kill with cold-blooded premeditation. Nor did they kill for profit. To do so violated the scale of values of The People. Beyond meeting simple immediate needs, the Navajo Way placed little worth on property. In fact, being richer than one's clansmen carried with it a social stigma. It was unnatural, and therefore suspicious. (page 133)

Why, then, was a man who was clearly a Navajo committing such a seemingly un-Navajo-like crime? In the end, this is explained quite understandably: the culprit is a Relocation Navajo, the product of a failed experiment in moving Navajo families to urban areas.

Early in the story, McKee and Leaphorn are almost coequal protagonists. As the story winds toward its climax, however, the focus shifts almost entirely to McKee. He and Ellen Leon are held captive in an Anasazi cliff dwelling. Leaphorn's function is to come to the rescue, but not before McKee has accomplished some heroism, surprising from a jaded, burnt-out college professor.

A traditional detective-story scene concludes the book. Leaphorn visits McKee in the hospital and ties up the loose ends of the mystery. The easy bantering relationship of the two old school friends is nicely handled. Says Leaphorn of McKee's extensive transfusions, "You've got more Navajo blood in you now than I do" (page 166). When Leaphorn second-guesses McKee's unnecessarily dramatic escape attempt, the professor counters, "How was I going to know you'd be wandering around out there? . . . It's supposed to be the cavalry that arrives in the nick of time, not the blanket-ass Indians" (page 167).

The Blessing Way was well reviewed. Among the early reviewers, Allen J. Hubin, writing in the *New York Times Book Review*,[3] was especially insightful, noting the similarity to Upfield's works and pointing to Leaphorn as a more interesting character than McKee. The novel was a nominee for the Best First Mystery Novel Edgar award by the Mystery Writers of America. It lost out to the debut of another perennial best-selling novelist, *The Anderson Tapes* by Lawrence Sanders, which Hillerman himself has said is a better book. *The Blessing Way* is undoubtedly a commendable first mystery, certainly not as good as the Hillerman novels to follow but just as surely not as bad as the comments Ernie Bulow and Hillerman himself suggest in *Talking Mysteries*.

Bulow called the book "a terrible disappointment. . . . The ethnography . . . was shaky, though some things were only slightly off center. It was

---

3. Allen J. Hubin, Review of *The Blessing Way*, *New York Times Book Review*, 19 April 1970, pp. 36–37.

something like reading a student paper with a lot of vocabulary freshly minted from a thesaurus. The definitions might be technically right—by the dictionary—but the usage wasn't quite in register." He also found that the mystery, "so absorbing and suspenseful as it unfolded, petered out with a lame denouement." In a footnote, Hillerman mildly disputes some of Bulow's ethnological arguments but shares his low opinion of the novel: "I like some parts of it, but a lot of it makes me flinch."[4]

Although the plot of *The Blessing Way* is better worked out than Bulow suggests, it is less satisfying as a mystery puzzle than the books to follow, providing no real surprises in the revelation of the villains and only a rather vague idea of what they were up to. The action parts are done efficiently enough, but they pale next to the almost Cornell Woolrich–like scenes of menace to come in Hillerman's second novel. The character of McKee may have seemed a necessary focal point for the novel's mostly Anglo readers, but from the start Leaphorn is indeed the more interesting character. In fact, as Hillerman notes in the interview that forms the next section of this volume, McKee was even more central in early drafts of the novel, and Leaphorn's role grew. In subsequent books, Leaphorn—and later Chee—are wisely given center stage without the need for white co-stars. McKee's implied romance with Ellen Leon seems a formulaic device. In *The Blessing Way*, it is the Navajo background that gives the book most of its special interest. One wonders what would have been left if Hillerman had followed his one-time (anonymous)

4. Tony Hillerman and Ernie Bulow, *Talking Mysteries: A Conversation with Tony Hillerman* (Albuquerque: University of New Mexico Press, 1991), pp. 13, 14, 17.

agent's notorious advice to "get rid of all the Indian stuff." If Hillerman had written only *The Blessing Way*, it would still be remembered as a unique and meritorious work.

The Fly on the Wall (1971)

Hillerman's second mystery novel is the only one not to feature the Navajo Tribal Police. In *The Fly on the Wall*, he draws on his experience as a journalist to create political reporter John Cotton, who does a regular column from the capital city of an unidentified midwestern state. There is still a New Mexico connection, however: Cotton is from that state and longs to return. He does, in fact, go back briefly, but it proves an unhappy occasion.

The opening chapter finds Cotton sitting in the capitol pressroom at work on his column, allowing him a chance to sketch the political climate of the state for the reader. Governor Paul Roark is considering a run for the Senate against incumbent Eugene Clark. His campaign is seen by Clark's friends as "a last-gasp effort of the once-dominant liberal-labor-populist-small-farmer coalition to retain its slipping control over the Democratic party machinery" (page 2). Among the friends pushing Roark to run is National Committeeman Joseph Korolenko, a former governor and ex-congressman. There already are hints that the progressive Roark is the good guy and Clark the bad guy in this battle, an impression that will be strengthened as the novel goes on.

Cotton's work is interrupted by fellow reporter Merrill McDaniels, who drunkenly proclaims he is on top of a big story that could win him the Pulitzer Prize. After McDaniels reels away, Cotton continues writing, only to be interrupted by a stranger in a blue topcoat who comes asking for McDaniels. The stranger's appearance does not seem significant until McDaniels falls to his death from the capitol rotunda.

Cotton tries to retrace McDaniels's steps with the use of the reporter's last notebook. As he gradually uncovers civic corruption, he realizes (as the reader will have figured from the first) that McDaniels was probably a murder victim. Cotton becomes a target himself. The title refers to the journalist's figurative role as well as a literal (and venerated) piece of graffiti on the capitol pressroom wall.

The background of politics and journalism is very effectively used. The reader sees exactly what steps an investigative reporter follows to get a story. The relationships of Cotton with his reporting colleagues and his governmental sources are believably sketched. The novel preceded the Watergate scandal by about a year; one wonders if it would have had a bigger impact with slightly different timing. In any event, Hillerman never returned to Cotton, devoting all his subsequent detective novels to one or both of his Navajo police heroes.

Cotton emerges as a heroic figure, though somewhat reluctantly. At one point, he is threatened with death unless he leaves the capital. Not given to reckless foolhardiness, he takes the advice. However, he finds he has been set up. In one of the book's two impressive sequences of menace and pursuit, he goes hunting back in New Mexico and finds a hired gun is trying to kill him. When he escapes, he goes back to the capital to finish his job while maintaining a low profile.

As in most of Hillerman's books, there is a muted romantic strain, with no explicit sex but a sensitive probing of feeling. Cotton's love interest is

Janey Janoski, an employee of the Legislative
Finance Office who aids him in some of his investigations and who has a memorable argument with him
in chapter 21, when he has fled to her apartment at
four in the morning following a terrifying stalked-by-
the-killer sequence in the capitol building.

Cotton has established most of the links in his
story of highway-construction fraud by this time and
works on rewriting it in Janey's apartment. Involved
as a project engineer on all the jobs in question is a
man named Singer. Janey wants to know more
about him. "Weren't you curious?" she asks. "Yes,"
Cotton answers. "But it was on the telephone. . . . He
had a nice voice. And he has a daughter in high
school" (page 182). Suddenly Janey can't understand
why Cotton wants to write the article, knowing it will
hurt a family man as well as a good governor whose
intended stand for the Senate will foil the present
senator's pernicious political machine.

Cotton becomes angry. "It's easy enough to
understand. Some bastard steals the public's money.
The public has a right to know about it" (page 182).
Janey accuses him of playing games, like her late
husband, a Navy combat flyer who finished his quota
of missions, then felt compelled to volunteer for
another tour. "He didn't hate anybody. The bombs
didn't really hurt anybody. It was Dick against the
anti-aircraft guns. It was a game you played" (page
183). She points out that by pursuing the story,
Cotton is apt to get himself killed. What he leaves
unsaid in response is that he has a motive for printing the story apart from journalistic purity: once the
facts are made public, there will be no reason for his
adversaries to require his elimination. He muses
that her real concern is not for him or for Singer but
for the political future of Governor Roark. Their conversation points up the question of political and
journalistic ethics that is the novel's major theme.

Cotton's Pulitzer Prize–winning colleague Leroy Hall believes in picking and choosing what facts to report in the interest of the greater good. Cotton, on the other hand, really believes that reporters have to be objective and even-handed, reporting the news regardless of whom it hurts. The dramatic conclusion of the novel brings the ethical problem into sharp relief. After Cotton's confrontation with the main antagonist—this novel has a stronger whodunit strain than most of the others—the culprit, many of whose political aims Cotton shares, takes steps to manipulate events for political benefit. And Cotton finds a way to help him without compromising his journalistic integrity.

Hillerman originally intended *The Fly on the Wall* to be a major mainstream novel. He did not achieve everything he had hoped in it, but it would rank high on any list of detective novels with backgrounds of politics or journalism. The author's mastery of pace and construction is surer than in *The Blessing Way*, and certainly the central mystery plot is stronger. The tension and power of the suspense sequences recall Cornell Woolrich.

The Fly on the Wall, like all Hillerman's books, was well received critically. A *New Yorker* reviewer praised its "stunning" scenes of menace and pursuit in the New Mexico mountains and the capitol as well as its "provocative ethical conundrum."[5] Jacques Barzun and Wendell Hertig Taylor, among the few commentators to be less than impressed with Hillerman's Navajo series, are enthusiastic about *The Fly*, finding the two scenes of menace "as good as any in the whole literature."[6] More than

5. Review of *The Fly on the Wall*. *The New Yorker*, 24 September 1971, pp. 142–143.
6. Jacques Barzun and Wendell Hertig Taylor, *A Catalogue of Crime*. Revised and enlarged edition (New York: Harper & Row, 1989).

The Blessing Way, The Fly on the Wall stands apart
from the novels that constitute Hillerman's greatest
achievement, but also, like *The Blessing Way*, if it
stood alone it would merit its own special niche in
the genre.

Dance Hall of the Dead (1973)

Hillerman's third novel, which marks his return to
Joe Leaphorn and the Navajo Tribal Police, also has
a well-explored central theme of professional
ethics, this time the ethics of scientific inquiry. As
in *The Blessing Way*, the opening chapter gives the
reader an immediate immersion into the exotic
background of Native American ritual.

A young Zuñi, preparing for the role of
Shulawitsi, the Little Fire God, in a tribal ceremony,
is running on the mesa and thinking about his crazy
friend George Bowlegs, a Navajo who wants to be a
Zuñi. The Fire God intends to run down the mesa
slope to rejoin George, then go home and do his
homework, but he is confronted by a figure who
appears from behind some boulders, not George but
"the Salamobia of the mole kiva, its mask painted
the color of darkness.... The Fire God stared at
the figure, the muscular body in the dark shirt, the
bristling ruff of turkey feathers surrounding the
neck, the black and empty eyes, the plumed feath-
ered topknot" (page 177). Still, he notes, the mask is
not quite right, and the wand the figure raises is
not made of woven yucca as it should be. The young
Fire God remembers that "Salamobia, like all of the
ancestor spirits which lived at the Zuñi masks, were
visible only to members of the Sorcery Fraternity,
and to those about to die" (page 177).

The focus shifts to Leaphorn, who is cooperat-
ing with Chief Ed Pasquaanti of the Zuñi Tribal

Police in searching for fourteen-year-old George Bowlegs, reported missing on Zuñi land. Leaphorn, who once had a Zuñi roommate at Arizona State, is convinced Zuñis feel superior to Navajos. Also missing is twelve-year-old Ernesto Cata, the in-training Fire God of the first chapter, whose bicycle along with a large amount of blood have been found. Both boys were seventh-graders, despite the disparity in their ages.

George's brother Cecil tells Leaphorn the boy was afraid of a kachina, which refers to ancestor spirits of the Zuñis as well as to masks and dolls. Cecil also says Ernesto may have stolen some artifacts from an anthropological dig the boys had frequented.

Leaphorn visits the dig, where graduate student Ted Isaacs tells him of the project, headed by maverick scholar Chester Reynolds, to find traces of the Folsom culture. Reynolds, though ridiculed by some of his colleagues, believes that Folsom Man did not die out as generally thought but *adapted* to his changing environment by an adjustment in the design of his lance point.

The boys had also been known to hang around Jason's Fleece, a hippie commune. Before visiting the commune, Leaphorn gets the opinion of a neighboring Navajo, a Vietnam veteran. The description illustrates the matter-of-fact, sympathetic, balanced view of their world Hillerman finds in the Navajos.

> He discussed these whites with an impersonal interest tinged with amusement, but with the detailed knowledge of neighbors common to those who live where fellow humans are scarce. In general, Young Husband rated the residents of Jason's Fleece as generous, ignorant, friendly, bad mannered but well intentioned.

• On the positive side of the balance, they provided a source of free rides into Ramah,
  Gallup, and once even to Albuquerque. On the
  negative, they had contaminated the spring
  above the Madman place with careless defeca-
  tion last summer, and had started a fire which
  burned off maybe fifty acres of pretty good
  sheep graze, and didn't know how to take care
  of their sheep. (page 207)

At Jason's Fleece, Leaphorn meets Susanne, a
young woman who had befriended the boys, and
Halsey, the leader of the commune. Susanne is
romantically involved with Ted Isaacs, although, in
these pre-AIDS days of casual sex, she also admits
she sleeps with Halsey.

When Leaphorn expresses concern about a
spaced-out member of the commune named Otis,
wondering if he is on peyote—if so, he'll be okay in
a couple of hours; if not, he should see a doctor—
Halsey indicates sardonically it couldn't be peyote,
since that is an illegal substance. Leaphorn implies
he might look the other way: "The way the Tribe
sees it, it's O.K. if it's used for religious purposes.
It's part of the ceremonial of the Native American
Church and some of The People belong to that. The
way it works, we don't notice people using peyote if
they're using it in their religion. I'm guessing Otis
here is a religious man" (page 211).

Shortly after Ernesto's body is found, George's
father, Shorty Bowlegs, is also found, murdered
like Ernesto by a blow to the head.

Leaphorn learns that two federal officers, FBI
agent O'Malley and drug enforcement agent
Baker, have become involved in the investigation.
Questions of jurisdiction are a constant concern of
the Navajo Tribal Police. Musing on the involvement
of the FBI, Leaphorn reveals a cynical attitude:

O'Malley would make his decisions with that ingrained FBI awareness that the rewards lay in good publicity, and the sensible attitude that other agencies were competitors for that publicity.... Usually the FBI would move into marginal areas only if someone somewhere was sure his batting average could be helped by a successful prosecution. Or if the case involved whatever held high agency priority of the season—and that these days would be either radical politics or narcotics. (page 271)

Leaphorn's conversation with Father Ingles at Saint Anthony's Mission about the religiously searching George Bowlegs touches on Christian, Greek, Navajo, and Zuñi religion. Though Leaphorn's cynicism about witchcraft is frequently noted, when Ingles asks him if he believes in witches, Leaphorn replies, "That's like me asking you if you believe in sin, Father" (page 262). The equivocal answer could be taken in two ways. It could mean that, of course, Leaphorn as a Navajo must believe in witchcraft, or that Ingles should not embarrass him by expecting him to confront the question, whatever the answer.

When Leaphorn remarks that the kachinas are like the Holy People of the Navajo, the priest replies:

"Not really. Your Holy People—Monster Slayer, Changing Woman, Born of Water, and all that—they're more like a cross between the Greek hero idea and the lesser Greek gods. More human than divine, you know. The kachinas aren't like anything in Navajo or white culture. We don't have a word for this concept, and neither do you. They're not gods.... Maybe you could call them ancestor spirits. Their attitude toward humans is friendly, fatherly. They bring blessings. They appear as rain clouds." (page 264)

In the course of this conversation, the novel's title is explained: Kothluwalawa, translated the Dance Hall of the Dead, is a sort of Zuñi heaven. It may be what George Bowlegs was looking for, to ask the kachinas to absolve his guilt for Ernesto's death, which he thinks may have been the result of Ernesto's breaking a taboo in telling a non-Zuñi too much about their religion. If so, Leaphorn must decide where George thinks this place is located. He gets Susanne, who has been expelled from the commune, to help him in his search.

In a prime example of the Navajo detective as tracker, Leaphorn tries to trace George by following the pattern of movement of a deer herd the boy would rely on for food. In the course of the search, Leaphorn steps on a booby trap and is shot with a tranquilizer dart of the kind used on animals. The experience is described in fascinating detail.

The novel proceeds to a strong finish. It is much superior to *The Blessing Way* in plot, putting the guilt on one principal and fully understood villain rather than on a team of relatively uninteresting baddies in a somewhat vague spy intrigue. Well worked out as the puzzle is, there is some disappointment that the very interesting villain, who appears only once earlier in the book, is offstage at the end.

Dance Hall of the Dead deservedly won an Edgar award for the best mystery novel of its year. The reviews again were glowing. Newgate Callendar in an otherwise overwhelmingly laudatory *New York Times Book Review* notice[7] (November 25, 1973,

7. Newgate Callendar, Review of *Dance Hall of the Dead, New York Times Book Review*, 25 November 1973, p. 49.

page 49) *did* find the murderer easily guessable (a reaction not all readers will share) but indicated it doesn't make much difference.

H. R. F. Keating listed *Dance Hall of the Dead* as one of the hundred best crime and mystery books.[8] Before I began rereading Hillerman's work for this article, I would certainly have chosen *Dance Hall* to represent Hillerman on any all-time list of favorites in the genre. In memory, it seemed the high point of the series. On rereading, though, I was surprised to find the books to follow even more impressive.

Hillerman's nonfiction collection *The Great Taos Bank Robbery*, whose title piece hilariously recounts the criminal history of the famous New Mexico artistic settlement, appeared in the same year as *Dance Hall of the Dead*. Five years would pass before the third Joe Leaphorn novel was published, but in that time the author would produce three more volumes of nonfiction: *New Mexico* (1974), *Rio Grande* (1975), and *The Spell of New Mexico* (1976).

Listening Woman (1978)

Listening Woman opens with the title character, blind medicine woman Margaret Cigaret, visiting the hogan of Hosteen Tso to diagnose and treat his illness. She believes some "messed-up" sand paintings may be the result of witchcraft and thus hold the key to his illness. Messing up, in this case, means preserving, a violation of Navajo religion: "If there was more than one sand painting at a time," she says, "then that would be doing the ceremonial

8. H. R. F. Keating, *Crime & Mystery: The 100 Best Books* (New York: Carroll & Graf, 1987).

wrong. That would be turning the blessing around"
(page 327). But Hosteen Tso refuses to answer any
question, saying he is keeping a promise he once
made. He tells Listening Woman he must get in
touch with his grandson, "who went on the Jesus
Road" (page 329), to tell him something before he
dies. She asks her niece Anna Atcitty to take her to
a place outside the hogan in the shadow of a cliff
where she can listen for the "voices in the wind"
that will enable her to diagnose Hosteen Tso's illness. When she is ready to return to the hogan, she
gets no answer. The reader learns what the blind
Listening Woman cannot see: both Anna and the
old man have been murdered.

Joe Leaphorn, en route to Tuba City with an
insouciant young prisoner bearing the common
Navajo name Begay, is nearly run off the road by
the driver of a Mercedes, a nemesis throughout the
book whom he will come to call Goldrims after his
glasses. It is the other car that winds up going off
the road and into the bushes. Leaphorn finds it
wrecked in a shallow arroyo, but Goldrims is gone
and the pursuit has also given his laughing prisoner a chance to escape.

Hillerman's third novel about the Tribal
Police is more of a police procedural than the first
two. The authority figure of Captain Largo appears
for the first time, and a sense of the organizational
problems and administrative decision-making necessary to any police force is introduced. To a
greater extent than the previous book, the balance
of cooperation and friction between law enforcement agencies (notably the Navajo Tribal Police
and the FBI) is explored. And, most significantly,
multiple cases are introduced.

A doctor in the Public Health Service wants his
daughter located. The FBI may have muffed the
Hosteen Tso murder case. Members of the Buffalo

Society, a militant offshoot of the American Indian Movement, have robbed a Wells Fargo armored truck and taken off in a helicopter that seems to have vanished. A package of heroin has been found taped behind the dashboard of a deserted car. A combination of these seemingly unconnected events permits Largo to relieve Leaphorn of his unwelcome assignment to keep the peace at a Boy Scout encampment in Canyon de Chelly.

In a conversation with Indian trader John McGinnis, more personal detail about Leaphorn is offered. As noted before, he belongs to the Slow Talking Dinee. His mother was Anna Gorman from Two Gray Hills, his grandfather Hosteen Klee-Thlumie.

The character of McGinnis injects some comedy relief into the narrative, giving the novel more humor than earlier ones. Hillerman, though enormously amusing as a public speaker and in conversation and attracted to absurd situations like that described in "The Great Taos Bank Robbery," is essentially not a funny writer.

McGinnis tells Leaphorn he doesn't believe a Navajo killed Hosteen Tso.

> "You Navajos will steal if you think you can get off with something, but I never heard of one going out to kill somebody. . . . That's one kind of white man's meanness the Navajos never took to. Any killings you have, there's either getting drunk and doing it, or getting mad and fighting. You don't have this planning in advance and going out to kill somebody like white folks. Right?" (page 363)

McGinnis gathers from Leaphorn's silence that the policeman agrees with him, which he does.

Among the traditional Dinee, the death of a

fellow human being was the ultimate evil. . . .
The Navajo didn't share the concept of his
Hopi-Zuñi-Pueblo Indian neighbors that the
human spirit transcended death in the fulfill-
ment of an eternal kachina, nor the Plains
Indian belief in joining with a personal God. In
the old tradition, death was unrelieved horror.
Even the death of an enemy in battle was
something the warrior cleansed himself of
with an Enemy Way ritual. Unless, of course, a
Navajo Wolf was involved. Witchcraft was a
reversal of the Navajo Way. (page 363)

This Navajo attitude toward murder helps
give weight and substance to the series. When commentators were claiming in the sixties, wrongly as
it turned out, that the spy novel would displace the
detective novel, one of the arguments advanced
was that one person's death was no longer enough
to engage a reader's interest, that the fate of the
world had to be in the balance to make today's
reader care. Not so in the Navajo culture, and not
so in the novels of Tony Hillerman.

Theodora Adams, the missing daughter of the
Public Health doctor, turns up around the trading
post expressing an interest in visiting the Tso
hogan. Leaphorn discovers she had stowed away in
his carryall, thinking he will take her there.

When Leaphorn goes to the Tso hogan before
dawn, he reveals he believed in Navajo witchcraft
as a child but came to disbelieve it while at Arizona
State. When he sees an owl, he reflects it might be
Hosteen Tso's ghost haunting the hogan. He discovers a stranger observing Catholic rituals. This
proves to be Tso's grandson, Father Benjamin Tso,
a priest who has returned from his post at the
Vatican and whom Theodora intends to marry.

In chapter 10, Leaphorn attends a Kinaalda cer-

emony at which Margaret Cig...
of passage of a girl into woma...
described in detail, proves as c...
the Enemy Way performed in *The* ...

Also as in *The Blessing Way*, ...
villains holding prisoners, with Lea...
a prisoner (along with some of the B...
than a rescuer. As he achieves his fi...
Goldrims and solves the case, it beco... that
Hillerman is not a proponent of the "mo...ar" police
procedural. All the disparate cases are brought
together in one well-worked-out plot.

Listening Woman is more of an action story
than *Dance Hall of the Dead*. Typical of Hillerman,
it points up a moral and religious theme in its dramatic climax, as the Navajo priest finds a way to
resolve his theological conflict.

Newgate Callendar ranked the book equal to
its Edgar-winning predecessor.[9] On recent rereading, it seemed to me even better, narrowly the best
of the three novels in which Joe Leaphorn appears
as solo sleuth, though not as impressive as the trio
of books about Jim Chee that were to follow it.

People of Darkness (1980)

Besides introducing a new central character,
Hillerman's fourth Navajo Tribal Police novel,
People of Darkness, varies his approach in other
ways. The first chapter occurs not out in open
country among the Indians but in Albuquerque at
the Cancer Research and Treatment Center of the
University of New Mexico, where a bacteriologist
working on her culture studies is interrupted by

9. Newgate Callendar, Review of *Listening Woman*, *New York
Times Book Review*, 7 May 1978, p. 26.

of a pickup truck in the parking lot.
first look at Jim Chee, a young tribal
man who holds to Navajo tradition but is
tensely curious about everything in the white
man's world, finds him visiting the most expensive
home in New Mexico, looking at a pair of head-
stones on the grounds and musing on odd burial
customs: "The Navajos lacked this sentimentality
about corpses. Death robbed the body of its value.
Even its identity was lost with the departing *chindi*.
What the ghost left behind was something to be disposed of with a minimum risk of contamination to
the living. The names of the dead were left unspo-
ken, certainly not carved in stone" (pages 5–6).

Chee's clan, like Leaphorn's, is the Slow Talking
Dinee, and he is learning to become a *yataalii*, a word
that none of the English synonyms (shaman, singer,
medicine man) approximate adequately.

Rosemary Vines, second wife of hugely
wealthy rancher and hunter Benjamin J. Vines,
wants to hire Chee during his thirty days of accrued
leave to find a stolen box of "keepsakes" belonging
to her husband. Mrs. Vines says the "People of
Darkness" (a literal translation of *dine'este'tle*, the
Navajo word for mole) stole the box, while leaving
many more valuable items untouched, and says
Vines had given something out of the mysterious
box to Dillon Charley, founder of a peyote-taking
cult, part of the Native American Church. Charley's
is one of the bodies buried on the grounds, along
with the first Mrs. Vines, his tombstone calling him
(with dubious humor) a "good Indian."

The local Navajos, says the current Mrs. Vines,
think her husband is a witch and will not work for
him; most of their servants are Lagunas or Acomas.
Thus she needs someone with a knowledge of
Navajo customs to take her case. She suggests that
Chee talk to Emerson Charley, Dillon's son, who

took over the church. As Chee leaves, an old servant gives him a message in Spanish to be careful.

The scene, reminiscent of the first chapter of Raymond Chandler's *The Big Sleep* and countless of its imitators in that the sleuth visits a rich person in an ostentatiously posh home and is offered a job, makes the novel feel more like a private-eye caper than a police procedural. But Chee doesn't explicitly agree to take the case and, ever the policeman, reports the burglary to the Valencia County sheriff although Mrs. Vines says she will not make a formal complaint.

Chee learns it was Emerson Charley's pickup truck that was blown up in Albuquerque at the University of New Mexico hospital and that Charley is now a cancer patient there. He subsequently learns that cancer seems to run in Charley's family.

Along with the crime, Chee and Sheriff Sena discuss the perennial subject of law enforcement jurisdiction problems:

> Even on the Big Reservation, which sprawled larger than all New England across the borders of New Mexico, Arizona, and Utah, jurisdiction was always a question. The serious felony brought in the FBI. If the suspect was non-Navajo, other questions were raised. Or the crime might lap into the territory of New Mexico State Police, Utah or Arizona Highway Patrol, or involve the Law and Order Division of the Bureau of Indian Affairs. Or even a Hopi constable, or Southern Ute Tribal Police, or an officer of the Jicarilla Apache tribe, or any of a dozen county sheriffs of the three states. (page 22)

Before Chee leaves his office, Sheriff Sena adds a second admonition to be careful.

Chee, like Leaphorn, is college-educated, with

an anthropology degree from the University of New Mexico, but unlike his older counterpart, the white man's schools have not turned him cynical about the Navajo Way. At one point, he receives a phone message from *Captain* Leaphorn at the Chinle station, but (in an inside joke for series readers) he never returns the call. Leaphorn, his promotion forgotten, will not return until *Skinwalkers*, three more novels down the line.

Chee also gets a call from B. J. Vines. Saying his wife stole the keepsake box herself, he tries to call Chee off the case.

In chapter 8, the focus shifts to Colton Wolf, a hired bomber who is himself hiring private eyes to find his long-lost brother Buddy and (through him) their mother. As the novel goes on, Wolf is the known antagonist, in the tradition of the Big Navajo in *The Blessing Way* or Goldrims in *Listening Woman*, though the person he is working for is in the shadows. The troubled Wolf is a much more intriguing character than either the Big Navajo or Goldrims.

Hillerman traces the origin of Colton Wolf to "First Lead Gasser," a "nonfiction short story" written during his days as a working journalist but published for the first time in April 1993 in *Ellery Queen's Mystery Magazine* and reprinted in the last section of this volume. In the story, a powerful work imbued with Hillerman's Roman Catholic faith and based on a true experience from his reporting days, condemned prisoner Toby Small implores a reporter to find his mother so she can claim his body and save it from being buried in the prison plot. Hillerman writes that Toby Small became Colton Wolf,

> reincarnated as he might have evolved if fate had allowed him to live a few murders longer. The plot required a professional hit man. Since it seems incredible to me that anyone

would kill for hire, I was finding it hard to conceive the character. Then the old memory of Small's yearning for his mother came to my rescue. I think I did a better job of communicating the tragedy of Small in the book than in the short story. A quarter century of additional practice should teach one something. But I'm still not skilled enough to do justice to that sad afternoon, listening to a damaged man wondering what he would find when he came out of the gas chamber.[10]

With Emerson Charley in a coma, Jim Chee seeks out his son Tomas Charley, his successor as peyote chief. Chee goes to the Crownpoint Elementary School, where Tomas is attending a rug auction, and there he meets a young teacher named Mary Landon and immediately stereotypes her.

A pretty lady . . . Chee recognized the look. He had seen it often at the University of New Mexico—and most often among Anglo coeds enrolled in Native American Studies courses. The courses attracted Anglo students, largely female, enjoying racial/ethnic guilt trips. Chee had concluded early that their interest was more in Indian males than in Indian mythology. Their eyes asked you if you were really any different from the blond boys they had grown up with. (page 66)

Of more substance than the stereotype suggests, Mary will become Jim Chee's up-and-down romantic interest in the stories to come.

Emerson Charley has died and his body has

10. Tony Hillerman, "First Lead Gasser," *Ellery Queen's Mystery Magazine*, April 1993, p. 14.

disappeared from the mortuary. Tomas Charley tells Chee he believes Vines killed his father by witchcraft and stole the body. He gives Chee directions to find the missing box.

In a nice get-acquainted scene with Mary, Chee tells her he has been accepted by the FBI but has not decided whether he will report for training. Chee begins to take Mary along on his investigations, their relationship at this point comparable to John Cotton and Janey Janoski's partnership in *The Fly on the Wall*. Together they follow Tomas Charley's directions to find the missing box. They find his body, shot to death, and they also see Colton Wolf, which makes them witnesses he must eliminate.

The Chandleresque opening is not the novel's only link to private-eye fiction. More than in any of Hillerman's other books, the plot has a Ross Macdonald feel, as a long-past event casts shadows in the present. The reader will divine early that the key to everything is an oil-field explosion in the forties that killed Sheriff Sena's brother and occurred on a day the chief of the Navajo crew (Dillon Charley) kept his men away, as if he knew what was going to happen.

In *People of Darkness*, Hillerman continues the pattern of continually topping himself. It is his best novel to date. A sequence of menace in which Colton Wolf comes after the hospitalized Chee and winds up killing a nurse and Chee's roommate is equal to the Woolrichian suspense scenes in *The Fly on the Wall*. And the solution, though it does not include a really surprising culprit, embodies one of the most elaborate and unusual murder weapons in fiction.

The Jim Chee Short Stories

Though the author himself is not certain whether

they were written before or after *People of Darkness*, this is an appropriate place to discuss Hillerman's two short stories about the Navajo police, both featuring Jim Chee (see last section of this book). Given the author's stature in the field, they have automatically become anthology staples. The first-published, longer, and better of the two is "The Witch, Yazzie, and the Nine of Clubs," which took third prize in a short-story contest sponsored by the Swedish Academy of Detection for the Third Crime Writers' International Congress, held in Stockholm in 1981, and was published with other winners in *Crime Wave* (Collins, 1981). Though this book was never published in the United States, the story has been reprinted in two anthologies edited by Bill Pronzini, *The Ethnic Detectives* (Dodd, Mead, 1985) and *Criminal Elements* (Ivy, 1988), and, most recently, in the nonfiction *Talking Mysteries* (University of New Mexico Press, 1991) by Hillerman and Ernie Bulow. The second, "Chee's Witch," first appeared in *The New Black Mask Number 7* (1986) and was anthologized by Pronzini in *Felonious Assaults* (Ivy, 1989) and by Jerome Charyn in the International Association of Crime Writers anthology *The New Mystery* (Dutton, 1993).

To say the two short stories have marked similarities is putting it mildly. Indeed, Hillerman in retrospect thinks of them as two versions of the same story. Each begins with Chee hearing rumors of witchcraft on the Rainbow Plateau, and the examples given are either identical or only slightly changed:[11] "Adeline Etcitty's mare had foaled a two-legged colt"

---

11. Quotes from "The Witch, Yazzie, and the Nine of Clubs" are from Hillerman and Bulow, *Talking Mysteries*, page 94; from "Chee's Witch" in Matthew J. Bruccoli and Richard Layman, eds., *The New Black Mask Number 7* (San Diego: Harcourt Brace Jovanovich, 1986), p. 87.

(both). "Rudolph Bisti's boys lost their best ram while driving their flocks into the high country, and when they found the body werewolf tracks were all around it" ("The Witch"). "Rudolph Bisti's boys lost three rams while driving their flocks up into the Chuska high pastures, and when they found the bodies, the huge tracks of a werewolf were all around them" ("Chee's Witch"). "The daughter of Rosemary Nakai had seen the witch, too. She shot her .22 rifle at a big dog bothering her horses and the dog turned into a man wearing a wolfskin and she'd run away without seeing what he did" ("The Witch"). "The daughter of Rosemary Nashibitti had seen a big dog bothering her horses and had shot at it with her .22 and the dog had turned into a man wearing a wolfskin and had fled, half running, half flying" ("Chee's Witch").

Though the stories diverge somewhat from there, each involves an alleged murder by the witch in question; each plot turns on mutilation of the corpse's fingerprints to prevent identification; and in each Chee figures this out by the same clue: the fact that the alleged witch took skin from the victim's fingers but left alone the skin from the corpse's feet, which would be equally necessary for making corpse powder.

This kind of permissible self-plagiarism, what Raymond Chandler called "cannibalizing," is not unusual when short stories are expanded into novels: contemporaries like John Lutz and Bill Pronzini do it all the time, and certainly writers like Agatha Christie and John Dickson Carr refined clues and plot elements for later use. However, for the same near-boilerplate language to appear in two short stories is more surprising—and more to be expected from a prolific pulpster than from a best-selling novelist who has published only a few short stories. The answer, as Hillerman reveals in his interview with Ernie Bulow, lies in the fact that both were attempts to sell a story to *Playboy*, solicited by the magazine, then rejected. In the introduction to "Chee's Witch," Hillerman describes the two ideas he was exploring in the story: "First, I wanted to use the Navajo belief that witches use the skin that has the 'wind marks' on the fingertips, palms, et cetera, to make 'corpse powder' and handle it as a way to avoid identification of a body; second, I wanted to try the notion of switching a protected witness under the noses of the federals" (*New Black Mask Number 7*, page 85). Hillerman goes on to point out he reused one of these ideas "later" in *The Dark Wind* (1982) and the other in *The Ghostway* (1984), indicating "Chee's Witch" was written several years before it was published. It is not clear, though, whether "Chee's Witch" was written before or after "The Witch, Yazzie, and the Nine of Clubs." Given the superior quality of the latter story and the fact that it was chosen for the contest entry, I suspect "Chee's Witch" came first. "The Witch, Yazzie, and the Nine of Clubs" is a fine example of the classical detective short story, but it is so dense with incident and necessary specialized information that it may take the less careful reader a couple of run-throughs to get it all straight. The same plot works better in *The Dark Wind*, where Hillerman has more elbow room to work in all the needed ethnological background.

The Dark Wind (1982)

The second of the solo Jim Chee novels, *The Dark Wind*, has a typical opening. A group of three Hopis, led by the elderly Lomatewa, are in the midst of a Niman Kachina ceremonial to end the drought when they find the dead body of a Navajo (a Tavasuh, or "head-pounder," in Hopi parlance), the skin of his hands and feet sliced away. Lomatewa insists they must not report the crime to the police until the ceremonial is concluded.

The second chapter finds a pilot named Pauling flying his Cessna low over Balakai Mesa, out of radar range, delivering a passenger and some suitcases with unknown contents (presumably narcotics) to a makeshift landing area on Oraibi Wash, discovering too late he's been led into a trap. Jim Chee, in the course of investigating vandalism to a Hopi windmill located on former Navajo land, sees the plane before it crashes.

A flashback to a meeting with Captain Largo, making his second appearance in the series and the first as Chee's superior officer, reestablishes the police procedural ambience that was strongest in *Listening Woman*. The Tribal Police have multiple cases under investigation apart from the windmill vandalization: an unidentified body found shot in the head on Black Mesa, a burglary at the Burnt Water Trading Post, bootlegging activity, and witchcraft gossip around Black Mesa. As in the two short stories, Chee indicates he is too new in the area for anyone to tell him anything about witches.

Largo and Chee are related. Chee's "born to" clan is the Slow Talking Dinee of his mother, his "born for" clan the Bitter Water People of his father, while Largo's "born to" is Standing Rock Dinee and his "born for" the Red Forehead Dinee. Since the latter is a secondary "born for" clan of Chee's father,

> that made kinsmen. Distant kinsmen, true enough, but kinsmen in a culture that made family of first importance and responsibility to relatives the highest value. . . . But [Chee] was remembering how a paternal uncle had once cheated him on a used-refrigerator sale, and

that the worst whipping he'd ever taken in the Two Gray Hills Boarding School was from a maternal cousin. (pages 13–14)

In the trading post robbery, Chee is seeking Joseph Musket, known as Ironfingers, a fired employee who apparently has stolen a large haul of jewelry from trader Jake West but, untypically, has not tried to dispose of it through the usual channels. On the John Doe corpse, so decayed and eaten when found as to be unrecognizable, Chee is working with Hopi Deputy Sheriff Cowboy Dashee, a flamboyant character who will recur in later books. Dashee displays sensitivity when he puts the corpse into the body bag by himself, freeing Chee of the necessity to handle it. "We Hopis have our hang-ups," Dashee says, "but we don't have the trouble you Navajos do handling dead bodies" (page 16–17).

Back in the present, Chee hears the plane explode, followed by a gunshot. He goes to the scene, sees a car driving away, and finds the bodies of the pilot and passenger. Subsequently, the FBI and DEA agents will suspect him of being involved in taking the drug shipment, which has disappeared.

During a visit to Jake West's trading post, Chee hears witch rumors similar to those in the two short stories. Also recurring from "The Witch, Yazzie, and the Nine of Clubs" are the proprietor's card tricks and the central problem of the trading post burglary.

On another visit to the crash site, Chee meets the pilot's sister and a lawyer, Ben Gaines. Chee deduces the pilot was murdered by the placing of a group of lanterns that led the plane straight into the rocks. Both Hillerman's Navajo detectives specialize in detection from physical evidence, which was widely practiced in the days of Sherlock Holmes and R. Austin Freeman's Dr. Thorndyke but sometimes seems a lost art in today's detective fiction.

When the lawyer patronizingly remarks, "I've always heard that Indians were good trackers" (page 52), Chee responds that he's a Navajo, that they have no word for Indians, and that some Navajos are good trackers and some not.

Since it involves non-Navajos, the plane crash is not in Chee's jurisdiction, but as in *People of Darkness* he is offered a freelance sleuthing job when Gaines tries to hire him to investigate further. When Chee says he'll check with his superior, Gaines asks him not to and raises the ante to $40 an hour, plus a generous bonus from the owners if the plane's cargo turns up. Chee's reply is intentionally ambiguous.

With the report from Cowboy Dashee that the windmill is being repaired by the Bureau of Indian Affairs, Chee is sure it will only be vandalized again. "With the BIA doing it, I thought it would be Christmas before they got it done," Chee says. "What the hell happened?" (page 59).

Dashee and Chee find and interview Albert Lomatewa, who originally found the John Doe body. Since the body had been well picked over by scavengers, this is the first they learn the skin of the hands and feet, ingredients for corpse powder, had been taken, proving a witch was at work.

When Chee is beaten by DEA agents who search his room, Largo tells him there is no point in filing a complaint because he won't be believed. Since the owners of the missing cargo will probably assume he has it, Chee is advised to leave the area and visit his relatives. Instead, he goes out to find the missing car that met the plane and presumably picked up the cargo. He finds it and another dead man.

A conversation with Miss Pauling, the pilot's

sister, points up the theme of the novel and also explains the title. She is determined the killers of her brother suffer for it. Chee does not understand the concept of revenge, which seems

> as strange to him as the idea that somebody with money would steal had seemed to Mrs. Musket [the missing man's mother]. Someone who violated basic rules of behavior and harmed you was, by Navajo definition, "out of control." The "dark wind" had entered him and destroyed his judgment. One avoided such persons, and worried about them, and was pleased if they were cured of this temporary insanity and returned again to *hozro*. But to Chee's Navajo mind, the idea of punishing them would be as insane as the original act. (page 109)

There may not be in the whole series a more succinct summation of the attractiveness of the Navajo worldview and its foreignness to that shared by most of Hillerman's readers.

The uneasy collaboration between Hopi and Navajo law enforcement is interestingly handled, with many references to their differences. For example, "Hopis collect, Navajos scatter" (page 135). Chee uses his own detailed knowledge of both Hopi and Navajo beliefs to get an old Hopi to tell what he saw the night of the crash.

Chee's reasoning in solving the mystery, with (as before) all disparate threads gathered together, is identical to that in "The Witch, Yazzie, and the Nine of Clubs," including the principal misdirection. At the end, Chee thinks various acts of revenge have been accomplished, but, not completely clear on exactly how this white man's concept is supposed to work, he isn't quite sure.

The plot is beautifully worked out, with a stronger whodunit element than usual and possibly Hillerman's best fair-play puzzle spinning in the tradition of writers like Ellery Queen, Agatha Christie, and John Dickson Carr. Whether he has once again topped all previous efforts is arguable, but the challenge-to-the-reader aspect achieves its pinnacle in the series to date. And Robin W. Winks, writing in *The New Republic*, found it his best book to that time.[12]

The Ghostway (1984)

At the opening of *The Ghostway*, Hosteen (meaning Old Man, to Navajos a term of respect) Joseph Joe witnesses a shooting outside a Shiprock laundromat. The driver of a truck who had asked Hosteen Joe about someone named Leroy Gorman has shot a man in a plaid coat who emerged from another car. The truck driver, who drove away, himself wounded, was obviously a Navajo, but one who spoke only English. Clearly this was white man's business.

In this third Jim Chee novel, we learn that his relationship with Mary Landon, who is not even mentioned in *The Dark Wind*, is going through a bad patch. He has decided not to mail his reapplication to the FBI, and she has decided he is another unambitious Navajo. Mary never appears in this book either, at least in the present tense, but Jim Chee is flashing back to their argument all through its course, trying to make sense of it, trying to decide what to do.

Chee and Sheriff's Deputy Bales are hunting

12. Robin W. Winks, Review of *People of Darkness*, *The New Republic*, 13 December 1980, p. 40.

an armed fugitive named Albert Gorman, sought by the FBI in a stolen car operation, in the Chuska Mountains. Captain Largo has emphasized that this is a federal case, not a Navajo Tribal Police operation, and Chee must not mess it up. Gorman is the man Hosteen Joe saw shoot the man in plaid, and they believe from Joe's account he might himself be wounded.

With Chee and Bales, Hillerman makes an interesting contrast of Navajo and white conversational habits.

> Chee was conscious again that Bales was waiting for him to say something. The white man's custom of expecting a listener to do more than listen was contrary to Chee's courteous Navajo conditioning. . . . While his people presume that if they're talking, you are listening, white people require periodic reassurance. . . . Bales was requiring such reassurance now, and Chee tried to think of something to say. (page 6–7)

Of course, what Chee is really thinking about is Mary Landon. She accuses him of putting being a Navajo ahead of his love for her, of expecting her to be an appendage. In a devastating argument, she reminds him that male Navajos "married into the wife's clan. The husband joined the wife's family" (pages 7–8). It is a hard point to refute.

The searchers find Gorman's body buried under some rocks near the abandoned hogan of Hosteen Ashie Begay. Gorman's moccasins have been reversed in the proper Navajo manner, "So the ghost can't follow the man after death" (page 23), but other customs have been ignored. The man should have been taken out of the hogan into the open sun to die, with "a death bed under the arbor, where no walls would have penned in his *chindi* when death released it, where the ghost could have lost itself in the vastness of the sky" (pages 22–23). And why was Gorman's dirty hair not washed in yucca seeds? What happened to Hosteen Begay and why his kinsman had been given only a partial Navajo send-off become the basic puzzles of the novel.

It develops that most of Hosteen Begay's clan were relocated to Los Angeles in the forties and fifties. Captain Largo's statement that there was talk of Begay's being a witch gets an interesting response from Chee: "There's some talk that just about everybody is a witch. . . . I've heard you were. And me" (page 28).

The disappearance of Begay's granddaughter, seventeen-year-old Margaret Billy Sosi, a probable runaway from Saint Catherine's Indian School, gives Chee the excuse he needs to interest himself officially in the Begay case. He returns to search the abandoned hogan, ostensibly because he is looking for the missing girl.

For Jim Chee—"an alumnus of the University of New Mexico, a subscriber to *Esquire* and *Newsweek*, an officer of the Navajo Tribal Police, lover of Mary Landon, holder of a Farmington Public Library card, student of anthropology and sociology, 'with distinction' graduate of the FBI Academy, holder of Social Security card 441-28-7272" (page 41)—entering this place of death should be no problem. But Jim Chee was "only what his uncle would call his 'white man name.' His real name, his secret name, his war name, was Long Thinker" (pages 41–42). And Long Thinker knows that Gorman's ghost, his *chindi*, is trapped inside the hogan, and all of "Long Thinker's training conditioned him to avoid *chindis*" (page 42). The internal conflict only brings him back to his quarrel with

Mary, who he is sure would say, "When you stepped through that corpse hole, you proved that you can be a Navajo on an emotional plane but an assimilated man intellectually" (page 42).

Chee discovers Hosteen Begay's granddaughter living in the hogan. She asks him for advice in exorcising the *chindi* but runs away while he is contemplating whether to enter the corpse hole. When evidence suggests Margaret has gone to Los Angeles to look for her grandfather, Chee goes there to look for her unofficially, taking vacation time.

While inquiring at Albert Gorman's Los Angeles address, he encounters some rest-home residents who live nearby and expresses puzzlement at the white custom of shutting away and segregating the old. He also meets detectives Wells and Shaw. The latter also has reasons for pursuing Gorman outside his normal assignment. Comments Wells, "The vigilantes ride again" (page 78).

At this point, Hillerman introduces another of his fascinatingly twisted career criminals, a nutty debt collector and enforcer named Eric Vaggan, among whose peculiarities is looking forward eagerly to a post-nuclear-holocaust world. In an extended chapter establishing what a mean character he is, he makes a grisly example of a TV talk show host named Jay Leonard. (This, bear in mind, was written several years before Jay Leno took over the *Tonight* show.) The sequence is more explicitly violent than most anything else in Hillerman's books, though the talk show host survives the attack, as he is intended to.

Chee meanwhile gets quite a bit of good information through very patient questioning of Mr. Berger, a rest-home resident who had been befriended by Gorman. Chee, whose tradition teaches him to revere the old, figures the Anglo LA cops would assume Berger, who communicates with difficulty, was senile and would not pursue serious questioning.

Chee makes the analogy of age stereotyping and racial stereotyping, but he understands why his urban colleagues see things differently. "On the Big Reservation, where people were scarce and scattered, one tended to know people as individuals and there was no reason to lump them into categories. Shaw had a different problem with swarming masses in his jurisdiction. People in West Hollywood were Koreans or Filipinos or some other category that could be labeled. Just like people in old folks' homes were senile" (page 106).

Back on the reservation, Chee does finally enter the corpse hole at Hosteen Begay's hogan, and he sees it as a choice both in his investigation and in his relationship with Mary Landon: "Having chosen Los Angeles over Shiprock, and Mary Landon over the loneliness of *hozro*" (page 163). The reader doesn't really believe it, isn't expected to, and by the end of the book Mary has made her own decision.

The novel has a good action finale and an interesting plot line regarding Albert Gorman's brother Leroy, who has been placed in the protected witness program, an angle first explored in "Chee's Witch." But on the whole, the book falls short of its immediate predecessors. While some of the Los Angeles sequences are interesting, the diversions from the usual scenes and themes into what T. J. Binyon called "some of the elements of more ordinary crime novels" (Vaggan and his gangster employers) may not have been advisable.[13] The novel is most memorable for Jim Chee's

13. T. J. Binyon, Review of *The Ghostway*, *Times Literary Supplement*, 27 December 1985, p. 1478.

exchanges with Mr. Berger and, in flashback, with Mary Landon. With the first two Chee novels, it makes a better trio than the three about Leaphorn.

Literary reputation is hard to define and certainly relative. Hillerman was not yet a regular on best-seller lists, and to the great world of literature, if you believe some recent accounts, at this stage of his career he was still a relatively obscure writer with a cult following. Inside the mystery field, though, he was established as a contemporary giant of the form. After all, he had already won one Edgar and been nominated for another, and he had been guest of honor at the 1979 Bouchercon mystery convention. Another indication of the kind of following he had developed is the fact that small publisher Dennis McMillan brought out *The Ghostway* in a signed limited edition in 1984, before its trade publication by Harper & Row the following year.

Skinwalkers (1986)

The next book, which would bring Leaphorn and Chee together in one volume and win an award not from the Mystery Writers but from the Western Writers of America, is generally considered Hillerman's breakthrough book.

Untypically, Jim Chee appears on the first page of *Skinwalkers*, awakened in the middle of the night by his cat clattering through the flap in the screen door of his trailer. The account of Chee's relationship with the cat is instructive both about the nature and personality of cats and the relationship to animal life in traditional Navajo culture. Chee is also looking forward with pleasure to the return of Mary Landon from Wisconsin in two weeks and without pleasure to the coming day's task of arresting Roosevelt Bistie on a charge of killing an old man with a butcher knife.

Wondering what has frightened the cat, Chee sees a form in the darkness outside his trailer, then hears a series of gunshots aimed through the skin of his trailer into his mattress. "And through the holes punched in the paper-thin aluminum walls, he could see lightning briefly illuminate the dying thunderhead on the northwest horizon. In Navajo mythology, lightning symbolized the wrath of the *yei*, the Holy People venting their malice against the earth" (page 8).

Lieutenant Joe Leaphorn has a different kind of problem. His wife Emma has been troubled with headaches and memory loss, and Leaphorn, fearing she has Alzheimer's, is on the point of insisting she see a doctor. Emma's sister Agnes is taking care of the house during Emma's sickness. Being around Agnes makes Leaphorn uneasy. Leaphorn is not a traditional Navajo but the Yazzies, his wife's family, are, and tradition would call for his taking another wife from the family if Emma were to die.

Leaphorn goes to his Window Rock police office and turns his attention to three seemingly unconnected and baffling homicides, only slightly diverted by a memo from Largo in Shiprock about the shots fired into Chee's trailer. Leaphorn is contemptuous of Chee's claim that he doesn't know what motive the attacker had. More administrative duties keep him from his crime problem: a councilwoman from the Canoncito Chapter House complaining about the lack of adequate police protection, a supplier of stock for the much-dreaded Navajo Rodeo who wants assurance his animals will be properly guarded at night, and the principal of a boarding school reporting that his students' favorite bootlegger has resumed operations.

Finally Leaphorn can return to consideration

of the homicides, represented by pins in the Auto Club of Southern California's "Indian Country" map mounted on his wall. (Such is Hillerman's admiration for this particular product he plugs it frequently in his writings.) The victims were killed in different ways—Irma Onesalt by shooting, Dugai Endocheeney by stabbing, Wilson Sam by a blow from a shovel—and at locations that form points of a triangle 120 miles apart. But their very rarity on the reservation, where violent deaths are almost always accidental, connects them. Sam and Endocheeney were killed, says the coroner, at about the same time, making the same killer virtually impossible. "Unless he was a skinwalker," FBI man Delbert Streib suggests, "and you guys are right about skinwalkers being able to fly, and outrun turbocharged pickup trucks, and so forth" (page 18). Leaphorn, who doesn't appreciate jokes about witches, is not amused.

Leaphorn continues to demonstrate to an extent unusual in fiction the administrative pressures on a ranking police officer when he is visited by Dr. Yellowhorse, a tribal councilman and founder and medical chief of the Badwater Clinic. Yellowhorse has two missions: to hector Leaphorn about progress in investigating one of the homicides committed in his area and to complain about the activities of Chee, the would-be *yataalii* who has reportedly been telling people Yellowhorse, who practices crystal gazing as an adjunct to his medical practice, is a fake and not to take their medical complaints to him. Since Leaphorn, much as the abrasive Yellowhorse aggravates him, admires the doctor's work, he is given another reason to be hostile to Chee.

In setting up a tension between two heroes already well established separately, Hillerman introduces a new angle that will enliven the series

45

for several books to come. On their first meeting, they discuss the attack on Chee's trailer and then the series of murders to which it may be connected. Leaphorn asks Largo to assign Chee to work on the killings. A major question is this: If a skinwalker is involved, is it as victim or as murderer?

In *Skinwalkers*, Leaphorn emerges as a much more fully developed character than in the first three books about him. For one thing, his relationship with Emma, who was only mentioned in passing in the earlier books, serves to humanize him. The contrast with Chee makes him seem more of an individual, as does the possibility of seeing him through the eyes of Chee, who has been a fully rounded figure from his very first appearance. Though they had not worked together before,

in the small universe of the Navajo Police, total membership perhaps less than 120 sworn officers, Lieutenant Leaphorn was a Fairly Important Person, and somewhat of a legend. Everybody knew he hated bootleggers. Chee shared that sentiment. Everybody also knew Leaphorn had no tolerance for witchcraft or anything about it—for those who believed in witches, or stories about skinwalkers, corpse sickness, the cures for same, and everything connected with the Navajo Wolves. There were two stories about how Leaphorn had acquired this obsession. It was said that when he was new on the force in the older days he had guessed wrong about some skinwalker rumors on the Checkerboard. He hadn't acted on what he'd heard, and a fellow had killed three witches and got a life term for murder and then committed suicide. That was supposed to be why the lieutenant didn't like witchcraft, which was a good enough reason.

> The other story was that he was a descendent
> of the great Chee Dodge and had inherited
> Dodge's determination that belief in skinwalk-
> ers had no part in the Navajo culture, that the
> tribe had been infected with the notion while it
> was held captive down at Fort Sumner. Chee
> suspected both stories were true. (page 56)

Leaphorn and Chee seem to work well
together from the beginning, having conflict only
when Leaphorn admonishes Chee about telling
people Yellowhorse is a fake, particularly while on
duty. Leaphorn points out there is no licensing of
Navajo shamans and thus they are no concern of
the Tribal Police; Chee replies he must expose anyone who cynically uses the Navajo religion. Chee
obviously will not desist without a specific order to
that effect.

Before Mary Landon can return from
Wisconsin, the second major woman in Jim Chee's
life is introduced: Janet Pete, a lawyer from DNA,
"the popular acronym for Dinebeiina Nahiilna be
Agaditahe, which translates roughly into 'People
Who Talk Fast and Help the People Out,' and which
was the Navajo Nation's version of Legal Aid
Society/public defender organization" (page 85).
She has been appointed to represent Roosevelt
Bistie, accused of the Endocheeney murder.

A short time later, Jim Chee receives good
news and bad news in his mail: a relative wishes to
hire him to do a Blessing Way sing, his second job
as a *yataalii*, and Mary Landon is starting graduate
school and won't be able to come back to visit until
Thanksgiving.

With Leaphorn and Chee alternating center
stage, the story rushes to an exciting conclusion.
The villain, though hardly a surprise, is one of
Hillerman's most interesting characters, and the

motive is both well-foreshadowed and credible. True to life, the two detectives' personal problems remain up in the air, though the novel ends on a hopeful note for Emma Leaphorn.

Skinwalkers ranks among the best of the series to date, certainly a better book than *The Ghostway* and in the same league as the first two Chees. Sales of the book put Hillerman onto bestseller lists for the first time. With the next book, there was no question he was there to stay.

A Thief of Time (1988)

A Thief of Time is Tony Hillerman's own favorite among his novels, and it may well be the high point of the series. It begins with a more typical opening chapter as anthropologist Eleanor Friedman-Bernal, illegally searching for Anasazi pots in a cliff dwelling, first discovers another "thief of time" has been there ahead of her, then confronts a "humped shape that was coming out of the moonlight into this pool of darkness" (page 10).

The first appearance of Joe Leaphorn reveals a changed man. There had been hope for Emma, diagnosed with a treatable brain tumor rather than the feared Alzheimer's, but after an operation that was longer and more difficult than expected, a blood clot has killed her. Losing interest in nearly everything, Leaphorn has decided to quit police work, but as a favor to a friend, L. D. Thatcher of the Bureau of Land Management, he joins in the search for Dr. Friedman-Bernal, who has been accused of illegal pot hunting and now has disappeared. In a search of Friedman-Bernal's apartment, they find she has been involved with Harrison Houk, a wealthy Mormon rancher whose family (wife, younger son, and daughter) had been murdered years before by his son Brigham.

Jim Chee meanwhile is test-driving a used Buick for Janet Pete and wondering if the attractive lawyer can fill the gap of the absent Mary Landon. Just after noting the car's steering is a bit slack, he meets a Plymouth driven by a wanted suspect (the Backhoe Bandit) coming the other way and makes a U-turn to follow him. When the sedate pursuit turns into a full-fledged chase, the steering fails and the Buick plows into the sagebrush, sustaining considerable damage. Chee denies to the garage mechanic that Janet is his girlfriend: "Tough as nails.... Not my type. Not unless I kill somebody and need a lawyer" (page 38).

Chee and Leaphorn cross paths when leads bring them to a revival meeting of Navajo evangelist Slick Nakai—the garage man had once towed the Backhoe Bandit's Plymouth from Nakai's camp, and the preacher is known as a dealer in Anasazi pots. Nakai's message embodies a shrewd interface of Navajo and Christian religion, while underlining poignantly the dilemma of any Navajo who wishes to preserve the traditional ways:

"Right up the highway here . . . you have Huerfano Mesa. We been taught, us Navajos, that that's where First Woman lived, and First Man, and some of the other Holy People, they lived there. An' so when I was a boy, I would go with my uncle and we'd carry a bundle of *aghaal* up there, and we'd stick those prayer sticks up in a shrine we made up there and we'd chant this prayer.... But I want you to remember something about Huerfano Mesa. Just close your eyes now and remember how that holy place looked the last time you saw it. Truck road runs up there. It's got radio towers

THE TONY HILLERMAN COMPANION

built all over the top of it. Oil companies built
'em. Whole forest of those antennae all along
the top of our holy place."

Nakai was shouting now, emphasizing
each word with a downward sweep of his fist.
"I can't pray to the mountain no more.... Not
after the white man built all over the top of it.
Remember what the stories tell us. Changing
Woman left us. She's gone away." (pages 48–49)

The idea that one should take on the religion of
another who has spoiled the possibility of practicing
your own may seem somewhat theologically skewed,
but Nakai's sermon is one of the most eloquent
statements of the Native American's plight in contemporary America in the whole Hillerman canon.
The rest of his message, as quoted, is more conven-
tionally evangelical but just as shrewd and eloquent.

Talking to some of the missing anthropologist's colleagues, Leaphorn learns she believed she
had identified an individual potter of the late
Anasazi period and that her discoveries could provide clues to where the Anasazis went when they
disappeared from the area. Leaphorn also visits the
powerful Mormon millionaire Harrison Houk, who
remembers him as the young Navajo cop who
found his drowned son's hat a quarter century
before, and goes to New York to trace the stolen
pot traffic with some art dealers. It is his first trip
out of the Southwest in the series.

Chee meanwhile concludes that neither he
nor Mary Landon can live in the other's world, and
his thoughts turn to Janet Pete.

Besides including one of Hillerman's best-
woven plots, with all elements coming together like
a perfect mosaic, *A Thief of Time* has some of his
deepest exploration of religious values and the
varieties of religious belief and expression.

Talking God (1989)

If *A Thief of Time* is one of the series' highspots, the next two collaborations in detection by Leaphorn and Chee have struck me as among the less impressive of the Navajo Tribal Police novels. Hillerman, though, is too fine a pro ever to produce less than solid work, and the least of his books belongs in the upper echelons of detective fiction.

Talking God has two distinctions to recommend it: one of Hillerman's most memorable antagonists and also one of the most striking of his always provocative opening chapters. In Washington, D.C., attorney Catherine Morris Perry, counsel to the Smithsonian's Museum of Natural History, receives a package in the mail containing the bones of her grandparents, dug up from a church cemetery. With them is a letter from Henry Highhawk of the Bitter Water People, who has dug up and shipped the bones to protest the museum's refusal to rebury their 18,000 Native American skeletons.

Highhawk, a conservator for the Smithsonian, is not a full-blooded Navajo but a fair-skinned quarter Navajo. Captain Largo remarks cynically, "Usually when they decide to turn Indian and call themselves something like Whitecloud, or Squatting Bear, or Highhawk, they decide they're going to be Cherokees. Or some dignified tribe that everybody knows about. But this jerk had to pick Navajo" (page 25).

Highhawk has said in a letter to his kinswoman Agnes Tsosie that he wants to become "officially a member of the tribe" (page 22). Agnes has been told she is dying, and a Yeibichai, or Night Chant, is to be sung in her behalf. She invites Highhawk to attend, and Jim Chee and Cowboy Dashee are dispatched to arrest him on a federal warrant. Though Chee grumbles about not having as much information from his superior as he might need, both officers have reasons for welcoming the assignment: Chee would like to learn the complicated multi-evening Night Chant, and Dashee is attracted by the prospect of meeting some Native American beauty contestants. Highhawk turns up as expected on the final evening of the ceremony, and Jim makes the arrest.

Joe Leaphorn, meanwhile, has decided not to leave the Navajo Tribal Police after all and is investigating a body found near the railroad tracks under a clump of chamiso. Though the victim is obviously not a Navajo and his body is found off reservation land, he has a note in his coat pocket reading *Yeabechay? Yeibeshay? Agnes Tsosie (correct). Should be near Windowrock, Arizona* (page 14). Emma Leaphorn continues to be a posthumous presence in the novels. Feeling pain in his knees when he crouches to look at the body, Leaphorn reflects he has not been getting much exercise since her death. They had taken walks together almost every evening.

Chee's love life is unchanged. He is still denying Janet Pete, now working in Washington, D.C., is his girlfriend, and he is planning to visit Mary Landon in Wisconsin. Shortly after receiving a crushing letter from Mary that she does not want to see him and reopen old wounds, Chee gets a call from Janet, who, by virtue of her Navajo blood, has been hired to represent Henry Highhawk. When Chee asks if she expects to get him off, she replies,

> "Not if he gets his way. He wants to make it a political debate. He wants to put the *belagaana* [white] grave robbers on trial for robbing Indian graves while he's on trial for digging up a couple of whites. It might work in Washington, if I could pick the right jury. But

> the trial will be up in New Haven or someplace
> up in New England. Up in that part of the
> country everybody's happy memories are of
> hearing great-granddaddy tell about killing off
> the redskins." (page 57)

In a touch out of a Perry Mason novel, Highhawk
has told Janet he also wants her representation for
a crime he hasn't committed yet. When she con-
fides someone is following her, Chee offers to come
to Washington and help her out by talking to
Highhawk. He still has his now-to-be-unused ticket
to Milwaukee to visit Mary.

It further develops that Janet feels she is
being used. She knows she got the job because she
is her firm's token Indian and because Highhawk
insisted on a Navajo lawyer. She also knows the
firm represents a development company called
Sunbelt Corporation that is trying to get a right-of-
way from the Tano Tribal Council, which is currently split on granting it. One of the contenders for
a vacant seat on the council, who favors the right-
of-way, is trying to get a Tano fetish currently in the
Smithsonian returned to the tribe. Chee "could
understand [Janet's] suspicion. The firm wanted
her to represent Highhawk because Highhawk
worked in a sensitive position for the museum
which held Tano sacred objects. Why? Did they
want Highhawk to steal the War Twin? Was Janet,
as his lawyer, supposed to talk him into doing
that?" (pages 78–79).

Leaphorn, too, goes to Washington, on the
same case but for different reasons, and most of
the rest of the novel plays itself out there. It may be
the use of a background away from the Southwest
that renders the book less impressive than its predecessors, not because of some minor errors in
Washington geography Hillerman says readers

found there but because continuing detectives, not only Hillerman's, often do not transplant well to other locales. Ironically, as with some other long-term mystery writers who have achieved best-sellerdom several years into their careers—Dick Francis, Agatha Christie, Ross Macdonald, John D. MacDonald, Elmore Leonard, Robert B. Parker, and P. D. James are some examples—the increased critical attention to later books gives them an inflated reputation at the expense of earlier and better books.

Coyote Waits (1990)

In *Coyote Waits*, for the second time in the series, Jim Chee is present on the first page, receiving a transmission on his patrol car radio from fellow officer Delbert Nez, who reports he is running low on gas and trying to "catch the son-of-a-bitch with the smoking paint gun in his hand" (page 2). When radio contact is lost, Chee is not overly concerned—it's a common occurrence among the mesas and buttes of the Big Reservation—and he takes his time looking for his colleague, stopping at a trading post for a mild flirtation with the girl at the cash register. "She was a Towering House Dineh, and therefore in no way linked to Chee's own Slow Talking Clan. Chee remembered that. It was the automatic checkoff any single young Navajo conducts—male or female—making sure the one who attracted you wasn't a sister, or cousin, or niece in the tribe's complex clan system, and thereby rendered taboo by incest rules" (pages 4–5).

But when Chee belatedly finds Nez again, the other officer's squad car is ablaze, and Chee's attempts to rescue him fail. Though burned in the rescue attempt, Chee arrests Hosteen Ashie Pinto, a Navajo shaman, for killing Nez. He takes the old man's repeated statement, *"'Shiyaazh. . . . Baa yanisin.' My son, I am ashamed"* (page 16), for a confession. Chee then contemplates quitting in the wake of his guilt over not getting to Nez sooner.

Janet Pete has returned to the reservation, now with the Department of Justice as a public defender in federal criminal cases. She is assigned the defense of Ashie Pinto. When Janet comes to see Chee, waiting for him as he leaves an examining room at the University of New Mexico Hospital Burn and Trauma Center, he is disappointed that it is in a professional rather than a personal capacity, while she wonders why it can't be both.

A new romantic interest also develops for Joe Leaphorn. Accompanying Mary Keeyani, a relative of Emma's who believes Ashie Pinto is innocent and wants Leaphorn to look into the matter, is Louisa Bourebonette, an American Studies professor at Northern Arizona University in Flagstaff, who had been getting Pinto's accounts of Navajo myth and tradition for a book. "He told me he knew the original correct version of one of the Coyote myths. The one about the red-winged blackbirds and the game they play with their eyeballs. Throwing them up in the air and catching them, and Coyote forcing them to teach him the game'" (page 60). Pinto had left a tape behind, speaking in Navajo: *"They say Coyote is funny, some of those people say that. But the old people who told me the stories, they didn't think Coyote was funny. Coyote was always causing trouble. He was mean. He caused hardship. He hurt people. He caused people to die. That's the way the stories go that I was told by my uncles when I was a boy"* (page 59).

The novel gives trial buffs a chance to see Janet Pete in action in court, albeit briefly, as she defends Ashie Pinto in Federal District Court in

Albuquerque. During jury selection, a Navajo woman is asked about her clan connections to establish she is no kin to the defendant, while the court interpreter's loose renderings into Navajo for Pinto's benefit give Chee a promising idea. Like the first Hillerman novel, this one belongs in the bottom third of his work, but that is not to imply it isn't rewarding reading.

Sacred Clowns (1993)

The first four collaborations in detection of Leaphorn and Chee had appeared annually from 1987 to 1990. For the fifth, impatient readers had to wait three years. Hillerman's twelfth novel overall and eleventh about the Navajo Tribal Police in some respects offers the mixture as before, but in others it takes the series in a fresh direction.

Sacred Clowns opens with Jim Chee sitting on the roof of a house in the Tano Pueblo watching the kachina dance ceremony while looking for Delmar Kanitewa, Tribal Council member Bertha Roanhorse's grandson, who has disappeared from school. With Chee, who is doing his best to mix business with pleasure, is tribal lawyer Janet Pete, but to his chagrin they are not alone. Sharing the rooftop are Hopi cop Cowboy Dashee and Asher Davis, introduced by Dashee as "what you college-educated people would call an oxymoron. He's an Honest Indian Trader" (page 8).

Chee is now working directly for Leaphorn in the Special Investigations Office, but it isn't going as well as he'd hoped. He feels underutilized, especially when he is assigned not to investigate the murder of Eric Dorsey, a shop teacher at Saint Bonaventure Indian Mission, but instead to seek out runaway schoolboys.

Part of the kachina dance performance is the appearance of the koshares, the sacred clowns of the title, the description of whose acrobatic and dangerous antics with a ladder sounds like a slapstick two-reeler from the Keystone days. When Janet objects that their knockabout comedy is disrupting the ceremony, Chee explains, "Not disrupting. It's part of the ritual. It's all symbolic. They represent humanity. Clowns. Doing everything wrong while the spirits do everything right" (page 14).

By the time the ceremony ends, Chee has spotted his schoolboy quarry and lost him, and one of the koshares has been clubbed to death. The victim's name is Francis Sayesva, and he proves to be the uncle of the missing schoolboy.

Thus Chee begins the story by adding to his mostly unjust reputation as a screwup—Leaphorn is impressed neither with his strategy of viewing the crowd from the roof nor with the fact that he had company at the time—and as the book goes on Chee continues to seem a less competent police officer than usual, doing little successful detecting. He serves primarily as a Dr. Watson figure, not only to supercop Leaphorn but also to his religious and cultural mentor, Hosteen Frank Sam Nakai, who does a sort of armchair detective number at the book's midpoint, giving Chee a hint of where Delmar Kanitewa might be found.

The clash between Chee the cop and Chee the shaman is brought into sharper relief than ever, and he begins to doubt if he can reconcile the two. This internal conflict, along with his personal romantic preoccupation with Janet Pete, accounts for his reduced effectiveness as a police officer. Indeed, the title of the book could refer to Chee as much as to the koshares. His role is that of the sacred clown, trying to get the moves right but failing.

One of the several matters in Chee's caseload

is a hit-and-run case. If Chee can solve it, Leaphorn says, he will enhance his prospects of promotion to sergeant. Chee likens the promise to a fairy story:

> You can marry the princess if you do something impossible—like putting a mountain in a pea pod. How in hell could you solve a hit-and-runner with no clues, no broken headlight glass, no scraped paint, no witnesses, no nothing? He thought of another parallel. How in hell could he expect to win the princess, a full-scale city girl lawyer, if he couldn't make sergeant? (pages 89–90)

How he finally solves the hit-and-run case, and the decision he makes about its disposition, points up the theme of clashing religious and secular roles.

The novel is more preoccupied with the personal and romantic relationships of Leaphorn and Chee than any other. Leaphorn is planning a trip to China with Louisa Bourebonette; veteran mystery readers will have a good guess as to whether the trip actually comes off. Meanwhile, Chee's increasing seriousness about Janet Pete forces him to consider whether their relationship violates Navajo incest taboos. As a "city Navajo," Janet doesn't even know her father's clans, and Jim devotes as much effort to working them out as to his police duties.

Another difference, one that is appropriate to the novel's title, is the increased use of humor, most notably in a chapter that is undoubtedly the funniest in any of Hillerman's novels. Jim and Janet attend a screening of John Ford's *Cheyenne Autumn* at a Gallup drive-in. In a continuation of the book's running gag about Jim's inability to get Janet alone, they are joined by Bureau of Indian Affairs Sergeant Harold Blizzard, himself a

Cheyenne and a temporary houseguest of Chee's. *Cheyenne Autumn* is a favorite movie of Navajos because of a durable practical joke carried out by some of the Navajo bit players cast as Cheyennes. As Chee explains to his companions, the somber responses to cavalry commander Richard Widmark in Navajo, translated into English as statements appropriate to the story, really "tended to have something to do with the size of the colonel's penis, or some other earthy and humorous irrelevancy" (page 122).

On a more serious note, Jim later remarks to Janet the differences between the Navajo audience's reactions to the film and those of Blizzard: "We Navajos would be laughing and honking our horns at our private joke, and he would be looking sad. Same scene, exactly. He'd be watching the destruction of his culture. We'd be watching our kinfolks making fun of the white folks in the movie" (page 131).

The whole novel is much lighter in tone than earlier books in the series. There are none of the Woolrichian-suspense set pieces that occur in many of the other novels. The requisite details of Native American belief and culture are presented, but there is less effort to evoke a supernatural aura. Though the mystery is complexly constructed, it is resolved by a final chapter of exposition, with the climax taking place offstage. The reader's considerable interest in the characters carries much more of the load than the plot. Rather than leaving romantic matters hanging, as has been Hillerman's practice in previous novels, there is more of a sense of reconciliation and closure at the story's end.

It is difficult to know where to rank this most recent novel among Hillerman's works. If it lacks the snap and urgency of early books in the series, its comparatively relaxed and mellow quality, together with its thematic interest and its wise decision to stick to the Southwestern locale, marks it in some respects superior to the pair that immediately preceded it.

Hillerman's Place in Crime Fiction

Tony Hillerman is far from being the only contemporary mystery writer who regularly makes the best-seller lists and is repeatedly profiled in national media. Indeed, mystery writers sometimes seem to be the rule rather than the exception on such lists in recent years. But he has achieved a unique niche. A survey of English teachers pronounced him their all-time favorite mystery writer by a wide margin, not just among contemporaries but for the whole history of the genre.[14] Hillerman's novels are commonly valued more for their Native American lore than for the mystery plots. Indeed, we are often told writers of detective fiction are read less for their puzzles than for their characters and background. While this is certainly true to an extent, the puzzle is still the element essential to making detective fiction a unique genre, and Hillerman's novels are as good as they are because he has not deserted the formal puzzle to indulge his anthropological specialty. If Hillerman had decided he could forgo or downplay the element of mystery and become a sort of southwestern Robert B. Parker, he might have gotten away with it for a time, but his books would be much less worthy of praise. Though constantly trying new approaches

14. Ben F. Nelms and Stephen L. Fisher, "Favorite Detective Story Writers: From Poe to the Present," *English Journal*, February 1992, pp. 91–95.

and growing as a writer, Hillerman has never renounced his adherence to the pattern and rules of classical detective fiction.

Hillerman has avoided another pitfall awaiting very successful writers, especially in the current market that encourages bigger books: excessive and self-indulgent length. His later novels are as crisp and spare and economical as the earlier ones, with no trace of blockbuster bloat.

The writer most comparable to Hillerman is of course his acknowledged precursor, Arthur W. Upfield. Though Hillerman's detectives do not share the semicomic Great Detective posture of Inspector Napoleon Bonaparte, the sympathetic and detailed depiction of a native culture is similar. Upfield, whose early books were florid and Victorian, developed into a spare and powerful writer. While it is true he sometimes patronizes his Aborigines, as Hillerman never does with his Native American subjects, allowance must be made for the times in which Upfield wrote. In novels like *The Bone Is Pointed* (1947), Upfield was way ahead of his time.

The less frequent but inevitable comparison to Agatha Christie, though such a comparison is an obvious and glib one for any writer working in the classical tradition, also has some merit. Aside from the skilled construction of puzzles, Hillerman has in common with Christie his family-audience sensibility: no explicit sex, no bad language to speak of, mostly muted violence, nothing you'd worry about your twelve-year-old picking up. He differs from Christie, though, in his emphasis on mysteries of motive over mysteries of identity.

Though Hillerman may or may not have been influenced directly by Cornell Woolrich, his scenes of suspense and menace sometimes suggest such an influence. Although Hillerman does not do locked rooms or impossible crimes per se, the continuing theme of the seemingly supernatural dispelled by a natural explanation parallels the method of John Dickson Carr. And Hillerman's achievement has something in common with that of Isaac Asimov and other writers of science-fiction detective novels: the need to introduce the reader to the rules and mores of an unfamiliar culture to which the problem and its solution are organic. Hillerman also has the challenge of reintroducing the culture in each book, telling enough for the new reader without losing the old reader through repetitiousness.

Hillerman, of course, also belongs among the writers of religious detective fiction. Few writers are as fully occupied with the practice of religion as Hillerman, and few bring real religious issues as strongly to the forefront in their plots. Hillerman has this emphasis on religion in common with writers on Jewish themes like Harry Kemelman, Joseph Telushkin, and Faye Kellerman; on Catholic themes like William X. Kienzle, Andrew Greeley, Ralph McInerny, and Sister Carol Anne O'Marie; on Protestant themes like the late Charles Merrill Smith, Gaylord Larsen, and Isabelle Holland. The difference is that the religion described with such detail and with such unpatronizing objectivity in Hillerman's fiction is not his own. He is a Roman Catholic, and while priests appear in prominent roles in a couple of the Navajo novels, and the Catholic theology comes through most strongly in the short story "First Lead Gasser," the spirit of his books is admirably ecumenical. Hillerman, one feels, would never deign to tell a person from another religious tradition how to believe, any more than would his Navajo characters.

2

INTERVIEW WITH
WITH
TONY HILLERMAN

Jon L. Breen

Tony Hillerman was interviewed by telephone by Jon L. Breen on March 7, 1993.

JB: Tony, you have something in common with another best-selling mystery writer, Harry Kemelman. People wrongly assume he must be a rabbi. Even now, some readers must still assume you're a Navajo. So I think the obvious first question is how you came by this extensive knowledge of Navajo culture.

TH: It took a long time, and it'll be a long answer.

JB: That's O.K.

TH: I was born in Pottawatomie County, Oklahoma, in a village called Sacred Heart, which was an old Benedictine mission. It was built on land provided by the Potawatomi, and the Benedictines built an Indian school there. My dad ran the crossroads store and we had a farm nearby. I grew up with Potawatomi and Seminole kids and went to the Indian school the first eight grades. The point is, I grew up knowing Indians are just like I am, just like everybody else is in all essential ways. Learn that as a child, it's easy. Try to learn it later, it's sometimes impossible. So given that basis, at the end of World War II, I was back in the States. I'd been sent home to recuperate and have an operation on a leg and I got a convalescent furlough. I had a job driving a truckload of oil field equipment onto the Navajo reservation, and I blundered into an Enemy Way ceremonial being held for a couple of Navajo marines back from the Pacific war. I saw a little bit of it. Then in 1952, when I got out here for good with the United Press, I thought, Here are Indians who still have their culture, and I was interested. So I began reading and making friends.

JB: Which values of the Navajo culture do you most value and which ones do you least value?

TH: What I most value is their central goal—to be in harmony with the circumstances that surround you. It's the idea of *hozho*, the word I often misspell in my books.[1] If you can't change it, you get in harmony with it. Then there's the high value they place on family and the extremely low value they place on material possessions. You don't measure a man's worth by what he owns in terms of pickup trucks and money. On the contrary, if he's got too much, he's probably not taking care of his primary responsibility, his family. The things about the culture that I think are negative, from my point of view, is the belief system that focuses so much on fearfulness. The witchcraft idea.

JB: Which recurs again and again in your books.

TH: It does. It's a pervasive notion.

JB: Now, I know you have a lot of fans among the Navajos. Is the feedback you get from Navajo readers always positive? Are they ever offended by anything you've written?

TH: I've had virtually all positive. In fact, they gave me an award—the only time they've ever given it—declaring me a Special Friend of the Navajos. They use my books in their schools. And I get a lot of letters from Navajo kids. In fact, I just

1. Sources on Navajo religion and culture give the spelling as *hozho* or *hozhoo*.

had a Navajo call me. They had a meeting with some senators here on preserving the Native American religion. They wanted me to write an essay for them. I'm considered kind of a second-string Navajo. But there have been instances—and I can only think of two—when Navajos were critical. They were young women, urban Navajos who hadn't actually grown up on the reservation. One thought I had the attitude about coyotes screwed up, and she had ideas about it. Another felt I shouldn't be writing this stuff, that a Navajo should be writing it, that it was exploitive.

JB: The same reaction that quite often comes up when a Caucasian writes about a minority.

TH: Well, yeah.

JB: Now, I know that for many years before your first novel was published, you were a journalist and freelance magazine writer. In the postscript to "First Lead Gasser," in the April 1993 *Ellery Queen's Mystery Magazine*, you said that the situation described in that story was what led you into writing fiction. What is the special satisfaction to you of doing fiction rather than nonfiction?

TH: Let me clarify the question. I don't get more satisfaction in writing fiction rather than nonfiction. I still write both quite a bit. I like to write nonfiction. I like to write fiction. The point was there are situations where objective journalism allows you to give people the facts—but it doesn't allow you to give them the truth as you see it. Fiction does. You can paint the picture for them as you see it in your own mind. The facts don't always allow that.

JB: In your first novel, *The Blessing Way*, Professor Bergen McKee is a character who in the early part of the novel is of about equal importance to Joe Leaphorn, and in the later stages of the book, he becomes sort of central to the story and

Leaphorn rescues him. In later books you let the Navajo cops take center stage. Did you think at the time that an Anglo protagonist was a commercial necessity? Or was it a viewpoint you were comfortable with?

TH: When I finished the first draft of that book and sent it to my agent, Joe Leaphorn was a very minor character. I had written a story about Bergen McKee, an anthropologist, in whose viewpoint I felt fairly comfortable. I set it on a Navajo reservation primarily because I thought the Navajos were so interesting, and their reservation was so interesting, that it would make a captivating setting for a mystery novel, which otherwise might not be very good, because I didn't know if I was going to be a good mystery writer. As the story began to jell I began learning two things. One was that this Leaphorn guy was a much better character than my plot gave him a chance to be. And two, I didn't know nearly as much about Navajo culture as I thought I did. When I got the manuscript back from Joan Kahn, she told me a lot of things—two pages, double-spaced—were wrong with it, but if I would give them a different ending they would be interested in publishing it. So now this is no longer a game. This is serious. This thing, believe it or not, is actually going to be published. So in revising it, I expanded the role of Leaphorn. Even when I finished it, I said, I've got to do another book and do the Navajo part right. That was the genesis.

JB: I've read that your original title was *Enemy Way* and the publisher thought *The Blessing Way* made a better title. Why in the world would they have thought that made a better title for a mystery than *Enemy Way*?

TH: I have not the slightest idea. I wish I knew the answer. I assume Joan Kahn, the editor, changed the name. She asked me for a list. I'd

already thought of *The Enemy Way*, but I typed up a
bunch of other names that came to mind. I must
have had *The Blessing Way* on the list. But I don't
know why. I was amazed when they made the
change.

JB: It seems baffling to me! In *Talking
Mysteries*, Ernie Bulow is really scathing about *The
Blessing Way* in his introduction, and you seem to
agree with his relatively low opinion of the book. To
me, as a reader, the book by itself seems a really
great achievement, and it only suffers when you
compare it with the books that came later. It's now
a little over twenty years after the book was first
published. What do you most like or dislike about
that first book now?

TH: What I most like about it is some really
good scenes. It has some of my best suspense. The
piece in the canyon when the guy wakes up in the
sleeping bag. I liked some of the descriptive stuff I
did. I liked the scene at the Enemy Way. I really
thought I gave a glimpse of the ceremonial that
revealed something about the Navajo culture. What
I didn't like about it, I think, was the same thing
Ernie didn't like about it. I put in some stuff that
was—let's see, how do I put this?—I was careless
with some of the stuff.

JB: He compared it in his article in *Talking
Mysteries* with a term paper or a thesis by a student
who was new to the vocabulary.

TH: Well, I don't know. I know he didn't like it.
I've said several times that if I wasn't doing something different, I wouldn't mind going back and
rewriting it. I didn't understand the nature of the
skinwalker as well then as I do now.

JB: You've always acknowledged Arthur W.
Upfield's books about Inspector Napoleon
Bonaparte, the Australian Aborigine sleuth. What
was it in Upfield that most appealed to you, and

also in what ways does your approach differ from his?

TH: It was his ability to make that outback, that desert, seem real. The same with the Aborigine culture. When I finished one of his better books I felt I had learned something. I felt I'd been to the outback and understood the culture better. I thought he stereotyped his character, made him a kind of superman. I didn't like that. The good books, the books that focus on the desert and the Abo culture, are really good—*The Bone Is Pointed, The Will of the Tribe, Death of a Lake*. But some of his books are just awful. Dennis McMillan reprinted one of the worst—*The Royal Affair* or something like that.[2]

JB: A very early one.

TH: *The New Shoe*, which the Mystery Library of the University of California brought out, was a loser.

JB: Really? That was the one that John Ball, who was the chief of that project, seemed to think was the best one.

TH: The mystery and detection was okay but that's not why you like Upfield. I say he influenced me, because he did. When I was a boy the Curtis Publishing Company published *Country Gentleman*, *Ladies' Home Journal*, *Collier's*, and *The Saturday Evening Post*—I think they published *Collier's*. You could send in this coupon and they would send you a book bag and start you in magazine sales. When you sold a certain amount of magazines, you got a dollar bonus. Well, in Sacred Heart, Oklahoma, where I lived, there was a population of only about sixty, including lots of people who couldn't really read or write, I'm sure. So I wouldn't sell very many

2. The title was *The Royal Abduction*, originally published in Britain in 1932 and published in the United States by Dennis McMillan in 1984.

magazines, except to sympathetic kinfolks and such. I would get my dollar and quit and start again for another dollar bonus. The point is that *The Saturday Evening Post* was serializing a novel about the Australian outback when I was doing that. I was about eleven or twelve. I read those things, and wow, I still remember those scenes. So I went through my young manhood with those memories vividly in my mind. I didn't remember who the hell wrote them. But after *Blessing Way* was published, the *Boston Globe* reviewer, I think it was, said it was reminiscent of Upfield. I went to the library and, sure enough, I had read a lot of his stuff as a boy. So I'm sure he influenced me.

JB: Your second novel, *The Fly on the Wall*, is the only adult novel you've done without a Navajo sleuth. At the time you wrote it, did you plan to return to reporter John Cotton in subsequent books?

TH: No, I didn't. My plan when I decided I'd try to write a novel was to write *The Fly on the Wall*, which would be a big important book. To get ready to write it since I wasn't sure how good I was, I thought I'd write a mystery first. They looked easier. So I wrote *The Blessing Way*. If I could finish that, I thought, then I'll write *The Fly on the Wall*. So I did finish it, and I did write *The Fly on the Wall*. But it didn't turn out to be a big important book. I still like it. And it's still in print, and I still get letters from newspaper reporters and stuff now and then.

JB: It's probably still one of the most realistic what you would call journalistic procedurals in the mystery field. I think that the question of journalistic ethics that's posed in it is very effectively done.

TH: The issue is still alive and well.

JB: Absolutely. In *Dance Hall of the Dead*, you

told me you changed the murderer in midstream. And in fact, the killer is offstage at the end of the book. When Newgate Callendar reviewed this in the *New York Times*, he said that only a dull reader would not figure out the murderer halfway through. But rereading it, it seemed to me that your original choice looked at least as likely a candidate as your final choice. How important is it to you to surprise the reader with the villain's identity?

TH: Not very. What I'd rather surprise him with is the question, What's going on here? Why is this happening? That sort of thing, instead of *who*.

JB: You've written on several occasions that you never know exactly where the plot of the book is going when you write the first chapter. About how far through are you when you have an idea of what the ending is going to be like?

TH: As we speak, I'm on page seventeen of a chapter in the book I'm now working on. And I quit to go for a walk with my wife. On the walk, I told her I finally knew how I was going to finish the book and I told her how. About two weeks ago, I told her I finally knew how to finish the book and I told her how. The endings are different. But this chapter I'm writing now is probably the second from the last of about twenty-eight or thirty chapters. Understand, I know what the crime is. And I know in this case what motivates it, but the way I'm going to work it out keeps changing.

JB: I gather this is another book about Leaphorn and Chee.

TH: Yes.

JB: Can you tell us the title?

TH: No. The working title is *Next Book*. This is the book—well, it's not the book. Last year, really *two* years ago, this book was called—believe it or not—"Mudhead Kiva." HarperCollins ran a big ad in *Publishers Weekly* and sent me a copy of the dust jacket, and I thought, My God, that's a terrible title. They tell me I suggested it but I figured we could change it. Then things happened. My brother died. He was older and my only brother and a great friend. That took some of the steam out of me. And then I had a couple of operations for cancer. I wasn't writing for a long time. When I started writing again, that so-called "Mudhead Kiva" was a dead book. It was just gone. I threw it away.

JB: So you abandoned it. Will you come back to it later?

TH: No. I salvaged some fingernail clippings and a few of the basic ideas and started over with a different concept. It's too complicated to get into here. But this book is very, very different from the book I was writing when all those bad things happened.

JB: After *Dance Hall of the Dead* won the Edgar award, there was a five-year gap before the third Leaphorn novel appeared. Was there any particular reason for that hiatus?

TH: Five-year gap?

JB: Yeah. *Dance Hall of the Dead* came out in 1973, *Listening Woman* was 1978, and *People of Darkness* was 1980.

TH: You're skipping *Dark Wind*.

JB: No, that's 1982. I'm sure I'm right on this.

TH: Hold on now. Hold on just a minute. Have you got that bibliography? [After checking the Louis Hieb bibliography of his works, Hillerman verifies the order of publication.]

JB: So I gather there wasn't any memorable reason for the five-year gap.

TH: Well, in that interim I wrote *The Boy Who Made Dragonfly* and maybe *The Spell of New Mexico*. I can't remember, really.

JB: In *People of Darkness*, you shifted from Leaphorn to Jim Chee as your central character.

There's quite an interesting inside joke for your regular readers. At one point Chee gets a message to call *Captain* Leaphorn in Chinle, but then he never returns his call. And of course later I think you rescinded Leaphorn's promotion to captain.

TH: I did. I rescinded Chee's promotion, too—he got promoted to sergeant in one book.

JB: That's right. Then he's an officer again. Now why did you switch characters at this point? And also, I'm wondering if you expected then that you would eventually return to Leaphorn.

TH: O.K., first question first. *The People of Darkness* was going to take place on the eastern side of the reservation: the Checkerboard Reservation, where it's all mixed up with Native American Church and Episcopalians and fundamentalists and Assembly of God and True Gospel and Mennonites and Roman Catholics religious-wise. And ethnically it's all a mixture of Lagunas and Mexicans and Germans and cantankerous old ranchers, a total melting-pot situation. So I thought that would be a great place to do something with these cultures rubbing together. It turned out it didn't work too well. I started using Leaphorn at first, and right away I realized he was too old and sophisticated to be amazed or interested. So I thought, Well, how about young Leaphorn, new to the force? But I'd been thinking of him in terms of a seasoned fellow, and I was just not comfortable. So I thought I'll start me a new guy. This time I'll give him a real Navajo name instead of that damned thing I called Joe. I'll try to give him a more traditional background. That was one of the important reasons. I had another reason. I had signed a movie/TV option—on *Dance Hall of the Dead*. The option had been renewed several times, enough to pay for the television rights. The way the contract was written, they had bought TV rights and continuing rights to the continuing characters. So I no longer owned the TV rights to Joe Leaphorn. This was no big deal, but it's irritating to think you've been screwed. And you don't want to continue buttering the bread of the screwer. I thought I'd quit using Leaphorn anyway. So I came up with Jim Chee.

JB: *People of Darkness* begins with Chee visiting the home of a rich man and being offered a job by the owner's wife. It has very much the feel of a private-eye novel more than a police procedural. Was this a conscious homage to Raymond Chandler on your part?

TH: No.

JB: It has a Ross Macdonald sort of plot, too, with the oil-field explosion buried in the past and influencing what happens in the present.

TH: You know what the genesis of that was?

JB: No.

TH: Understand, I wasn't making money off those first books. I had six children and a faculty job. If you've ever been on a faculty, you know you don't make any money.

JB: Right. I agree.

TH: So I was writing all kinds of stuff. I had been retained by a bank holding company to do a biography of the founder of the bank. His name was Luthy. He had made some loans on oil-drilling operations—this is back in the Depression, the dollar-a-barrel oil—and he'd gone down to inspect one. They were shooting the well to bring it in, which is when you'd want to be there if you were the banker. The damned nitro went off before they got in the hole, just as it did in the story, and it killed some people and blinded Luthy. I had that in my mind. Item two, my brother was a petroleum geologist and a well logger. One of these guys who sits on the well and analyzes the drill stem. I had been to a well he was working watching him analyze drill stem, and I was thinking of all kinds of possibilities for chicanery. So that's the genesis of that plot.

JB: I wanted to ask you about the two Jim Chee short stories. Were those written after *People of Darkness* or before? Or do you recall?

TH: I don't really recall. I think they were written before. I think *People of Darkness* kind of grew out of them.

JB: The plot elements, though, turn up in *The Dark Wind* and *The Ghostway*.

TH: Gosh, I don't remember when I wrote those. You'd have to look. You can dig up the copyright.

JB: It's not crucial. I know you did reuse a lot of material from them. I also noticed that in the two stories some of the language where you described the rumored witch sightings is identical, and also the clue of the mutilation of the bodies turns up in both stories. Did you think at the time that the stories would ever be published, or were they just something that would be fodder for some of your books?

TH: Again, I'm relying on memory. I'm like a lot of people who write—who think they can write short stories. So I'd gone through that period early on of trying to write the damned things, and it finally dawned on me that while I could write them I couldn't sell them. One of those things I wrote because I got a letter from the fiction editor of *Playboy* asking me for a short story. One of them was written for that purpose. At the same time—that must have been in the late seventies—the International Crime Writers had a contest. I said I would enter it. They'd written me and said, Where's your entry? I thought, Well, two birds with one stone. I did it for *Playboy* and got a wonderful rejection letter. Then I rewrote it and got another wonderful rejection letter. And then I thought, Well, I'll enter it in the competition. That's how it came to be written. I really don't remember much about the chronology of any of that stuff.

JB: You think of it mainly as two versions of the same story?

TH: Yeah, you keep trying to get the damned thing written—to find a way to make it work.

JB: Now, *Dark Wind*, I would say, in contrast to *People of Darkness*, is more like a police procedural novel in the sense that there are a number of different cases being investigated at the same time. Some police procedural writers will do that and never connect up the various strands, but you invariably tie all of them together at the end. Is that something that's more satisfactory to you? Do you think you owe it to your readers to bring all the cases together?

TH: I wouldn't say exactly. I wouldn't think of using that language. I kind of write for an invisible reader. I'm building a structure, I'm entertaining him or her, I'm providing a scene. I want the reader to look out my window and see this. Also, in a sense, I'm satisfying my own urgings—this sounds kind of pretentious—to get a kind of symmetry in the book. Before *The Dark Wind* I had never been content with the way I had made plot and subplot work together. In this one I couldn't make the plot go either. I was really stuck. I don't think I've ever been stuck harder in a book. Marie [Mrs. Hillerman], who knows me very well, said, Why don't you go out on the Big Res and spend some time? You always come back with new ideas. So I said, How about going along? She said O.K., she'd go along. Winter was just coming. We got out on the Hopi reservation, and while we were there somebody vandalized a windmill. The Hopis put out a little weekly—I forget the name of it—and they had a little piece in there. When I saw it, I said, Marie, let's go home.

JB: That solved it.

TH: Yeah, it gave me a reason for the cop to be where he had to be. And then, as the story developed, when I began thinking why the mill would be vandalized, I began seeing how it could be as important as the plot. In the final book, I think, more people are going to remember the subplot than the main plot.

JB: When we get to *The Ghostway,* which was the third of the novels where Chee appears by himself, it becomes clear his relationship with Mary Landon, the Anglo schoolteacher, is in trouble, because she wants him to leave the reservation and become an FBI agent. I thought some of her reasoning was quite interesting. She said he follows the Navajo way only when it suits what he wants to do anyway, and then she points out that the Navajo tradition is for the husband to join the wife's clan, rather than the wife becoming part of the husband's family. Do you think she had a point there?

TH: Damned right!

JB: Yeah. She didn't convince Chee, though.

TH: He wanted to be a *hataalii,* a singer, a medicine man. You can't perform those ceremonies outside the sacred mountains, and a lot of Navajos feel people who leave the reservation are no longer Navajo. It's very difficult for a Navajo to remain a Navajo when he moves to the city. One of my good sources, in fact, was a young man who really had a lot of promise, I thought, a student at the University of New Mexico. I hadn't seen him for a while. I ran into his brother and I asked him where he was, and he said, Oh, he committed suicide. It's tough. That's why I think Mary and Jim both had a point.

JB: Your first six Navajo novels follow a sort of

neat pattern. You've got three about Leaphorn, then you've got three about Chee, and in the seventh they join forces. How did you come to the decision to use both characters in the same book? You weren't planning at that point that you wanted three of each?

TH: No, that thought hadn't occurred to me. They came together in what?

JB: It's in *Skinwalkers* where they were first together.

TH: It was going to be basically about Chee, and it *was* basically about Chee. But I needed a superior for him to deal with. And there was good old Joe Leaphorn on the shelf, whom I knew very well, so I just started using him. I can't remember doing any advance planning on it, or thinking about it. And I've never had the least interest in numbers.

JB: I don't know if you'll agree with me about this, but I thought when I read your books the first time, when you switched from Leaphorn to Chee, I was a little bit disappointed. Rereading the books, though, it seems to me that Chee is a fully realized character from his very first appearance, whereas the Leaphorn of the first three books is a much less rounded character than the Leaphorn of the later books.

TH: I think you're right. Until you reach a certain age where your brain cells are dying too fast, if you're interested in something, you continue learning. I was learning. With every book I wrote, I think I learned something. Now I do remember why I stuck Leaphorn in that book. I remember it very vividly. I was in California at a book signing, and a woman asked me why I started using Chee instead of Leaphorn. I gave her the same explanation I gave you. She said, I can't tell them apart. And oh, boy, that was a dagger to the heart.

JB: I don't think she was reading very carefully.

TH: I couldn't get that out of my mind. Nobody had ever said anything like that to me before. I thought, Have I been kidding myself? I went back and looked at them, and *I* could tell them apart. So I thought, You know what I'm gonna do? I'm going to resurrect Leaphorn, stick him in this book, put 'em in there side by side, and I'll see if I can tell them apart. That's how he got off the shelf. Thanks to that lady.

JB: Another thing about Leaphorn. It seems a pity to me that Mrs. Leaphorn, who's only mentioned in passing a couple of places in the first three books, only becomes a real character when she's dying. Do you regret at all that you didn't use Mrs. Leaphorn earlier?

TH: No, I don't. I would have to look back. She was only there by sheer accident anyway in *Dance Hall of the Dead*. I had Leaphorn talking to his dispatcher on the radio, exchanging information, and I wanted to stretch it out a little bit and make Leaphorn seem kind of like a real person. I stuck in the dispatcher telling him that Emma wanted to remind him he had a dental appointment. That's where Emma came from. It was sheer whimsy. Pure accident.

JB: It seems sort of ironic that the younger detective, Chee, is the more conservative and the one who hews to the old ways, and the older one, Leaphorn, is more ambivalent. We see today that young people are more conservative than their parents were. Would you say that Leaphorn is essentially a sixties person and Chee is essentially an eighties or nineties person?

TH: Yeah, except I think I'd change the calendar dates some. Chee is sort of an amalgam of twenty years of students. But mostly of those students of the sixties and seventies, who were reading *Ivanhoe* and that awful Hermann Hesse—the romantic writers. They were idealists, they were full of dreams, they were true believers, they were rebels. They were fascinating people to teach, but they wore you out. That's Chee. They were in a sense traditional in that they wanted to go back to the nineteenth century, when everybody was honest and honorable, and there weren't any atomic bombs and—you know. Leaphorn was more the person of the—

JB: Fifties?

TH: Or forties—a pragmatist, a rationalist, a fellow who looked through the mythology at the reason the mythology was created. And as a matter of fact, I think that's the way reality is. Oddly enough, you find tradition among the Navajos in the very old and the young guys, and the guys in the middle are less traditional. Often they don't speak the language as well either.

JB: *Skinwalkers* won a Spur award from the Western Writers of America, which is an unusual honor for a detective novel. Are you attracted to the Western genre, and have you ever considered doing a historical Western?

TH: No. I admire some of them, but they're not my bag. Neither is fantasy or science fiction.

JB: It seems to me, and see if you agree with this, in your recent novels, since you became a best seller, you have avoided two of the major pitfalls that sometimes await mystery writers when they make the best-seller list: either stinting on the mystery and detection element, which you have not done, or writing at excessive length. I'm wondering, are you under any pressure to write longer books?

TH: No, not really. I don't think so. HarperCollins has been waiting for this book forever. To let them know that I'd come alive and was actually writing, I sent the first hundred pages to my agent, and he showed it to them. Then subsequently I told my agent I was on page two hundred or so, and he told the editor at HarperCollins. The editor then wrote me and said something about me being two thirds finished. That would indicate he's expecting three hundred pages, but I don't know if you'd say that's pressure to write longer books. I just finished reading a novel at nine hundred and something. But the one I'm writing—well, I just write them until they're written, and they tend to run about three hundred pages.

JB: I'm going to ask you a question that sometimes invites a particular answer, but I'll risk asking it anyway. Do you have a favorite among your books? Is there one in particular where you thought all the elements came together particularly well?

TH: I do. It's *The Thief of Time*. Every one of my books has good places in it and bad places in it. There are places where, boy, it really worked and places I wish I could go back and rewrite. But in general I think *The Thief of Time* was clean and clear, and it has less of those draggy spots. I guess I'd say that would be my pet.

JB: Are there any that you're less than happy with, in retrospect?

TH: *The Blessing Way*.

JB: Besides that.

TH: Well, again there's parts in several of them I could have done better on. I think, I should have had this guy say this, or done this. There's places where you can fix them. But the only one I— well, when people say where should I start, I say, Don't start with *The Blessing Way*.

JB: Even though it's the first one in order.

TH: Yeah.

JB: I notice that one of the characteristics of the books with the Navajo background is that certain surnames recur over and over again among the Navajos, like Yazzie and Begay and Bitsi.

TH: That bothers me too, even though they are very common Navajo names. There's a radio station at Farmington where you just walk up to an open mike and make announcements over the air. I collected out of the wastebasket there a whole stack of these. I went through them and wrote down names. I use names of people I know, and I've got a Navajo Communications Company telephone book, and I use it for names. I went through all these sources and wrote down names: Shorty Begay, Curtis Benny, Charlie B. Joe, George Bluehorse, Beulah Sunrise, Kee Shaggy, Joseph Redhead. I'm trying to expand my vocabulary of Navajo names. It's amazing how many Navajos you know are named Begay or Tsosie or Joe or Billy or something like that. It's similar to the Smiths, Joneses, Johnsons, and Lees.

JB: Sometimes when they recur in the books, I wonder, Is this the same person that is in some other book or is it just someone else with the same name? With your background as a professor of journalism and also as assistant to the President of the University of New Mexico, you could do quite an academic novel. Have you had any thoughts of making Leaphorn or Chee a visiting professor somewhere?

TH: No. I had a thought once of having a crime committed at Rhein-Main Air Base or someplace in Germany and a Navajo enlisted man accused of it and have it involve some sort of esoteric business with the Navajo religion and have Chee sent back there to investigate it. It'd give me a tax deductible excuse to go to Germany.

JB: So far, if memory serves, you've taken your Navajo detectives away from their normal stamping grounds twice. In *The Ghostway*, Chee goes to Los Angeles, and of course *Talking God* is partly set in Washington, D.C.

TH: I had no problem much with Los Angeles, because I put Chee in a neighborhood I'm very familiar with. Marie's had an aunt living there who was elderly, living alone and in poor health. We used to go out and spend some time trying to get her straightened out. So I knew the neighborhood. I made a lot of mistakes in Washington. People there were very cooperative. The working stiffs at the Museum of Natural History, after I got smart enough to know that's the people to talk to, not the big shots, they gathered me in and turned me loose so I could look behind the scenes. I stayed in a real shoddy kind of hotel that Chee would stay in, and walked the streets and rode the subways. But I still made a lot of mistakes. Washington cabs don't have meters. I put in a Walgreen drugstore. They don't have them.

JB: Which to most readers wouldn't make the slightest bit of difference.

TH: No, but to the people who know Washington, it screws up the book.

JB: I know you must regularly receive advance copies of books from publishers, certainly those with Native American themes, in hopes you will give them a quote.

TH: I get about eight a week.

JB: Are there any authors of mystery fiction writing about a Native American background whom you particularly like?

TH: I like Jean Hager a lot. I haven't seen her most recent work, but I liked what she was doing with the Oklahoma tribes I grew up around. And Jake Page, who knows Hopis as well as any white man except perhaps Frank Waters, is out with a good book set in Hopi country. Earlier he and his wife, Susanne, did an outstanding photo essay on the tribe.[3] Outside of mysteries, there's Ron Querry's *The Death of Bernadette Lefthand*, a powerful book. And Tom King, the Canadian novelist. He's an important writer, but I can't remember his tribe. I always say every literate American should have a copy of N. Scott Momaday's *The Way to Rainy Mountain* in his library. It's as much an American classic as *Leaves of Grass*

JB: Any mystery writers you'd like to mention?

TH: I'm excited about James Girard and *The Late Man*, an innovative book. Judith Van Giesen is very good, and Sue Grafton and a host of the new women writers.

JB: What kinds of things do you enjoy reading—apart from, I assume, anthropology texts and all those galleys you get from publishers?

TH: I read mostly nonfiction. However, I just finished a novel, one of these reader's copies, that one I mentioned that's going to be nine hundred pages. What a book! The name of it is *Gospel*. It's his second novel. I can't think of his name or the first book.[4] The characters are almost all academic theologians: the University of Chicago, Hebrew University, that big university in Cairo. One principal character is an ex-Jesuit, and the plot concerns a scroll that's been floating around the black market for years. Now it dawns on some people that it is

3. The collaborative book Hillerman is referring to is *Hopi* (Abrams, 1982) by Susanne and Jake Page. Jake Page is also the author of a mystery novel with a Native American background, *Shoot the Moon* (Bobbs-Merrill, 1979). Three titles by Jake Page were published in 1993, *Songs to Birds* (Godine), *The Stolen Gods* (Ballantine/Del Rey), and *Tales of the Earth* (Oxford University Press), written with Charles Officer.

4. The author is Wilton Barnhardt, and the book was published in 1993 by St. Martin's Press.

probably a gospel written by Matthias, the disciple who replaced Judas. The author is really steeped in esoteric knowledge of this first century of Christianity. Something is always happening. It's a great book. But then, as I said, I don't read much fiction anymore. I read some poetry. I've been reading Robert Frost and Stephen Spender.

JB: Given your current status in publishing, I have a hunch you could probably get anything you've ever written in print, if you wanted to. You could probably collect your Purina Pig Chow commercials and get them published as a book. Is there anything in your files that you'd like to see published that you wrote a long time ago?

TH: My master's thesis was something called *The Great Taos Bank Robbery*. Well, a long time ago, I had the idea of putting together a kind of darker edition of this. And starting out with a couple of long essays I wrote. One of them is about a murder, and the title would be "Who Killed Cricket Coogler?" It would concern a 1949 murder of a teenage bar girl in New Mexico. The crime turned this state upside down. And the fact that it did is so illuminating of what's happening in American culture. Hell, now you'd find somebody like that in the ditch and it would make page 92 and be forgotten in three days. But it was a strange case. I've got a long start on that. I'd use that as the title essay and then do one about a guy who was misidentified in a murder case in a strange way. The result was that a very savage killer went free. I have several others but I don't know when I'll do it. I've got the start of two novels in my files. One of them is the typical coming-of-age story, about sort of a redneck *Catcher in the Rye*. The other one is about a man whose brother is just deceased in Thailand, the discovery by the grandmother that she has a grandchild in Asia, and the efforts of the reluctant

surviving brother to go back there and get this kid.
The year is 1975, when, as you may remember, the
South Vietnamese government collapsed, two
years after we withdrew. I want to put this guy in
the chaotic situation. I went to Asia and did some
research and said, No, I'm not ready for this. I think
maybe I might be ready for it now.

JB: What kind of feedback on your books do
you get from your family? How has your writing
affected your family?

TH: In various ways. Not much. They like the
idea that I've been successful. We have six great
kids and they're very fond of me and the feeling is
mutual, so they're pleased that Dad's doing all
right. I'm almost sure my oldest daughter has read
all of my books. I wouldn't swear to it. Both of my
other daughters have read some of them. But more
out of family duty. My youngest son claims he's
read them.

JB: But you don't believe him?

TH: He wouldn't lie. My oldest son said, Dad, I
wish you'd write more like Louis L'Amour.

JB: Some of us are glad you don't. Are any of
your children writers or aspiring writers?

TH: My oldest daughter is the editorial page
editor—or something like that, I don't know what
her title is—for the *Albuquerque Journal North*
which is the Santa Fe and points north edition of
the *Albuquerque Journal*. She has had a couple of
children's books published and is working on a
book about transoceanic balloon flights. My middle
daughter is an artist, except she's a full-time
mother. She illustrated *The Boy Who Made
Dragonfly*. And the youngest daughter is a house-
wife. She has four daughters herself, so they keep
her busy. None of my sons are writers. One is a
pharmacist, and one is a cable installer, and one
keeps American Airliners flying.

JB: What would you most want a reader to get out of your books?

TH: A respect for the Navajo culture.

JB: I noticed in *The Ghostway* there was one memorable scene where Jim Chee is in Los Angeles and he's questioning Mr. Bergen, the elderly man in the rest home next to the apartment where the guy lived, and he assumes or he believes that probably the LA police had stereotyped the elderly people as all being senile and not knowing what's going on and therefore would not have questioned the man as thoroughly as they should. That would be an example—

TH: Exactly.

JB: —of a Navajo value that helps Chee to solve the case.

TH: I'm always looking for that sort of stuff.

JB: I've run through my questions. Is there anything you'd particularly like to add at this point?

TH: Oh, man, I think you've pretty well covered it.

In October 1993, the interview resumed by mail.

JB: In Jack Hitt's *The Perfect Murder,* you were the contributor to point out that hotel room keys have changed significantly in recent years, suggesting you spend a lot of time on the road promoting your books. Do you enjoy going on the bookstore and talk show circuit? What do you most and least like about the book promotion process?

TH: I enjoy small book signings ... in which there's no long line and there's an opportunity to talk to people. But, alas, small book signings became impossible several books ago and big book signings are an awful ordeal. I no longer do them. The talk show circuit is also an ordeal, but now it can be done mostly via satellite.

JB: Since we last talked, *Sacred Clowns* has

appeared. It seems to differ from the other novels in that there is a great deal more humor. The scene regarding the screening of *Cheyenne Autumn* is especially funny. Was the inclusion of more humorous content a conscious decision on your part or did it just develop with the action or theme of the story?

TH: The humor in *Sacred Clowns* simply developed with the plot. Its mood was less grim and tense than most of the others.

JB: The mention of *Cheyenne Autumn* reminds me to bring up something we didn't get into in our earlier interview: Hillerman and the movies. I know *Dark Wind* was being adapted for the screen a couple of years ago and there was some controversy over the actor playing Chee, Lou Diamond Phillips, not being a Navajo. How has that film-making process gone and what has been your involvement in it? And what was your view on the casting controversy?

TH: All I know for sure about the movies is this: (a) Robert Redford holds an option on the Navajo Tribal Police books. (b) R.R. told me he wants to make a sequence of three films based on three of the books. *The Dark Wind* was filmed on the Navajo and Hopi reservations a couple of years ago with Lou Diamond Phillips as Chee, Fred Ward as Leaphorn, and Gary Farmer as Cowboy Dashee. I had a three-line role as warden which didn't survive the cutting. I understand that Redford was not pleased with the film and it wasn't released in U.S. theaters. Now I hear the videotape is being released for rental.

Meanwhile, I understand a scriptwriter named Beebe is doing the screenplay for Redford on *A Thief of Time* and that Redford intends to direct this one himself summer of '95. I am not particularly interested in the casting (or in movies, for that matter). Obviously, I would prefer that Navajos be cast to play Navajos, but they have to know how to act.

The Dark Wind must have been released in

England, since someone sent me a moderately favorable review. And a friend in France wrote that he had seen it there.

JB: At one point in *Sacred Clowns*, you refer by name to a TV weathercaster, something I recall you've done in other books. Am I right that these are real people? And why weathercasters as opposed to, say, news anchors?

TH: Country people are *very* interested in the weather. So I mention it and, to show the common humanity Navajos share with all of us, show that they also get it from the TV set. Why not the names of actual TV weather people?

JB: *Sacred Clowns,* untypically, finishes with a sense of resolution of Leaphorn's and Chee's romantic storylines, though not of Jim Chee's professional career clash between cop and shaman. Is it possible Chee's future will take him away from the Navajo Tribal Police, though not (I hope) from fictional detection completely?

TH: Who knows? I have not yet planned his role in the next book. I'd think he would still be Navajo Police.

JB: At present, what do you plan for your next book? Another Leaphorn and Chee adventure or a non-series project?

TH: I am now working on an untitled novel not involving the Navajos. It involves a small-town newspaperman who, in April 1975, when the South Vietnam government is going bad and Pol Pot is surrounding Phnom-Penh, is thrust into the rescue role—and into the chaos of a collapsing society. When that's done, I'll work on a book using Chee and Leaphorn and involving the surreptitious climbing of the Shiprock monolith, and a vector control specialist hunting the source of a new outbreak of bubonic plague (which has plagued the reservation episodically since about 1915).

3

THE NAVAJO NATION

George Hardeen

When we asked Tony Hillerman to recommend a good essay on the Navajo, he said that the following selection by a Navajo writer from the APA Insight Guide Native America was the finest short account available anywhere. We are pleased to make it available to Hillerman's readers.

Entering the Navajo Reservation from any direction, on any road, you quickly sense its most striking quality: space, openness, unbounded landscape. Everywhere you look there are dramatic views of distant, angular mesas, expansive plateaus and wide, pale-green valleys. No other land in the Southwest quite compares in scale or beauty to the 17-million-acre Navajo Reservation, the largest in the country. After seeing it, being within it, you may wonder why it remains so unknown and empty.

Today's Navajoland (*Dine' bikeyah*) dominates the northeast corner of Arizona and spills over into New Mexico and Utah. In every direction, the treeless Navajo horizon stretches out before you in a landscape of tawny dunes, orange-and-pink canyons, and faraway blue mountains rising more than 10,000 ft.

On most days, the land is flooded in brilliant sunlight and domed by a nearly cloudless blue sky. But in the summer, when moist air arriving from the Gulf of Mexico collides with hot air rising from the desert floor, ominous thunderheads gather overhead. Then entire weather systems are created before your eyes. Huge anvil-shaped clouds rise to a center point in the sky and then spread, darkening like blue-black mountains in the air. Desert rainclouds can open at any time and pour out their burden in a 15- or 20-minute thunderstorm, pelting the ground with the hard "male" rains that send torrents rushing across slickrock and into arroyos.

Geologically, Navajoland is absolutely awe-inspiring. Buttes and cliffs dwarf human figures. Huge slabs of sandstone and limestone appear freshly broken from rocky abutments, making them look as if they have emerged through heaps of geological debris. From a distance, these huge chunks of rock take on a different aspect, like sleeping giants occupying the earth.

In fact, Navajo mythology teaches that the huge expanses of mesa and plateau are the petrified bodies of monsters who inhabited the earth before it was fit for humans. The Navajos' Hero Twins—Monster Slayer and Child Born of Water—slew the monsters of the third or Yellow World to make the land safe for the emergence of the "five-fingered people" into the fourth or Glittering World.

The land was an obstacle to the earliest white visitors—the Spanish in the 1500s followed by the Mexicans and Americans. But the indigenous people—the Navajos, Hopis and Paiutes—held it in reverence and adapted to the vagaries of climate, precipitation and resources.

The Navajos, relatives of the Athabascan people who migrated to the Southwest from the frozen arctic north, made the land their religion. It is home to their deities, the Holy People, an immense pantheon of supernatural personalities still remembered today in the chants of Navajo medicine men, singers, hand tremblers and crystal gazers, all known simply as *hatahli*.

Over the past 600 years, the Navajos have embraced this land with as much reverence as tenacity, adapting to it with a light touch. Today, the most common symbol of their relationship with the land is the hogan, the traditional domed dwelling once made exclusively of stacked or standing logs and covered with mud. Although dwindling in number, these ancient homes can still be seen across the reservation, especially in areas where modern facilities have arrived late.

Since the 1970s, though, the old mud hogan has been used by Navajos more for ceremonial and religious purposes and less for housing. Today, federally subsidized housing and mobile homes are proliferating as the Navajo population mushrooms. But this change is more indicative of Navajo adaptability than of an abandonment of culture. In fact, modern eight-sided hogans, usually built of plywood and lumber, are still quite common. Traditional or modern, with its entrance always facing the rising sun, the hogan symbolizes the security of the Navajo mother, *shimah*—Mother Earth as much as the woman who serves as the anchor of the Navajo family.

Holy People

In Navajo cosmology, the land lies between two protective parents. Below, supporting and nurturing the people, is Mother Earth, provider of sustenance—corn, water, grazing land. Above is Father Sky, providing life-giving rain to make the plants grow and the water run. In the morning, before sunrise, traditional Navajos still offer a few sprinkles of corn pollen and, in their prayers to the rising sun, ask for the blessings of the Holy People.

Navajos believe they emerged from an underworld known as the first or Black World. This was a timeless place known only to spirit-beings and the Holy People. Here lived First Man and First Woman, but separately, in the east and west. They were united when First Man burned a crystal (symbolizing the awakening of the mind) and First Woman burned a piece of turquoise. Seeing each other's fire, they were united after four attempts.

But soon, the insect-beings of the First World began to quarrel and create chaos, forcing First Man and First Woman to leave through the east. Their migrations, brought on by disunity, led them to the Blue World, and then to the Yellow World, where they found the six sacred mountains still revered by the Navajos. These are Blanco Peak in Colorado to the east, Mount Taylor in New Mexico to the south, the San Francisco Peaks of Arizona to the west, and the La Plata Range of Colorado to the north. Within this area is Huerfano Mesa in New Mexico at the center, and Gobernador Knob, also in New Mexico, as the inner mountain.

It was Coyote who began the turmoil of the Yellow World by stealing the child of Water Monster. Furious, Water Monster flooded the world. First Man planted a female reed that grew to the sky, permitting the living things to escape the rising waters. As the flood receded, the First People found themselves in the Glittering World, where the Navajos live today.

First Man and First Woman are also the parents of Changing Woman, who they found as a baby atop Gobernador Knob and who is the mother of the four principal Navajo clans. Together with her sister, White Shell Woman, these are the most important figures in the Navajo pantheon.

Despite the influx of various Christian denominations, most Navajos continue to practice their own religion, remain superstitious, respect taboos, and try to adhere to the teachings handed down from previous generations. Most families still have medicine men they rely on to perform any number of ceremonies that help restore a sense of harmony, balance, beauty and prosperity—the highest ideals of Navajo life, expressed by the concept of *hozjo*.

Among the most common ceremonies still practiced by the Navajos are the *kinaalda*, a girl's puberty rite; the *nidaa*, or squaw dance, a three-day ceremony performed in the summer; and the *yei-be-chei*, a winter healing ceremony that lasts up to nine days and features masked dancers that are somewhat similar to Hopi kachina dancers.

Although sacred to the Navajos, some ceremonies also serve as social gatherings. The *nidaa*, for instance, is often advertised on hand-painted signs posted along the highway. Visitors may attend, but it is highly recommended that they come with someone who is already familiar with the ceremony. (Bear in mind that in the past some Squaw Dances have been the site of alcohol-related disturbances.) The *yei-be-chei* is also open to outsiders, but tends to be less common these days because of its nine-day length and expense. It may cost a Navajo family as much as $5,000 to pay for preparations, food, helpers and the services of a medicine man.

The Long Walk

Navajos have long been known for their ability to adapt to the changing circumstances of their lives. They borrowed from all the people with whom they have been in contact—the Spanish, Hopis, Americans—adopting and transforming various aspects of their cultures. From the Spanish they acquired sheep and horses and became some of the best herdsmen and riders in the Southwest. It's uncertain from whom they learned silversmithing, possibly the Spanish, Mexicans or eastern tribes, but it continues to be one of the most popular and distinctive Navajo art forms. From the Hopis and other Pueblo people, they learned desert agriculture and weaving. For more than a century now, the Navajos have been renowned for their exquisite, hand-woven rugs. Certain aspects of Navajo religion also seem influenced by Pueblo belief.

But like other native people, the Navajos did not always enjoy peaceful relations with their neighbors. In the 1770s, the Spanish were able to subdue them brutally, beginning a long and bitter period of slave-raiding and territorial encroachment. In 1804, the Navajos made war on them, but suffered a bloody defeat at Canyon de Chelly, where the Spanish shot people retreating into caves and then destroyed hogans, burned crops, seized sheep and horse herds, and captured dozens of women and children. In 1821, at a truce conference with a Spanish commander, 24 Navajos were treacherously murdered, each stabbed in the heart as he smoked in peace and hope.

When Americans started moving toward Navajo territory in the 1840s, there was hope that they would dispatch the Mexicans and free their relatives from slavery. In less than 10 years of their coming, however, relations between the white people, or *bilagaana*, and the Navajos were already dismal. The Americans had failed not only to free Navajo slaves as promised in treaties, but were instrumental in allowing slave-raiding to continue. They had also invaded Navajo land and destroyed crops, and, in 1849, shot and killed the aged Narbona, the most prominent Navajo leader of his time.

The first American military post built in Navajo territory, Fort Defiance, was established in 1851. Several treaties followed, but none of them held the peace for more than a few years. Then, in 1862, General James H. Carleton took command and immediately set about clearing the Indians off the land. It was Carleton who devised the ill-fated plan to march 8,000 Navajos 300 miles to the flat, featureless no-man's-land called Bosque Redondo, east of Santa Fe. This was the infamous Long Walk, remembered bitterly to this day. Carleton wrote that the only peace the Indians would find was imprisonment at the Bosque, where they would supposedly learn to farm. "Entire subjugation, or destruction of all the men, are the alternatives," he said.

In 1863, Colonel Christopher "Kit" Carson was assigned to carry out Carleton's orders by slashing, burning and shooting his way across Navajo territory. As winter came, Carson's patrols hunted the Navajos like animals, forcing them to surrender a few at a time after weeks of cold and hunger. The campaign's most bitter episode came in January 1864, when Carson and 300 soldiers swept through Canyon de Chelly, repeating the destruction of the Spanish years earlier. Those who tried to escape were shot down. Many of the elderly, too weak to make the Long Walk, were left behind to die. Only a few Navajos are known to have made it into the rugged canyon country around Monument Valley, led by the well-known headman Manuelito.

Within four years, Carleton's plan ended in disaster. A quarter of the Navajos imprisoned at Bosque Redondo (renamed Fort Sumner) starved or died of illness. Their crops failed from drought. The little water available was too brackish to drink. There was no wood. A grief-stricken Ganado Mucho told the government superintendent that the Navajos would live on a reservation if it could be in their own country.

Outcry over the Navajos' fate finally reached Washington, and on June 1, 1868, Navajo headmen agreed to peace by signing the Treaty of 1868, a document still held sacred by the tribe. The US government granted the Navajos a reservation in their old country and allowed the survivors to return.

The early decades of the 1900s saw more lands added to the reservation and improvement of the Navajos' condition, although confrontations with whites continued. In the 1930s, for example, the federal government implemented a livestock-reduction program designed to reverse the effects of over-grazing. Thousands of sheep were bought by the government for a dollar a head, and then slaughtered in canyons and left to rot. The Navajos were horrified as the source of their wealth and sustenance was destroyed before their eyes.

The Navajos also became involved in a long-term land dispute with the Hopis, whose mesa-top homes are completely surrounded by the larger Navajo Reservation. For years the Hopis had charged that Navajos were robbing their fields and stealing their cattle. Tensions escalated to a high point in 1974 when the US Congress passed the Navajo-Hopi Relocation Act. The law, which divided nearly 2 million acres between the tribes, will eventually force 11,000 Navajos and about 100 Hopis to leave homes they have known for generations. About half the Navajos have already received new government housing, but many who moved, called "refugees" by the tribe, are still waiting. Others have vowed never to leave and continue to resist from strongholds at Big Mountain and Teesto.

Finally, in the late 1980s, the Navajos seemed to turn on each other. At the height of a fractious corruption scandal involving former chairman Peter MacDonald, two MacDonald supporters were shot and killed by police at a demonstration that turned violent. MacDonald's downfall was sealed in 1990, when he was convicted on 41 charges of corruption in the Navajos' own court. The following month, his arch-rival, former chairman Peterson Zah, was chosen to lead the tribe as its first elected president.

THE NAVAJO NATION

Canyon de Chelly and East

Today, calm has returned to tribal politics, although great challenges lie ahead for Navajos. Window Rock, next to the New Mexico state line, is the seat of Navajo government and the most impressive of all tribal capitals. Navajo government offices and federal Bureau of Indian Affairs offices are housed in historic sandstone buildings of classic Southwestern design tucked into a small canyon where the famed "window rock" arch rises above. The Navajo Tribal Council is a one-of-a-kind, hogan-shaped building with a high log ceiling. Around the eight interior walls is a mural depicting the history of the tribe.

Window Rock is the home of the tribally-owned Navajo Arts and Crafts Enterprise, an excellent place to purchase all kinds of Navajo rugs, jewelry, sand paintings, pottery and beadwork. The building also houses the Navajo Tribal Museum and art museum, well worth a stop.

Over the Fourth of July, Window Rock is the site of one of the biggest all-Indian rodeos in the country. Rodeo, it goes without saying, is the most popular sport on the reservation, and travelers can find one any summer weekend. For nine days in September, Window Rock also hosts the Navajo Nation Fair, the largest in the country. It is like a county fair with an Indian flavor, bringing together as many as 50,000 Navajos and members of neighboring tribes, a cornucopia of produce, rugs, jewelry, continuous powwows, traditional dancing and one booth after another selling mutton stew and fry bread, Navajo favorites.

Twenty-eight miles west of Window Rock on Highway 264 is Ganado, site of the Hubbell Trading Post. The post was opened by the legendary John Lorenzo Hubbell in 1876 and has been open for business ever since. The most important trader of his day,

Hubbell was much loved by the Navajos, whom he tended during the devastating smallpox epidemic of 1886. His biggest influence on the tribe was popularizing Navajo rugs and blankets, encouraging weavers to use color, and essentially creating the distinctive Ganado Red design that became so popular with the outside world. Hubbell's place retains the look and feel of an old-time trading post, and Navajos still travel for miles to do business here. The post is now administered by the National Park Service.

Perhaps the most important destination on the reservation is Canyon de Chelly, the very heart of Navajoland. The main entrance is about 2 miles from the large town of Chinle, and about 30 miles north of Highway 264. This extraordinary three-branched canyon, enclosed within 800-ft sandstone walls, has been home to desert people for more than 1,000 years. The prehistoric Anasazi left behind hundreds of cliff-dwellings and thousands of artifacts. Like the Navajos, who moved in centuries later, the Anasazi farmed the canyon's bottomland (for additional information see *Ancestral Ground*).

Travel within the canyon is restricted to guided tours by the National Park Service, because Canyon de Chelly remains home to many Navajo families who still herd sheep and raise crops within its confines. Good paved roads along the rim offer excellent views of the canyon's depths. There is one hiking trail to the bottom of the canyon at White House Ruin.

It takes about two hours to make the trip down and across the wide, shaded stream to the ancient Anasazi pueblo tucked into a ledge in the cliff face.

The Canyon de Chelly visitors' center is an excellent place to learn about the Anasazi people who occupied the entire Four Corners region. The Thunderbird Lodge, just inside the park, sells hundreds of Navajo rugs at reasonable prices, often better than those at local trading posts. Many talented Navajo weavers live in the Chinle area and earn their entire incomes with their looms.

Canyon de Chelly's north-rim drive takes you 10 miles east to Tsaile, home of Navajo Community College. Founded 20 years ago, this is the country's first Indian community college, offering two-year associate degrees. Although humble, the campus features a gleaming glass hogan-shaped building surrounded by several traditional hogans. This is another good place to learn more about Navajos and the reservation. The college runs an excellent book store packed with titles on Native American cultures. It also is host to two annual powwows; for exact dates consult the college.

East of Tsaile, across the heavily wooded Chuska Mountains, you can pick up Highway 666. To the south is Gallup, New Mexico, the so-called "Indian Capital of the World," where Navajos, Zunis and other Pueblo people do a good deal of trading. Gallup pawn shops and trading posts usually carry an extensive stock of Navajo jewelry and rugs, Hopi kachina dolls and Pueblo pottery, although prices are never as good as buying directly from the artists. For excellent buys on Navajo rugs, try the town of Crownpoint, about 50 miles northwest of Gallup, where six times a year a rug auction attracts buyers from all over the U.S. Crownpoint is also a convenient stepping-off point for the magnificent Anasazi ruins at Chaco Culture National Historical Park, located at the end of a rutted 20-mile dirt road.

About 80 miles north of Crownpoint, past the bizarre, twisted rock formations of the Bisti Badlands, is Farmington, a major agricultural center though not very interesting. Another Anasazi site, Aztec Ruins National Monument, is about 15 miles to the east. The little town of Shiprock, named after the jagged cinder cone that soars to an elevation of some 7,000 ft, is located about 25 miles west.

Monument Valley and West

Starting back at Canyon de Chelly, you can head north to Many Farms and catch Highway 59 to Kayenta. This is a 66-mile trip through some of the area's most spectacular landscape. The road skirts the northeast flank of huge Black Mesa, perhaps the most significant and isolated land mass on the reservation. When you get to the intersection of Highways 59 and 160, take a few minutes to look around. Across a wide expanse to the north is Monument Valley; to the west, beyond Kayenta, is the remote canyon-land of Skeleton Mesa. Before you is Church Rock, one of several volcanic plugs jutting out of the area's bright orange sandstone.

Kayenta is not only one of the reservation's prettiest towns, it's a remarkable blend of traditional and modern ways of life. Kayenta's economy is fueled by the Peabody Coal Company, which operates the two largest mines in the country atop Black Mesa. Many of the company's 800 miners live here, giving the town an air of prosperity. With a number of motels, restaurants and service stations, Kayenta also does a brisk business with travelers.

From Kayenta, Highway 163 takes you through wide sandy valleys enclosed by giant plateaus and buttes to Monument Valley, the crown jewel of the Navajos' spectacular red-rock country and familiar from countless John Ford westerns. Today it's a tribal park, requiring a $1 fee to travel along the dusty loop road. While the unpaved road may seem inconvenient, especially in the heat of summer, it adds to the ambience and helps retain some of the park's natural quality. Like Canyon de Chelly,

Monument Valley is the home of several Navajo families. Children may flag you down to offer a cedar-bead necklace for a few dollars. The money this and other items brings may be a significant addition to their family's income. If you would rather not drive yourself, a number of companies offer van tours with Navajo guides. For many tourists, this is the best way to get off the main trail and see some of the less-traveled areas.

To the west of Kayenta, there is another, perhaps less well-known site, every bit as beautiful and culturally rich as Monument Valley. This is Navajo National Monument, site of the Southwest's largest and prettiest prehistoric Indian ruins. From the visitors' center high on the rim of Tsegi Canyon, you can see Betatakin ("Ledge House" in Navajo), a ruin of 135 rooms built into a 500-ft-high, scallop-shaped cave hollowed into the canyon wall. Built around AD 1300, Betatakin is thought to be one of three major centers of Anasazi culture, the other two being Chaco Canyon, New Mexico, and Mesa Verde, Colorado (see *Ancestral Ground*). For a closer look at the ruins, the Park Service offers at least one guided trip daily during the summer months.

For those seeking more adventure, the 160-room Keet Seel ruin is down an 8-mile trail into Dowozhiebito Canyon. Horses and local guides can be hired to make the trip in a single day. Backpackers usually camp the night. Check with park rangers to make the necessary arrangements.

West of Kayenta, in the low-lying Klethla valley, Highway 98 turns toward the town of Page, just over the reservation's northwestern border. Page is the site of Glen Canyon Dam and gateway to Lake Powell, perhaps the most beautiful body of water in the entire Southwest. The dam is a 710-ft-high concrete plug jammed into a narrow section of Glen Canyon. It was designed to deliver a regular supply of water to downstream users, produce a clean source of electricity, and provide recreation for millions.

But since the dam's completion in 1963, environmentalists have decried the loss of the enchanted Glen Canyon, now sunk in a watery grave beneath Lake Powell. They have also criticized the dam's impact on the Colorado River. More than 40 federally-sponsored environmental impact studies are currently under way.

The most convenient way to explore Lake Powell is by boat. Both houseboats and motorboats may be rented at Wahweap Marina, 5 miles from Page. It is possible to spend weeks exploring the winding sandstone canyons, isolated beaches, remote trails and hidden ruins. Of particular interest is the famed Rainbow Bridge National Monument, tucked deep into the recesses of Forbidding Canyon. At 309 feet, Rainbow Bridge is the world's largest natural stone arch. If time is limited, you can catch a one-day tour boat to Rainbow Bridge at Wahweap Marina. Hardy backpackers can also reach it by land on two of the prettiest trails in Arizona. One is 13 miles long, the other 16 miles. Guides can be obtained by inquiring a few days in advance at the Tuba Trading Post (Tuba City) or Navajo Mountain Trading Post (Navajo Mountain).

Leaving Page on Highway 89 south takes you across more miles of beautiful open desert rising into the Navajo sandstone formations high above House Rock Valley and the Colorado River. About 24 miles south of Page the road passes through the giant "cut" blasted into the cliff face. Pullouts here offer stunning views of the valley below, the high Kaibab and Paria plateaus 10 miles across, and the tips of the San Francisco Peaks more than 100 miles south.

A quick detour on Highway 89A leads you north again across the dangerously narrow Navajo Bridge, spanning Marble Canyon Gorge and the

Colorado River 467 ft below. Historic Lee's Ferry, where all raft trips into the Grand Canyon begin, is another 6 miles north.

Returning to Highway 89 and continuing south, the road quickly descends to the desert floor and is bounded by the rocky face of Echo Cliffs. Aside from a couple of old trading posts, Navajo hogans and cornfields, there is nothing but lovely scenery all the way to the bright-red badlands around the little settlement of Moenave. Dinosaur tracks at the Moenave turnoff have been a popular attraction since the turn of the century. The 12-inch, three-toed tracks were left by a dilophosaurus about 60 million years ago.

Nearby, Tuba City is the major town in the western portion of the reservation. It was settled in 1870 by Mormon pioneers and named after a Hopi chief. In addition to government offices and medical facilities, Tuba City has one motel, several restaurants, a theater and large supermarket. If you happen to be passing through on a Friday, be sure to stop at the local flea market behind the big white community center. Dozens of vendors and hundreds of shoppers gather here to buy and sell everything from herbal medicines and Indian art to hot mutton sandwiches. It's a cultural treat to drift through the booths, enjoy the smell of cooking fires, and hear the old people talking in their native languages.

Across the road from Tuba City is the Hopi village of Moenkopi, the Hopi Indians' westernmost settlement. Hopis say they have used the lovely canyon as a farming satellite for some 300 years before the Navajos arrived in this region. A ruin high on a promontory across from the village shows evidence of prehistoric habitation.

This small Hopi town was permanently settled about the time the Mormons arrived in 1870. In fact, the old Mormon church still stands in the village next to the cemetery where Tuba's first pioneers now rest. Just past the entrance, you can see that the village is divided into upper and lower sections. The old stone pueblos of Lower Moenkopi are considered to be the most traditional part of the village, similar in appearance to the original settlement. This is a good place to buy kachina carvings, paintings and other Hopi art directly from the makers, and for very reasonable prices. Ask for the information at the Clifford Honahnie Building as you enter the village.

South of Tuba City, the highway heads across the ice-cream-colored rocks of the Painted Desert. This is where 200-million-year-old shale, mudstone and sandstone streak the landscape with bands of brilliant red, green and tawny rock. Although bare and alkaline, the desert is scattered with bits of petrified wood, a survival of the ancient forest that once flourished here. To the east, Petrified Forest National Park offers trails, information and some of the most dramatic vistas in the Painted Desert.

Travelers have convenient access to Grand Canyon National Park, adjacent to the reservation's western border; the ancient ruins at Wupatki and Walnut Canyon national monuments; and the cities of Flagstaff and Sedona.

If you want to find out more about the Navajos, two excellent museums are within reasonable driving distance of the reservation: the Museum of Northern Arizona in Flagstaff and the Heard Museum in Phoenix. The Museum of Northern Arizona sponsors an annual Navajo art show and exhibition, usually in July. Farther afield, the Museum of Indian Arts and Culture and the Wheelwright Museum in Santa Fe, and the great Southwest Museum in Los Angeles all maintain first-class collections of Navajo art and artifacts.

4

NATIVE AMERICAN CLANS IN TONY HILLERMAN'S FICTION

A GUIDE

Elizabeth A. Gaines
and Diane Hammer

Elizabeth A. Gaines taught first grade through college-level mathematics and computer science for fifteen years. A resident of Columbus, Ohio, she prepared the concordance section of The Robert Ludlum Companion *(1992) and is busily at work on* The 87th Precinct Companion, *a major study of the work of Ed McBain. Her collaborator, Diane Hammer, is an Administrative Program Manager at the Pediatric Pulmonary Center at the University of Wisconsin, Madison. This concordance is greatly expanded from a database developed by Diane for Tony Hillerman.*

Clan identification is important among the Navajo and other Native Americans of the Southwest featured in Hillerman's books. One's maternal ("born to") clan determines the primary kin relationship; a child's maternal uncle plays an especially important role (for example, Hosteen Frank Sam Nakai, Jim Chee's mother's older brother). A man typically becomes a member of his wife's family upon marriage; nevertheless, strict prohibitions govern the interaction of a man and his mother-in-law in traditional families. (See *People of Darkness*, chapter 5, for the traditional taboo, and *Talking God*, chapter 2, for a looser interpretation.)

The paternal ("born for") clan is also taken into account in determining who a person is. Men and women may have only a formal relationship with opposite-sex members of the same maternal clan, and a sexual relationship between members of the same maternal clan is considered incestuous (see *The Dark Wind*, chapter 24). Even a shared paternal clan kinship is sufficient to prohibit dating. Thus Chee, as an eligible bachelor, automatically does a mental clan check when he meets a young woman (see *Coyote Waits*, chapter 1). The issue becomes prominent in *Sacred Clowns*.

Clan links between people of the same sex or of the extended family serve to strengthen relationships. Hillerman writes in *The Ghostway* that "he takes care of his relatives" is a high compliment, while "he acts like he doesn't have any relatives" is the ultimate insult. Kinship carries with it obligation; for example, Leaphorn feels a responsibility to help Mary Keeyani, a distant relative of his deceased wife, in *Coyote Waits*. Kinship may also engender favoritism or nepotism; for instance, in *Coyote Waits*, Leaphorn thinks perhaps Largo is defending Chee because of their clan ties (in *The Dark Wind* there is a secondary paternal link), although in *Listening Woman*, Leaphorn and Largo are also related.

According to Navajo mythology, Changing Woman created the first four clans from the skin of her breast: the Salt, Mud, Bitter Water, and Bead People (*Coyote Waits*). Hillerman states there are now approximately sixty Navajo clans. Many of the clan names are related in some way to the area in which the clans live.

In the following pages clans are arranged alphabetically within tribes by name of clan, and the people are listed alphabetically by book abbreviation; you can see not only which characters are in the same clan in the same book but also who they are related to in the other books. Under each clan is listed the name of the character, followed by (m) for maternal clan, and then the father's clan followed by (p) for paternal clan; then comes the abbreviation for the book (or books) in which the character is found. For characters for whom no paternal clan is known, just the maternal clan is listed. Characters for whom we have found conflicts are so noted.

Also, there are clans referred to in these books for which no character is listed. We have saved these for the last in their own group and have added the information we have found about them. Please note some characters have neither (m) nor (p); these characters were simply identified as belonging to or being a member of a certain clan. (Notice that in

People of Darkness, "born to" designated the father's clan; this was corrected in later books. Hillerman states that he usually uses the common translations of existing Navajo clan names, but on rare occasions invents a clan, as with Leaphorn's Red Forehead People. With the exception of Leaphorn, family names used are those of extant Navajo families. "Leaphorn" was so named because Hillerman was reading of ancient Crete's version of rodeo games while writing *The Blessing Way.*)

NAVAJO CLANS

BEAD (YOO'L DINEE)
Eleanor Billie (m)	SW

BITTER WATER
Emma Leaphorn (m)	CW, TT
Anges Yazzie (m)	CW
Standing Medicine	LW
Gray Old Lady Benally (m)	SC
Jim Chee's father (m)	SC
Delmar Kanitewa's father	SC
Sergeant Yazzie	SC
Bent Woman (m) Deer Spring (p)	SW
Alice Onesalt (m)	SW
Irma Onesalt (m) Towering House (p)	SW
Agnes Tsosie (m)	TG
Jolene Yellow (m)	TG
Henry Highhawk's grandmother (m)	TG

In WY the Bitter Water Clan lives along the Utah border.

BLUE BIRD PEOPLE (DOLII DINEE)
Bahe Yellowhorse (m)	SW
(Father an Oglala Sioux)	
Bahe Yellowhorse's mother	SW

COYOTE PASS

Franklin Begay (m)	SW
Monster (p)	

EARS STICKING UP (SLEEP ROCK DINEE)

Leonard Skeet (m)	SW

HIGH STANDING HOUSE

Shorty Bowlegs (m)	DD
Old Woman Running (m)	DD

HUNGER PEOPLE (DICHIN DINEE)

Hosteen Barbone's grandmother	SC
Janet Pete's paternal grandmother (possibly)	SC

LEAF PEOPLE

Kayonnie brothers (m)	SW
Mud (p)	

MANY GOATS

Agnes (Elsie) Tso Horseman (m)	BW
Lilly Tso	BW
Minnie Tso	BW
Cowboy	WY

The young woman in Los Angeles (GW) belongs to the Many Goats Clan and the Streams Come Together Clan. The Many Goats Clan is mentioned in LW; in PD it is a clan on the east side of the reservation; in WI, Chee talked with the people of this clan; and in WY it is a clan along the Utah border.

MUD

Anna Atcitty	LW
Emerson Begay	LW
Margaret Cigaret (m)	LW

Alice Endischee (m)	LW
Eileen Endischee (m)	LW
Old Lady Nakai	LW
Old Lady Nakai's daughter	LW
Alice Frank Pino	LW
Mustache Tsossie (m)	LW
Rudolph Becenti	PD
Chee's uncle's wife	PD
Joseph Sam	PD
Windy Tsossie	PD
Dugai Endocheeney (m) Streams Come Together (p)	SW
Iron Woman Ginsberg	SW[1]
Lizzie Tonale	SW

In CW, Odell Redd says Ashie Pinto was born to the Mud Clan. Historically, the Utes tried to capture the Mud People, who lived around Sweetwater. In PD it was listed as a clan on the east side of the reservation. In WI, Chee talked with the people of this clan.

ONE WALKS AROUND

Wilson Sam (m) Turning Mountain (p)	SW

PAIUTE (PIAUTE)[2]

Kicks His Horse	CW

1. If Lizzie Tonale was born to the Mud Clan (SW), then Iron Woman Ginsberg should also be born to the Mud Clan. In the same book Iron Woman is listed as being born to the People of the Valley Clan.

2. Piaute may be a spelling variation of Paiute. The Paiute are a separate linguistic and cultural group from the Navajo and want their own identity; the Navajo have engulfed them and consider them Navajo.

THE TONY HILLERMAN COMPANION

Left-Handed	CW
Amos Whistler	T T

This clan figures prominently in the Butch Cassidy legend.

PEACHTREE
Moenkopi woman[3]	BW

PEOPLE OF THE VALLEY (HALGAI DINEE)
Iron Woman Ginsberg (m)	SW
(Father is Jewish)	

POLES TOGETHER
Walker Pinto's wife	WY

RED FOREHEAD
Annie Horseman	BW
Luis Horseman (m)	BW
Billy Horseman Nez (m)	BW
Frank Bob Madman	DD
Chee's father	PD
Joe Leaphorn (m)	TG,T T[4]

In WY it is a clan along the Utah border.

SAGE BRUSH HILL
Mrs. Greyeyes (m)	CW
Towering House (p)	

3. Moenkopi is a Hopi village. The assumption is made that the woman is a Navajo who is living there and belongs to the Peachtree Clan as she is romantically involved with a Navajo male.

4. Leaphorn's maternal clan is listed both as Red Forehead and as Slow Talking Dinee. His mother, Anna Gorman, is born to the Slow Talking Dinee, so his maternal clan should also be Slow Talking Dinee.

116

Salt (Salt Dinee)

Jefferson Tom	GW
Joseph Sam's wife (m)	PD

In PD it was a clan on the east side of the reservation.

Salt Cedar

Boy who worked at Short Mountain	LW
Benjamin Tso	LW
Ford Tso's wife	LW
Jimmy Tso	LW
Mustache Tsossie's wife	LW
Chee's father	WI
Virgie Endecheenie	WI

The middle-aged woman in Los Angeles (GW) was born for this clan.

Slow Talking (Taadii Dinee)

Jim Chee (m)	CW, DW, GW, SC, SW, TG, TT, WI, WY[5]
Captain Largo (m)	LW, SW[6]
Joe Leaphorn (m)	CW, DD, LW
Frank Sam Nakai (m)	DW, GW, PD
Anna Gorman	LW
Tessie Chee (m)	PD, SW

This clan produced more singers than any of the other sixty-plus clans.

5. In PD he is listed as belonging to the Bitter Water Dinee and Red Forehead Clan (p); in SW he belongs to the Salts and the Red Forehead Clan (p); in WY Mud Dinee is (p); in WI Salt Cedar is (p); and in SC Bitter Water is (p). His maternal grandmother and his mother are Slow Talking Dinee, so he should also be Slow Talking Dinee.
6. Captain Largo's maternal clan is listed as both Slow Talking and Standing Rock.

STANDING ROCK

Captain Largo (m)	DW
Red Forehead (p)	
Fannie Tsossie Musket (m)	DW
Mud (p)	
Joseph Musket (m)	DW
Edna Nezzie (m)	DW
Graywoman Nezzie (m)	DW[7]
Bitter Water (p)	
Windy Tsossie's wife (m)	LW
Girl who stuck knife into	SW
Gorman (m)	
Young woman at Girl Dance (m)	WY
Bitter Water (p)	

This clan was located on the east side of the reservation (PD), along the Utah border (WY); Chee talked with the people of this clan in WI.

STREAMS COME TOGETHER

Old Woman Mustache	SC
Roosevelt Bistie (m)	SW
Standing Rock (p)	
Alice Yazzie (m)	SW
Old Lady George (m)	TT[8]

TOWERING HOUSE (KIN YAA AANII)

Shirley Thompson	CW
Jimmy Chester	SC
Captain Dodge	SC
Bootlegging woman (m)	SW
Rock Gap (p)	
Navajo police sergeant	SW

7. In DW, Graywoman Nezzie's father is listed as Many Poles Clan.
8. Related to Chee through his father's clan.

Robert Bates's wife (m)	T T[9]
Gorman, the 7-Eleven cashier (m)	T T
Irene Musket (m)	T T
Paiute (p)	

TURKEY (TAZHII)

Ashie Begay (m)	GW
Albert A. Gorman (m)	GW
Leroy Gorman (m)	GW
Bentwoman Tsossie (m)	GW
Bentwoman Tsossie's daughter (m)	GW
Salt (p)	
Margaret Billy Sosi	GW
Billy Yellow (probably)	GW

One of the smallest Navajo clans. Many in this clan were relocated by the BIA to Los Angeles, and some moved to the Cañoncito Reservation; the clan was virtually extinct.

TURNING MOUNTAIN

Narbona Begay (m)	CW
Mary Keeyani (m)	CW
Mary Keeyani's daughter (m)	CW
Ashie Pinto (m)	CW
Bitter Water (p)	

WATER RUNS TOGETHER

Graywoman Nezzie's husband (m)	DW
Many Poles (p)	

YUCCA FRUIT

Old Man Joseph (probably)	CW
Delbito Willie's wife (m)	CW

9. Jim Chee was related to Mrs. Bates through his grandfather and the Waters Flow Together Clan.

OTHER NAVAJO CLANS

Linked Clans: Salt and Bitter Water (SW); Turning Mountain and Bitter Water (CW). In TT, Chee's grandfather belonged to the Waters Flow Together Clan (To'aheedlinii; this was probably also a linked clan). The Many Hogans Clan is mentioned in SW as being involved in a land dispute with the Weaver Clan. In WY the Monster Clan is said to live along the Utah border. According to Bergen McKee in BW, the totem of the Reed Clan was a crouching frog. In WY the Tangle Clan lives along the Utah border.

ZUÑI CLANS

BADGER

Ernesto Cata (m)   DD

OTHER ZUÑI CLANS

In DF the Badger, Turkey, Yellow-wood, and Tobacco clans were listed as clans who took part in the great food battle at Ha'wi-k'uh. In the author's endnotes the Macaw Clan is also mentioned.

HOPI CLANS

FLUTE

Flute Clan Boy   DW

FOG

Taylor Sawkatewa (m)   DW

SIDE CORN

Cowboy Dashee (m)   DW, SC

OTHER HOPI CLANS

The following clans were mentioned in *The Dark Wind:* Arrowshaft (now extinct), Bear, Bow,

Cloud, Coyote, Drift Sand, Fire, Snake, and Water. The Bear Clan initially denied the Bow Clan and the Fog Clan a home at the Hopi mesas; the Bow Clan was an aggressive clan; the Fog Clan brought the Hopis the gift of sorcery and nearly died out. The Fog Clan is linked to the Cloud and Water clans. In "Chee's Witch," stories of "two-hearted" witchcraft were associated with the Fog Clan.

Four religious fraternities were mentioned in *The Dark Wind:* the Flute, One Horn, Two Horn, and Wuchim. Eddie Tuvi (DW) and Cowboy Dashee (TG) both belonged to the Antelope Society.

5

CHARACTERS IN TONY HILLERMAN'S FICTION

A CONCORDANCE

Elizabeth A. Gaines
and Diane Hammer

We have listed all people who appear as characters or who are mentioned in Hillerman's works of fiction. To our knowledge only two characters are named after real people: Ernie Bulow and Bernard St. Germain, both in *Talking God*. Many real people are referred to in the books, however, and we have included their names here. Some are historical figures, such as Kit Carson; some are contemporaries, such as modern Western historian Patricia Limerick. Since Hillerman usually does not distinguish the real from the fabricated, neither do we.

We do not know, for example, whether often-mentioned Channel 7 weatherman Howard Morgan really exists or not, and we have not tried to guess.

Each entry is followed by an abbreviation that indicates the book or short story in which it occurs:

BW	*The Blessing Way* (1970)
CW	*Coyote Waits* (1990)
DD	*Dance Hall of the Dead* (1973)
DF	*The Boy Who Made Dragonfly* (1972)
DW	*The Dark Wind* (1982)
FLG	"First Lead Gasser" (1993)
FW	*The Fly on the Wall* (1971)
GW	*The Ghostway* (1984)
LW	*Listening Woman* (1978)
PD	*People of Darkness* (1980)
SC	*Sacred Clowns* (1993)

THE TONY HILLERMAN COMPANION

SW	*Skinwalkers* (1986)
TG	*Talking God* (1989)
TT	*A Thief of Time* (1988)
WI	"Chee's Witch" (1986)
WY	"The Witch, Yazzie, and the Nine of Clubs" (1981)

   Computer-type alphabetization is used in the concordance, since that system is in common use today. Blank spaces come before characters, characters come before alphabeticals: thus, Ha, Ha'tchi, Haas. Titles preceding a first name are not considered in alphabetizing—for example, "Hosteen" is a Navajo title indicating veneration for a person's age or wisdom. Although he was less than thirty years old, Nashibitti was known as Hosteen Nashibitti, because of his great wisdom; Ashie Pinto was known as Hosteen Ashie Pinto because of his age. To use Ashie Pinto as an example: he is listed as **Pinto, Hosteen Ashie,** alphabetized by the last name and then the first.
   All Native Americans listed in the concordance are assumed to be Navajo unless specifically listed as members of another tribe. Native Americans before the coming of the white man appear to have a single given name; some people after that time are also referred to in the same way. You will find them listed alphabetically by the first word in their name: for example, **Afraid of His Horse** is listed under A.
   Certain people are referred to by a descriptive name only and never by their real name; they are listed alphabetically by the first letter in the descriptive name; **Blue Policeman,** for example, is found under B. Occasionally we have invented our own descriptive name for a character. We have also listed significant terms, such as **Navajo Wolf** and **Fly on the Wall.** These are alphabetized by the first

126

word of the term; **Navajo Wolf** is under N, **Fly on the Wall** is under F.

Characters whose first name only is known are listed alphabetically under the first name, as are characters whose name could be either a first or last name.

Some characters are referred to by more than one name in the text; their name is alphabetized as usual, followed by the other names or nicknames in parentheses.

A few characters have the same name in different books. If the characters are different people with the same name, they are listed as separate entries. If the characters are the same people with the same name, they are combined into one entry, the books in which they appear are noted in chronological order, and the books are usually referred to in the entry.

We have not used linguistic symbols for the Indian languages but have tried to use their equivalent in English. You will notice that some terms have more than one spelling, which is the spelling used in that particular book (spellings change from book to book because Navajo terms are transliterations from Navajo characters and thus English equivalents change over time).

And—if someone was killed, we have stated how it was done but not who did it. If you haven't read the books yet, we don't want to spoil the endings for you.

A'shi-wa-ni priests (DF)

Rain Priests were one of the most powerful and important groups in Zuñi society, valuable members of the A'shiwi Tribal Council. In *The Boy Who Made Dragonfly* there were six A'shi-wa-ni priests. According to another source there are sixteen rain priesthoods, each containing from two to six members who have inherited their position through matrilineal household groups. Each priesthood has one fetish, which is their source of power from the Rain Gods.

A'shiwi (DF)

The Zuñi were called the A'shiwi before they became known as the Zuñi. According to Hillerman, A'shiwi means "the Flesh of the Flesh." Two other sources translate it simply as "the Flesh."

A'wonawil'ona (DF)

Zuñi. Hillerman describes A'wonawil'ona as the Great God and Container of All Things, creator of the Sun Father and Moon, creator of Shi-wa-ni and Shi-wa-no-kia, supernatural beings who created the starry skies and the earth and all living things deep inside the earth. Another source defines A'wonawil'ona as "holder of the paths of life" and says the term is used to include primarily the Sun Father and Moon Mother and sometimes a much wider group of supernatural beings.

Adams (FW)

An organization man, Adams sat next to Cotton on the flight from Chicago to Albuquerque. He seemed to be a seasoned traveler; he took an aisle seat and was easy to talk to. He said he was a salesman for National Cash Register, worked out of Denver, and was heading home. He liked hunting, so Cotton told him about his favorite fishing spot up on the Brazos.

The next time Cotton saw him, Adams was dressed in a red cap and jacket, carried a long-barreled rifle with a telescopic sight, and was hunting John Cotton. Cotton managed to evade Adams, leaving him in a stream with a broken arm; he then slashed the tires of Adams's truck and drove back to Sante Fe. When he returned home he identified Adams from police photos as a man listed as Randolph Harge.

Adams, Theodora (LW)

Theodora and her father had met Father Benjamin Tso in Rome, through the brother of her college roommate. Theodora stayed behind when her father, a doctor with the Public Health Service, returned to Washington. She was determined that Ben break his vows and marry her. When Ben returned to the reservation, she tracked him down and persuaded him to let her move in with him for a little while.

Largo had asked Leaphorn to check on her whereabouts and make sure she was safe; the request had come from her father. Theodora was a pretty young woman who drove a midnight-blue Corvette Stingray; she had intended to drive herself to Tso's hogan, but the car was too low for the rough roads. Theodora had flashing white teeth in a perfect tanned face, a mass of blond hair, and unusually deep blue eyes; she was high-breasted and slender and appeared expensive, competent, and assured. Leaphorn thought she was formidable, that she was tough and shrewd and would reveal only what she wanted to reveal. He felt Ben didn't have a chance to remain a priest with Theodora pursuing him. She was captured and held captive along with Ben and the Boy Scout group.

Adcock, Eddie (FW)

An ex-Associated Press reporter, now syndicated, writing for twenty-five or thirty dailies, he specialized in embarrassing county chairmen whose patronage efforts showed.

Addington (FW)

A *Capitol-Press* police reporter at the central

station, Addington was a very young man with a sandy mustache, sandy eyebrows, and pale blue eyes. He told Cotton there was no notebook among McDaniels's belongings. When Cotton's car was found, Addington called the Associated Press and gave them the news about the car being registered in Cotton's name and other details about Cotton's supposed death.

Afraid of His Horse (BW)

This son-in-law of Old Woman Gray Rocks saw the Navajo Wolf killing his penned-up rams with a knife. Old Woman Gray Rocks didn't want his name connected with a Navajo Wolf, so she was evasive with her replies to Bergen McKee.

Afraid of His Horses (WI)

Hearing a witch on the roof of his hogan and seeing dirt fall through the smokehole as the witch tried to throw corpse powder down on him, this Navajo followed the Navajo Wolf's tracks, which disappeared after a mile or so.

Agoyo, Henry (SC)

Tano. Henry's current job was running a road grader for the county. He knew Francis Sayesva very well; they had been in the same class in school and had driven trucks at the Jacks Wild Mine before Francis left for the university. For the ceremonial Henry was the chief clown, in charge of the team that put on the skits. Teddy Sayesva had asked him why the clowns had put the Lincoln cane in the clown wagon. Henry hadn't wanted it there but had put it in at Francis's insistence. Francis had told Henry he hoped what he was thinking was wrong.

Ahkeah, Eugene (SC)

Eugene was a suspect in the murder of Eric

Dorsey; he lived in Thoreau and his family lived out toward Coyote Canyon. Eugene was in his thirties but looked over forty because of alcoholism. He was slightly overweight and seedy-looking. According to Mrs. Montoya, he had been married at one time and maybe had a couple of girlfriends. Although he was a friend of Eric's, he was not his lover.

Eugene worked at Saint Bonaventure Indian Mission as a handyman. Supposedly he had killed Eric Dorsey for silver ingots and jewelry that would enable him to buy alcohol. A box with the ingots and jewelry, plus a ball peen hammer with blood-stains on it, was found under his mobile home. Eugene had no idea how the box had gotten there or who had called the police to report it. He was taken into custody at Crownpoint. He told Lieutenant Toddy that Eric was his friend and he would never do anything to harm him. He refused to say anything more until he could see a lawyer.

Leaphorn was upset because Janet Pete of DNA was assigned to defend him, and Chee was dating Janet. Leaphorn felt Eugene might not have killed Eric, despite all the evidence to the contrary, and requested his release, but Eugene was resentful. He felt he'd been arrested just because he was nearby.

Ainsley, Judge (FW)

Republican Ainsley beat Korolenko in the special election for the Senate during the McCarthy days. He wouldn't use the information about Korolenko's communist relatives in his campaign. Two years later he was defeated by Eugene Clark.

Akron, Agent (TG)

Blond FBI man, Dillon's partner in Washington, D.C., Akron was sent to talk to Leaphorn about Santillanes.

Al (SW)

Al was the police officer on the evening shift at the Farmington jail; he checked in Roosevelt Bistie and inventoried his belongings.

Albertson, Eloy R. (LW)

Frank Hoski sent one letter a week from Washington, D.C., to this alleged person, c/o General Delivery, West Covina, CA. No one ever claimed the letters.

Albino boy (DW)

Hopi. A ten- or twelve-year-old albino boy assisted Sawkatewa with daily chores. When Chee and Dashee visited him, the boy made coffee for them and brought them cigarettes.

Alding, Bailey, Hackler, Mygatt, Peterman, Peterson (FW)

Cotton had celebrated the end of another week with these reporters, after the Sunday edition had gone to press, in Frank's Lounge in Santa Fe, when he was younger. While drinking in Al's Backdoor, Cotton wondered where they all had gone.

Alvis, Kenneth (FW)

Part of the family that owned Alvis Materials (supplier of building and construction materials to Reevis-Smith), old man Alvis had once been state adjutant general. A small white-haired man with skin weathered from being outdoors frequently, he told Cotton he followed his column in the *Tribune* but checked with his company before inviting Cotton in to look through their invoices. When Alvis saw what Cotton had discovered, he ran the totals himself on all five of the Reevis-Smith jobs.

Angie (CW)

Angie worked at the Navajo Tribal Police

Station in Shiprock. She had lived in the area for ten or twelve years, but that wasn't long enough for the residents there to feel safe talking to her about skinwalkers.

Apache people (DF)

Zuñi. The A'shiwi knew the Apache and the Navajo were their younger brothers; the tribes arrived in the area after the A'shiwi had become well established. The Apache and the Navajo raided the A'shiwi, as they were hunters and gatherers rather than farmers.

Applebee, Roger (SC)

Applebee was a lawyer who worked the reservation territory out of Santa Fe, a save-the-planet environmentalist and a big gun in Nature First. He'd talked to Janet Pete about Continental Collectors Corporation's proposed toxic-waste dump last year. When Chee met him the Tribal Council was in session, and Applebee was in Window Rock lobbying to stop the proposal. He had seen and liked Chee's letter on the same subject in the *Navajo Times*.

Applebee was a handsome man, perhaps fifty-five, healthy-looking, small and slender, with long blond hair. When he came over to Janet's table in the coffee shop of the Navajo Nation Inn, he was wearing polished boots, faded jeans, and a pale blue shirt with a silver bear claw on a bolo tie. Chee thought Applebee was the type of man who got right to the heart of the matter when he spoke. He mentioned to Chee that he was a collector and had bought a very old silver pollen flask. He ordered hot herbal tea but had to settle for ordinary tea.

Applebee had heard that Councilman Jimmy Chester was a consultant for Continental and was in favor of the dump proposal. Applebee had been hoping that Chester would go to jail because he had accepted money from Continental, creating a conflict of interest. Since this was not going to happen he thought he could provide evidence that would make the people at Horse Mesa suspicious of Chester's motives, and then they would direct Chester to vote against the proposal.

Chee figured it was Applebee who broadcast the illegally obtained audio tape of Chester and Ed Zeck discussing what appeared to be a bribe. After Leaphorn was suspended, he tried to contact Applebee about the tape. Applebee was staying in room 127 at the Navajo Nation Inn. When Leaphorn arrived, Asher Davis was knocking on his door and Applebee's dark blue English Land Rover with its environmental bumper sticker was parked outside. No one answered the door, and Leaphorn asked Davis to have Applebee contact him when he found him. Later, when Leaphorn called Dilly Streib at home, he learned Applebee had been shot three times in the chest with a .45 and was dead.

Archer (DW)

Boyfriend of Tom West in prison, Archer was around forty, big, with a body developed by lifting weights; his nose had been broken twice. He said T. L. Johnson had set up West, making it look like West had snitched. West was scared. He decided to take his chances in the regular prison environment because the other inmates respected him. West was Joseph Musket's friend, but Archer didn't know if the reverse was true; Archer thought Musket was "too damn clever." Archer wouldn't say who he thought killed West.

Archibald, James (FW)

Captain Archibald was spokesman for the capital city police who identified the car in the river as Cotton's; they assumed it was Cotton who had drowned because they could not locate him.

Armijo (DW)

Armijo had an office in the New Mexico State Penitentiary at Santa Fe. He was plump, around forty, with coarse black hair and very white teeth. He told Chee he had known Joseph Musket personally because Musket, a trusty, worked in the records section; Musket had friends in prison because he had money; there was more money in his canteen fund than he could have earned doing prison jobs. Armijo had no idea if Tom West had any friends in prison and called the deputy warden to find out. Armijo was busy trying to complete his annual report, which was late.

Armstrong, C. J. Delos (Chick) (FW)

As soon as he became state executive engineer, Armstrong moved Larry Houghton to second district maintenance engineer and put Herman Gay in as state construction engineer. The quality experiment was his idea, to test an enriched mix of cement to prevent chipping.

Arnett, Grace and Bad Dude (DD)

The Arnetts were members of the Jason's Fleece commune.

Arnold, Bo (TT)

"Dr." Arnold was a part-time botanist with the Bureau of Land Management while he worked on his dissertation on lichens; finishing his dissertation was all he really cared about. Ellie Friedman-Bernal had met him at the University of Wisconsin in Madison. Bo was around forty, a lanky man "with an array of white teeth in a face of weathered brown leather"; he typically wore jeans and a faded red shirt and drove an old jeep. He had lived in one of the temporary housing units and worked at Chaco, but now he lived in an old house out on the highway near Bluff, Utah. He was looking for Ellie because she had borrowed first his saddle and then his kayak, and the kayak was still missing.

Atarque, Thomas (DD)

Zuñi. One of Ernesto Cata's uncles, he helped dig out Ernesto's body and refused Leaphorn's offer of help.

Atcitty, Anna (LW)

Daughter of Margaret Cigaret's sister and a Listener-in-training, Anna was a pretty girl, perhaps sixteen years old, who attended Tuba City High School; she was a typical teenager, with a couple of boyfriends and no enemies. Margaret said she was "a good student in some ways" and "when she got over being crazy about boys, she would be an effective Listener." Anna "had the rare gift of hearing voices in the wind and getting the visions that came out of the earth." The gift of divining the cause of illness ran in Anna's family; her mother's uncle was a famous Hand Trembler who could diagnose lightning sickness.

On the spring day they visited Hosteen Tso, Anna drove Margaret's Dodge pickup, did the ritual painting on Hosteen Tso's chest, and guided Margaret to the listening place on the cliff wall. Anna had not wanted to accompany Margaret that day; she wanted to meet a boy of the Salt Cedar Dinee who worked at Short Mountain. Anna was killed because she was a witness to Tso's murder.

Atcitty, Curtis (SW)

Atcitty called Janet Pete and told her he was Roosevelt Bistie's friend; Bistie had asked him to find a lawyer. Janet knew he'd lied to her because Bistie later told Janet he didn't know any Atcitty.

Baca, Delbert (TG)

Undersheriff of McKinley County, New Mexico, Baca was at the site near the Amtrak rails where Santillanes's body was found. He found the note referring to the Yeibichai for Agnes Tsosie in the handkerchief pocket of the man's suit.

Backhoe Bandit (TT)

Chee was test-driving a Buick for Janet Pete when he spotted the Backhoe Bandit, a young man with long blond hair hanging down from under a dark-billed cap and suggestions of pockmarks on his jaw. The Bandit had once given Bernie Tso two $100 bills to tow his car and fix the transmission and told him to leave the car and his change with Slick Nakai, whom he saw fairly often. The Bandit told Bernie he worked in the Blanco gas field. Slick said his name was Joey or Jody and he sometimes bought pots from him.

Bacobi (DD)

Zuñi. One of Ernesto Cata's uncles, he helped dig out Ernesto's body.

Bacteriologist (PD)

Using a wheelchair to get around, she had worked in the Communicable Disease Laboratory at the University of New Mexico for two years. While she waited for cultures to develop, she had developed the habit of looking out at the parking lot. She saw a blond man put a grocery sack in the back of Emerson Charley's green pickup; then the window through which she was watching was blown out by an explosion.

Bailey, Markie (TG)

Receptionist-secretary for Catherine Morris Perry, Markie Bailey was curious about her boss's weekend in Vermont. Mrs. Perry wanted to fire her but couldn't because Mrs. Bailey was protected by civil service rules.

Baker, Agent (DD)

John O'Malley implied that Baker was just another FBI agent, but Baker was really a narcotics agent with the Treasury Department. He was "maybe fifty, with a pink, freckled, sagging, hound-dog face and a shock of sandy hair . . . bad teeth, irregular and discolored, and an air of casual sloppiness, and . . . a quick, inquisitive, impatient intelligence." Leaphorn remembered he'd met him in Utah in connection with a death caused by an overdose of heroin; Baker was smarter than one would expect and apparently more ruthless as well. Leaphorn watched him work undercover at the Shalako ceremony and decided he wouldn't care to have Baker pursuing him.

Bales, Deputy Sheriff (GW)

Bales, a deputy sheriff of San Juan County, New Mexico, went with Jim Chee and Agent Sharkey to capture Albert Gorman; he was afraid one of the law officers would get shot. An older white man with weathered skin, easygoing and talkative, a cigarette smoker, he'd been a deputy for thirty years.

Barbone, Hosteen (SC)

Hosteen Barbone was an *hataalii*, an ancient man with an old, cracked, scratchy voice. His daughter appeared to Chee to be at least seventy. He lived over by Crystal and knew about the Hunger People and their clan relationships from his grandmother, who had been captured and sold in Santa Fe for $150. She had escaped and returned to her family, but her family was gone, so she joined with other escapees to start their own clan, the Hunger People.

Barzun, Rick (FW)
Barzun and Cotton had celebrated blanking the Associated Press on a major accident at the finish of the Pan-American Road Race in Ciudad Juárez. While drinking in Al's Backdoor years later, Cotton wondered where Rick was.

Bates, Robert (TT)
An undersheriff in the San Juan County sheriff's office, Bates usually handled homicides. Bates's wife was born to the Towering House People, which was linked to Chee's grandfather's Waters Flow Together Clan, which made Bates's wife and Chee distant relatives. Bates and Chee had worked together a time or two and liked each other.

Becenti, Henry (PD)
Jim Chee was Lieutenant Henry Becenti's replacement at Crownpoint. Becenti had spent more than forty years as a policeman; he thought the white men had some weird customs. Sheriff Sena told Chee he had once had problems with Becenti because their jurisdictions overlapped; Becenti had been arresting members of the Peyote Church, and Sena wanted to hold them to find out what they knew about the oil rig explosion. Chee visited Becenti to find out what he knew before agreeing to work for Rosemary Vines.

Becenti, Rudolph (PD)
One of the Navajos who did not report for work at the oil rig the day it exploded in 1948, he was of the Mud Clan. He died of leukemia.

Beck, Alice (FW)

As a young man, John Cotton had intended to marry this blond, slender, sexy, silly young woman. He was more distraught about Charley Graff's betrayal than about losing Alice.

Begay, Hosteen Ashie (GW)

Born to the Turkey Clan (Tazhii Dinee), Begay lived near Two Gray Hills. His aunt was *ahnii* (matriarch) of their clan, and one of his grandmothers was Tewa. Begay very carefully followed the Navajo Way. His family had lived in the area longer than anyone could remember; he had a grazing permit, ran his sheep, and kept to himself. Begay was honest, well-liked, and took care of his relatives, although some said he was a witch. He enjoyed dipping snuff and didn't drink alcohol; he suffered from bunions and took more sweat baths than most Navajos.

Albert Gorman's tracks led to his hogan, and Begay had bought pain medication for him at the trading post. Begay had built on a beautiful site and had taken good care of his home, yet he had abandoned it, as if someone died there. Begay would have dragged Gorman outside the hogan before he died rather than abandoning it; he would never have left his Four Mountains bundle in a death hogan if he was alive. Chee found Begay dead, shot in the head, his body dumped in the wash.

Begay, Eddie (DW)

Eddie Begay was the Navajo policeman who questioned Edna Nezzie about the squash-blossom necklace she'd pawned.

Begay, Emerson (LW)

Emerson Begay, a young man born to the Mud Clan, had a "flat Mongolian face with tiny lines around the eyes, giving it a sardonic cast." When Leaphorn picked him up, he was wearing a black felt Stetson hat, a denim jacket, a rodeo-style shirt, and a $12.95 Timex watch with a heavy sand-cast silver watchband on his left wrist. Leaphorn had him handcuffed because Begay had been in jail twice before for stealing white men's sheep and because Begay had a reputation for making escapes. Leaphorn had caught Begay at the Kinaalda for Eileen Endischee, his niece, and had no choice but to take him along when he pursued the man in the gray Mercedes. While Tomas Charley and Leaphorn were examining the abandoned Mercedes, Begay slipped away.

Begay, Frank (SW)
Frank Begay was from the Lukachukai area. Irma Onesalt wanted him to testify that the Many Hogans Dinee had the right to some land in that area. She was furious when Chee brought in Franklin instead of Frank. She didn't know Frank had died on October 3 from complications of diabetes.

Begay, Franklin (SW)
Born to the Coyote Pass People and born for the Monster People, he lived on the Checkerboard reservation. Chee brought him from the Badwater Clinic to the Chapter House instead of Frank Begay.

Begay, Joseph (BW)
Joseph, a short round-faced man with a barrel chest, found the body of Luis Horseman near Ganado. He was married, with one daughter and two sons. A third son, Long Fingers, died in childhood.

Begay, Largewhiskers (DW)
Mary Joe Natonabah accused Largewhiskers

of grazing his sheep on her land. When Chee arrived in the Begay camp, Largewhiskers was not there, so Chee told his son-in-law of the complaint and of the consequences and promised he'd come back and check on it.

Begay, Long Fingers (BW)
Young son of Joseph Begay, he died of the choking sickness one night in their hogan. His family had to abandon the hogan and build a new one because his *chindi* was trapped in the old one.

Begay, Narbona (CW)
Ashie Pinto's maternal uncle, Narbona had taught Ashie many stories of the old times.

Begay, Simon (the City Navajo) (WI)
When the FBI broke a car theft ring in Los Angeles, Begay had been one of the men who stole the expensive cars, which were then shipped to South America. He had seen some things that tied the bosses of the ring into the crime so the Justice Department had made a deal with him: In exchange for his testimony they would hide him on the reservation in one of the government houses. The reservation Navajos immediately spotted him as a relocation Navajo, a stranger; when odd things began to happen on the reservation, the Navajos said Simon Begay was a witch and was causing the problems.

Begay, Hosteen Tallman (DW)
Joseph Musket hired this singer to perform an Enemy Way sing for him when he came home from prison.

Begay, Tsosie (BW)
It was Tsosie Begay who found the Navajo Wolf's tracks around his sheep pen.

CHARACTERS IN TONY HILLERMAN'S FICTION

Begay, Woody (PD)

One of the Navajos who did not report for work at the oil rig the day it exploded in 1948, Woody was said by his sister, Fannie Kinlicheenie, to have died in 1953 in a Gallup hospital from leukemia.

Begay family (DW)

This family had a reputation for causing trouble on the Joint Use Reservation.

Bell, Eddie (SC)

Sergeant Bell of the Farmington police told Chee the department had already tried unsuccessfully to find out whether the bumper sticker ERNIE IS THE GREATEST had been made in Farmington, Albuquerque, Gallup, Flagstaff, or Phoenix. He also told Chee the tape of Councilman Jimmy Chester and Ed Zeck discussing money had been broadcast from the Kirtland public access line of KNDN.

Beloved Ones (DF)

Zuñi. The Beloved Ones were the souls of people who had completed their lives and now lived happily in the Dance Hall of the Dead. They had given the A'shiwi an abundance of water blessings.

Benally, Sergeant (TT)

Captain Largo told Chee not to do anything about the backhoe, that Benally would handle it. Benally told Chee about Joe Nails and the rented truck from U-Haul. He thought maybe they could persuade Nails to admit he took the backhoe.

Benally, Gray Old Lady (SC)

Gray Old Lady Benally was related to Delmar Kanitewa's father through the Bitter Water People. She lived more than fifteen miles west of the

143

Torreon Trading Post off Navajo Road 7028. She
had a log hogan with a dirt roof, an unused corral,
and a small frame house with most of its white
paint missing. Two fifty-five-gallon water cans, one
empty, one with just six inches of water in it, stood
by the door of the house. She offered Chee and
Blizzard each a half cup of coffee, although she
drank none herself.

Gray Old Lady wore a shawl over her head
and looked about eighty; her once-round face was
shrunken by the years and she was toothless. She
said her husband, asleep in the bedroom, was so
old he couldn't walk, didn't know who he was, and
had forgotten how to say words. She hadn't seen
Delmar, her great-grandson, for a long time.

She and her husband had relied on Eric
Dorsey to bring them food and water from the mission. They called him *begadoche*, their water sprin-
kler. He made them laugh with his duck puppet. He
had made Gray Old Lady a rocking chair to help
her back, had taken her husband to the doctor, and
had helped them sell things profitably. She cried
when Chee told her Eric was dead.

Benaly, George (SW)

A Navajo Tribal policeman in Shiprock, Benaly
had worked with Leaphorn out of Many Farms. He
was more observant than Officer Al Gorman.

Beno, Aileen (Mrs. Leonard Skeet) (SW)

Hildegarde Goldtooth was Aileen Beno's
father's sister. Aileen told Leaphorn that Goldtooth
had recently died and there was no one living there
now, where Chee was going to make arrangements
for the sing.

Beno, Robert (GW)

Robert Beno ran the car-stealing operation

for McNair Factoring. He was indicted by the grand jury through the efforts of Kenneth Upchurch but was never picked up; there was no arrest record and no pictures or fingerprints on file for him.

Beno, Shy Girl (SW)
The younger, unmarried daughter of Theresa Beno, she followed Chee in a gray Chevy pickup when Chee left the Beno camp; Chee felt she wanted to tell him something about the sheep stealing but was too shy.

Beno, Theresa (SW)
Theresa Beno was head of her camp. She was married; her elder daughter was married, and her younger daughter was Shy Girl. Jim Chee visited her to ask about sheep stealing.

Bent Woman (SW)
Born to the Bitter Water People, born for the Deer Spring Clan, Bent Woman was thin and stooped, partially blind from glaucoma and cataracts. She was pleased to find that Chee was her nephew, distantly related through his father's family, the Salt Clan. Her mother was Gray Woman Nez.

Bentwoman's Daughter (GW)
Born to the Turkey Clan, her mother was Bentwoman Tsossie and her father was Jefferson Tom of the Salt Dinee. She was an eighty-year-old Navajo woman living in Los Angeles "with a round, plump face framed with graying hair" and a rusty old-person's voice; her hands were wrinkled and she had pain when she moved. She spoke Navajo. Ashie Begay was her nephew, and at first she denied having seen Margaret Sosi.

Berger (GW)
A resident of the Silver Threads Rest Home on La Monica Street in Los Angeles, Berger was frail and bony, with white hair and pale blue eyes. His body was bent and skinny, and his hands were twisted and trembly; he used an aluminum walking frame and dragged his legs. He was frustrated by how hard it was to speak and move around; he'd had a stroke. Berger liked Albert Gorman because he'd stop and talk to him when no one else would; he knew Gorman was in bad trouble. By using a combination of pantomime and head nodding, Berger was able to give Chee information about Gorman.

Bernal, Eduardo (Eddie) (TT)
Before Eddie Bernal and Ellie Friedman were married they were part of a site-mapping team in the Anasazi ruins as graduate students and lovers. Ellie thought of him as "tough little Ed." Leaphorn thought from his wedding photo he was a good-looking Mexican.

Bierly, Lieutenant (FW)
Cotton was to call this capital city policeman for assistance if Captain Whan was unavailable.

Bifocals (PD)
This nurse was on duty on the fifth floor at the Bernalillo County Medical Center in Albuquerque, where Jim Chee was recovering from a gunshot wound. She was a white woman in her mid-forties, with a round placid face and skin wrinkled from the sun; she wore bifocals. She told Chee what she knew about the disappearance of Emerson Charley's body.

Big Hat (WY)
Big Hat was scalp carrier for the scalp shooting part of the Enemy Way ceremony for Emerson

Nez. The "scalp" was a strip of red plastic 1 inch wide by $1/2$ inch thick by 18 inches long that had fallen off the bumper of the witch's truck. Chee wanted Big Hat to give him the scalp after the ceremony, but Big Hat was killed. (A variation of this story appears in *The Blessing Way*, in which Billy Nez stole the scalp.)

Big Navajo (BW)

Big Navajo was a tall man who looked like a Tuba City Navajo: long-faced, rawboned, with heavy eyebrows and a wide mouth; he wore his hair in short braids with red bands on them. He was usually seen wearing a black shirt, flat-heeled boots, and a black felt hat with a silver concha hatband. He drove a gray Land Rover and carried a .38 pistol and a rifle with a telescopic sight. He had to visit Old Man Shoemaker's trading post to pick up supplies and to buy a new hat when his was stolen.

He had hoped to pass as a reservation Navajo but was quickly spotted as a stranger because he couldn't speak Navajo fluently. It was thought he was a relocation Navajo, born and raised in Los Angeles; most of his knowledge of the Navajos seemed to have been acquired from books. The Big Navajo had a long history of violent juvenile and adult crimes and was associated with the Mafia. His real name was George Jackson, but he also used the names Amos Raven, Big Raven, and George Thomas. It was said he never broke a contract or screwed up a job, but on this job he received a lance wound that killed him.

Bigthumb, Thomasina (CW)

Thomasina thought witches caused radio signal breakup; the old lady blamed witches for just about everything.

Billie, Eleanor (SW)
A woman from the Yoo'l Dinee, the Bead People, this receptionist at Badwater Clinic had a good memory. She remembered Chee and the wrong Begay incident. She was plump and had beautiful clear writing; she obtained a copy of the patient list for Chee.

Billy, Ellison (TT)
A Navajo Tribal Policeman at Window Rock, subordinate to Major Ronald Nez, Corporal Billy handled office work for him and called Leaphorn for Nez.

Birdie, T. J. (CW)
Deputy Birdie, on duty at San Juan County jail in Aztec when Chee came in to examine Ashie Pinto's file, was half White Mountain Apache. The sheriff had hired him not to get Apache votes but because he was smart; unfortunately he was also lazy. He was a stubby young man with short-cut black hair.

Bishbito, Al (BW)
Al owned and operated the diner in Chinle; his cook quit so Al had to do all the cooking himself, only he wasn't very good at it. Leaphorn used Al's telephone to make a long-distance call.

Bisti, Blackie (DD)
A friend of Leaphorn's at Arizona State, Bisti attended a meeting of the Native American Church with Tom Bob and Leaphorn and sampled peyote.

Bisti, Emerson (LW)
Bisti had been born at Kaibito Wash and grown up there, herding his mother's sheep. After the Korean War he patrolled this same area.

Corporal Bisti furnished Leaphorn with a map of all the known water holes in that region; Leaphorn figured Goldrims would head for water after abandoning the gray Mercedes.

Bisti, Priscilla (DW)
Chee came close to catching Priscilla bootlegging, but she and her boys had removed the evidence from her pickup before he arrived. At a later date they were seen loading six cases of wine into her truck in Winslow, Arizona.

Bisti, Roosevelt (CW)
Bisti was a former client of Janet Pete. Chee finally admitted to Janet that he had searched Bisti's sack while she had Bisti with her at the telephone. See also **Bistie, Roosevelt.**

Bisti, Rudolph (WI) (WY)
In the short story "The Witch, Yazzie, and the Nine of Clubs," Bisti's boys had lost three rams while driving their sheep up into the Chuska high pastures. When they found the rams' bodies, they were surrounded by werewolf tracks. The same character with the same name appeared in the short story "Chee's Witch."

Bistie, Roosevelt (SW)
Born to the Streams Come Together Dinee and born for the Standing Rock People, Bistie was part of a very large family. He had at least two daughters; one lived on his land with him, one lived at Shiprock (see **Bistie's Daughter**). Bistie was old and thin, a tall man stooped by age and illness; his face was copper-colored from jaundice. He had a small scar on his chest where a corpse bone had been removed; he carried the bone in his billfold. At the Badwater Clinic, Bistie had been told he

THE TONY HILLERMAN COMPANION

had cancer of the liver and would die; he was angry.

Bistie drove a rusty old green GMC pickup with a .30-.30 carbine in a rack across the back window; he didn't own a shotgun. When Chee and Kennedy arrested him for killing Dugai Endocheeney, he told Chee he had shot Endocheeney off the roof of his hogan but wouldn't say why. Witnesses said Bistie's truck was at Endocheeney's hogan when Endocheeney was killed, and Bistie had been heard saying he intended to kill Endocheeney. Endocheeney, however, was killed with a butcher knife. Janet Pete was asked to represent Bistie, and he was released from Farmington jail and went back to his hogan. When Leaphorn and Chee went there to question him, they found Bistie had been shot by a .38 pistol and his body had been dragged up the hill behind his hogan. See also **Bisti, Roosevelt.**

Bistie's Daughter (SW)

Roosevelt Bistie was described as having two daughters; one daughter appeared to live with him at his hogan. The first time she talked to Chee she told him her father had gone into Farmington to buy medicine, then stayed overnight with her sister at Shiprock; when she talked to Chee just after her father's death she told him she had been in Gallup visiting her sister. (Either there is a third daughter or an error in where the second daughter lives.)

The daughter at the hogan was a sturdy young woman with crooked teeth, bent ankles, and a pigeon-toed stance. When Chee spoke to her, she was dressed in an I LOVE HAWAII T-shirt, jeans, and squaw boots. When Chee and Jay Kennedy went to Roosevelt Bistie's hogan the first time, the daughter spoke to Chee in Navajo, as she had not associated with many white people and felt uncomfortable speaking in English. She was very reluctant to speak about dead people, including her own father, whom she loved very much; she was relieved when Chee told her that her father had died outside the hogan. She had not hired Janet Pete to represent her father.

Bitsi, Rudolph (BW)
    Coroner–justice of the peace who was sent to examine Luis Horseman's body, he was a "short, middle-aged man, tending to fat."

Bizett, Allen (GW)
    A detective with the Los Angeles Police Department, Lieutenant Bizett reported on the radio in his gravelly voice only the most basic details of Eric Vaggan's attack on Jay Leonard.

Black, Van (LW)
    This was one of the many aliases of Jimmy Tso, aka Frank Hoski.

Blind Eyes (LW)
    Margaret Cigaret, the Listening Woman, was also known as Blind Eyes.

Blizzard, Harold (SC)
    Sergeant Blizzard worked for the Bureau of Indian Affairs Law and Order Division and had an office in Albuquerque. He was a Cheyenne, with long legs and a hard, bony face with a profile like a hatchet. He was too large and loud to be ignored and wore a New York Yankees cap with his uniform. While waiting for Chee at Crownpoint he passed the time by reading a science fiction book by Roger Zelazny.
    Blizzard was new to adobe country, and Chee

at first thought he was a hard-ass. Chee softened a bit after Blizzard asked him for help, saying he was a city Indian who didn't know much about Indians in the Southwest. Blizzard was frustrated because he didn't know how to talk to these people and get information from them.

His father had worked for the post office in Chicago. Blizzard had been to the Cheyenne Reservation only once, for the funeral of his father's mother, when he was a little boy. He remembered how cold it had been in his uncle's shack and how unfriendly the other children had seemed.

Blizzard and Chee had both been assigned to locate Delmar Kanitewa for questioning; Blizzard had found Delmar and returned him to his school. While he was talking to the federal agents the boy took off again, and Blizzard called Chee for help. The two of them had covered a lot of miles that day, and Chee asked Blizzard if he'd like to stay overnight at his trailer.

That evening Blizzard enthusiastically accepted Janet's invitation to accompany Chee and Janet to see the movie *Cheyenne Autumn*, which he had heard about but never seen. Janet Pete liked him because they had similar backgrounds. Chee noticed that Blizzard's reaction to the movie seemed to be sadness at seeing the destruction of his people's culture. When the three of them returned to the trailer, Chee was grateful when Blizzard quickly excused himself so he could be alone with Janet.

Blue Policeman (BW)

This descriptive name is used by the Navajo to designate any police officer anywhere; in particular, they used it to address Leaphorn when they didn't know his name.

Blue Topcoat (FW)

An Organization man, he was tall and dark-haired, wore a blue topcoat, and drove a dark blue Cadillac. He walked into the capitol newsroom and looked on McDaniels's desk for his notebook; he then sat in the Cadillac and watched Cotton going to meet Janey Janoski at the Copper Pot, and later he hunted for Cotton inside the statehouse with Randolph Harge.

Blue Woman (CW)

For Ashie Pinto's trial, a middle-aged woman in a dark blue dress in the federal building in Albuquerque spun the bingo cage and pulled out names of prospective jurors. (In *The Ghostway*, Mrs. Frank Sam Nakai was called Blue Woman by her friends.)

Bluehorse, Felix (SC)

Delmar Kanitewa's best friend, first at the Crownpoint school and then after Felix had transferred to the school at Thoreau, Felix was small, about sixteen years old, with enough white blood mixed with the Navajo to make him prone to acne. He lived with his mother, who worked for the Navajo Communications Company, in a mobile home in Crownpoint. Felix was anxious to talk to someone but was cautious, because the man who had killed Eric Dorsey was after Delmar and could come after him.

Felix had made a silver bracelet in Dorsey's class for his girlfriend and asked Delmar to pick it up for him. After Delmar picked up the bracelet, he was in a hurry and asked Felix to come for him at the video rental place in Thoreau. He had the newspaper-wrapped object with him. Felix dropped Delmar at the Giant Truck Stop on Interstate 40, where he could get a ride to Tano Pueblo.

Bourebonette, Louisa (CW) (SC)

In *Coyote Waits*, Louisa is an associate professor of American Studies at Northern Arizona University at Flagstaff; she lives just south of Flagstaff and has been a friend of Ashie Pinto's family for over twenty-five years. At her first meeting with Leaphorn, the professor is angry, haughty, and arrogant. Her accent is slightly southern. She is trim and gray-haired, with sharp blue eyes in an austere face. Louisa had studied mythology in Cambodia, Thailand, and Vietnam, before the intensifying war had made that impossible. She'd been compiling a biography and memoir of Ashie Pinto for over twenty years.

She and Pinto were collaborating on a book about the evolution of witchcraft beliefs; she comments that the book is mostly Pinto's and it won't be as solid without his input. She accompanies Mary Keeyani to Leaphorn's office in Window Rock; the FBI had not been helpful, and Pinto's attorney had given her the impression that Pinto would not be very well represented. She is willing to hire a private investigator, as she is sure Pinto did not kill Delbert Nez. She accompanies Leaphorn on several excursions to gather information about Pinto and shares her interest in mythology with him; he appreciates her alertness and tolerance for long silences.

In *Sacred Clowns*, Louisa, now a professor, has a research project in Asia, and she and Leaphorn are planning a one-month trip to China. They will first spend three days in Beijing where she intends to work in the libraries and meet other folklorists; she will then head south to Xian and Nanjing to continue work in that area. Meanwhile Leaphorn will travel north from Beijing into Mongolia, then meet her in Shanghai for the trip home together. Dilly Streib describes Louisa as a nice-looking woman. He tells Leaphorn he's been alone long enough and he should get involved with the professor.

Joe notices that Louisa's hair is becoming gray but looks alive, clean and healthy, and that she needs to get the prescription for her bifocals changed because she has to get close to the map to read it. She persuades Joe to stay overnight, and he follows her Honda Civic to the small old brick bungalow four blocks from the campus of Northern Arizona University. The guestroom is really an office and is small and crowded. After drinking some hot herbal tea and discussing the Dorsey and Sayesva murders with her, Joe falls asleep in her recliner.

Everything is ready for the big trip when Joe is suspended because of the audio cassette that Jim Chee left in Joe's recorder. Joe is unable to contact Louisa and leaves messages for her on answering machines. He figures she will leave without him. When she hears the message about his suspension, however, she cancels the trip and comes to find him, thinking he might need her.

Bowlegs, Cecil (DD)
    Eleven-year-old brother of George Bowlegs and son of Shorty Bowlegs, Cecil told Leaphorn that George ran away because of the kachina; he thought Ernesto Cata had broken a taboo, the kachina had caught Ernesto, and George was trying to find the kachina. Cecil didn't know where George was. He didn't like his Zuñi schoolmates because they made fun of him, and he didn't like Ernesto because he felt Ernesto was a bad influence on George. Cecil's only possessions were in his yellow Snoopy lunch box, which he took with him to Saint Anthony's, where he was to stay until

he could be returned to Old Woman Running's people.

Bowlegs, George (DD)

Son of Shorty Bowlegs, brother of Cecil Bowlegs, and best friend of Ernesto Cata, George was fourteen years old and attended Zuñi Consolidated School with Ernesto. He and Ernesto spent a lot of time together. He was curious about the Zuñi religion and had learned many things from Ernesto; he wanted to quit being a Navajo and become a Zuñi. Ernesto encouraged his curiosity but didn't see how George could ever become a Zuñi. George visited an old Zuñi man and tried to persuade him to teach him how to become a sorcerer; he collected cactus buttons for the Jason's Fleece commune and tried them himself in search of visions. He and Ernesto visited Ted Isaacs frequently, and George persuaded Ernesto to go through a box of artifacts and take a lance point made by the Old People.

When Ernesto trained for the Shalako ceremony, George waited for him with his bike so they could go home and do their homework; when Ernesto didn't show up, George left the bike and went home. When Ernesto didn't go to school the next day, George became frightened and left school early. He thought the kachina had killed Ernesto for breaking the taboo, and he wanted to find the kachina and propitiate it, at the lake that was said to be the location of the Dance Hall of the Dead. He told Cecil he would be gone for a few days on business and took his father's rifle and his big bay horse; he stopped by the commune to ask for supplies but went away without any because of Halsey.

Leaphorn was afraid George would freeze to death and was somewhat relieved when Susanne told him how much George knew about deer hunting; George had provided deer for his family for years. Leaphorn knew someone was hunting George, to question him and then kill him, so he was trying to find George first. Leaphorn did find George at the Shalako ceremony—but not quickly enough.

Bowlegs, Shorty (DD)

Member of the High Standing House Clan, this alcoholic father of George and Cecil Bowlegs drank so much that most of the time he couldn't hold a coherent conversation. He had taken a job tending someone else's sheep, then relied on the boys to do the sheepherding for him. When he was sober he was a friendly man, a man who tried to be helpful, and his sons loved him. One night after George disappeared, Shorty was hit on the head and his hogan was searched.

Bowlegs, Mrs. Shorty (DD)

Leaphorn had heard that the absentee mother of George and Cecil Bowlegs was no good. Father Ingles said she started hitching rides into Gallup for drinking bouts with men or she moved in with two brothers who were witches or a combination of both. Shorty didn't get along with his wife's people, so he and the boys moved back to the Ramah area.

Bowles, Volney (FW)

A reporter for the *Journal*, Bowles was sitting at the press table in the House of Representatives working a Double-Crostic in the *Saturday Review* during one of the morning legislative sessions. During another session he asked Governor Roark why Tommy Gianini wanted the position on the parole board and if Gianini had any relatives in stir; Cotton said Bowles's diet was making him mean.

Boxholder (PD)
Colton Wolf's contact in El Paso, he gave Colton his assignments. Colton was curious to see what he looked like, as they had always talked by telephone.

Boyden, Roger (FW)
Boyden had been the AP's second man at the statehouse for ten years before becoming Clark's press secretary and hatchet man. He had moved back to the midwest capital from Washington to mobilize Clark's supporters for a primary battle against Roark.

Bracken (PD)
A person named Bracken died at the Bernalillo County Medical Center; his or her belongings were in a red plastic bag kept in storage.

Bryce, George W. (FW)
One of Clark's people, district attorney of the Third Judicial District, Bryce had once been a partner in Clark's law firm and was in control of law enforcement in the state's most politically sensitive area, including the state capital. Korolenko figured Bryce would use Cotton's story to ruin Roark's chances of winning the Senate primary race.

Buffalo Society (LW)
A militant political group that split off from the American Indian Movement, it formally declared war against whites, pulling a series of bombings, kidnappings, and bank robberies. Their most recent robbery was of a Wells Fargo

armored truck in Santa Fe; their getaway helicopter was last seen over the Navajo reservation. The Buffalo Society declared itself the avenger of the Sun God; when seven symbolic crimes had been avenged, the earth would be cleansed of the white man and left for the buffalo herds and Indians to repopulate.

Bulow, Ernie (TG)
A real person that Hillerman wrote into the story, Bulow attended the Yeibichai ceremony for old Agnes Tsosie. He was "a towering, gray-bearded desert rat who'd been raised on the Big Reservation and had written a book about Navajo taboos. Bulow spoke coherent Navajo and had developed close personal relationships with Navajo families." He arrived at the ceremony in a station wagon.

Bundy (SC)
An art dealer in Chicago, he was primarily interested in Lincoln artifacts and had been in the business about forty years. His voice was old and hoarse from smoke damage and too much whiskey. At an annual meeting of Lincoln buffs he'd heard the rumor that one of the Lincoln canes had been bought by a man from Miami, Florida.

Burgoyne, John Neldine and Jane (TG)
Henry Highhawk sent lawyer Catherine Perry a box containing the bones of her grandparents, the Burgoynes, to let her know what it felt like to have one's ancestors disinterred.

Bush, George (TG)
FBI Agent Jay Kennedy wondered why President Bush had picked what's-his-name for

THE TONY HILLERMAN COMPANION

Vice President, among other things he was pondering—like why he was having lunch with Leaphorn when he knew Leaphorn was going to ask him a favor.

Caldwell (PD)

A person named Caldwell died at the Bernalillo County Medical Center; his or her belongings were in a red plastic bag kept in storage.

Campbell, Professor (TT)

At the University of New Mexico, he had told Chee's class there were forty thousand sites in New Mexico alone with New Mexico Laboratory of Anthropology registry numbers.

Canfield, Jeremy Robert (BW)

An associate and friend of Bergen McKee in the anthropology department at the University of New Mexico, Dr. Canfield was looking for Folsom Man artifacts in the burial sites of the Anasazi. He was "a very small man, bent slightly by a spinal deformity, with a round, cheerful face made rounder by utter baldness." When he was in the field working he liked to smoke his pipe, wear a plaid canvas fishing hat with an oversize feather in the band, play his guitar and sing ribald songs, and drive his camper. He asked McKee to give him a totem to protect him from the Navajo Wolf; McKee found him dead inside his truck in an isolated canyon.

Captain, the (TG)

The black man who shined Leroy Fleck's shoes in Washington, D.C., had lined skin, and his hair was a thick mass of tight gray curls. He didn't believe Fleck was really an undercover cop; he enjoyed the money Fleck gave him for acting as a neighborhood lookout.

160

Cardona, Ramon Huerta (TG)

Head of the secret police in Chile, General Cardona was going to visit the Smithsonian to see the display of masks. Some American tycoon had obtained a priceless Inca mask that had belonged to his family and given it to the Smithsonian; he wanted it back.

Carson, Kit (LW) (CW) (SC)

According to *Listening Woman*, when Kit Carson and the U.S. Army came into the territory in 1864 they used the Utes to help them track down and kill the Navajos; there had been long-standing enmity between Ute and Navajo ever since. In *Coyote Waits*, Leaphorn stated that Kit Carson was worse than even Colonel John Macrae Washington; Washington was at least an honest enemy of the Navajos; Carson pretended to be a friend.

Christopher "Kit" Carson was born December 24, 1809, in Madison County, Kentucky, and died May 23, 1868, at Fort Lyon, Colorado. At the age of fifteen he ran away from home to join traders bound for Santa Fe; he was a trapper for the next fifteen years and considered Taos, New Mexico, his home. After 1840 the fur business died down and Carson married an Arapaho woman. In 1842 he had a chance encounter with John Frémont and served as guide on Frémont's exploratory trips of the West in 1842, 1843–44, and 1846. He was en route with dispatches from Frémont's command to Washington, D.C., when he met General Stephen Kearny and agreed to act as Kearny's guide to California. From 1846 to 1848 he alternated duties, became friends with many people in high office, and established his reputation as an Indian fighter. In March of 1854 he was made Indian Agent at Taos, and in 1861 he became Colonel Carson of the

THE TONY HILLERMAN COMPANION

1st New Mexico Volunteers. On July 22, 1863, he began his "scorched earth" policy against the Navajos; they called him Red Shirt and Ahdilohee, the Rope-thrower. One source says he was known for his fairness and sympathy for the plight of the Indian, a statement undoubtedly disputed by the Navajo. He was appointed Superintendent of Indian Affairs for the Colorado Territory in January 1868 and held that position for the last months of his life.[1]

Cassidy (TG)

Cassidy and two other men, Dalkin and Neal, raped and beat Leroy Fleck at Joliet. Cassidy was a macho 240-pounder who could bench-press 400 pounds. Fleck got even by luring him around a corner and slipping a narrow flat blade between his ribs.

Cassidy, Butch (CW)

This American outlaw who escaped to South America was of great interest to Dr. Tagert. It was rumored that Cassidy returned to the United States in 1909 and was seen at a train robbery at Fry Creek near Blanding and in a stagecoach robbery. He was then seen escaping onto the Navajo reservation. The Navajos said he was a very good shot, even on horseback.

Robert LeRoy Parker was born April 13, 1866, in Beaver, Utah, and died in 1909(?), Concordia Tin

---

1. See *The New Encyclopedia Britannica*, Vol. 2 (Chicago: Encyclopedia Britannica, 1992), p. 903; *The Book of the American West*, ed. by Jay Monaghan (New York: Julian Messner, 1963), pp. 74, 75, 77, 82; *Great Western Indian Fights*, by members of the Potomac Corral of the Westerners (May 1969), p. 99; and "Winds of Change: A Matter of Promises," PBS Home Video 262, Wisconsin Educational Communications Board and Board of Regents, University of Wisconsin system, 1990, 60 min.

CHARACTERS IN TONY HILLERMAN'S FICTION

Mines, near San Vicente, Bolivia(?). Cassidy was known as the foremost member of the Wild Bunch and took his alias from Mike Cassidy, an older outlaw from whom he learned cattle rustling and gunslinging (1884–1887). From 1887 onward, except for 1891–92 when he worked as a cowboy and 1894–96, which he spent in the Wyoming State Prison, he was an outlaw. In 1899 he teamed up with Harry Longbaugh, the Sundance Kid. At this time the law was effectively reducing the number of outlaws, and Cassidy and Sundance escaped in 1901 to New York and then to South America. In 1902 they bought a ranch in Argentina and worked it until 1906, by which time they evidently were bored or broke and returned to outlawry. The stories of Cassidy's death vary. One story says he was trapped by Pinkerton agents and killed in Bolivia; another says he was cut down in December 1911 by soldiers during a bank robbery in Mercedes, Uruguay; still other stories have Cassidy (alone or with Sundance) returning to the United States, drifting from Mexico to Alaska, and dying in obscurity in 1937, either in Johnny, Nevada, or Spokane, Washington.[2]

Cata (DD)

A Zuñi and father of Ernesto, he and his family probably lived in Zuñi, as that is where the Niman Kachina ceremony was to take place. He and Ernesto's uncles shoveled dirt from the landslide off Ernesto's body.

Cata, Ernesto (DD)

Born into the Badger Clan of the Zuñis, thirteen-year-old Ernesto was given the high honor of

2. See *The New Encyclopedia Britannica*, Vol. 2 (Chicago: Encyclopedia Britannica, 1992), p. 926.

portraying Shulawitsi, the Little Fire God, for the Shalako ceremony. The seventh-grader ran every evening to condition himself for his role. He was an altar boy at Saint Anthony's and had confessed to Father Ingles that he might have broken a taboo by telling George too much about the Zuñi religion. Ernesto had many friends, but his oldest and best friend was Crazy George Bowlegs, who was supposed to meet him with his bike after his last run. Ernesto's body was found buried under the rubble of an earth slide on a ridge above Galestina Canyon; his head had been nearly severed from his body with an ax and George had disappeared.

Cayodito, Gracie (SC)

Chee accompanied Hosteen Frank Sam Nakai to Gracie Cayodito's cabin to meet Hosteen Barbone and other elders. Barbone had gone there to decide the kind of ceremony needed to cure a Cayodito grandchild's illness. Gracie was very much against modern adaptations of ceremonials and warned against the violation of incest taboos. Chee had been hoping to find out what the relationship was between his clans and those of Janet Pete's father.

Charley, Dillon (PD)

Father of Emerson Charley, grandfather of Tomas and Rudolph Charley, Dillon Charley had a vision the night before the oil rig exploded and warned the Navajo workers not to go there the next day. When Deputy Sheriff Sena heard this he thought the Indians had caused the explosion; Sena was suspended for roughing up Dillon while questioning him. Dillon started the Peyote Church, an offshoot of the Native American Church; peyote was used during services to provide visions. When the church members were arrested for using peyote, B. J. Vines worked to get them released. Dillon then worked with Vines to defeat Sena in his race for sheriff, and later went to work for Vines as foreman of his ranch. Dillon died of cancer December 11, 1953, and was buried in a small grassy plot near Vines's garage. After Dillon died, none of the other Navajos would work for Vines; they said he was a witch.

Charley, Emerson (PD)
Dillon Charley's son, father of Tomas and Rudolph Charley, Emerson had taken his dead father's place as peyote chief. Emerson was a large man with the heavy torso and slender hips of a Navajo. When he entered the Cancer Research and Treatment Center at the University of New Mexico in August he was wearing jeans and a denim jacket; he left his suitcase in his green pickup and walked slowly and laboriously to the entrance. While Emerson was in the hospital, dying from cancer, the keepsake box was stolen from the Vines, and before anyone could claim Charley's body it mysteriously disappeared from the hospital morgue.

Charley, Hosteen George (BW)
Hosteen Charley had to move his sheep to another grazing area because an oil company was running seismographic tests in his area.

Charley, Rudolph (PD)
Younger brother of Tomas Charley, Rudolph looked a lot like Tomas, only a little thinner. He conducted the Peyote Way services after Tomas was killed.

Charley, Tomas (LW)
Leaphorn asked Corporal Charley, a stocky Navajo policeman, to set up a roadblock for the

gray Mercedes; he warned Charley that the man was armed and might be dangerous. The car never arrived at the roadblock. Later, Charley found the Indian woman who had seen the helicopter and questioned her.

Charley, Tomas (PD)

The grandson of Dillon Charley became peyote chief of the Peyote Church after his father, Emerson Charley, became ill. Emerson Charley was Navajo and Tomas's mother was Acoma. Henry Becenti said Tomas was a member of one of the Laguna kiva societies. One of Tomas's paternal uncles was a *yataalii* and had taught him the Blessing Way. He had a nephew and a sister who sold her weavings at the Crownpoint rug auction.

Tomas drove an ore loader for Kerrmac Nuclear Fuels; he lived on a rural route between Grants and San Mateo village, drove an F-150 blue 1975 Ford pickup, and had no telephone. He was a small man, not over five-and-half-a-feet tall, skinny, with a bony face, small deep-set black eyes, and a narrow forehead; he had an alert look about him. Becenti had said Tomas was the craziest one of the Charleys, from too much peyote. Tomas told Chee some witch was making his father sick and he wanted to turn it around. Chee found him shot in the head where he had told Chee the keepsake box that belonged to Vines would be found.

Chee, Dolores (CW)

Chee is a common name on the Navajo Reservation. Taka Ji knew a junior high school teacher by that name but didn't think his father knew her.

Chee, Jim (Jimmy)
(PD) (WY) (WI) (DW) (GW) (SW) (TT) (TG) (CW) (SC)

CHARACTERS IN TONY HILLERMAN'S FICTION

When first introduced (*People of Darkness*), Jim Chee is a sergeant in the Navajo Tribal Police, recently transferred to Crownpoint. He has been tested, interviewed, and accepted for admission to the FBI Academy in Virginia and has to decide whether to report there in four weeks. In the two stories that followed ("The Witch, Yazzie, and the Nine of Clubs" and "Chee's Witch") he is a corporal, assigned to the Tuba City subagency and given the Short Mountain territory. He remains at Tuba City subagency through *The Dark Wind*, then is transferred once again, from Tuba City to Shiprock (GW). At the time of *Skinwalkers*, he has been a Navajo Tribal Policeman for seven years, ever since his graduation from the University of New Mexico in Albuquerque. In the remaining books (except for *Sacred Clowns*), he continues to work out of Shiprock (mostly east and south) for Captain Largo.

In *Sacred Clowns*, Chee is second in command to Lieutenant Joe Leaphorn in the Special Investigations Office at Window Rock. His office is upstairs in the station, and he has a window through which he can see the southern end of the Chuska Range. Chee is new to the job and is afraid Leaphorn will send him back to being a patrolman the first time he makes a mistake. He's even filed applications with the BIA, the Arizona State Police, and the Apache County Sheriff's Office in case the job with Leaphorn doesn't work out.

He shows his concern for the Tano people by writing a letter to the *Navajo Times* opposing a proposal to use the open pit of the abandoned Jacks Wild Mine as a toxic-waste dump. He enjoys the praise he receives from Janet Pete for the letter but is disgruntled because Leaphorn has him working on the disappearance of the Kanitewa boy and the Todachene vehicular homicide case. He feels he should be concentrating on the Dorsey murder

167

and matters related to the dump problem. He'd like to make sergeant because that might help him persuade Janet Pete to marry him.

Chee grew up in his mother's home near the Chuska Mountains, in the area of Rough Rock, south of Kayenta (PD, GW); Ship Rock was a landmark of his childhood. His mother, Tessie Chee (SW), has at least two sisters and one brother. Her brother, Frank Sam Nakai, married into the Mud Clan. One of Chee's aunts, a "real tiger," was on the Tribal Council from the Greasy Water district. In *Sacred Clowns,* Chee states his aunt is now a former councilwoman.

Chee has two older sisters and no brothers; the elder, Irma, had a bit part in the movie *Cheyenne Autumn* (SC). His father is dead. Relatives are expected to treat you better than people from other clans, but Chee had "a paternal uncle [who] had once cheated him on a used refrigerator deal, and the worst whipping he'd ever taken in the Two Gray Hills Boarding School was from a maternal cousin" (DW).

His mother's clan is the Slow Talking People, his father's clan the Bitter Water Dinee. He is also a member of the Red Forehead Clan because his father was (PD). In the story "The Witch, Yazzie, and the Nine of Clubs," Chee is said to have been "born for" the Mud Dinee (or for the Salts, in *Skinwalkers*). Other paternal clan links include Streams Come Together/Waters Flow Together (TT). Chee's maternal clan is consistently identified as Slow Talking People, and his paternal clan is usually identified as Bitter Water (PD, DW, GW, SC). He is distantly related to Largo through the Red Forehead Clan (DW).

When he was a boy Chee's mother would wake him, take him outside, and teach him star lore. He learned the names of the constellations from his grandfather. But of all his family, the one most important to Chee is his uncle, Hosteen Frank Sam Nakai, his mother's older brother; Nakai has been a teacher and friend since earliest boyhood (as his key clan uncle). Nakai is a well-known, highly respected Singer; he chose Chee's war name, Long Thinker (PD). As a boy Chee accompanied Hosteen Nakai into the Blue Gap country to collect herbs and minerals for the Mountain Way ceremony and sacred objects for Nakai's *jish*, or medicine bundle (DW). Nakai's winter hogan is beyond Dennehotso, where he lives with his second wife, Blue Woman, whom Chee calls Little Mother (GW).

Chee's family hoped he would become a Singer; his dinee had produced more Singers than any of the sixty other Navajo clans. His nickname at Rough Rock had been a Navajo word meaning One Who Studies to Be a Singer (PD). He had been taught since infancy to remember things, because this was a skill much needed by a *yataalii* (GW). He had early memories of an Enemy Way ceremony for his father's mother, Old Lady Many Mules, who later died of lung cancer or tuberculosis; it was then he first thought of learning the curing ways (CW).

Chee is curious about the white man's world; he spent two years with whites at Two Gray Hills Boarding School (DW, GW), then Shiprock High School (PD) and the University of New Mexico, where he completed a degree in anthropology (WI and elsewhere). He had taken a course in Southwestern Ethnology at the University of New Mexico (DW). During the summer of his junior year he collected sacred objects he needed for his Four Mountains bundle (GW). He understood why white men thought all Indians looked alike; although in his freshman year he had dated a white girl from his sociology class (GW), he'd had difficulty distinguishing between similar-looking groups of white people (WI, DW). His family held an Enemy Way for him after he returned home from the University of New Mexico (WY) because of his exposure to alien ways and cultures. It had taken Chee seven years on and off to get his bachelor's degree, because he kept running out of money and had to work; Albuquerque never felt like home.

The tension in *People of Darkness* and other books in the series is created by the conflict between Chee's very traditional Navajo identity and the pressure, particularly from Mary Landon, to embrace a white way of life off the reservation. He struggles, too, to reconcile his work as a policeman with his desire to be a medicine man for his people. In *People of Darkness*, Chee has passed the FBI tests and been accepted at the Academy; he is also training to be a Singer. He has to decide which one he is going to do; he knows he can't do both at once.

When he worked out of Tuba City, the setting for *The Dark Wind*, Largo was his superior and Chee frequently worked with Cowboy Dashee. Largo had tried Chee as acting sergeant, but it hadn't lasted; Chee was a loner, not an organization man (CW). Upon his transfer to Crownpoint, he drives the usual white van with the emblem of the Navajo nation on its doors (PD). In Shiprock, he is a patrolman, driving patrol car units 4 (SW) and 11 (TT). Leaphorn, his superior, thinks Chee would work well in criminal investigations (CW) and gives him that opportunity in *Sacred Clowns*.

Chee carries a medium-barrel Ruger .38, but he has never really decided what he would do if he had to fire on a fellow human being (DW). (Chee's only violent act occurs in the short story "The Witch, Yazzie, and the Nine of Clubs," in which he shoots and kills Yost.) Chee doesn't like pistols in general but was reassured by the presence of his pistol when it was needed (TT). He is not a very good shot; he barely made a qualifying score (DW), and keeping up his marksmanship certificate was an annual chore (GW). Chee has frequently been injured in the line of duty and has had to be hospitalized: in Albuquerque for a gunshot wound (PD); in Los Angeles for a concussion, after being hit on the head by Eric Vaggan (GW); at the Badwater Clinic for wounds to his skull and right arm (SW); in Farmington for the treatment of burns (CW).

In *Skinwalkers*, Chee is the target of a killer. Someone put a shotgun blast through his trailer but misses him; there is a piece of bone in the cartridge case, implying Chee is a witch. Later someone shoots him twice with a shotgun. Chee can't understand why anyone would want to kill him. He admits to Leaphorn, however, that he has told people Dr. Yellowhorse is a false Crystal Gazer; Leaphorn reminds him forcefully that there is no law against Crystal Gazers.

After Delbert Nez died in *Coyote Waits*, Chee filed a report saying Nez hadn't asked for a backup; the rules said Chee should have given him a backup anyway. He feels guilty because he hadn't been there to help. After pulling Nez out of the burning patrol car, Chee immediately got back into his own patrol car and went out to look for Nez's killer. Chee tries to turn in his badge and resign, but Largo tells him he can't do that until after Ashie Pinto's trial. Chee thinks Leaphorn's inquiry about Professor Tagert is a vote of no confidence in him; he is pleased when Leaphorn asks his opinion about why Nez was killed.

Chee is known for bending the rules to suit himself; he's not a team player, according to Leaphorn. Although Chee doesn't particularly like either Largo (DW) or Leaphorn (SW, TT, SC), he respects them and is very sensitive to what they think of him; he doesn't want them to think him incompetent (DW, SW). He especially wants Leaphorn's approval (TT, CW, SC). In *Sacred Clowns*, Chee's originality helps him solve crimes, but his disregard of procedures nearly costs Leaphorn his job and interferes with his trip to China. Chee is deeply dismayed over this.

In all the books in which he appears, Chee is studying to be a Singer (*yataalii*, *hataalii*, *hatathali*—one who performs healing ceremonies). This involves memorizing scores of chants and rituals that last many days and learning how to make complicated sand paintings in the prescribed way. Chee's uncle, Hosteen Frank Sam Nakai, has taught him the Blessing Way. In *People of Darkness* and *Talking God*, Chee is trying to learn the Night Chant, sometimes by listening to his uncle's performance on audio tapes while he drives (also DW). In *The Ghostway* he is learning the Mountain Way, the Shooting Way, and the Stalking Way. Chee feels a heavy responsibility to continue his studies, as once there were at least sixty shamans but few now remain. Leaphorn says in *Sacred Clowns* that Chee wants to save his people from the future.

Chee knows, and uses, traditional Navajo prayers, songs, and blessings (such as the Stalking Song in *People of Darkness*, Talking God songs in *Coyote Waits*, and sweat lodge songs in *The Dark Wind* and *A Thief of Time*). Before pursuing the killer in *The Dark Wind*, Chee takes a sweat bath and sings the Stalking Way songs. He keeps a medicine pouch inside his trousers (PD) or under his shirt (DW) in which he carries pollen for greeting the dawn (DW) and a soapstone badger fetish given him by his father (PD). He is proud of his deerskin *jish* case containing ceremonial items (such as his Four Mountain bundle) for performing the Blessing Way (SW, CW).

On the business cards he had printed, Chee advertised he was available to perform a Blessing Way; he had no telephone at that time so he used the number of the Shiprock police station. He successfully performed a Blessing Way for the niece of Old Grandmother Nez, and Alice Yazzie wanted him to perform a Blessing Way for her uncle, Frazier Denetsone. In *Skinwalkers* he feels his career as a *yataalii* has really started.

Outside his trailer he has a leveled area the size and shape of a hogan floor where he practices his sand painting; Largo calls it his "laboratory." His ceremonial regalia is kept in an outside compartment of his trailer. Chee dresses up for his meeting with Alice Yazzie—new jeans, red and white shirt, polished go-to-town boots, and black felt hat; he wishes he looked older and wiser (SW).

Chee wanted to find a *hataalii* who would be willing to take him on to learn the Yeibichai, even though it meant he would have to take time off from work to do it. Chee was somewhat discouraged, because in the four years since he proclaimed himself a *hataalii* he's had only three customers: a maternal cousin, the niece of a friend, and Leaphorn (TG). In *Sacred Clowns* he begins to doubt whether he can be a medicine man and a policeman at the same time, and he comes away from his meeting with Frank Sam Nakai and the other elders feeling he is not traditional enough in their eyes to become a *hataalii*.

Witchcraft is a potent force on the reservation; Chee believes witchcraft was explained in the origin story. He believes in the poetic metaphor of human genesis and in the lessons the Origin Myth teaches (SW). He knows witches exist (in a metaphorical sense) and are dangerous because they are a violation of the Navajo Way (CW). Like most Navajos, he is reluctant to touch a dead body or to enter a place where someone has died; the *chindi* (ghost) may remain. Although he had very little water, Chee was determined to take a sweat bath to cleanse himself after being exposed to the *chindi* of Joe Nails and Jimmy Etcitty and the Anasazi graves (TT).

Chee can't understand the white man's attitude toward a corpse; his uncle told him to learn to understand all people and then he would be able to understand the white man. Although Chee is very much a part of the Navajo world, he is not immune to white culture; he subscribes to *Esquire* and *Newsweek*, has a Farmington Public Library card and a Social Security Card (#441-28-7272), and graduated from the FBI Academy with distinction. With all his education and contact with the white world, he still didn't want to enter Ashie Begay's hogan where the *chindi* was; nevertheless, he promised Bentwoman Tsossie he would go inside and examine it (GW).

Chee lives in an aluminum trailer parked under a cottonwood tree for privacy and isolation (DW); in most of the books he has no telephone. After seven years in the Navajo Tribal Police, Chee is transferred to Shiprock (GW, SW), where he locates his battered trailer on the north bank of the San Juan River about a mile south of town. He is still living in the trailer in *Sacred Clowns* but is now in Window Rock. The post office won't deliver mail to his trailer in *Talking God*; in *Skinwalkers* he receives mail at his office, and in *A Thief of Time* he picks up his mail at P.O. Box 112, Shiprock.

The trailer is described in some detail in many of the books: a picture emerges of a tidy monastic home, with a small shower, a shelf crowded with books, equipment for making filtered coffee, and a battery-powered TV (on which he watches weather forecasts by Howard Morgan on

Channel 7 or Bill Eisenhood on Channel 4). When he adopts a Manx cat some Anglo had lost, he tries to help it learn to survive on its own, like a Navajo; he decides the cat won't make it unless it has better shelter and cuts a door in the trailer so the cat can enter and leave by itself (SW).

In *The Ghostway*, Chee is in his early thirties; he weighs approximately 175 pounds (GW) and wears size 10 boots (DW). Off duty he wears jeans and a plaid shirt (GW), work shirt (DW), or torn Coors T-shirt (TT). In Washington, D.C., he wears town jeans, a leather jacket, bolo tie, and a felt reservation hat with a silver band—and feels out of place in his Western clothes (TG). Chee is at least a head taller than Janet Pete (CW). Leaphorn describes him as young and good-looking with a long, sensitive face (CW). In *Talking God* he is described as tall, slender, and dark with a narrow face; he looks like an Indian. His physique is that of a typical Tuba City Navajo (an anthropologist's label)—longish, narrow body, all shoulders and no hips—destined to be a skinny old man (SW). Janet Pete tells him she likes him because of his pearly white teeth, long, lean, lanky frame, and muscles (SC).

When he was performing the Blessing Way for Leaphorn, he wore his hair tied in a knot at the back of his head. While pulling Nez out of the burning police car, he was burned on both hands, one arm, one leg, and his chest, and his eyebrows were burned off. His left hand was especially badly burned, and he worried, despite doctors' assurances, about how much use of the hand he would recover (CW).

Chee smokes but doesn't drink whiskey (PD, DW); he drinks soft drinks warm or cold and drinks too much coffee. He also drinks the rinse water from a coffee cup, because he has been taught never to waste water (SW). He likes Lottaburgers because they're covered with onions (SC).

He drives a pickup truck with a rifle on a rack across the back window (DW). On one occasion he was driving and listening to a ballad about trouble and a worried mind by Willie Nelson; it matched his mood (WI). He had priced a GMC four-by-four in Farmington but couldn't come close to affording it (SW). Chee couldn't survive without a vehicle to drive. In Albuquerque he didn't understand the bus system and was uneasy in taxis, so he called Janet Pete for a ride (CW). He had his first subway ride in Washington, D.C.; he had always wanted to ride the New York City subway system because of the rumors he had heard about it (TG).

Chee is fluent in the Navajo language and speaks some Spanish but no Keresan, the language of the Acoma (PD). He does not understand or speak the language of the Tano (SC) or the Hopi (DD). In *Coyote Waits* he follows the testimony at Ashie Pinto's trial and knows when the Navajo translator is cutting corners; he is also able to detect when important parts are left out of Ashie Pinto's taped stories. In *Sacred Clowns* he listens to the Navajo-language radio station, KNDN, on the radio in his pickup.

Chee is alert and known to be smart; he's a perfectionist (SW). Normally he doesn't let his temper show (CW). He has been taught that it is rude to look someone in the face while they are talking to you, and also rude to say anything before they have finished speaking. And he has been taught "All things in moderation" (SW).

For a while, Mary Landon was the love of his life. He met Mary, an elementary school teacher, at the Crownpoint rug auction. He had not known any white women well, so he decided to study her; a deep friendship developed between them. Mary made him happy, she made him feel like singing (PD), she made him feel like the ultimate man

(CW). Chee wanted to spend the rest of his life with her; he took her home to meet his mother, assuming Mary would join him on the reservation and he would become a *yataalii*. Mary, however, wanted him to take the FBI job and join her in the white man's world. He decided he loved Mary too much to let her go and so would take the FBI job—but he couldn't bring himself to tell his uncle that he would not become a *yataalii* (GW).

Mary returned to Wisconsin, where Chee visited her and met her family; Chee was very uncomfortable because her father looked at him like he was a creature from another planet (SW). Chee was happy when Mary said she would be coming back to the reservation in two weeks and numb when he received her letter saying she *wasn't* coming. He wasn't surprised when he heard she was going to stay in Wisconsin and go to graduate school; it was inevitable. She asked him to visit her again over Thanksgiving break. Chee decided the cat he had adopted was *belagaana* and not able to survive in the desert, just as he couldn't survive away from his people, so he sent her the cat. He realized he was now her former lover (GW). He suffered feelings of anger and loss over the breakup of their relationship (TT), and he was disappointed when he received another letter telling him not to make the trip to Wisconsin; he couldn't seem to get over her (TG). In *Sacred Clowns* he tells Janet Pete the only contact he'd had with Mary had been a Christmas card.

Chee met Janet Pete in *Skinwalkers* while he was working on the Roosevelt Bistie case. Their relationship at first was adversarial: Janet was Bistie's lawyer, and Chee was investigating the murder of Dugai Endocheeney. Members of the DNA were not especially friendly toward the Navajo Tribal Police, and Janet appeared somewhat hostile. Chee wanted to hold Bistie long enough to question him about witchcraft and find out why he wanted to kill Endocheeney; Janet wanted Bistie released right away. Janet was puzzled over Chee's questions about the bone pieces but somewhat mollified when Chee stated that the police knew her client didn't kill Endocheeney; she thought witchcraft was nonsense.

Chee decided to ask Janet Pete who had asked her to be Bistie's lawyer, as Bistie's daughter had denied hiring her. He met Janet at her car and couldn't help noticing her very nice legs. She was shocked when Chee told her it was Bistie who had been killed, especially since this was the second of her clients to die recently; she couldn't understand why someone would want to kill Bistie when he was already dying of cancer. She was willing to discuss this over coffee with Chee in the Turquoise Café. Chee noticed she had nice slender feminine hands, even though he was thinking about Mary Landon while he was talking to Janet.

Chee was uncomfortable when Janet studied his face while he was talking to her; he realized she had been taught in law school to search for nonverbal signals. He tried to keep his face blank and felt her behavior was rude. He noticed she put two teaspoons of sugar in her coffee and wondered how she stayed so slim, then realized that, like Mary Landon, she was always moving around. He noticed her beautiful Navajo complexion. He was so intrigued with her remarks about Irma Onesalt that he spilled coffee on his shirt, which was just what he *didn't* want to do in front of her. He delayed Janet's departure by telling her about the problem with the *belagaana* cat and asking her to help him find a solution.

In *A Thief of Time*, Chee sat in his office in Shiprock and daydreamed about Janet. He was willing to check out the Buick she wanted to buy; after he wrecked the car he was more concerned about how to tell her about the wrecked car than how to pay for repairs. Although he told Bernie Tso that Janet was not his type, the thought that she had spent the night with her boyfriend hurt his feelings. When she told him John McDermott wanted to marry her but she was uncertain, Chee told her he was available if she was interested.

In *Talking God*, Janet was working in Washington and called Chee to tell him he had arrested her client, Henry Highhawk. Janet liked to know what she was getting into and wanted to know what Chee knew about Rudolfo Gomez. Chee decided to go to Washington to help her instead of going to Wisconsin to visit Mary Landon; he was also still flirting with the idea of joining the FBI and wanted to visit the FBI building. He thought of himself and Janet as friends but resented the plans she had made with McDermott because he felt McDermott was using her.

In *Coyote Waits*, Chee was delighted when Janet came back to New Mexico. He was very upset, however, when he discovered that Janet was to defend Ashie Pinto. If Pinto was found innocent, Chee felt he would be guilty of allowing Delbert Nez to die and of allowing his killer, Ashie Pinto, to go free. He had some difficulty dealing with this situation; he wished he wasn't so attracted to Janet because of his job, yet he enjoyed the affectionate hugs she gave him when she found out he had been trying to help her client.

In *Sacred Clowns*, Chee is uneasy about asking Janet to marry him, because she is a well-educated, sophisticated city Indian and he is a country-boy Navajo Tribal cop. When Janet indicates she is interested, Chee then begins to worry about their clan relationships. At the meeting of the elders at the Cayodito hogan, one wise old lady tells him that only the mother's clan relationships are important. He is still uneasy about Janet's father's clan relationships but is ready to bend traditional Navajo beliefs to marry her.

Chee, Tessie (SW)
Jim Chee's mother, Tessie Chee, was born to the Slow Talking Dinee.

Cherry, George (FW)
Temporary replacement for McDaniels, he was pulled off general assignment until the *Capitol-Press* could get a political reporter. Cotton met him at the press table in the State House of Representatives. He hardly knew McDaniels and seemed to know nothing about McDaniels's missing notebook.

Chester, Jimmy (SC)
Councilman Chester, from the Horse Mesa Chapter, was working hard to get the proposal for the toxic-waste dump passed. Chee knew he was a big operator in the cattle business in the Checkerboard, and many people thought he was a jerk. Applebee thought he was a consultant for Continental Collectors Corporation and was taking money from them. Janet Pete said this was legal, but he couldn't vote on the proposal in council.
The audio tape that was broadcast made it sound like Chester wanted bribery money from Ed Zeck, that he had signed a paper and the payment was now due. Chester was in the chief's office at Window Rock when Leaphorn came back from Thoreau and Tano. Chester was wearing his black hat with a silver band, and he glowered at Leaphorn as he came into the office. He accused Leaphorn of trying to ruin his reputation and

wanted him charged with illegally tapping his telephone, a third-degree felony.

He also wanted Leaphorn dismissed from the police department. As Chairman of the Justice Committee, he had been opposed to setting up Leaphorn's Special Investigations Office. Chester had presided over many investigations during his thirty years on the council and knew an investigation might take time, and he was impatient. The chief promised him that Captain Dodge would complete an investigation of his allegations within ten days and Leaphorn would be suspended in the meantime. Chester accepted this plan, in part because Dodge was a Towering House Clan relative.

Chester had reason to be angry. He and Ed Zeck had been in the cattle business together for almost twenty years. The conversation on the audio tape was about twenty-two thousand dollars needed to pay off a loan Chester had signed for. Zeck had sold their heifers but hadn't deposited the money in the account yet, and Chester was paying interest on the loan.

Chief, the (SC)

The Chief is Leaphorn's boss at the Window Rock Tribal Police station. Although Virginia Toledo had told the Chief for years that he needed to lock the doors at the station, the doors remained unsecured. The Chief was especially interested in having the Victor Todachene hit-and-run case solved, because the driver had left Todachene to bleed to death in the road. Finding the driver seemed hopeless, so he gave the case to Leaphorn to solve.

The Chief was worried and puzzled about Jimmy Chester's allegations that Leaphorn had illegally tapped his telephone. He gave Captain Dodge ten days to investigate these allegations and suspended Leaphorn until Dodge's work was completed. The Chief had picked Dodge to assuage Chester, since they were members of the same clan.

Chief Priest of the Bow Priesthood (DF)

Zuñi. The Chief Bow Priest was proud of all the corn his people had grown and decided that his people should fix a great feast, inviting all the other Indian tribes. He proposed to the Tribal Council that the people should then engage in a mock battle with the other tribes, using their abundant corn products as weapons; he wanted the other tribes to marvel at their wealth.

The Bow Priesthood, *apila a'shi-wan-ni,* was associated with war and with the twin gods, *ahayuta.* The priests were recruited from warriors who had killed and scalped an enemy; at the time they were initiated into the priesthood there was a scalp dance, to protect them from the ghost of the enemy they had killed. One of the main jobs of the priesthood was to protect the people from enemies and later to protect them from witches.

All diseases not the result of an accident were believed to have been caused by witches; it was the job of the Bow Priest to find the witch and punish him. People who did not properly perform the rituals and join the various societies were suspected of being witches and could be removed from the tribe or even killed. Another of the Bow Priest's duties was to choose the men to impersonate the kachinas at the Shalako festival.

Chinle High School Girl (BW)

Plump, pretty fifteen-year-old who danced with Joe Leaphorn and Billy Nez at the Girl Dance at the Enemy Way for Charley Nez. She was Billy's girlfriend; she told Leaphorn that Billy had stolen the

Navajo Wolf's hat. (Similar to **Young Woman at the Girl Dance** in "The Witch, Yazzie, and the Nine of Clubs.")

Cigaret, Margaret (Blind Eyes, Listening Woman)
(LW)

Navajo born to the Mud Clan, Margaret was widely known on the reservation for her skills as a Listener. She was a large woman, handsome once, with gray hair and a weathered face; she was now blind from glaucoma and walked with a cane. The day she visited Hosteen Tso she was wearing a voluminous skirt, a blue velvet blouse, and blue tennis shoes; she carried her ceremonial items in a black plastic purse. When Anna Atcitty was killed, Margaret hadn't heard her screams, because Margaret had been at the cliff, in a trance, listening to the earth.

At the Kinaalda for Alice Endischee, Margaret wore a purple velvet blouse and supervised the making of the ritual cake for the menstruation ceremony.

City Navajo (WI)

See **Begay, Simon.**

Clans (DF)

Zuñi. In 1987 there were fourteen clans subsumed under the six Zuñi kivas; in the past there had been many more. Clans associated with a particular direction lived in that particular kiva; for example the Crane, Grouse, and Evergreen clans were associated with the North and would live in the kiva associated with that direction. The clans mentioned in this story were the Badger Clan, Turkey Clan, Yellow-wood Clan, and Tobacco Clan; they were among those divided into teams for the great food battle at Ha'wi-k'uh. The Macaw Clan and Bow Society are mentioned in the author's notes. For Hopi and Navajo clans, see the separate section on Clans that precedes this concordance.

Clark, Desmond (SC)

Clark was proprietor of the Clark Gallery in Santa Fe and an old friend of Joe Leaphorn's; they had gone deer hunting together. Leaphorn inquired of him how much a Lincoln cane would sell for on the underground market. Clark guessed that bidding would start at a hundred thousand for a legitimate object with a certificate of authenticity. He was no authority on Lincoln canes, however, and referred Leaphorn to Bundy, a dealer who sometimes bought items from him.

Clark, Eugene (Gene) (FW)

U.S. Senator Clark's friends thought Governor Roark would battle him for the nomination in the next election. If Clark won he "would be superbly financed by banking and defense industries, as always." He was "a sophisticated, urbane political creature, with a sort of country-club, Hamiltonian distaste for mass man." He was an opportunist, a person who voted for his own benefit. Although he was a Democrat, he voted with the Republicans on the forestry conservation bill because the Hefrons had lumber interests and were connected with Citybank.

Cloud-Swallower (DF)

In Zuñi mythology, Cloud-Swallower was the monster who would rise up into the sky and drink down all the clouds. Cloud-Swallower was at work during the drought at Ha'wi-k'uh.

Collins, Larry (DW)

DEA agent and partner of T. L. Johnson, Collins

was twenty-five years old, a big man with unkempt blond hair and a face with a mass of freckles. He wore a dirty cowboy hat. Collins searched Chee's trailer for drugs, then pinned him down and handcuffed his hands behind his back.

Commander, the (GW)

Eric Vaggan always referred to his father as the Commander. His father was a small man with bristling blond hair, blue eyes, and a trim mustache; Vaggan remembered him wearing his dress whites with a row of ribbons on them. Vaggan had never known his mother; she may have been dead or she may have left; his father would never talk about her.

The Commander believed the next world war would start over Berlin. He trained Vaggan to be strong, and he disowned Vaggan when he was thrown out of West Point; his father told him he had buried him beside "the woman." He hadn't spoken to Vaggan in twenty years.

Corn Maidens (Mothers of Corn) (DF)

Zuñi. The White Corn Maiden and the Yellow Corn Maiden lived south of the village in the Land of Everlasting Summer and looked after the A'shiwi people. The Corn Maidens were saddened that the people would waste the food of the water blessing, and they caused a great drought to occur, forcing the people to ask the Hopi for help.

Corn Mountain (DF)

Zuñi. Sacred mountain of the A'shiwi. The Zuñi chief priest, the Pekwin, observed changes in the times of sunrise and sunset over specific parts of Corn Mountain to decide when to celebrate the winter and summer solstices.

Cornstalk Insect (Being That Flies, Cornstalk Being, Dragonfly) (DF)

Zuñi. The Cornstalk Insect was created by the boy because he couldn't find a butterfly for his sister in the middle of winter. When the boy discovered he couldn't make butterfly wings, he made two pairs of long thin wings and attached them to the body; then he painted the insect and the paint ran and the eyes were very large and the wings developed stripes. The boy made a cage out of cornstalks and dried grass and hung the insect inside. When the insect asked the boy to let him go, the boy couldn't believe he'd heard the insect speak. After the boy let him out of the cage, the insect promised to find a way to help the boy and his sister and promised he would return before dawn.

The Cornstalk Insect found the Sacred Lake, dove below the surface, and entered the Dance Hall of the Dead. There he told the gods how the boy was keeping his sister alive and told them how the children needed seed food for the winter. The gods instructed the Cornstalk Insect to help the children learn their duties to the gods and sent messengers to the village with corn for the Cornstalk Insect to give to the children.

The Cornstalk Insect taught the boy how to make the prayer plume bundles; when the bundles were completed the Cornstalk Insect carried them to the Dance Hall of the Dead and laid them at the feet of Shulawitsi, who was pleased with his work. The chief god, Pa'u-ti-wa, informed the insect he would send rain for the fields and seeds to be planted for the children.

The insect next flew to the Land of Everlasting Summer and talked to the Corn Maidens, who said they would visit within three days and chase away the cold snows of winter. Then he asked the boy to make another insect like him and send her forth;

her name would be Dragonfly. The boy told him he would paint dragonflies on sacred objects as a symbol of the god-given rains of springtime, and the companion would be the symbol of summer and summer showers.

Cotton, John (FW)

Forty-year-old political reporter for the Twin Cities *Tribune*, he'd been in the capitol pressroom for seven years and was senior man among the P.M. reporters. His "At the Capitol" column had wide readership. Cotton thought there was some "Señor Maestas" in everybody, whereas Hall saw the infinitely corruptible citizen (see **Maestas, Cirilio**).

Cotton was a native of Santa Fe, New Mexico; he'd grown up there and been best friends for a while with Charley Graff. He had then gone through boot training at Camp Pendleton and worked on a newspaper in Santa Fe. His next post was police and general assignment reporter for the *Denver Post*; it was probably during one of these first two jobs that he had written movie reviews for a brief time. For the past nine years he had been working for the *Tribune* in a capital city in the Midwest; he didn't like the city where he was and wanted to return to Santa Fe, where he could go trout fishing.

Cotton was "a tall, wiry man with a longish, freckled, somber face." He was lanky and blond, with long, thin legs; he didn't tend to fat, which was good, because he liked to eat. His face wasn't one he'd have chosen for himself—his jaw was a little long, his nose bony and slightly bent, and his ears were more prominent than necessary. He drank margaritas or bourbon and water and usually drank by himself; he didn't like drunkenness. He'd been trying to stop smoking—he'd gone eighteen days without a cigarette and he wanted one badly.

He had inexpensive vices, so he had built up his savings. He was a cautious poker player—he'd learned to resist his hunches; he was at Roy Hall's house playing poker when he learned that Whitey Robbins had been killed in Cotton's battered old borrowed Plymouth sedan.

Cotton didn't like people putting their hands on him, but he might have made an exception for Janey Janoski. Cotton had never married, and he was attracted by Janey. He asked her to accompany him to the Highway Building to help him trace the story McDaniels had uncovered; he also asked her to go to New Mexico with him. When he learned that he, rather than Whitey Robbins, had been reported drowned, he realized how few people were close enough to him to mourn his death; he didn't need to call anyone to assure them he was still alive. He needed to have Janey believe in him; he gave her the option of giving his big story to his newspaper or to the governor.

Council of the Gods (DF)

Zuñi. The Council of the Gods is the governing group of the kachina spirits in the Sacred Lake. Pa'u-ti-wa is the chief god.

Councilwoman from Cañoncito (SW)

She was a "burly, big-bosomed woman about Leaphorn's middle age and middle size, dressed in an old-fashioned purple reservation blouse and wearing a heavy silver squash blossom necklace." She came to Leaphorn to complain that the people of the Cañoncito Band were unhappy with the Navajo Tribal Police because they felt they were getting no protection. They had no Navajo policemen; all they had was a part-time Laguna, a Bureau of Indian Affairs employee who was rarely in his office. This was an old complaint Leaphorn had heard before.

Cowboy (WY)

Assistant county agriculture agent and Chee's friend for the past few months, Cowboy belonged to the Many Goats Clan and was a member of the Native American Rodeo Cowboys Association. He had an outdated Arizona State University parking sticker on his Ford pickup. While he was driving his truck he liked to listen to Willie Nelson; he went to the Girl Dance to try to find a new girlfriend. He told Chee about the witch who had killed a man and mutilated his corpse the past spring (similar to later **Cowboy Dashee** character).

Crichton (FW)

Company auditor for Alvis Materials, Crichton ran the totals for Cotton for the cement deliveries they made to Reevis-Smith.

Dalkin (TG)

One of the inmates at Joliet who raped and beat Leroy Fleck.

Dance Hall of the Dead (Dance Hall of the Gods in the Lake of the Dead) (DF)

Zuñi. The kachina spirits lived in the Sacred Lake, the Dance Hall of the Dead. When the Cornstalk Insect entered it, it was blazing as if lit by a thousand fires. The happy souls of the Beloved Ones, the souls of men who had completed their lives, celebrated their happiness there. At one end was the Council of the Gods with Shalako Messenger Birds attending them. The Little Fire God, Shulawitsi, was also there.

Danilov, Ernie (FW)

When Cotton was returning from Santa Fe he called Danilov, managing editor of the *Tribune*, as a security measure, to let him know when he was arriving and who would be meeting him. After Captain Whan found Cotton a secure place to stay, Cotton called Danilov again and let him know where he was and what his telephone number was. Danilov didn't sound happy or friendly, but then he never did. He agreed to put a notice in the paper saying Cotton was on an indeterminate leave because of illness; he wanted Cotton to outline what had happened to him, put it in a memo, and get it to him as soon as possible. He grudgingly admitted Cotton's story would go on page 1; Danilov wasn't known for giving compliments.

Danley, Glen (FW)

Night city editor for the *Journal*, he called Hall during the poker game and read Cotton the story that had come over the AP wire about his supposed death.

Dashee, Albert (Cowboy) Jr. (DW) (TG) (CW) (SC)

Hopi. In *The Dark Wind*, Dashee is a Coconino County deputy sheriff headquartered in Flagstaff, Arizona. His Indian name is Angushtiyo, or Crow Boy, and he is a member of the Side Corn Clan and Kachina Society in Shipaulovi. He had attended Northern Arizona University and completed sixty credit hours before he quit. Dashee is known for driving at fast speeds and stopping abruptly. He is a bachelor.

Dashee and Chee were building a friendship, but there were still some things Dashee didn't like to discuss with Chee because of his being a Navajo. Dashee and Chee had found a body near the Hopi village; he knew Navajos had an aversion to handling the dead, so he put the body in the body bag by himself. Dashee is a talker; Chee figured he'd told Jake West about the plane crash. Dashee showed Chee a picture of Richard Palanzer, and

Chee told him where Palanzer's car could be found. Dashee is uneasy about taking Chee out to talk to Sawkatewa, even if it is on police business.

In *Talking God*, Dashee is a deputy sheriff of Apache County, Arizona, and a citizen of Mishongnovi on the Hopi Second Mesa; he was born into the Side Corn Clan and is a valuable man in the Hopi Antelope Society. He is a good friend of Chee's from their high school days. He tags along with Chee when Chee goes to pick up Henry Highhawk at the Yeibichai ceremony for Agnes Tsosie, partly because it is a good place to meet young women. Dashee doesn't like the waiting, which is part of the job, so he curls up and goes to sleep in his patrol car until the excitement starts.

In *Coyote Waits*, Dashee is convinced that the radio signal breakup that occurs when he tries to reach Chee or headquarters is caused by magnetism in the old volcanic outcrops.

In *Sacred Clowns*, Dashee is a sworn deputy sheriff of Apache County, Arizona, and Jim Chee's best friend. He jokingly says that, whatever it is, "Hopis do it best." Dashee accompanies Chee to the ceremonial at Tano Pueblo and intends to help Chee catch Delmar Kanitewa. He suggests they sit on a rooftop where they can see the kachina dancers and watch for Kanitewa.

Davenport, Roger (CW)
Professor of Anthropology at the University of Utah, Davenport had used Ashie Pinto for information about the Navajos. Their audio tape was in the library at the University of New Mexico.

Davis (CW)
In the early 1900s, Davis was shot in the back, off his horse, after the train robbery at Fry Creek; he'd been carrying most of the payroll money for the Parker Mine, which was recovered. He said

THE TONY HILLERMAN COMPANION

Butch Cassidy was leading the group of bandits. Davis died in the hospital at Blanding, according to old newspaper reports in Dr. Tagert's files.

Davis, Officer (GW)

Eric Vaggan told Margaret Sosi he was Officer Davis from the Los Angeles County Sheriff's Office and he wanted to take her to her grandfather.

Davis, Asher (SC)

Asher Davis's occupation was Indian trader. Cowboy Dashee introduced him to Jim Chee and Janet Pete as an "Honest Indian Trader," then jokingly modified that to "Fairly Honest Indian Trader." Mister Fair Price was another of Davis's nicknames. Joe Leaphorn remembered he had first heard about Davis twenty years ago when Sergeant Largo had advised an old woman not to sell her grandfather's concha belt until she asked Asher Davis what it was worth. Desmond Clark, the art dealer, named Davis as one of a number of honest dealers that he knew. Davis's honest-looking face also helped his dealings.

Davis rode along with Jim Chee, Janet Pete, and Cowboy Dashee to the ceremonial at Tano Pueblo. Davis said that Tano was an unusually good market for old pots and Jicarilla baskets. He wondered if the teacher from Saint Bonaventure who had been killed was Eric Dorsey. Dorsey had asked him to get a good price for some item an old-timer had for sale.

Davis had a sunburned neck and wore an eighteen-inch-neck triple-x-width sport shirt. He was afraid to sit on a rooftop at Tano Pueblo because of his size. Davis had attended school with Roger Applebee. At Santa Fe High School they had played on the Santa Fe Demons football team, Davis as fullback and Applebee as quarterback.

Davis stated that Applebee was the kind of friend who kept life interesting. Because of a scheme of Applebee's to avoid taking an algebra test when they were in high school, Davis had been suspended. Leaphorn had first encountered Davis when Davis called the Chinle police station. Applebee had used Davis's credit card to rent a car and had then left the car at Canyon de Chelly. Davis had asked Leaphorn to help retrieve it. Leaphorn arranged for the jailer's wife to drive the car to Farmington for him.

When Leaphorn was looking for Applebee at the Navajo Nation Inn, he found Davis outside the door of Applebee's room. Since it was evident that Applebee was not inside, Leaphorn decided to ask Davis to do him a favor and tell Applebee when he saw him that Leaphorn needed to see him right away. The next time Leaphorn heard about Davis, Applebee had been shot and killed.

Davis, Maxie (TT)

Co-worker of Randall Elliot and Ellie Friedman-Bernal at the Chaco dig, Maxie was going to write the definitive book on the Anasazi culture with Elliot. She worked as much on the computer, programming statistical projections for the population study, as she did in the field.

Maxie was a small, beautiful young woman; her oval face was almost as dark as Leaphorn's and was surrounded by short dark hair. Her small hands and fingers were battered and scarred from work in the dirt. In the field she often wore a blue work shirt and a cap.

Bob Luna said Maxie was the ultimate self-made woman. She had lived on a worn-out Nebraska farm with her widowed father and younger siblings and helped him raise the children while she went to the nearby rural high school.

While attending the University of Nebraska on a scholarship, she worked as a housekeeper in a sorority. She then studied at the University of Wisconsin at Madison, again on a scholarship, and again worked her way through, attempting all the while to send money home to her family. It was at the University of Wisconsin, in graduate school, that she met and became friends with Ellie Friedman.

Maxie was at the opposite end of the economic scale from Randall Elliot; he wanted them to get married, she didn't. She felt bitterly that anything Elliot did didn't count because he'd had everything given to him. Elliot had received decorations for his part in the Vietnam War; her younger brother was killed in the same war and no one had given him any decorations.

Day, Mrs. (GW)

Albert Gorman's tall, gaunt, gray-haired landlady, she had a bony, exotic face, mixed Negro and Chinese or possibly Filipino. When Chee tried to interview her, she was uncooperative; when Sergeant Willie Shaw interviewed her she was more helpful, because Shaw threatened to have her rental properties inspected by the fire marshal. She gave Margaret Sosi and Shaw the address Albert Gorman had given her for his relatives in Los Angeles. Shaw had asked her to watch Gorman and report whatever she saw, but so had someone else. The other party paid her $100 down and another $100 for the same service. The phone number she was to call for the other party was an answering service.

Dead Navajo (WI)

By the time the police found the body, the scavengers hadn't left much. The autopsy said he

was a male Navajo in his thirties; there was no
identification on him and no sign of foul play. The
skin was flayed on his hands but not his feet, and
his neckbones were not removed. He was wearing
size 10D shoes and a hat (similar to **John Doe** in the
short story "The Witch, Yazzie, and the Nine of
Clubs" and in *The Dark Wind*).

Degenhardt, William (CW)
Prospective juror in the Ashie Pinto trial in
Albuquerque, Degenhardt was a conservative-look-
ing man with a conservative haircut, dressed in a
conservative gray suit.

Dendahl, Hugh (CW)
Lawyer prosecuting the Ashie Pinto case for
the U.S. Attorney's office, he questioned Mrs.
Greyeyes to determine whether she was related to
Ashie Pinto, as she was also Navajo.

Denetsone, Frazier (SW)
According to Alice Yazzie's letter to Jim
Chee, her Uncle Frazier had been ill all summer
and wasn't any better. He had gone to the Crystal
Gazer at the Badwater Clinic, who had given him
medicine and recommended a Blessing Way sing.

Denny (SC)
Mr. Denny had helped Eric Dorsey with driving the school buses.

Desbah (SC)
Desbah had an office in the Window Rock
Tribal Police station. Virginia Toledo knew when
Desbah was there or why he was not.

Devanti, Delbert (TT)
Devanti was the top expert in human migration

patterns. Maxie Davis and Randall Elliot had to answer to him in their field as Ellie Friedman-Bernal did to Professor Lehman. Dr. Devanti was from Arkansas, had worked his way up the hard way, and "sounded like corn pone."

Dillon, Agent (TG)

A blond FBI agent in Washington, D.C., and Akron's partner, Dillon was bigger and older than Akron and was the one in charge. He told Leaphorn that the Navajos had no jurisdiction in the case of Santillanes and that Santillanes was with a terrorist organization. Dillon didn't know about the note in Santillanes's suit pocket, Agnes Tsosie, Henry Highhawk, or the small red-haired man.

Dineyahze, Jenifer (CW)

Taka Ji hoped to impress this Navajo girl, a junior at Shiprock High School and a cheerleader. Ji had many pictures of her taken from afar or enlarged from the high school yearbook.

Dockery, Roland (TG)

The Amtrak official who gave Leaphorn access to the baggage left by Pointed Shoes seemed to enjoy the departure from his normal work schedule. Dockery was about forty, plump and balding; he wore bifocals and looked slightly disheveled. He was interested in the disappearing passenger and was also interested in Indians, since he'd never known any. He told Leaphorn he was Christian but didn't go to church much; Leaphorn felt like a hypocrite, talking to him about the Navajo religion.

Dodge, Captain (SC)

Captain Dodge worked at the Navajo Tribal Police station at Window Rock. He was assigned by

the chief to investigate the allegations of illegal
wiretapping against Joe Leaphorn. The assignment
was to be completed in ten days. Leaphorn wished
someone a little brighter had been assigned, but
Dodge was reliable. Leaphorn realized that Dodge
and Chester were both members of the Towering
House Clan. He left a detailed three-page report
for Dodge before leaving the building. During the
investigation Leaphorn was relieved to find that
Dodge was doing a good job getting Chester qui-
eted down and was not revealing the internal business of the Navajo Tribal Police to the public.

Dodge, Chee (SW)

Leaphorn was rumored to be a descendent of
the famous Chee Dodge, who said that witchcraft
had no place in the Navajo culture and that the
tribe had been infected with it while it was held
captive at Fort Sumner.

According to dates found in the calendar "The
People: Indians of the American Southwest" by
Stephen Trimble, Chee Dodge was born February
22, 1860, and died January 7, 1947. Assuming that
Chee Dodge was also known as Henry Chee Dodge,
he served on the Business Council established by
the Navajo people on July 7, 1923; this council led to
the establishment of the Navajo Tribal Council in
1938. Chee was an influential man who served as a
Navajo interpreter for many years; he was intelligent, educated, and had great leadership abilities.
He was a leader of the Navajo for over seventy
years.[3]

Dodge, Trixie (PD)

When asked by Chee about the People of

3. See Bertha P. Dutton, *Indians of the American Southwest*
(Englewood Cliffs, N.J.: Prentice-Hall, 1975), p. 84.

Darkness and moles, Officer Dodge said she had a cousin who was "into" the Peyote Church. She wondered what kind of Navajo would use a mole for an amulet. Trixie had a variety of duties in the office at Crownpoint.

Domenici, Pete (TG)

The senior Senator from New Mexico was the ranking Republican on the committee that oversees the budget for the FBI. In order to extract some information, Leaphorn told FBI agents he was going to have lunch with Domenici.

Dorsey, Eric (SC)

Thirty-seven-year-old volunteer shop teacher at Saint Bonaventure Indian Mission School in Thoreau, he was killed by a blow to the back of his head; silver ingots and his students' silver projects had been stolen from a locked cabinet. His body was found on the floor of his shop by students arriving for an afternoon class. His death was a great shock to his students and the community because of the help he had given them.

Dorsey had been not only a shop teacher but also a school bus driver and had worked in maintenance. He had encouraged his students to make useful things or something they could sell. He tried to make the youngsters feel more artistic than they actually were. If they needed something special, like turquoise, Eric would find the money somewhere to buy them some. He taught his students that if they wanted to be craftsmen they would have to be neat. He set the example by cleaning up his woodshop every evening and kept a list of what each student was working on.

Mrs. Montoya described him as the school comedian. He had a duck puppet and wasn't a very good ventriloquist, but the kids thought he was great. He was the master of ceremonies for their school programs. On the weekends he took water and food out to elderly people's hogans and paid for the gasoline out of his own pocket. He took his duck puppet along and made them laugh, too. Mrs. Montoya thought he was a lonely but a kind, gentle, and talented man, well-liked. He frequently talked to Father Haines but he wasn't Catholic. She thought he was gay but knew Eugene Ahkeah was not his boyfriend. There had never been any problem from Eric's being homosexual.

Eric had come from Fort Worth, Texas, where he had been a laboratory equipment maintenance technician at Texas Christian University. He was not a rich man. He had an old Chevy and lived in an old mobile home. He earned only $300 per month, yet he managed to furnish the truck for his water and food deliveries to the elderly. Eugene evidently depended on him, because he had one of his nephews call Eric when he was having car trouble. Eric interrupted his dinner at the Giant Truck Stop beside I-40 and immediately went to help him, even though he suspected Eugene might have been drinking. Father Haines said Eric's primary purpose in life was to help others.

The dilapidated little trailer was Eric's home and office. Everything was tidy and neat, nothing relaxed or comfortable. There were three pictures on the wall. One was a family photo of himself, his mother and father, two brothers, and a sister. He was the oldest child. A photo beside that one showed a bearded young man wearing a sweatband and long hair. Next to that was a picture of Saint Francis of Assisi with a poem under it. There was a desk, probably made by Dorsey, and files for his school papers on top of it.

Leaphorn found drawings, specifications, and an order for ebony for two Lincoln canes. One had been made two years before. Leaphorn also found a number of letters from Fort Worth and from a VA hospital in Amarillo with just the name *George* above the return address. Eric had only twenty-some dollars in his billfold the day he died, and no one came to claim his belongings.

Dorsey, Mr. and Mrs. Robert (SC)

Parents of Eric Dorsey, they lived in Springfield, Illinois, where Mr. Dorsey had retired from the fire department.

Downey, Judge (CW)

Ashie Pinto's case was to be heard by Judge Downey, a female federal court judge in Albuquerque.

Drabner, Dr. (CW)

Anthropologist from Tucson. He worked with Ashie Pinto gathering information about Navajo culture and history. The last time he worked with Pinto had been months ago.

Dragonfly (DF)

See **Cornstalk Insect.**

DuMont, Richard (TT)

DuMont bought the Anasazi pot Ellie Friedman-Bernal was interested in and agreed to see Leaphorn. He lived on East 78th Street in New York City, in a very expensive house. When Leaphorn saw him, he was dressed in a dark blue dressing gown, sitting in a wheelchair at the end of a very long library table. He had a pinched, narrow face, perfect teeth, small gray eyes, and eyebrows almost the same color as his pale skin; his voice was soft but clear, precise, and easy to understand.

Before he would show Leaphorn the documentation for the pot he insisted that Leaphorn tell him all the grisly details of the killings, so he would have a good story to tell his friends when he showed them the pot. He told Leaphorn that Ellie Friedman-Bernal had been there, and she had told him the documentation was false. He had Edgar, his butler, make a copy of the documentation for Leaphorn, gave him his business card, and insisted that Leaphorn call him back when he found out what had happened to Ellie.

Duncan, Dr. (PD)

Colton Wolf pretended to be Dr. Duncan, dressed in a blue cotton hospital coat checking on medications, to get by the nurse on the fifth floor at the Bernalillo County Medical Center so he could get to Chee and kill him.

Ebaar, Professor (TG)

Dr. Ebaar, Jim Chee's sociology professor at the University of New Mexico, had taught him about intraspecies hostility. Chee thought man had evolved to survive overcrowding in the D.C. subway.

Eddie (GW)

Eddie had a tip for Chee about bootleggers loading their trucks at the Blue Door Bar outside Farmington. Eddie's mother was an alcoholic, and he didn't like bootleggers. Unfortunately, his tips never seemed to lead anywhere.

Edgar (TT)

Edgar was the stooped, elderly, gray-haired man who was Richard DuMont's butler and servant.

Eisenhood, Bill (GW)

Chee watched this Channel 4 weathercaster; he told Mary Landon the Indians got their weather information the same way white men did.

Elkins, Eddy (TG)

Tall, slender, and slightly stooped, Elkins was a Dartmouth man with a law degree from Harvard, a man who looked like a teacher and liked to teach. He had been disbarred and sentenced to four to eight years on a felony count for fixing jurors or witnesses for someone in the rackets. He'd kept his mouth shut and served his time in prison; as a result he'd had connections and money inside and out.

He was working in the infirmary at Joliet when he met Leroy Fleck; he got Leroy a job in the infirmary and taught him how to kill people efficiently and quietly. When Elkins left prison he couldn't practice law himself but he was able to work for a Chicago law firm. Elkins hired Leroy for various jobs after he left prison; he kept a protective insulation between Leroy and the clients. Leroy believed Elkins's group would get rid of him when they decided it was necessary.

Ellie (SC)

Ellie worked at station KNDN in Farmington. She appeared to be about a year out of high school and liked talking to young, good-looking cops like Jim Chee. She considered anyone past thirty as kind of old. She told Chee about the broken bill of the man's cap and the way his clothes smelled of onions. Even though she had already made two copies of the open mike announcement the hit-and-run driver had made, she willingly made another one for Chee at no cost.

Elliot, Howard (FW)

McDaniels's last words in his notebook were a quote from Representative Elliot, a "half-senile country banker-politician," about the amount needed to balance the general fund for the next fiscal year.

Elliot, Randall (TT)

Elliot worked with Ellie Friedman-Bernal on the Keet Katl dig and with Maxie Davis on the population and migration studies. Ellie thought of Elliot as brainy but nuts, a blueblood, the Man Who Could Do Anything—but none of that counted with Maxie. Elliot was obsessed with Maxie; he had left a job in Washington and worked his way into this project to be near her.

Elliot was in his middle to late thirties, a couple of inches over six feet tall, and slender and athletic, with sun-bleached light brown hair. He had an upper-class face, a little narrow, unscarred, and large blue eyes. He wore jeans and a denim jacket; his boots were dusty and scarred but perfectly fitted of some expensive soft brown leather.

Elliot said Maxie never tired of reminding him of the silver spoon in his crib. He had attended Phillips Exeter Academy, played football at Princeton, and made a name for himself in physical anthropology in graduate school at Harvard. In Vietnam he'd flown a Navy helicopter and won a Navy Cross as well as other decorations. Maxie said he had to aim high because he had so many influential relatives. She felt he might be a nice man, but how could you know, since he'd never really had to do anything on his own?

Ellis, Mrs. (FW)

Korolenko's housekeeper, she was always off on Tuesdays to visit her sister.

Ellis, Mrs. (GW)

An elderly lady in a wheelchair at the Silver Threads Nursing Home on La Monica Street in Los Angeles, she had thin white hair, pale-blue vacant eyes, and a happy smile. She was physically capable of wheeling herself around. Mr. Berger said she was smart sometimes; her senility seemed to come and go. He said her son had been in the Navy and was now a rich big shot. She told Chee she had seen Margaret Sosi and that Albert Gorman had shown Mr. Berger a picture. She then denied she had a son.

Elwood, Robert (FW)
Cotton was registered at the Southside Inn under the name Robert Elwood; one of the capital city policemen moonlighted there as the night clerk.

Emily (CW)
When Janet Pete worked in Window Rock she shared an apartment with Emily.

Emmett (TG)
When Chee was a child, he remembered his Cousin Emmett sitting beside him, listening to the stories of Frank Sam Nakai.

Endecheenie, Virgie (WI)
Police dispatcher at Window Rock, Virgie was very pretty and had a pretty voice. She was born to the Salt Cedar Clan, Chee's father's clan, so dating between Virgie and Chee was forbidden. She relayed the message to Chee that he was to meet Jake Wells at Kayenta.

Endicott, Mrs. (TG)
Mama Fleck had hurt this resident of the Eldercare Manor by twisting her arm.

Endicott, Officer (FW)
A young capital city police officer sent to pick up John Cotton after Robbins's death and take him down to headquarters to be questioned, he was "very young, very neat, and very officious."

Endischee, Alice (LW)

A Navajo born to the Mud Clan. The Kinaalda took place at her home, so Eileen was probably her daughter.

Endischee, Eileen (LW)

Eileen was a pretty girl, Emerson Begay's niece, Navajo born to the Mud Clan. She was enjoying her Kinaalda, the ceremony for a girl just entering womanhood.

Endocheeney, Dugai (SW)

Born to the Mud People, born for the Streams Come Together Clan, Endocheeney was between seventy-five and seventy-seven years old and wasn't a thief or a drunkard. He had once laid rails for the Santa Fe Railroad but now received government food stamps and occasionally sold firewood. He had never been in trouble and had always tried to help others; everyone liked him, but once he was dead there were a few people who said he was a skinwalker. Iron Woman Ginsberg told Chee it was just gossip, that Endocheeney was a harmless old man who rarely came into the trading post after his wife died; when he did, two or three times a year, he came with a relative. Because he had no daughters he lived alone.

He had a Red Ant Way sing to cure him of something after his wife died. He had fallen off a fence the past autumn and broken his leg and had had it set at the Badwater Clinic. Iron Woman said he only received one letter that she knew about, from the Office of Social Services, and his pawn was still at the trading post unclaimed. Endocheeney died near his hogan from a knife wound; there was a corpse bone found in the knife wound during the autopsy.

Ernie (SC)

Grandson of Clement Hoski, he was about fourteen, tall and skinny. When Chee saw him he had on a black jacket, blue pants, and a blue backpack. He rode the Bloomfield School District bus for Special Education kids—Ernie had fetal alcohol syndrome. His mother and father had left him with his grandfather, who was trying to teach him how to cook, read, do numbers, and take care of himself. His grandfather also played games with him, took him hunting, and was teaching him how to drive his truck.

Ernie was proud of the bumper sticker his grandfather had on the back of his truck: ERNIE IS THE GREATEST. Chee gave Ernie instructions to give to his grandfather, to take off the old bumper sticker and replace it with a new one Chee had had printed: I HAVE THE WORLD CHAMPION GRANDSON.

Etcitty, Addison (SW)

Etcitty's name was on Irma Onesalt's list of patients who had been treated at the Badwater Clinic before they died.

Etcitty, Adeline (WY) (WI)

In the short story "The Witch, Yazzie, and the Nine of Clubs," Etcitty's mare had foaled a two-headed colt, evidence of witchcraft occurring. The same character with the same name also occurs in the short story "Chee's Witch."

Etcitty, Jimmy (TT)

Etcitty was a Navajo who worked at the Chaco dig; he also played guitar for Slick Nakai's revivals and helped Joe Nails dig for pots with the backhoe. Etcitty had worked at the park for less than a year, and Bob Luna said he was a good hand and a good man. He was a fundamentalist born-again Christian and didn't believe in *chindi*. He lived in Arizona between Tes Nez Iah and Dinnehotso with his mother-in-law's outfit. Etcitty had sold a pot to Houk and said it had been found on private land; the documentation he constructed for it was false. Ellie Friedman-Bernal had wanted to talk to him about where he obtained the pot. He was killed by a .25 caliber gun at the same time as Joe Nails at the same site; he was thirty-seven.

Everett, George (BW)

An associate of Bergen McKee's in the anthropology department at the University of New Mexico, Everett assumed McKee would take over his summer classes while he enjoyed supervising an excavation in Guatemala.

Farmer (GW)

Farmer was formerly an assistant U.S. district attorney; he had quit the Justice Department and gone to work for a law firm in San Francisco. Willie Shaw had wanted to contact him about the George McNair case. Farmer's replacement was unfamiliar with the file; after flipping through it, he decided he didn't want to talk to Shaw about Leroy Gorman.

Fat Man (TG)

The Fat Man was in charge of Eldercare Manor where Mama Fleck was living. He wanted Leroy to take her out of there because Mama was just too much trouble. Leroy threatened to kill him and twisted his arm, to force him to keep Mama there until he could find another place for her.

Feeney, Jim (LW)

This FBI agent out of Flagstaff, plus a BIA agent and two of Largo's men, investigated the Tso-Atcitty murders. Leaphorn knew Feeney and considered him to be brighter than the usual FBI man; Feeney's investigation was as thorough as Leaphorn's would have been. Feeney's group decided that Anna Atcitty was killed because she was a witness to Hosteen Tso's murder. Feeney recorded his interview with Margaret Cigaret, and Leaphorn later listened to it carefully; Feeney hadn't realized the information about the sand paintings and Tso's grandson was important.

First Cavalry (PD)

A young helicopter pilot for the El Paso Natural Gas Company, he had a scarred nose, walrus mustache, and First Cavalry Division emblem on his jacket. First Cavalry transported Chee and Mary Landon from the Bisti badlands to B. J. Vines's ranch, where he and Mary created a diversion to cover Chee's approach to the house.

Fishbein (SC)

Desmond Clark told Leaphorn that old man Fishbein was an honest and reputable art dealer.

Fleck, Delmar (TG)

When the family was evicted from their house in Tampa, Mama Fleck loosened the cap on the gas line; later Delmar, Leroy's older brother, came back and threw in a lit match. The neighbors saw him around the house, and the police picked him up and took him to jail. Then Leroy and Mama went to the police station and told them Leroy did it, because Leroy was under age and would get a lesser penalty; Delmar had already been arrested for shoplifting, car theft, and assault. Delmar tried to go straight, hold a job, and have a family. He told Leroy not to call him; he refused to have anything to do with his brother or his mother. He had told Leroy to let the government take care of Mama, that he couldn't afford to pay for her care on what he made at the car lot.

Fleck, Faye Lynn (TG)
Beautician wife of Delmar Fleck, she would have hung up immediately if she had known it was Leroy on the phone.

Fleck, Leroy (Little Red Shrimp) (TG)
Leroy was Delmar Fleck's younger brother. He was devoted to his mama, who had taught him the only way to keep his head up was to get even with the ruling class. Leroy had served time in detention centers, jails, and finally Joliet. He learned how to be an efficient killer at Joliet and had worked for Eddy Elkins for seventeen years afterward.

Leroy was a very small man with a rosy, freckled, rotund face, short, curly red hair, and greenish-blue eyes; he lifted weights and appeared stocky and burly, although he weighed 130 pounds or less. He was fast and quick, and that had helped him survive. Chee described him as a "freak," a dangerous, unpredictable man. Chee saw him following Janet Pete and questioned him; Leaphorn saw him watching the Santillanes apartment and also questioned him.

Leroy drove an aging, dented 1976 Chevy two-door sedan. All his furniture folded up and fit in the trunk, and he kept his cash in a child's plastic purse under the spare tire. He knew how to stretch his money and he took care of Mama, even if he had to do without things himself. He felt that Elkins was in his debt, and he was angry when the Chileans wouldn't pay him the $10,000 they still owed him, so he set up a plan to get even.

Fleck, Mama (TG)
Mother of Delmar and Leroy Fleck, she had

once weighed 140 pounds and was strong; after the strokes she was skinny and helpless. She didn't recognize Leroy and talked about Delmar. Whatever rest home she was in wanted to get rid of her after a while, because she always made trouble. She believed in getting even with anyone she thought had harmed her and had taught her sons to be the same way.

Flowers, Jason (FW)

Highway Commission Chairman Flowers was a "prominent capital lawyer, big in the social set, who had feuded with the local paper for years over a dozen civic issues and once sued the editor for libel." His animosity toward the *Capitol-Press* and everyone associated with it was well known. He was paid no salary; the chairmanship was usually sought as a launching platform for a statewide political candidacy.

According to one of the letters McDaniels received, Flowers no longer had political ambitions; when Flowers was attorney general, he and Governor Newton had hushed up a scandal in the Highway Department. Flowers had not been reelected. After that he had built a lucrative corporate law practice; when he took the chairmanship he had had to farm out some of the law firm's work. He wasn't losing any money, however, since the people who had been involved in the Highway Department scandal had been promoted and Flowers was being paid more for these services than he lost in legal fees. Cotton called him to check on the highway contract story; Flowers wouldn't comment until he "looked into it."

Flute Clan Boy (DW)

Hopi. Flute Clan Boy was one of the guards for Lomatewa, the Messenger. He was the first to see

the boots of the dead man on the trail. Flute Clan
Boy had attended school in Flagstaff and had a job
at the post office. Lomatewa felt he had to instruct
him not to report the body, because he had heard
Flute Clan Boy didn't know how to plant his corn
patches properly and didn't know his proper role
in the Kachina Society.

Fly on the Wall (FW)
There was a two-foot-square ink drawing of a
fly on the wall above John Cotton's desk, glued into
its position back in the 1930s. Cotton thought it represented Walter Lippmann's concept of the
reporter as seeing all but remaining detached and
objective.

Four Underworlds (DF)
Zuñi. In one version of the Emergence Myth
the four underworlds are Water Moss World, Mud
World, World of Wings, and the Lake; the people
ascended to the surface through reeds. The four
underworlds are the four wombs of Mother Earth,
where the lives of the ancestors and all other living
beings were conceived; this makes animals, birds,
and insects the brothers of the people, and as such
they are to be treated with respect.

Friedman-Bernal, Eleanor (Ellie) (TT)
An anthropologist whose specialty was
Anasazi ceramic pots, she hated pot hunters. Ellie
had a long face with prominent bones; the skin of
her hands and face was that of a person always out
under the sun, working in the dirt. She usually carried a small leather notebook containing details of
her work in her shirt pocket and appeared to be a
highly intelligent person. Her mother had wanted
her either to be a medical doctor or to marry one;

she was disappointed when Ellie, who was Jewish, married Eddie Bernal, a Puerto Rican archaeologist. The marriage had ended after a few years when Eddie ran off with another woman.

Ellie thought she had identified one specific potter who had been making pots of the St. John Polychrome type, and she believed she knew where the potter had gone when the Anasazis left the Chaco site. She was eager to get Professor Lehman's approval of her work. The day she disappeared she told everyone she was going into Farmington. When the police searched her room they found she had taken her working clothes, sleeping bag, leather notebook, a borrowed saddle, and a .25-caliber gun. She had left sauerbraten marinating in the refrigerator for her dinner with Lehman. Leaphorn discovered that she had stopped at Bo Arnold's, to drop off the saddle and borrow his kayak, and that only Harrison Houk saw her after that.

Fry (PD)

Colton Wolf's mother had lived for a while in San Jose with a man whose last name was Fry; Colton thought Fry was his father and had used the name when he attended school there. Fry had a round, dark, pockmarked face, a round belly, and a sullen, unhappy mouth. Colton barely remembered him. See **Small, George Tobias**.

Fry, Linda Betty (PD)

Colton Wolf's mother used this name when she lived in San Jose with a man named Fry. See **Maddox, Linda Betty, Shaw, Linda Betty**, and **Small, Mama**.

Fuchs, Klaus (FW)

Dr. Fuchs was a British physicist who worked

at Los Alamos. He had stood on the Delgado Street Bridge in Santa Fe and handed the secrets of the atomic bomb to Russian agents. Cotton looked at the plaque commemorating the event while walking around Santa Fe.

Gaines, Ben (DW)

Ben Gaines told Gail Pauling that he was her brother Robert's attorney. Gaines drove a dark blue Ford Bronco, a rental car. He was tall and gray-haired, in his early fifties, in good physical shape; he had a long face with deep lines along his nose and luminous eyes with large black pupils. When Chee saw him he was wearing jeans and a white shirt and was hatless. He had stopped at the Burnt Water Trading Post to get directions to the site where Robert's airplane had crashed, and he had also stopped in Tuba City to read the police report Chee had filed. Gaines had wanted to meet Chee to ask about the plane crash and to hire him to find the cargo.

Garcia, Gilberto (PD)

Garcia was sheriff of Valencia County, New Mexico, in 1948 when the oil-rig explosion occurred.

Garcia, Junior (FW)

A reporter at the Thursday morning press conference, he wanted to know if the governor was going to veto House Bill 178 legalizing parimutuel racetrack betting and what the governor was going to do about the incident in LeFlore County. He was smoking his cigar and playing poker with Cotton and others when Whitey Robbins was killed. He said he had seen McDaniels's car parked at the Highway Maintenance Division Office several times recently.

Gavin, William Jennings (Bill) (FW)

Gavin was a veteran politician; he'd been governor over twenty-five years ago, had served thirteen consecutive terms in Congress, and had kept the Democrats in the state from splintering along factional lines. He was a latter-day populist who'd never lost his rapport with blue-collar workers. He was also a close friend of Roark and had supported Roark's previous run for governor. He hated Clark and thought Roark could beat Clark in a senatorial primary race. Gavin died unexpectedly, early one Sunday morning; his body lay in state in the House Chamber on Monday.

Gay, Herman (FW)

A letter to McDaniels said that when Gay was the Sixth Division construction engineer, he and two project engineers were taking payoffs from contractors. He was transferred into the Right of Way Division, where he stayed until a month after Flowers became chairman of the Highway Commission, when he was promoted to state construction engineer. When Cotton called him he at first denied Cotton's story, then said his office couldn't keep an eye on everything at once. He wasn't as concerned as Singer was, because he didn't sign any of the falsified documents, but Singer would almost certainly implicate him.

George, Eldon (CW)

Sergeant George of the Navajo Tribal Police was sent to pick up Chee and examine the site of Delbert Nez's death. He found Chee half unconscious from shock and tried to treat Chee's burns with his first-aid kit; Ashie Pinto was asleep, sitting handcuffed in the back of Chee's patrol car.

George, Old Lady (TT)

Old Lady George was Streams Come Together Clan, related to Chee through his father's clan. She'd been a very helpful witness in an auto theft case Chee had once worked on; another time, when Chee was looking for one of her grandsons wanted on an assault charge, Old Lady George had sent the grandson to the police station to turn himself in. Chee had been sent to the 7-Eleven store in Shiprock to stop the disturbance; when Chee arrived he found Old Lady George, drunk and sitting on a culvert. Chee put her in the patrol car and took her home to her worried granddaughter.

Gianini, Delmar (FW)

Delmar was Tahash County Democratic Party Chairman, brother of Tommy Gianini.

Gianini, Tommy (FW)

A prominent Tahash County civic leader and businessman, Tommy was appointed to the State Pardon and Parole Board by Governor Roark. He was the brother of the Tahash County Democratic Party Chairman and stated he had no relatives in prison.

Gibbons, Eloise (CW)

Mrs. Gibbons, a prospective juror in the Ashie Pinto trial in Albuquerque, was a slender young woman in a gray pantsuit.

Ginsberg, Iron Woman (SW)

Daughter of Isaac Ginsberg and Lizzie Tonale, member of the People of the Valley Clan, she was a bulky woman, stout and ramrod straight. She remembered Chee had been out there before about the Dugai Endocheeney murder; she didn't believe he had come "just to poke around." Although she was nominally Jewish and had been educated at the College of Ganado, she didn't like talking about witches to a stranger.

Ginsberg, Isaac (Afraid of His Wife) (SW)

Ginsberg had built the Badwater Wash Trading Post of red sandstone in Utah, just thirty feet north of the Arizona border. During the winter he lived in a hogan one hundred yards to the south of the trading post. He was Jewish and his wife, Lizzie Tonale, had converted to Judaism; they had one daughter. Ginsberg died of natural causes.

Girlie (BW)

Member of the Los Angeles gang who relayed messages to Big Navajo and Eddie Poher by radio.

Gishi, Eddie (DW)

Jake West said that Eddie became violent when he drank, but he didn't think Eddie had pulled down the windmill.

Gishi, Emma (DW)

Jake West said Emma was tough and couldn't be pushed around; she was a practical woman and wouldn't let anyone in her group destroy the windmill.

Gishi, Patricia (DW)

The windmill and the Hopi shrine were on what had been Navajo grazing land allocated to Patricia Gishi in the Joint Use area.

Gishi family (DW)

The Hopis thought the Gishis or the Yazzies might be vandalizing the windmill, since they had a reputation for causing trouble on the Joint Use Reservation.

Goldrims (LW)

Leaphorn referred to Frank Hoski as Goldrims because he saw his gold-rimmed glasses before he knew anything else about him.

Goldtooth, Hildegarde (SW)

According to Alice Yazzie's letter, Chee was to meet her at Goldtooth's hogan, to conclude the financial arrangements for the sing for Denetsone. He didn't know Goldtooth's daughter and son-in-law had left the area after she died and her hogan was empty.

Gomez, Norbert Juan (LW)

One of the Boy Scouts held hostage by the Buffalo Society, he was twelve years old, four feet eleven inches tall, weighed eighty pounds, and had black hair and eyes.

Gomez, Rudolfo (Bad Hands) (TG)

The first time Chee saw Gomez was at the Yeibichai ceremony for Agnes Tsosie. Gomez had arrived early for the ceremony in a rented green four-door Jeep Cherokee and appeared nervous. He was slender and dark with black hair and looked part Indian or Asiatic; he seemed to have several false fingers on each hand, and his thumbs and little fingers jutted out stiffly. He was wearing a neatly fitted business suit with white shirt and a tie, thin black leather gloves, a snap-brim felt hat, and a fur-collared overcoat.

Chee surmised that Gomez had not known Henry Highhawk before this occasion, because Gomez walked over to Highhawk and introduced himself. Later Chee observed that Gomez had paid Highhawk's jail bond in Arizona and done various jobs for him, such as driving him to his lawyer and answering the telephone; he always seemed to be around Highhawk. Leroy Fleck knew Gomez as Santero.

Gorman (SC)

Fictitious hit-and-run driver in Chee's story to Janet Pete, he represented Clement Hoski.

Gorman (SW)

A young man attending a wedding at Teec Nos Pos, he was fooling around with a Standing Rock girl and she stuck him in the arm with a knife. Iron Woman Ginsberg heard about it on the radio.

Gorman (TG)

A Yeibichai ceremony was being performed in December near Burnt Water for a Navajo with this name.

Gorman (TT)

Middle-aged female cashier at the 7-Eleven store in Shiprock, member of the Towering House Clan, she called the police to report a drunk causing a disturbance in the store.

Gorman, Al (Plump Cop) (SW)

Officer Gorman was a Navajo Tribal Policeman who worked out of Shiprock, a "jolly looking, plump young man with a thin mustache" who was investigating the murder of Wilson Sam with Jay Kennedy. Leaphorn made Gorman nervous. Leaphorn watched Gorman and didn't think he was very observant; he made him go over the scene of Sam's murder with him and re-examine it.

Gorman, Albert A. (GW)

Younger brother of Leroy Gorman, uncle of Margaret Sosi, son of Ashie Begay's youngest sister, and probably a relocation Navajo, he lived in West Hollywood, California, and spoke only English. Albert worked for George McNair's car-theft ring and was wanted by the FBI for questioning in regard to the death of an FBI agent in Los Angeles. He'd been arrested several times and convicted once for grand larceny, motor vehicles.

Albert drove into Shiprock in a rented green

Plymouth sedan, looking for his brother Leroy. Albert wasn't a witness against McNair, but Eric Vaggan had warned him not to go looking for Leroy. Albert had just talked to Hosteen Joe in front of the laundromat when Lerner drove up. Lerner told Albert he had to go back, and Albert pulled out his gun. They exchanged shots, and Albert was injured. He drove out to his uncle's hogan and bled to death or was murdered. Chee found his body under some talus. Albert was in his mid-thirties and had on jeans, a jacket, and low-cut brown jogging shoes; he had the usual ID and $2,700 in his billfold. His hair had not been washed with yucca as was the usual Navajo custom, but his shoes had been reversed on his feet.

Gorman, Anna (LW) (SW)

Anna Gorman was Joe Leaphorn's mother, a member of the Slow Talking Dinee from Two Gray Hills. In *Skinwalkers* she was referred to only as Joe Leaphorn's mother; she buried his umbilical cord at the roots of a piñon tree near their hogan after he was born, to bind him to his family and his people.

Gorman, Eddie (LW)

Eddie was the boy wearing a black felt reservation hat who attended the Kinaalda for Eileen Endischee; he had to leave to refill the water barrels, which was a twelve-mile round trip. Eddie had seen the missing helicopter dive into an arm of Lake Powell; he also had a battery lantern with the name Haas on it. Leaphorn wanted to talk to him.

Gorman, Leroy (GW)

Leroy was the older brother of Albert Gorman, nephew of Ashie Begay, uncle of Margaret Sosi, and son of Begay's youngest sister; he was also a relocation Navajo. Leroy and Albert made their living stealing cars for George McNair. Kenneth Upchurch caught Leroy red-handed, convinced him to be a witness against McNair, and put him into the Witness Protection Program. He was to assume the name Grayson and live in a house trailer near Shiprock.

When Chee went out to the trailer, the man called Grayson told him he had taken a Polaroid picture of himself in front of the trailer and sent it to Albert. He told Chee his father had run off, his mother was sickly, and they had never met their relatives; Chee gave him directions to the Ghostway sing for Margaret Sosi so he could meet his family.

Gorman, Old Lady (CW)
Jim Chee found Delbert Nez's burning car on the dirt road leading out to where Old Lady Gorman's family lived.

Graff, Charles Albright (Charley) (FW)
Cotton described this boyhood friend as "frail, witty, happy, ineffable." As youngsters they built a treehouse in the cottonwood tree beside Cotton's home. When they were older he and Cotton spent three years working and pooling their funds to buy a car; they were going to take a trip to Canada to celebrate their manhood. Charley knew Cotton intended to marry Alice Beck; Cotton felt betrayed and beat him severely when he found Charley in the back seat of their car making love to Alice.

Gray Rocks, Old Woman (or Old Lady) (BW)
McKee went to talk to her because she was the source of one of the better Navajo Wolf rumors; she knew the Navajo Wolf was a stranger but didn't know that Luis Horseman was dead. Old Woman

Gray Rocks was married, had grandchildren, and was related to Horseman through her nephews.

Grayson (GW)
      Grayson lived in an aluminum house trailer under a cottonwood tree, like the one shown in the Polaroid picture of Leroy Gorman. He was a "man on the young side of middle age, clean-shaven, slender, distinctly Navajo in bone, with a narrow, intelligent face"; he walked with an easy grace and wore "neatly fitted denims, a long-sleeved shirt of blue flannel, a denim vest, and a black felt hat with a feather jutting from its band." He was Navajo but didn't understand the language. He told Chee he didn't know Leroy Gorman and said a "cute little skinny girl had also been looking for Gorman." Chee left a note with him addressed to Leroy because he thought Grayson might be Albert Gorman; later on Chee thought Grayson could be Robert Beno.

Green, Dr. (BW)
      Head of the anthropology department at the University of New Mexico, he expected Bergen McKee and Jeremy Canfield to keep him informed about their changing locations during the summer.

Greyeyes, Mrs. (CW)
      Prospective juror for the Ashie Pinto trial in Albuquerque, she lived close to Coyote Canyon on the reservation. She was born to the Sage Brush Hill People and born for the Towering House Clan.

Ha, Doan Van (CW)
      After his father's death, Taka Ji was supposed to be staying with his uncle, Doan Van Ha, in Albuquerque, but he had left there to stay with his aunt.

Ha, Janice (CW)

Daughter of Thuy Ha and Taka Ji's cousin, she was a single young woman and drove an elderly blue Chevy sedan. She acted as her mother's translator.

Ha, Jimmy (CW)

Young man at the Doan Van Ha home, he told Leaphorn his family had taken Taka Ji to his aunt's house in the South Valley and gave Leaphorn his aunt's telephone number.

Ha, Khanh (CW)

An elderly lady in the Doan Van Ha household, she had only a rudimentary knowledge of English.

Ha, Thuy (CW)

Older sister of Huan Ji, she was a smaller, slightly older, female version. Thuy had only recently been released by the Communists and had been in the United States for about a year. She was convinced that the Communists had come to the United States and killed Huan Ji. She didn't speak English.

Ha'wi-k'uh (DF)

This ancient Zuñi village is in the Valley of Hot Waters where the young boy, his sister, his parents, the old woman, and the old uncle lived. It was the next-to-last stop for the Zuñi people looking for the heart of the world. Ha'wi-k'uh was founded around A.D. 1300 and abandoned about 1672. At one time the Shalako ceremony was associated exclusively with this village.

Haas, Edward (Ed) (LW)

Pilot of the helicopter that disappeared, Ed

had flown helicopters in Vietnam. He was married and had two children. He had no criminal record and seemed to have won small amounts of money in Las Vegas in three trips there during the past two years. Leaphorn spotted a battery lantern on the blanket in the Endischee hogan; it had Haas's name on it.

Haines, Father (SC)

Father Haines was in charge of Saint Bonaventure Indian Mission at Thoreau but was not there when Leaphorn first inquired about the murder of Eric Dorsey. On Leaphorn's next visit he met Father Haines, "a thin, gray man, slightly bent." Father Haines waited patiently while Leaphorn examined Eric's workshop and then answered questions about Eric Dorsey and Eugene Ahkeah. He wondered whether it was possible for Eugene to have killed Eric in a drunken rage. Leaphorn wondered what would have caused the rage.

Hair in Bun (DD)

Young man in bib overalls with peeling sunburn and blond hair tied in a bun who was trying to weld a seat in a school bus at Jason's Fleece commune, he didn't like talking to the "Navajo Fuzz" and didn't hesitate to show it.

Hall, James W. (Jim, Jimmie Willie) (BW)

Electrical engineer from UCLA and fiancé of Ellen Leon, Jim was tall and rather slim with blond hair and blue eyes, a very handsome man. He was originally from Hall, New Mexico, and had met Ellen at the Pennsylvania State University; she realized he was a long way from home and might be lonely, so she spoke to him, starting a long relationship. Jim graduated magna cum laude from college and was very smart and ambitious; he was also very moody. He was angry to be in a system that would keep him on a treadmill for forty years; his goal in life was now to earn a million dollars. Jim told Ellen he was going to work for an electronics communications products company, taking along one of his own patents. He was installing radar equipment in the Many Ruins area when Leaphorn found him; Jim jumped into his truck and shot himself to death before Leaphorn could stop him.

Hall, Leroy (Roy) (FW)

Hall was chief of the *Journal*'s capitol bureau, number one in the pressroom, and winner of a Pulitzer prize for exposing a land-zoning bribery affair. His "Politics" column reached 450,000 readers daily. Hall was five feet nine, in his fifties, a slender man with gray hair cut in a bristling burr; he was married. His first law of political reporting was "If his lips move, he's lying"; his second was "Find the one who got screwed."

Hall had worked with McDaniels on the *Portland Oregonian*; he wondered if McDaniels's fall was really an accident. He'd written the story on Peters and the disappearance of the cigarette tax stamps, acting on an anonymous tip that McDaniels and Cotton had also received. He was hosting the poker game the night Whitey Robbins was murdered; while they were playing he received a call from his night editor telling him there was a story Cotton had been killed.

Hall had liked Gavin; he put together a memorial column recalling incidents from Gavin's career. He liked Korolenko, respected Roark, and couldn't stomach Clark. He was pessimistic about how well the public can decide matters for themselves, given just the facts. He had added up the haulage figures for Alvis Materials six weeks before Cotton saw them, leaving his characteristic dagger doodles in the margin of the hauling slip. Cotton noticed Hall was bitter and wondered if he had taken a payoff.

Halona It'a-wa-na (DF)

Zuñi. The Zuñis built the pueblo, "Ant Hill of the Middle Place," of stone and adobe on top of the hill (where Water Strider touched his body) along the north side of the Upper Zuñi River, in McKinley and Cibola counties near the Arizona border. This is the last place the Zuñi lived on their long trek from the underworld and is to be their home until time ends.

Halsey (DD)

Halsey was head of the Jason's Fleece commune living on Frank Bob Madman's old property; he was in charge because he'd had the money to make a deal for the allotment and he bought the groceries. He controlled the money and supplies and decided how much each person should receive. When George Bowlegs stopped by to ask for some provisions before his trip to the sacred lake of the Zuñi, Halsey refused to give him any supplies even though George had recently brought them a deer; Halsey was afraid George was being hunted by the law and didn't want the law to examine the commune.

Halsey had a mustache and was a big young man, tall and heavy in the shoulders. He wore an army fatigue jacket and boots that were dirty but of good quality. He didn't want Leaphorn talking to Susanne or visiting the commune; he finally threw Susanne out, hungry and penniless.

Hand Man (CW)

A specialist at the University of New Mexico Burn and Trauma Center, he examined Chee's burned left hand. He was from India and had traces of a British accent.

Hardin, John (FLG)

Hardin was a reporter covering the execution of George Tobias Small at the New Mexico State Penitentiary at Santa Fe shortly after midnight on March 28; he transmitted his story to the news service in Albuquerque by teletype. Although it was not a high-interest story, he was having difficulty trying to compress it into 300 words; Hardin and Thompson had talked to Small the afternoon before the execution and had learned about his past. (In the afterword Hillerman says he was Hardin and covered the execution of a man like Small when he was New Mexico manager of the United Press.)

Harge, Randolph Allen (FW)

Cotton identified Adams as Harge from photos at the capital city police station. Harge was born in Okeene, Oklahoma, March 11, 1930. He had been arrested and imprisoned several times for auto theft, extortion, and assault with intent to kill; he'd been acquitted of charges of armed robbery with intent to kill, murder, and kidnapping and extortion. He worked for the rackets in Chicago (the Organization). He was a tall man, stocky, with heavy shoulders, an intelligent face, about thirty-five years old; he looked like an office machine salesman. He had his left wrist in a cast. He'd been in the statehouse with Blue Topcoat hunting Cotton and then had been summoned to Korolenko's house to pick up Cotton.

Harper, Joe (FW)

Alvis introduced Cotton to Harper, saying he was "in cement." Harper looked nervous and slightly belligerent. He told Cotton that Reevis-

Smith had worked both the highway and the resort concession jobs out of the same cement batch plant.

Harris, Joe (SW)
    Dr. Harris, the San Juan County Coroner in Farmington, did the autopsies on Wilson Sam and Dugai Endocheeney. There had been foreign objects, including a dime, in Endocheeney's knife wounds.

Hartman, Carolyn (TG)
    Curator in charge of setting up the mask exhibit at the Smithsonian, Dr. Hartman called in Sandoval to check the accuracy of the exhibit. She was a slender, handsome, middle-aged woman whose specialty was the Incas. Henry Highhawk introduced her to Chee; she approved of giving Highhawk back the 18,000 Indian skeletons in the Smithsonian collection but did not want to give the Inca mask back to Chile.

He'hea-kwe (DF)
    Zuñi. The Runners-of-the-Sacred-Dance who carried the corn grains from the Sacred Lake to the village for food for the boy and his sister. The Runners were also instructed to plant the fields for them.

Hebert, Dr. (TG)
    Mrs. Perry's superior, Dr. Hebert, called to congratulate her on how well she'd handled the *Washington Post* with regard to the museum's Native American skeletons.

Hefron, Randolph (FW)
    His family owned a new shopping center and Commercial Credit; they also had a lot of small

loan interests, real estate, and big investments with Federal Citybank in paper and lumber in the capital city. Clark voted with the Hefron interests.

Hefron, Richard (FW)
Richard and Randolph were both involved in the family businesses.

Henderson, Dr. (CW)
Specialist on law and order in the Old West at the University of California at Berkeley, Henderson wrote a textbook. Professor Tagert criticized part of it, then Henderson criticized Tagert's paper on the Hole-in-the-Wall Gang; he and Tagert hated each other. Henderson had a new book out about the Pinkertons; he had found evidence in La Paz that Butch Cassidy and the Sundance Kid were shot to death in Bolivia. Tagert was determined to disprove Henderson's theory.

Henry (GW)
Henry was one of George McNair's underlings; he was a plump man with a soft voice and shrewd eyes that displayed a haughty contempt. When Eric Vaggan was invited to McNair's home, Henry resented being asked to bring him a glass of water.

Highhawk, Henry (TG)
Trouble-making conservator in the Smithsonian Museum of Natural History in Washington, D.C., he was impossible to get rid of, as Mrs. Perry discovered. Highhawk was one fourth Navajo: his grandmother was Bitter Water Clan, granddaughter of Ganado Mucho; her father had been Streams Come Together Clan. Highhawk sent his picture with a letter to Agnes Tsosie, asking her how he could join the Navajo Tribe; she invited him to the last night of her Yeibichai ceremony.

Highhawk had a long slender boyish face, large blue eyes, and long blond hair woven into braids or tucked into a bun. Because his left leg was shorter than his right, he limped and had to wear a metal brace and a boot with a lift. When Chee saw him at the Yeibichai, Highhawk was dressed like a Hollywood Indian, in a dark blue velvet shirt with silver buttons circa 1920, a reservation hat, silver concha belt, jeans, boots, and a leather jacket with fringes.

Because Highhawk had dug up the bones of Catherine Perry's grandparents, there was a federal warrant for his arrest for flight across state lines to avoid prosecution for the desecration of graves. Highhawk said he represented the Paho Society. He had told everyone he was going to attend the Yeibichai, which is where Chee arrested him. Chee noticed Highhawk knew some of the words to the chant and used a tape recorder at the ceremony.

After Rudolfo Gomez paid his bail, Highhawk returned to his home in the Eastern Market neighborhood on Capitol Hill in Washington, D.C. When Janet Pete and Chee visited him, he invited Chee to look at his kachina collection; Chee was surprised to see a copy of the Talking God mask in the collection. He surmised some of the other figures were also skillful copies made by Highhawk.

Highhawk didn't want Chee to know of his interest in the Tano War God figure. He was extremely well informed about Navajo metaphysics, as could be seen by his sketches. His exhibit at the Smithsonian, "The Masked Gods of the Americas," included the Talking God mask. Chee and Leaphorn found Highhawk dead, with a replica of the Talking God mask and his tape recorder, inside one of the cases at the Smithsonian; he had been shot above the eye.

Highsmith, J. D. (DD)

A New Mexico state policeman whose real job was traffic safety, Sergeant Highsmith filed descriptions of Ernesto Cata and George Bowlegs and alerted the highway patrol to watch for hitchhikers.

Hill, Governor (FW)

Hill had vetoed the income tax bill and cut the Welfare Department budget six years ago when he was governor. A woman on welfare killed herself and her three children when her benefits were slashed so much she didn't have enough money to buy food for them.

Hopi people (DF)

Zuñi. When the A'shiwi could no longer care for themselves because of the drought, they asked the Hopi people if they would help them. The Hopi agreed, and the A'shiwi made the long trek to their village, where they had to work very hard for the Hopi.

Horn Rims (BW)

This plump young man with horn-rimmed glasses was a second cousin to Luis Horseman. He'd been out looking for a stray mule when he came across Luis walking along a sheep track. Horn Rims shared his tobacco with Luis, even though he thought Luis was worthless.

Horse Kicker (LW)

Hosteen Klee was also known as Horse Kicker when he was young. See **Klee, Hosteen,** and **Klah, Hosteen.**

Horseman, Agnes Tso (BW)

Member of the Many Goats Clan, Elsie Horseman was listed as Agnes Tso Horseman on the autopsy report on Luis Horseman.

Horseman, Annie (BW)

Member of the Red Forehead Clan, she was mother of Luis Horseman and Billy Nez. Old Woman Gray Rocks said Annie wasn't any good because she ran off and deserted her children.

Horseman, Billy (BW)

Billy Nez went by the name Horseman until he went to live with his uncle and took his uncle's name.

Horseman, Elsie Tso (BW)

Member of the Many Goats Clan, estranged wife of Luis Horseman, she—and Luis—lived in the Klagetoh area. See **Horseman, Agnes Tso.**

Horseman, Luis (BW)

Member of the Red Forehead Clan, son of Annie Horseman, husband of Elsie (Agnes) Tso, and brother of Billy Nez, Luis had "a young face, thin and sensitive, with large black eyes and a sullen mouth." His forehead was high and his nose curved and thin, hawklike. He was seen wearing denims and a red shirt and had his hair pulled back the old way, secured with a red sweatband. Luis had attended school on the reservation and worked at short-term jobs. He had been arrested for drunk and disorderly, assault and battery, and operating a motor vehicle while under the influence of alcohol.

He was drunk the night he knifed the Mexican in Gallup; he thought he'd killed the man, so he stole a car to get away, then later abandoned it. Luis headed back to his mother's clan's area of the reservation to hide; he knew his wife's people would not help him. He was only twenty-three when he was killed.

Horst, Willie (FW)

Willie Horst was in charge of the highway

records room where John Cotton and Janey Janoski were examining records to find bid figures to match the ones in McDaniels's notebook. He was "a tall, stooped man with large ears and a habit of allowing long pauses between sentences while he sorted out exactly what he wanted to say." He repeatedly told John and Janey not to get his file materials out of order.

Hoski, Clement (SC)

Clement Hoski was the man who ran over Victor Todachene. When he heard about Todachene's death, he went to KNDN in Farmington and confessed over the open mike that he had heard his truck hit something; he had gone back to look and seen nothing, so he left. He said he was drunk, although he normally didn't drink; if he had known Todachene was there he would have helped him. He said he was sorry and would send money every two weeks to Todachene's relatives to help them. He did not give his name, and he sounded as if he was holding back tears. He had no difficulty using the microphone, and he was able to speak Navajo very well.

Hoski was medium in size, middle-aged, dressed in jeans, a jean jacket, a cap with a CAT symbol on the crown, dark-rimmed glasses, and high-top work shoes. His cap looked as if someone had sat on the bill, and his clothes smelled strongly of onions. He drove a dirty green pickup truck with a brand-new ERNIE IS THE GREATEST bumper sticker on it. The license plates were covered with dirt.

Chee found Hoski at one of the Navajo Agricultural Industries produce warehouses, where he appeared to be a foreman. He didn't drive his truck but participated in a carpool with a group of workers who lived in NAI housing. He and his grandson, Ernie, lived farther out in a plank house with a pitched tin roof and an outhouse. It had electricity but probably not gas, as there was firewood stacked against the wall. Hoski had taken on the responsibility of raising Ernie by himself and had sent a first payment of $145 to the family of Todachene. Chee told Leaphorn he thought he had the driver but couldn't find the truck and provided Hoski with a new bumper sticker for his truck, actions that Janet Pete strongly supported.

Hoski, Frank (or Colton) (LW)
These were aliases of Jimmy Tso, Henry Kelongy's right-hand man and friend of John Tull; Hoski had participated in the robbery of the Wells Fargo armored truck in Santa Fe. The FBI had no idea who Hoski really was, as he never used his real name; his aliases included Colton Hoski, Frank Morris, Van Black, and Theodore Parker. Hoski had first appeared as one of the "violents" at Wounded Knee.

He was a trim but stocky man with black hair, and he looked Indian. He was five feet eleven inches tall, weighed 190 pounds, and had possible heavy scar tissue under his hairline above his right cheek. Hoski had been a demolitions expert and a radioman in the infantry during the Vietnam War. He smoked cigars, was a moderate drinker, had a pugnacious disposition, and enjoyed telling jokes. He had lived in Los Angeles, Memphis, and Provo, Utah. Hoski wasn't homosexual, but the FBI had no record of relationships with women, other than Rosemary Rita Oliveras, whom he may have fallen in love with while he was working as a janitor at Safety Systems in Washington, D.C. See **Goldrims**.

Houghton, Lawrence (Larry) (FW)
Houghton, Second Highway District maintenance engineer, was an oversized man, six feet

four, with a shock of carefully combed hair, a brigadier's mustache, a handsome, scrubbed pink face, and a clear, clipped, loud voice. His name was at the top of two different pages in McDaniels's notebook; McDaniels had interviewed him. Houghton had been one of the long-timers hired as a political patronage appointment before the merit personnel system had been enacted; he'd been active in politics and was one of the "good old boys." One of the letters to McDaniels said Houghton was moved out of his job of state construction engineer to his present position so Flowers could put Herman Gay in that job.

Houk, Alice (TT)

Wife of Harrison Houk, mother of Elmore, Dessie, and Brigham Houk, she had wanted Brigham to be locked up, but Harrison wouldn't agree. Brigham killed her.

Houk, Brigham (TT)

Son of Alice and Harrison Houk, he was the youngest of the Houk children. In many of his pictures he didn't smile and was shown with an animal he had killed; he loved the outdoors but was shy around people. Harrison regretted that he hadn't gotten him any help; Brigham was schizophrenic and heard voices. He was a loner; the only person he was happy around was his father. He enjoyed music and played the piano, guitar, and clarinet. When he was fourteen he killed the entire family, except for Harrison; it was thought Brigham drowned in the San Juan River that same day.

When Leaphorn saw him in the canyon he was a middle-aged man, wearing a new nylon jacket, worn jeans, and moccasins of deerhide; his beard and hair had been cut straight across by his father. He was a small, tightly built man, with short arms and legs and a thick, strong torso; his eyes were the same odd blue-gray as his father's. His father had told him Leaphorn was coming. Brigham had found Ellie Friedman-Bernal after she was hurt and had taken care of her; he described the person who hurt her as a devil.

Houk, Della (TT)

Leaphorn thought the name of Harrison Houk's wife was Della. Houk said his wife's name was Alice.

Houk, Dessie (TT)

Daughter of Harrison and Alice Houk, sister of Elmore and Brigham, she was killed by Brigham Houk. Harrison had a picture of her in a cheer-leader's uniform when she was in high school.

Houk, Elmore (TT)

Son of Harrison and Alice Houk, brother of Dessie and Brigham Houk, he was killed by his brother, Brigham. Harrison had a picture of Elmore in a football jacket when he attended Montezuma Creek High School.

Houk, Harrison (TT)

Houk had a ranch just outside of Bluff, Utah, in the heart of the Anasazi ruins country. He was a "cattleman, pillar of the Church of Christ of Latter-Day Saints, potent Republican, subject of assorted gossip, county commissioner, holder of (many) Bureau of Land Management grazing permits, legendary shrewd operator," and former Utah state senator. Knowing that he was smarter than most other people had been a major source of satisfaction in his life; he'd become richer and others had become poorer.

He was not always honest in his business dealings, and the Mormon Church had come down on him about this. Houk collected Indian pots. To keep from being implicated in a violation of the Antiquities Preservation Act, he gave the documentation form to the seller to fill out and send in. He complained that every time there was a case of pot stealing, the authorities bothered him. Ellie Friedman-Bernal had come to see him about a pot he'd obtained from Slick Nakai.

Houk was not a young man, but he intended to live to be very old. He had to use a cane because he had arthritis in his hip; this didn't prevent him from using his kayak on the San Juan River. Although he was paunchy and there was a slight slump to his shoulders, his body had a blocky sturdiness. His hair was gray, and there was a ragged walrus mustache on his round bulldog face. His face was lined, and he wore steel-rimmed glasses over his small blue eyes.

He remembered Leaphorn from twenty years before, because of Leaphorn's kindness to him the day Brigham had killed his family. Leaphorn had found his son's hat by the San Juan River. Houk blamed himself for his son's murderous rages and regretted that he had not obtained help for him when he was young. Then Irene Musket, his housekeeper, found Houk dead in his barn one morning; he'd been shot twice with a .25 caliber pistol. Houk had written a note for Leaphorn on the back of a business card and tucked it inside the top of his underwear, where it was later found by the coroner.

Howard (CW)

The CIA thought Howard, a defrocked CIA agent, had sold out to the Russians. The FBI staked him out, but his wife drove the getaway car and Howard escaped to safety behind the Iron Curtain.

Hudson, Jimmy (BW)
A Hand Trembler, he told Charley Tsosie he had been witched.

Huerta, Ramon (TG)
See **Cardona, Ramon Huerta.**

Huff, Sherman (PD)
An epidemiologist who had his office in the basement of the Cancer Research and Treatment Center in Albuquerque, he was a burly man with a gray mustache, bushy gray beard, sun-weathered skin, and bright blue eyes. He did not smoke and was very anti-smoking, as evidenced by the posters on his walls. Dr. Huff was extremely interested in the incidence of leukemia deaths in the six Navajos who had worked at the oil rig in 1948.

Hunt, Sergeant (PD)
Sergeant Hunt worked for the Albuquerque Police Department. He was a "small man, with pale-gray eyes and a narrow, bony face"; he had a soft, polite voice. Hunt's job was to keep track of old unsolved homicides and see if anything new fitted in. He visited Chee in the Bernalillo County Medical Center and wanted him to go over the blond man's description again. He thought the blond man might be the one who had blown up Emerson Charley's pickup, killing two men. Chee told him about Emerson Charley's body disappearing.

Ice God (Sun-i-a-shi'wa-ni) (DF)
Zuñi. Deity of winter, the Ice God rarely blew his breath toward the fields of Ha'wi-k'uh because the Corn Maidens looked after them.

Ingles, Father (DD)
Father Ingles had been a Franciscan priest for

almost forty years. He was a "wiry, tidy, tough-looking little man, his face a background of old pockmarks overlaid with two generations of damage by sun and wind." He was a cigar smoker and wore an old secondhand navy blue jacket. Father Ingles had worked for years out of Saint Michael's Mission at Window Rock and spoke Navajo almost as fluently as the Navajos did; the Navajos affectionately referred to him as Narrowbutt, because of his bony posterior. He was currently working at Saint Anthony's Mission, where he had become well acquainted with both Ernesto Cata and George Bowlegs; he had spent hours discussing the Navajo, Zuñi, and Catholic religions with George and remarked that George was highly intelligent and a mystic. He thought Ernesto's breaking the taboo was a trivial matter; Ernesto knew the legend said the taboo breaker had his head chopped off by the Salamobia.

Irma (SC)

Chee's oldest sister played the drums as an extra in one scene of the movie *Cheyenne Autumn*.

Isaacs, Ted (DD)

A young anthropology graduate student with a dig close to the mesa where Ernesto Cata was killed, Ted was hunting for Folsom Man lance points to support Dr. Reynolds's modification theory. Ted was a tall, bony young man in his late twenties; although he usually wore a hat, his face was tanned from the sun. He sometimes had a wizened old-man look, and he had slightly protruding buck teeth which he vowed one day he would have fixed. He was determined to finish his project and get a good faculty appointment.

Ted's parents had been "east Tennessee white trash"; he wasn't sure who his father was, and anyway his father had run off and left him. He'd lived with a drunken uncle in a sharecropper's shack, chopped cotton, and pleaded with his uncle to allow him to finish high school. As a student at Memphis State University he worked as a janitor and washed dishes; he even tried to get into the army, just to see how it would feel to eat regularly.

Reynolds gave Ted a way out. He gave Ted $400 to use for his dig; Ted put a down payment on an old Chevy truck and built a wooden box on the back to live and work in. Reynolds praised Ted for his work but demanded that Ted keep Susanne and the boys away so no one would have reason to challenge its scientific authenticity. Ted cared deeply for Susanne, but when he was asked to help her he decided his career had to come first; Leaphorn was disappointed in Ted's choice.

It'a-wa-na (DF)

Zuñi "heart of the world" or navel of the earth, where Water Strider touched the earth with his body, this sacred site is preserved in one of the ceremonial rooms and contains two columns of rock, one of crystal and the other of turquoise. Only the highest priest of the Rain Priesthood is allowed to enter it.

Jackson, Deputy Sheriff (TG)

As Deputy Sheriff of McKinley County, New Mexico, Jackson, a plump young man, was driving by the site where Santillanes's body was found. He was ordered to guard the site and the evidence.

Jackson, George (BW)

George Jackson was the real name of the Big Navajo.

Jacobs, Jean (CW)

Dr. Tagert's teaching assistant at the University

of New Mexico and girlfriend of Odell Redd, Jean seemed to like Odell more than he liked her. She was a plump woman in her late twenties with a round good-natured face and short brown hair; she wore reading glasses. Chee found her to be a talented listener, unusual in white people. She had heard it was Chee who arrested Ashie Pinto.

She hadn't seen Tagert since the end of summer session; he had left early, and she had graded his papers and turned in his grades for him. The department chairman asked Jean to start teaching Tagert's class on the Trans-Mississippi West; he wanted to know where Tagert was, as if it were Jean's fault that Tagert hadn't returned. She didn't like Tagert very much, but she was trying to get a doctorate in history, specializing in the impact of the trading post system on the Western tribes, which fell into Tagert's area.

Janoski, Dick (FW)

Janey told Cotton her husband had been a fighter-bomber pilot for the navy. He had told Janey somebody had to do it; then, when his hundred missions were over, he volunteered for another tour. He rationalized that he didn't hate anyone and the bombs didn't really hurt anyone; it was a game he played against the antiaircraft guns. He lost.

Janoski, Janey (FW)

Janey was executive secretary in the Legislative Finance Committee Office. She was a pretty woman, with dark eyes behind square horn-rim glasses—a skinny, emotional, unpredictable brunette. Cotton liked her. There was something reckless and vulnerable about her. It was rumored that she was the governor's mistress.

Cotton enlisted her help to do research on Gay and Singer. After he escaped from Harge and Blue Topcoat in the statehouse, he made his way to Janey's apartment and rewrote his story on her old portable typewriter; Janey called the police for him. Janey believed reporters didn't care who they hurt with their stories; she felt Cotton could give his story to Roark and he would clean up the situation.

Jansen (DW)

Jerry Jansen's brother, the man who put the narcotics deal together, he was middle-aged and wore a straw hat. Chee found him dead from stab wounds in the front seat of his blue Lincoln in the village of Sityatki the night of the Washing of the Hair ceremony.

Jansen, Jerald R. (Jerry) (DW)

Jansen was a lawyer from Houston, in the narcotics business with his brother. He represented the sellers of the cargo in the Cessna and was to signal Robert Pauling if it was safe for him to land. Chee found Jansen dead, shot in the back by a .38 or larger gun, slumped against an outcropping of basalt. Jansen was a white man, dressed in a business suit and tie, with smooth-soled pointy-toed shoes; he was between forty-five and fifty, wore eyeglasses, and held in one of his hands a small white card from the Hopi Cultural Center with a message on the back.

Jenks, Randall (SW)

Pathologist at the Indian Health Service hospital at Gallup, Dr. Jenks came to the reservation because his student loan demanded two years of service in the military or in the Indian Health Service; he'd stayed beyond the two years. Leaphorn tried not to stereotype him as an "Indian lover." Jenks wore glasses and had shoulder-length blond hair held in place by a red headband with Corn Beetle woven into it; he was wearing a frayed denim jacket under his blue lab coat.

Jenks had the laboratory report on the bone bead shot at Jim Chee. He startled Leaphorn when he asked if Leaphorn's investigation was connected to Irma Onesalt; Leaphorn felt Jenks's business was public health, not police business. Jenks had seen Irma Onesalt's death list but couldn't remember many of the names on it.

Ji, Huan (CW)

Ji was a Vietnamese, a teacher of mathematics for four years at Shiprock High School. Chee had seen his beat-up white Jeepster turning off the road a short distance from where Delbert Nez's burning patrol car had been found. Ji didn't remember much about what he saw the night Nez was killed. Ji was a small thin man with short-cropped black hair and a short-cropped mustache showing gray; he stood rigidly erect. When Chee saw him he was dressed neatly in gray slacks, blue jacket, white shirt, and tie. He was a widower with a teenage son; they lived in Shiprock, in a freshly painted house with an orderly interior and well-tended garden.

Ji had been a colonel in the South Vietnamese army, commanding a Ranger battalion and gathering intelligence for Washington. When Saigon fell, the CIA got him out and helped him get a start in the United States. The day Ji died he had walked home from school alone; he had been in the house and was shot twice and died before help came. He left two messages in blood on the wall, one for Taka Ji, his son, and one for Jim Chee.

Ji, Taka (CW)

Huan Ji's teenage son was a slender boy who wore jeans and a black leather jacket and drove his father's white Jeepster. His bedroom was neat and filled with books and pictures; there were many pictures of the same sixteen-year-old Navajo girl. He and his father both enjoyed photography and had a well-equipped darkroom in their home; in the darkroom there were telescopic pictures of a volcanic outcropping.

Taka had not seen his father since they drove to school together in the morning; he had kept the car after school. He had heard a shot fired and had passed Chee on the road in the white Jeepster, but he hadn't told the police because his father didn't want him to get mixed up in it. If his father had enemies, Taka didn't think his father would have told him about them. The police sent him to live with his only remaining relatives, in Albuquerque.

Jim, Haskie (CW)

Leaphorn's father's older brother, Haskie Jim had told Leaphorn the rain seemed random from where they stood, but if they stood somewhere else it might not be random. He reinforced the Navajo concept that there is order in everything.

Joe, Hosteen Joseph (GW)

This eighty-one-year-old man who lived with his daughter near Shiprock had driven into town in his daughter's pickup to use the Shiprock Economy Wash-O-Mat. When he came out of the Wash-O-Mat a stranger stopped him, showed him a Polaroid of Leroy Gorman, and asked Hosteen Joe if he'd seen the man.

John Doe (WY) (DW)

In the short story "The Witch, Yazzie, and the

Nine of Clubs," John Doe was the unidentified man Chee picked up on Paiute Mesa, dead for two months before his body was recovered. It appeared he had died from natural causes—too much booze and too much high-altitude cold. He was about forty. No skin was removed from his feet because his boots had been left on. Chee knew he hadn't been killed by a witch.

In *The Dark Wind*, a young Navajo man was found dead on Black Mesa by the Hopis, shot in the head by a .38 pistol, his boots removed, and the soles of his hands and feet flayed, as if killed by a Navajo witch. He was thirty to thirty-two years old, five feet seven inches tall, and weighed between 155 and 160 pounds; there was no billfold or other identification on him, hence the name John Doe. No effort had been made to hide the body, which lay on the trail to a Hopi shrine. He had been killed July 10 but had not been found until two to four weeks later.

Johns, Dr. (Burn Doctor) (CW)

Female physician at the University of New Mexico who treated Chee's burns, she consulted with the Hand Man about treatment and told Chee they'd let him know what they thought about surgery for his hand.

Johnson, Senator (FW)

Johnson died in office. The Democratic Central Committee gave Korolenko the nomination for the special election, to finish the two years left in Johnson's term.

Johnson, Randy A. (PD)

A twenty-three-year-old from Roswell, New Mexico, he died from injuries in a motorcycle accident. His body was next to Emerson Charley's

The author, sitting at left in wagon, with big brother Barney holding handle and big sister Margaret Mary hiding eyes. Other participants are cousins Joe, Elizabeth, Emma, and Monica Grove at Uncle Arthur's farm.

Family picnic at Sacred Heart, with author (crying because he didn't get to sit on the tricycle) showing talent at getting front/center spot when pictures are taken.

The author displaying skill at holding fish closer to camera to augment size. Left to right, cousin Joe Grove, the author, Barney, and cousins Monica and Johnnie Grove.

What was left, in 1990, of the Sacred Heart store Gus Hillerman operated during the Depression.

Konawa High owned twelve baseball uniforms, which went to nine starters, two relief pitchers, and a utility infielder. The author (top row, sixth from left) was substitute right fielder, where the damage done by his inability to judge fly balls was minimized. World War II took a heavy toll on the team.

Part of Fourth Platoon, C Company, 410th Infantry, looking uncharacteristically tidy, in a French village during its conquest of the Third Reich. The author (grenade in lapel) is on the jeep hood at the center.

A rainy February 9, 1945. Hillerman receiving Silver Star from General Anthony McAuliffe. The general had just become famous for his one-word ("Nuts") response to German demands that he surrender his forces in Bastogne during the Battle of the Bulge. Unknown to the general, the author was Absent Without Leave, having slipped away from the Army hospital at Saverne to rejoin his platoon.

August 16, 1948. Author marries Marie Unzer, the greatest coup of his life.

Summer 1951. On the night shift in the United Press bureau in Oklahoma City.

Winter 1952.
United Press
Bureau
Manager in
Santa Fe.

Winter 1954. In uncharacteristically double-breasted attire, photographed by the governor's press secretary while covering politics for *The New Mexican*.

Deer season in the Brazos high country. The author never actually shot at a deer, but the rifle gave him an excuse to be out there after fishing season ended.

Author with wife Marie, his mother, and daughter Anne at his brother Barney's wedding.

Author showing grandson Brandon Strel the art of holding a fish closer to camera to augment its size.

The author, center as usual, with Scott Turow and Studs Terkel, laughing at their own witticisms at a library fundraising event.

The Navajo Tribal Police headquarters at Window Rock, where Joe Leaphorn and Jim Chee have offices in more recent books.

Some of the secondhand buildings of St. Bonaventure School, scene of a fictional murder in *Sacred Clowns*.

in the morgue at the University of New Mexico hospital.

Johnson, T. L. (DW)

Johnson said he was an FBI agent looking for the cargo from the plane crash; he was actually a DEA agent. He was a tall, lean, red-haired man; he had a well-trimmed pale mustache, pale blue eyes, and even white teeth in a sunburned freckled face. He was dressed in denims and black boots made of some exotic leather and appeared confident and competent. He thought Chee might have been involved in the robbery, since he was there at the time the plane crashed, and he thought the cargo was still near the crash area. Johnson and Larry Collins walked into Chee's trailer while he was sleeping and searched his trailer; when Collins didn't find the drugs, Johnson struck Chee across the face and told him if he'd tell them where the drugs were, he wouldn't report it and Chee could continue in his job as a Navajo policeman.

Joseph, Old Man (CW)

According to Ashie Pinto's old stories, Old Man Joseph was thrown from his horse during the trip with Delbito Willie to raid the Utes. While they were returning home, two white men tried to steal their horses. Old Man Joseph shot one of them, and the one with the yellow mustache shot Old Man Joseph in the chest and killed him.

Kanitewa, Mrs. (SC)

Tano. Delmar Kanitewa's mother had divorced his father, apparently without hard feelings. Delmar had kept his Tano name and lived with his mother until high school; then he went to live with his father, the son of Bertha Roanhorse. Mrs.

Kanitewa's home was one street south of the plaza in Tano Pueblo. She had both an Indian Service frame-and-stucco house and one made of adobe. The government wanted her to live in the frame house, but she used it only for storage. She lived in the adobe house because it was warmer in winter and cooler in summer.

Under Chee's skillful and sensitive questioning, Mrs. Kanitewa gave Chee more information than she had the BIA. Her son Delmar had come home and gone to visit her brother, Francis Sayesva. She hadn't seen Delmar again after the ceremonial. She had expected him to stay for his uncle's funeral before returning to school. Delmar had never disappeared like this before, she didn't know where he was, and she was worried. She wanted Chee and Blizzard to leave messages with the Senas, neighbors who had a telephone, when they discovered anything about his whereabouts.

Kanitewa, Delmar (SC)

Navajo/Tano. Delmar Kanitewa was a teenage boy who had run off from boarding school. Chee's assignment was simply to locate him, find out why he had left, and determine where he was staying. Delmar's paternal grandmother, Bertha Roanhorse, was a very important member of the Navajo Tribal Council and was quite concerned for his safety. Chee was annoyed because he felt he was being used as a truant officer. He figured Delmar would be as nervous as Chee himself had been, when he had run away from boarding school, but harder to catch.

Delmar's parents were divorced and his father had remarried. When he entered high school Delmar had decided to live with his father and stepmother. Delmar's portrait in the Crownpoint High School yearbook showed a fifteen-year-old boy with a "wide grin, white but slightly crooked teeth, high cheekbones, a slightly cleft chin, and a bad haircut." Chee noticed that although Delmar resembled his mother he was five feet eight inches tall, taller than the usual Pueblo boy. His great-grandmother said the family name for Delmar was Sheep Chaser.

While living at Tano Pueblo, Delmar had been initiated into the same kiva as his uncles, Francis and Teddy Sayesva. Delmar had left Eric Dorsey's workshop with a newspaper-wrapped package under his arm and gone directly to his Uncle Francis with it. He had stopped by his mother's home and told her he had to see his uncle about a religious matter and would then return to school. After hearing a report on the radio about Dorsey's death, Delmar disappeared. He was wearing a red shirt at the time and no one seemed to know where he was hiding.

Kayonnie (Brother of Young Man) (SW)
    Born to the Leaf People, born for the Mud Clan, Kayonnie was dressed like his brother and looked the same, except for being a little heavier and not having the white scar on his face. Both brothers were unemployed and had been drinking. Chee felt no kinship to them.

Kayonnie (Young Man) (SW)
    Born to the Leaf People, born for the Mud Clan, he was standing on the front porch of Iron Woman Ginsberg's trading post; he was in his late teens and smelled of alcohol and was rude and sullen. He had a thin face and a half-moon of white scar tissue beside his left eye socket; he was wearing a red sweatband, a faded red shirt, jeans, and cowboy boots. He had beer in his four-by-four, but not from Iron Woman's trading post.

Keeyani, Dillon (WY)

Keeyani was the shaman in charge of the Enemy Way ceremony for Emerson Nez. He was a tall, gaunt man.

Keeyani, Mary (CW)

Mrs. Keeyani was Ashie Pinto's niece, Turning Mountain People with a connection to Bitter Water People, thus Emma Leaphorn's kin. She was a small bony woman who dressed traditionally; she wore only a single bracelet of narrow silver and a squash-blossom necklace with very little turquoise.

She visited Joe Leaphorn's office in Window Rock with Professor Bourebonette; she wanted some help finding evidence that Ashie Pinto was innocent of the murder of Delbert Nez. She knew about Ashie Pinto's prison term when he was young; Ashie Pinto was her mother's brother. Mary usually read her uncle's letters to him and answered them for him.

Mary was married and had several children; her husband tended their sheep, and her youngest daughter helped him when she wasn't attending school. The daughter had seen a vehicle stop at Ashie Pinto's place.

Kelly, Gary (FW)

Kelly was vice-president of Reevis-Smith. When Cotton contacted him with his story, Kelly offered him $25,000 to be Reevis-Smith's public relations consultant. When Cotton declined the offer, Kelly told him he wanted to get together and talk about it.

Kelongy, Henry (the Kiowa) (LW)

Henry Kelongy was the fanatic disbarred lawyer who started the Buffalo Society. He was half-Kiowa and was raised in Anadarko, Oklahoma.

Henry attended the University of Oklahoma law school and served in the 45th Division during World War II; he was promoted to first lieutenant during the war, then killed someone in Le Havre, was court-martialed, and lost his commission. When he came back to the United States, he entered politics; during the Vietnam War he ran an Indian draft-resister group. He then spent some time as an evangelist for the Church of the Nazarene, after which he became a minister for the Native American Church; in his church they worshiped the Kiowa Sun God. He went to Wounded Knee with the American Indian Movement in 1973 and preached violence; when AIM backed off, he called them cowards and started the Buffalo Society, taking many of the most violent AIM members with him.

Kendall, Pete (FW)

A reporter in the capitol pressroom, he had a collection of erroneous headlines tacked above his desk. Kendall was playing poker with Cotton and others when Whitey Robbins was killed. Hall remarked on Kendall's frequent use of simile, saying Kendall had learned it on the *Corpus Christi Caller*.

Kennedy, Jay (SW) (TG) (CW)

In *Skinwalkers*, Kennedy was an FBI agent stationed at the Farmington office. Chee thought Kennedy was a better sort than most FBI men and a lot smarter, even if he didn't understand Navajo humor; Chee was with Kennedy when he arrested Roosevelt Bistie. Kennedy had sun-bleached short blond hair, and his skin was peeling from the sun; he enjoyed playing bridge. Like most FBI agents, he wore a pistol in a shoulder holster under his jacket.

In *Talking God* he was stationed at Gallup; he

had been with the FBI for at least twenty-eight years, and he and Leaphorn had been friends for several years. Kennedy was married, and his wife had convinced him to start drinking tea because caffeine was making him jumpy. He told Leaphorn he was glad Leaphorn hadn't resigned and asked him to track for them at the scene of the murder near the Amtrak rails. Later, Leaphorn told him the dead man's name was Santillanes and asked Kennedy to find out what he could about him.

In *Coyote Waits*, Kennedy was still an FBI agent at the Gallup office and now an old friend of Leaphorn's. Kennedy had become quite gray and needed a haircut. Leaphorn invited him to lunch to learn what Kennedy knew about the Ashie Pinto case.

In this book we find out that the FBI had sent Kennedy west because his ex-wife had been active in the American Civil Liberties Union; she had then left Kennedy to marry a real estate broker. When Kennedy and Leaphorn were talking about wanting to trace their ancestors, Kennedy said he used to want to go back to Ireland where his great-great-grandfather had come from, but he had outgrown the idea.

Kicks-Her-Horse (WY)

In "The Witch, Yazzie, and the Nine of Clubs" the person who sees the Navajo Wolf turn into an owl is Kicks-Her-Horse. In "Chee's Witch," the person who sees the owl is Hosteen Musket.

Kicks His Horse (CW)

Paiute Clan headman in the days of Butch Cassidy, Kicks His Horse told Delbito Willie he should wait until the Season When Thunder Sleeps to go after their livestock, because neither the curing ceremony nor the Enemy Way sing could be performed until then. The men of Kicks His Horse's clan didn't go with Willie's group because Willie wouldn't wait.

King, Ed (TT)

Substitute pilot for the air ambulance service in Farmington, he agreed to fly the helicopter for Chee on short notice, even in less than good weather. He was a "burly, bald-headed man with a great yellow mustache."

Kinlicheenie, Fannie (PD)

Woody Begay's sister, married in 1953, Fannie lived north of the Borrego Pass chapter house. She tied her hair in a bun and wore a heavy silver squash-blossom necklace and a wide silver and turquoise bracelet; she was wearing several layers of clothing. She told Chee she had been a water carrier in the Peyote Church and that Dillon Charley was a witch and had given her brother corpse sickness.

Kirby, Nelson (PD)

Forty-year-old crew chief on the oil rig in 1948, he was killed in the explosion.

Kiva societies (DF)

Zuñi. Kiva societies represent the kachina society. All young males are introduced into one of six kiva groups; usually the kiva group the boy enters is chosen by his parents. There is one kiva group per sacred direction and each group has a chief who belongs to the Antelope clan, a speaker who belongs to the Badger clan, and two Bow Priests. Meetings are held in rectangular rooms aboveground. During his first initiation a boy between the ages of five and nine is whipped by the kachinas to purify him and signify the boy has been put in the care of the kachinas. At a second initiation, between the ages of ten and twelve, the boy is whipped a second time and taught the secrets of the kachina society.

Klah, Hosteen (SW)

Frank Sam Nakai referred to Hosteen Klee as Hosteen Klah. Nakai told Chee that all famous Singers like Klee had started when they were young. See also **Klee, Hosteen,** and **Horse Kicker.**

Klee, Hosteen (Hosteen Klee-Thlumie, Horse Kicker) (LW)

Klee was Joe Leaphorn's maternal grandfather. John McGinnis had known him well when Klee was learning to be a Singer, and Klee and McGinnis had helped each other at various times. See also **Horse Kicker** and **Klah, Hosteen.**

Knoll, Marty (FW)

Knoll worked in the Park Board Information Office. He confirmed that he had given McDaniels the hearing files on the Wit's End State Park resort concessions.

Korolenko, Catherine (FW)

Joe's wife had acted as his hostess. She stayed away from politics as much as possible; she didn't understand it. When she found out her husband would lose the election because she had mentioned Joe's Communist Party relatives in Yugoslavia to Clark's wife, she was devastated. She was never the same after that—she didn't want to live. She eventually died of pneumonia.

Korolenko, Joseph (Joe) (FW)

Former governor, ex-Congressman, and now National Committeeman, Korolenko was a close friend of Roark and was depressed about Gavin's death; he and Gavin had been friends for over forty years. Korolenko was in his seventies, with frail hands and dark brown eyes behind a film of age; part of the lobe of his left ear was missing. He did not look well, and there were rumors he had an incurable disease. Korolenko had been a widower for five or six years; he had been deeply in love with Catherine. He blamed Clark for Catherine's depression and death.

Korolenko also hated Clark because Clark had no political principles, and he thought Roark could beat Clark in the primary race. He told Cotton he would kill him if it would prevent Clark from getting reelected to the Senate. Korolenko had run for the Senate when he was fifty-four, during the Joe McCarthy days. Clark had spread the rumor that Korolenko had cousins who were officials in the Communist Party in Yugoslavia, and Korolenko had lost the election.

Koshare (SC)

According to Hillerman's account in *Sacred Clowns*, koshares are the sacred clowns of the Pueblo people. Men who live outside of the pueblo frequently do not have time to be members of kachina societies, so many become koshares. The four koshares of the Tano wore breechcloths and had black-and-white zebra-striped bodies and white faces with huge black smiles. Their hair jutted upward into two long conical horns, surmounted with corn shucks.

The koshares do everything wrong while the kachinas do everything right. Their role is to show how far human beings are from perfection. One example is when a koshare grabbed a kachina, to make fun of how humans try to possess everything. Another is the clown skit that portrayed the Tano people's willingness to sell their tribal treasures.

The koshares follow tradition. They don't normally get involved in politics and don't get personally insulting. This was why the incident with the Lincoln cane was so unusual.

Koyemshi (DF)

Zuñi. These impersonators of the Mudhead Clowns precede the Shalako figures into town during the Shalako festival in late November or early December. At the New Year celebration in the winter, the priests appoint a leader of the clowns, Father Koyemshi, who appoints nine other clowns. These men form a cult group that serves for four years, entertaining the people between the rain dances with their comic performances. The Koyemshi are dangerous, however—whoever touches one of them will become crazy. The clowns represent the trickster in mythology.

In their Emergence Myth, at the second place the people stopped on their migration, the son and daughter of a Rain Chief had incestuous relations with each other and were changed into clowns (Mudheads). The Mudheads then formed two mountains with a river in between, which the people had to cross.

Kreutzer, Mrs. (BW)

Secretary in the anthropology department at the University of New Mexico, she was an older lady who wore bifocals and worried about people, many times giving them unsolicited and unwanted advice.

Landon (SW)

When Chee visited Mary's home in May, her father had been painfully polite. Mr. Landon had asked endless questions about the Navajo religion and looked at Chee as if he were a man from another planet.

Landon, Mary (PD) (GW) (SW) (TG) (CW)

In *People of Darkness*, Mary was a young teacher at Crownpoint Elementary School who taught fifth-grade English and social studies. She was a small woman with an oval face, soft blond hair, and large blue eyes. She was new to Crownpoint but had taught the past spring at Laguna Pueblo School.

Mary had graduated from the University of Wisconsin. Her home was near Milwaukee, where her father ran a sporting goods store; she knew how to shoot a pistol and a .30-.30 rifle. Chee met her at the rug auction at the Crownpoint school, when he was looking for Tomas Charley; when Chee drove out on the reservation to find Vines's keepsake box, Mary went along and then brought help when Chee collapsed from a gunshot wound. She liked Chee very much.

In *The Ghostway*, Mary was in love with Jim Chee, but they had to work out a lot of problems before they could get married. Mary was disappointed that Chee hadn't accepted the FBI job yet; she told Chee she had thought he was an assimilated man intellectually, yet he was more interested in being a Navajo than in marrying her. She reminded him that a Navajo male joins his wife's family.

Even though she had worked several years in Native American schools, Mary still had stereotypical images of Indians; she didn't think the education in those schools would be good enough for her children. She decided she wouldn't marry Chee if it meant he would be unhappy because he couldn't be a *yataalii*; she didn't know if she could become part of his world and she was going home to Wisconsin to think about it for a while.

In *Skinwalkers*, Mary had taken a leave from her teaching job at Crownpoint. Although she had promised to come back, she told Chee in a letter that she was going back to school in Wisconsin to get her master's degree. She wanted him to come visit her in the fall because she wouldn't be able to visit him in New Mexico until Thanksgiving break; she was living in Stevens Point. Chee noticed she had changed her greeting from "Darling" to "Dearest Jim"; Chee decided to send her the pregnant *beligaana* cat so it would survive.

In *Talking God*, Chee and Mary write frequently to each other. Chee had intended to visit her again in Wisconsin; her letter told him not to come because nothing had changed and the visit would just make both of them miserable. Chee remembered he had decided to marry her the final night of an Enemy Way they had attended. Mary called Chee in Washington and wanted to see him, to talk to him in person, because she felt she shouldn't have told him in a letter. She didn't make the trip to Washington, because they both decided it was hopeless.

In *Coyote Waits*, Chee was mourning the loss of Mary Landon but becoming more interested in Janet Pete.

Langer, Fritz (SW)

Officer on the jail information desk at Farmington, he was asked by Chee to stall in getting Roosevelt Bistie checked out to his lawyer until Chee could get there. Chee wanted to question Bistie before he left, so Langer agreed to try. Langer enjoyed watching Chee getting chewed out by Janet Pete; it wasn't so funny when Janet Pete sailed into Langer for being so slow releasing Bistie and for being part of the old boys' network.

Largewhiskers, Ethelmary (SW)

Dr. Jenks remembered that Ethelmary's name was on Irma Onesalt's list of dead people, for whom she wanted dates of death.

Largo, Howard (or A. D.)
(LW) (PD) (DW) (GW) (SW) (TT) (TG) (CW) (SC)

   Listening Woman referred to Captain Howard
Largo as a Navajo Tribal Policeman whose office is in
Tuba City; he wears horned-rimmed bifocals and
smokes cigarettes. Largo and Leaphorn were both
born to the Slow Talking Dinee, so they readily did
favors for each other. Leaphorn wanted Largo to
request his help in Tuba City so he could find the man
with the gold-rimmed glasses who had tried to run
him down with the gray Mercedes. Largo wanted his
own men to hunt the driver but honored the request
because he owed Leaphorn some favors.

   In *People of Darkness* and *The Dark Wind*,
Largo is stationed at Tuba City and is Chee's superior. In *The Dark Wind*, Chee and Largo are distant
kinsmen, related through the secondary Red
Forehead Clan of Chee's father. Largo was born to
the Standing Rock Dinee and born for the Red
Forehead Clan. He is a short plump man, with a
barrel chest, narrow hips, and a round face with
crooked white teeth. He tells Chee to write and
sign a report about his mistreatment by agents
Johnson and Collins, then take a week off and get
away from the area; he is afraid Chee won't be
treated fairly by the whites and doesn't want Chee
interfering in federal jurisdiction.

   In *The Ghostway*, Largo has been Chee's
superior for two years, first at Tuba City and then
at Shiprock. Largo has black eyes and the top-
heavy wedge shape common to western Navajos.
He holds Monday morning meetings, and Chee has
come to expect Largo to say strange things. He tells
Chee to find Leroy Gorman and call back so they
can report to the FBI; he emphasizes it is not a case
for the Navajo Tribal Police or Jim Chee. Largo also
tells Chee to find Margaret Sosi but to be careful
because the FBI is so touchy about this case. It

makes Largo angry when Agent Sharkey denies knowing anything about Leroy Gorman.

In *Skinwalkers*, Largo is referred to as Captain A. D. Largo, the commanding officer at the Shiprock subagency. Largo reports to Leaphorn that someone has used a shotgun on Chee's trailer, trying to kill him. Largo doesn't want Chee pulled off his regular work to work on FBI cases, but he goes along because he doesn't want Chee killed. He sends Chee out to work around the Utah part of the reservation.

In *A Thief of Time*, Captain Largo wants Chee to hang around the motor pool during his shift and have it recorded that he'd been there, so the motor pool couldn't blame their losses on a lack of security by the police department. When a backhoe was stolen while Chee was on duty, Largo was *not* pleased.

In *Talking God*, Largo tells Chee he wants him to go to the Yeibichai for Agnes Tsosie and arrest Henry Highhawk; he thinks it is ironic that Highhawk wants to become a Navajo yet is to be arrested for desecrating graves. He tells Chee not to try to figure out why the feds do what they do; he was paid to do what Largo told him to do. In *Coyote Waits*, Largo is still Chee's superior at Shiprock, a neat, large, bulky man with a round dark face. He investigates Huan Ji's death. In *Sacred Clowns* Leaphorn remembers that Largo used to complain about the difficulty he had getting Chee to follow regulations.

Leaphorn, Emma (SW) (TT) (TG) (CW) (SC)

In *Skinwalkers*, Joe and Emma Leaphorn had been happily married for almost thirty years; they met while students on the campus of Arizona State University. Emma followed the Navajo Way. She could not be happy away from the Sacred

Mountains, and Joe could not be happy away from Emma.

Emma was ill. Joe was certain she had Alzheimer's disease; she had all the symptoms. He was afraid he was going to have to watch her slowly die. Emma had severe headaches and nightmares and was extremely forgetful; at times she didn't recognize Joe. She had lost weight because she would forget to eat. Joe asked her sister Agnes to stay with her while he worked. Emma was afraid to go to a *belagaana* doctor, and Joe finally had to force her to see a neurologist at the Indian Health Service hospital at Gallup. After running tests they told Joe that Emma had a brain tumor, and there was a chance they could remove it and Emma would recover.

In *A Thief of Time*, Joe thought about their lives together. Emma was nineteen when Joe met her; she had a unique and remarkable beauty. When Joe was attending the FBI Academy he had taken Emma to New York City, and they had visited the Museum of Modern Art and discovered Picasso's goat. Emma had thought it was a perfect mascot for the Dineh: starved, gaunt, bony, and ugly but a tough and defiant survivor. Emma had disliked bats and admired lizards, had battled roaches endlessly, and had given names to the spiders around and in their house. She had been a neat housekeeper and hadn't liked dirty windows. She didn't like Joe to eat sausage and eggs, and he had done it only when she was away visiting her kinfolks. She used to make sauerbraten occasionally, but Joe didn't care for it.

Emma had been practical and had common sense; Joe missed bouncing his problems off her. It had helped him and it had been fun. He and Emma had talked about taking a boat excursion down into the deep canyons of the San Juan River someday but had never done it. Joe wondered what he would do without Emma.

She had died from a blood clot; there was too much infection and strain after the operation for the brain tumor. Her brothers and family buried Emma in the traditional way. After cleansing and dressing her, they took her to a high spot in the cliffs where the predators couldn't reach her and came home and took sweat baths. Four days of silent mourning followed; Joe couldn't stand it and had to leave after two days.

In *Talking God*, Joe remembered Emma sitting in her brown chair making baby clothes; it was a little over a year since she died.

In *Coyote Waits*, Joe remembered that Emma, a small, lovely woman, had been an amateur bird watcher and had kept three feeders stocked in their backyard. Emma hadn't been a traveler, so Joe had given up on his desire to hunt his origins in the Far East. Every day Joe looked at the enlarged map of Indian Country hung behind his desk in his office; Emma had fastened it to a piece of corkboard for him.

In *Sacred Clowns*, Emma had been dead one year, eight months, and eleven days. Joe and the nurse had both been sleeping when Emma died in her sleep. When he looked at Louisa's graying hair he remembered that Emma's hair had remained glossy black to the end. He could never think of Emma as a malevolent ghost no matter what Navajo tradition taught. Louisa Bourebonette's problem with bifocals reminded him how Emma had always balked at getting her eyes examined. When he was packing for his trip to Asia he pulled out a pair of pajamas that Emma had bought him. She'd kept him supplied with pajamas ever since the first pair she had given him for his birthday two weeks after their wedding. Joe had always worn pajamas, in deference to Emma's modesty.

CHARACTERS IN TONY HILLERMAN'S FICTION

Leaphorn, Joseph (Joe)
(BW) (DD) (LW) (PD) (SW) (TT) (TG) (CW) (SC)

Leaphorn is said to be a member of the Slow Talking People in (DD), (LW), and (CW); in (TT) and (TG), however, his mother's clan was identified as Red Forehead. He was raised in a traditional manner by his mother, Anna Gorman, and his father near Two Gray Hills (LW, SW) among the sheepmen and hunters of Beautiful Mesa (DD). The women of his clan were proud and known for retaining their own last names even after they married. His other relatives include cousins and nephews (BW, LW, SW, CW); Haskie Jim, a paternal uncle (CW); two uncles who are Singers (LW); his maternal grandmother, a famous Hand Trembler (LW) who told him about Navajo superstitions (SW); and two maternal grandfathers, Nashibitti and Klee-Thlumie.

Hosteen Nashibitti, a great Singer, was seventy years old when Leaphorn knew him (DD). He told Leaphorn the stories of the People; he also taught him the Navajo Way, beauty through the complex harmony of nature, and lessons of interdependency, cause and effect, reason, and pattern (DD). Hosteen Klee-Thlumie ("Horse Kicker") was also a Singer (LW, SW). Leaphorn is rumored to be a descendent of the famous Chee Dodge, who tried to rid the Navajo people of skinwalker beliefs instilled at Fort Sumner.

For almost thirty years he was married to Emma, a member of a traditional Bitter Water family, the Yazzies. In *Skinwalkers* he is certain that Emma has Alzheimer's disease and is almost relieved when neurologists discover she has an operable brain tumor. Leaphorn loved Emma dearly. He is devastated by her sudden death, as revealed at the beginning of *A Thief of Time*; the doctors had predicted a 90 percent chance of recovery. By the time of Emma's death, the Red

Forehead Clan is nearly extinct, and few relatives attend his Blessing Way ceremonial (TG).

Leaphorn had attended the Kayenta Boarding School (LW); he didn't like school as a boy, and bitter feelings remained from a sign in the hall of his BIA high school that read TRADITION IS THE ENEMY OF PROGRESS (DD). At Arizona State University he focused on cultural anthropology and had twelve credit hours of Spanish; nonetheless, his Spanish as an adult was of the Gallup-Flagstaff wetback variety, and he couldn't make himself understood to a Chilean (TG). During his freshman year in college he had a Zuñi roommate, Rounder, who made him feel inferior. He went with Rounder to a Shalako ceremonial and with Tom Bob and Blackie Bisti to a meeting of the Native American Church, where he sampled peyote (DD). As a junior he ran around, drank, and chased girls (CW). He completed B.A. and M.S. degrees and had begun a Ph.D. graduate fellowship when he met nineteen-year-old Emma (TT); he left college then and joined the Navajo Tribal Police. Emma became his real tie to the Navajo people (SW).

In all the books in which he appears, with the exception of *People of Darkness*, Leaphorn is a lieutenant in the Navajo Tribal Police Law and Order Division and is stationed at Window Rock; in *People of Darkness* he is Captain Leaphorn and calls Jim Chee from the Chinle substation. Leaphorn's office is on the second floor of the Navajo Tribal Police building (TG) with a window overlooking Window Rock Ridge (CW) and the tribal barns on Navajo Route 3. His office is neat and tidy, the desk is clear, and there is no sign of dust. He figures the contents of a police station should be safe, so the door to his office is always open (SC).

When he was a newlywed, Leaphorn worked out of Crownpoint (TT) and, as a young patrolman,

Tuba City (LW, SW). He had worked out of Kayenta at least twenty years ago (TT, CW) and had also worked out of Many Farms (SW); early in his career he had been in charge of the Shiprock subagency (BW). He joined the recruit class of the Navajo Tribal Police soon after meeting Emma (TT), but at some point as a young man he had also attended the FBI Academy (SW, TT, TG). After more than two decades of police work he is something of a legend among the 120 members of the Navajo Tribal Police (SW). After Emma's death, word spreads throughout the department (now 400 in number) that he has had a nervous breakdown and has decided to retire (TT); he suspects there are some people who will be happy to see him go (CW). He is on a thirty-day terminal leave at the beginning of *A Thief of Time*. In *Sacred Clowns* he is running the Special Investigations Office, getting ready to take that long-awaited trip to Asia with Professor Bourebonette.

Mounted on the wall behind Leaphorn's desk is an enlarged map of the reservation, an Indian Country map from the Southern California Automobile Club. On it he has 100 colored pins and notes marking the crimes and complaints he has investigated. Scarlet, red, and pink pins denote alcohol-related crimes; blue pins show cattle thefts; black ones are for witchcraft complaints; brown pins with white centers stand for homicides and violent deaths (SW). Yellow pins mark oddities (CW). Largo says that Leaphorn uses the pins in his map to work out mathematical solutions to crimes. Leaphorn isn't sure how it works, other than help him think (SC). He eventually has a twenty-five-year accumulation of pins on his map (CW); the map itself is seen as a symbol of his eccentricity (SW).

Leaphorn is not inclined to tell Jim Chee any more than he has to know because he doesn't quite trust Chee; he recognizes him from his photo and knows everything about him from his personnel file before they first meet (GW). He thinks Chee's notion of becoming a Singer is totally impractical and that Chee is a dreamer to think he can live the old way in a white man's world; he tries not to show he is impressed by Chee's police work in *A Thief of Time*. He thinks Chee is an unusually bright young man but also an individualist and a romantic. He is not sure whether Chee is reliable and blames him for the death of Delbert Nez because Chee didn't follow standard police procedures. Ultimately he concedes that Chee is brave and creative and thinks he might work out well in his own area, criminal investigation (CW).

In *Sacred Clowns*, Chee has become Leaphorn's assistant in the Special Investigations Office. Leaphorn realizes he has become accustomed to working alone and needs to establish some policies between himself and Chee so they will function better. When Chee neglects to leave a note for Leaphorn about the audiocassette he found on his desk, Leaphorn is accused of illegal wiretapping and is suspended for ten days while Captain Dodge runs an investigation of the allegations. Councilman Chester wants Leaphorn dismissed from the department. Leaphorn is forced to remain in the area, thus canceling his trip to Asia. In the meantime Chee has been out of touch with the office on a trip with his uncle to discover Janet Pete's clan relationships. When he returns he admits leaving the audiotape cassette in Leaphorn's tape player, and the charges against Leaphorn are dropped.

Leaphorn dislikes FBI agents most of the time. In *Dance Hall of the Dead*, John O'Malley refuses to share information with him, interrupts him, and doesn't want him to interfere with FBI "experts"; neither man respects the other. Leaphorn thinks FBI men are incompetent and have their own solution in mind; they don't care what really happened on various cases. Though his attitude seems to mellow through contact and even friendship with agents Jim Feeney (LW), Dilly Streib (SW, SC), and Jay Kennedy (SW, TG, CW), Leaphorn remains convinced that the agency's prime directives are to employ clean-cut, conventional agents and assure good publicity. When he attended the FBI Academy, all the other agents had blue eyes; he and his black friend P. J. Rodney were the country-cousin outsiders (TG).

At the beginning of the series he is forty years old (BW). He has a "Checkerboard-type body," a Navajo/Pueblo mix typical of the eastern reservation (SW): taller than most Zuñis, and with heavy shoulders. His hair is cut in the style of the white men (BW), and he is lanky and raw-boned, with a square Navajo face, Roman nose, and dark brown (or black) patient eyes (DD, TG). As he reaches middle age he feels he is getting old; his back hurts when he sits too long, and Emma is pressing him to take off some pounds and inches (SW). He feels guilty in *A Thief of Time* for violating his diet by fixing himself a breakfast of sausage and eggs. He has an inner ear problem that makes it difficult for him to fly in anything but big jets, and small planes make him sick (TT).

Although he loses weight after Emma dies, he still gets out of breath following Chee, and his knees hurt when he squats; his hair is gray (TG) and short-cropped (CW), and he puts on glasses to examine a photograph (CW) or read (SC). He almost always wears his khaki NTP uniform and is rather embarrassed by the looks it receives in New York City (TT). When he goes to Washington, he wears the DC uniform: a three-piece suit (mid-1970s vintage Sears), and black, shiny wing-tip shoes that look as though they hurt his feet (TG).

For twenty years he had worn a comfortable pair of Justin boots that Emma bought for him (CW). In *Sacred Clowns* he comments on the accuracy of his $13.99 Casio digital watch, and he drives a GMC Jimmy.

Leaphorn has a fierce pride in the Navajo people, but he is irritated by their close-mouthed ways and their superstitions, especially the widespread belief they have in witches. As a sophomore in college he overcame his belief in witches and ghosts; he believes that people choose the evil way. He dislikes illogic and detests it in himself; he is curious, skeptical of coincidences, methodical, patient, and precise. He is a good listener (DD), rarely argues, and has an excellent memory (LW); he tells people only what he wants them to know (TG). John McGinnis says he got right to the point, which is rare in a Navajo (CW); Jim Chee says he is never quite satisfied with anything, and Leaphorn admits he has the non-Navajo habit of doing things to save time (TG). Emma fussed with him about being a cynic (CW).

Other religions interest him. While he was in college he had studied the religion of the Kiowa, in a graduate seminar on Native American Religions, and had attended a Catholic mass and thought about it for weeks (LW). He wished he knew more about the Zuñi religion and found the Native American Church boring (DD); he respected their First Amendment rights, however, and was glad when the federal court overthrew the law against ceremonial peyote use (SW). Christian fundamentalism doesn't appeal to him, but he finds its methods of persuasion intriguing (TT).

Some people think Leaphorn is hard to get along with: Janet Pete calls him "Grouchy Joe" (TG); Jim Chee is defensive and rather intimidated by him (TT); and Captain Largo thinks he is too hard on Jim Chee (CW). Leaphorn enjoys making Officer Gorman nervous (SW) but is unfailingly polite to elderly people (e.g., Sandoval in BW) and the downtrodden (Susanne in DD) and is compassionate toward the insane (Brigham Houk in (TT). In *Sacred Clowns* he is at first annoyed because Janet Pete is defending Eugene Ahkeah and she is Chee's girlfriend. He later decides he likes Janet Pete because of the way she works for her clients and surprises her by agreeing to obtain the release of Eugene Ahkeah.

Leaphorn was once addicted to cigarettes (two packs a day of Pall Malls, then three packs of filtered cigarettes), but he stopped as an offering to Emma early in her terminal illness. Smoking was replaced by a coffee addiction, four cups before noon and decaf after (CW); he even drinks bad instant coffee at home (TG). He drank beer in college (BW, DD, CW) but not afterward; he detests whiskey and hates bootleggers (SW). He says if he could have just one wish it would be to get rid of booze (SC). He swears "with feeling and eloquence" in Navajo (DD) and in Spanish, then in English, because Navajo is too precise (BW). He tries to break habits associated with Emma and thinks he should sell their house or burn it down after she dies (TT). He watches TV (CW), sometimes just as background noise (TT), and realizes he has started talking to himself. He takes a vacation only because he doesn't want his friends and the people at work to pity him; he has no desire to go anywhere without Emma (TG).

In *Coyote Waits* he meets Louisa Bourebonette when she accompanies Mary Keeyani to his office to ask his help for Ashie Pinto. After considerable doubt about her motives and personality, he finds he enjoys their conversation and likes to show off for her. He decides he would like her to go to China with him to explore his Athabascan roots (CW). In *Sacred Clowns*, he and Louisa are making the final preparations for their trip. He thinks Louisa is a lovely lady and surprises himself by asking her opinion on the Dorsey and Sayesva murder cases. When he has to leave a message for Louisa telling her he has been suspended and can't go with her to China, he realizes he will miss her and maybe he loves her.

Leaphorn's mother (SW)
    See **Gorman, Anna.**

Lebeck, Carl (PD)
    The geologist who was logging the well the day the oil rig exploded in 1948, he was presumed to have died in the explosion. His age was unknown. Mary Landon's sister had dated someone with the same or a similar name.

Left-Handed (CW)
    According to Ashie Pinto's story, Left-Handed was a Navajo who lived during the time of Butch Cassidy. He was a Paiute Clan man; when he was working in his fields, the Utes shot at him and he ran away. He had a son, Delbito Willie.

Lehman, Professor (TT)
    A professor at the University of New Mexico, he had written books on Mimbres, Hohokam, and Anasazi pottery evolution. He was the top guru in the ceramics field and had been chairman of Ellie Friedman-Bernal's doctoral dissertation committee. He was big, ugly, smart, gray, and sexy. He was to meet Ellie at the Chaco ruins; she intended to impress him with what she had found. He was her project supervisor, and Ellie felt she needed his approval before going to publication. He was angry when he arrived and Ellie wasn't there.

Leon, Ellen (BW)

Bergen McKee first described Ellen, daughter of a friend of Jeremy Canfield and fiancée of Jim Hall, as "five feet five, slim, with long blackish hair"; later he noticed she had short dark hair, dark blue eyes, and a slender smooth neck and weighed about 110 pounds. She drove a baby-blue Volkswagen.

Ellen's father was a pharmacist, and he and his family lived on a shaded street in a Philadelphia suburb. Ellen had met Jim Hall at Pennsylvania State University on the first day of a Shakespeare Tragedies class. They had been engaged for some time when Ellen decided to locate Jim and tell him he had to choose between her and his pursuit of a million dollars.

Leonard, Jay (GW)

Jay Leonard was a big TV talk-show host in Los Angeles; he lived in Beverly Hills and enjoyed alcoholic drinks and cocaine. He owed $120,000 plus interest, but had told the Man to take him to court because he wasn't going to pay. Leonard had a rent-a-cop staying with him, a new burglar alarm system, and two nonbarking Doberman guard dogs. Eric Vaggan was able to get past the security systems and stapled cattle tags in Leonard's ears.

Lerner (Plaid Coat) (GW)

Lerner was a longtime hood who was a collection man for George McNair. He had worked in extortion for the longshoremen, had been a bodyguard for somebody in Vegas, and then worked for McNair; he had a long rap sheet. When he came into Shiprock he was driving a new Ford sedan he had rented at the Farmington airport. He found Albert Gorman in front of the Shiprock laundromat and told him he hadn't done what he

THE TONY HILLERMAN COMPANION

had been told to do, so Albert had to go back with him. Albert pulled out a gun, they exchanged shots, and Lerner was killed. (In *Talking God* there is also a character named Plaid Coat.)

Liebling, A. J. (FW)

Kendall said that he once stole an outrageous simile from Liebling, which he got past the front desk and had published.

Limerick, Patricia (CW)

A Western history expert from the University of Colorado, she disputed Frederick Jackson Turner's theory of land ownership.

Linington, A. J. (FW)

One of the attorneys in the civil case McDaniels had checked, Linington had represented the Amalgamated Haulers and Handlers Union, which had been sued by a construction company in some sort of labor dispute. He owned a small law firm in the Exchange Building and was the agent of record for both Midcentral Surety and Wit's End, subsidiaries of Highlands Corporation, which also owned Reevis-Smith.

Listening Woman (LW)

Margaret Cigaret was also known as Blind Eyes and Listening Woman.

Little Boy (Brother, Father of His People) (DF)

Zuñi. When the Corn Maidens came into town disguised as old women, the little boy and his sister offered them some of their corn cake; the Corn Maidens remembered their kindness. During the drought, after the people had left the two children behind, the boy managed to catch birds and roast them for his sister; he didn't go near the Old

Woman's house because he thought perhaps she had left with the others, and besides, she might have been a sorceress.

When he couldn't stand his sister's crying anymore, he offered to get her anything she wanted; she wanted a butterfly. He knew he couldn't find a butterfly during the winter so he made her a Cornstalk Insect in a little cage. When the creature came to life and begged to be released, promising it would return, the boy was kind and let it out of the cage. When the insect returned with corn for them, he and his sister feasted happily on it.

From the Cornstalk Insect the boy learned how to make prayer plumes. He prayed to the Council of the Gods, and the gods were pleased and sent runners who brought food for the children and planted their fields with seed. When Old Uncle brought the people home from the land of the Hopi, the little boy was recognized as the Father of His People. He chose three from among the strangers who returned to the village to be his counselors, and he chose a great warrior and placed him under Old Uncle; the warrior and Old Uncle were to supervise the harvest. When the boy became an adult he married the most beautiful maiden in the village, and they had beautiful daughters.

Little Shirley (TG)

Little Shirley, a relative of Jim Chee, sat with Cousin Emmett and Chee when they were children, listening to the stories of Frank Sam Nakai.

Little Sister (Mother of Seed, Seed Priestess of Earth) (DF)

Zuñi. The boy and his little sister had worked hard all night, preparing for the journey to the land of the Hopi; they lay down in a corner and slept and were forgotten by the people in their rush to leave.

When Little Sister awakened she wanted her mother and wanted some parched corn to eat. Her brother caught wild birds and cooked them for her, but Little Sister became sadder and sadder, wishing for her usual diet of corn dishes. Her brother promised her anything she wanted if she would stop crying; she asked him to find her a butterfly. Since the boy couldn't get a butterfly in the middle of the winter, he made a Cornstalk Insect for her and hung it in a little cage; she laughed when she saw it and called it "Being-which-flies-on-double-wings." All day long she talked to it and made it swing in its cage. At night when she became hungry she told it to fly away and find some yellow corn for her brother to parch for her breakfast. Little did she know that it would come to life and help them. When the people came back, her brother made her the Mother of Seed. Later she became Seed Priestess of the Earth, provider of fertility.

Littleben, Leo Junior (GW)

Littleben, a *yataalii* who knew the Ghostway, the Blessing Way, and the Mountaintop Way, was not a young man, but he was the younger of the only two *yataaliis* who knew the Ghostway. Unless Chee became a *yataalii*, Littleben would be the last person alive to know it. Littleben was short and fat and limped when he walked, because of a stiff leg; he had two black pigtails, a mustache almost gray, and deep-cut lines on his face. He lived at Two Story, near Window Rock, and he was listed in the Navajo-Hopi phone book. When Chee called him, he was performing a Ghostway sing on the Cañoncito reservation, practically in Albuquerque. It was a five-day Ghostway, and he had been hired by Margaret Sosi.

Lomatewa, Albert (DW)

Hopi. Lomatewa was seventy-three years old, a

smoker, and had nine grandchildren and one great-grandchild. He was disappointed to see his grand-children living in the city acting like white people.

His ceremonial role was the Messenger. He was on a pilgrimage to find spruce for the Niman Kachina ceremony and was accompanied by his two guards, Eddie Tuvi and the Flute Clan Boy, when they found the body of the Navajo man beside the path. He had never seen this particular Navajo before; the soles of his hands and feet were flayed as if by a Navajo witch. He took care to instruct the Flute Clan Boy not to report the body so it wouldn't ruin the ceremony, which was to take place at Third Mesa.

Lone Rangers (TG)

A liberal/intellectual covey had flocked into the Navajo Mountain territory and declared them-selves spokesmen and guardians for Navajo fami-lies facing eviction from the old Joint Use Reservation. They were a nuisance.

Long Thinker (GW)

Jim Chee's uncle, Hosteen Frank Sam Nakai, gave him this secret war name.

Lord Ben (DD)

Lord Ben was another member of the Jason's Fleece commune.

Lowden (or Logan) (FW)

This fat, frightened Carter County sheriff had been exposed fifteen years ago for falsifying prison meal records and was removed from office, indicted, and destroyed. It was Cotton's first (and hardest) exposé.

Ludlow, Sheriff Lester (CW)

Chee read in the early 1900s Blanding newspaper that Sheriff Ludlow was confident that the posse would catch Butch Cassidy and the remaining bandit after a Mormon reported seeing them at Montezuma Creek.

Lum, Nagani (BW)

Lum, an old man who came in a wagon to Shoemaker's Trading Post, seemed to know about Luis Horseman and told Bergen McKee about a witching case that probably involved Billy Nez.

Luna, Allen (TT)

Son of Bob Luna and his wife, Allen was around eleven, blond-haired and freckled like his mother. He was interested so much in the adult conversation that he laid down his fork during the meal to listen. When his father asked him if he had done his homework, he said he had finished it on the bus; his father asked him to find something to do, so he politely excused himself from the table.

Luna, Bob (TT)

U.S. Park Service Superintendent at the Chaco Culture National Historical Park, he was medium-sized with a round, good-humored face, and lines around his eyes and the corners of his mouth. Leaphorn thought he looked surprisingly young to be the superintendent of such an important park. He lived with his wife, son, and daughter and knew Ellie Friedman-Bernal quite well; she had been gone for two weeks, and he had called the sheriff of San Juan County in Farmington to report her missing.

Luna, Mrs. Bob (TT)

A "handsome woman with a friendly, intelligent face," blond hair, and freckles, she was polite but full of questions about Ellie Friedman-Bernal. Ellie had picked up the Lunas' mail and shopping list to take into Farmington the day she disappeared. She said their community was so small that everyone knew everything about one another, but maybe Ellie had a man they didn't know about.

Luna, Sue (TT)
Daughter of Bob Luna and his wife, she was nine or ten years old and denied she had any homework; she didn't want to miss the adults' conversation after dinner. Her father sent her to take care of her horse. She and her brother, Allen, had an eighty-mile round-trip bus ride to school every day. They had talked to Ellie Friedman-Bernal and seen her leave early the day she disappeared.

Lynch, Frederick (LW)
Lynch employed Frank Hoski at the security company, Safety Systems, Inc., in Washington, D.C. The only complaint the police had received about him was that he kept vicious dogs; he trained dogs for security duty. His gray Mercedes was found abandoned alongside a road on the Navajo reservation with a large dog muzzle and the smell of dog urine in the back seat; Lynch and one of his dogs were not found.

Mackensen, R. J. (PD)
Mackensen, a sixty-year-old employee of Petrolab, the company that supplied the nitroglycerin charge for the oil rig, was killed in the explosion in 1948.

Mackinnon, Susy (TG)
Susy was Leaphorn's cabdriver in Washington, D.C. She drove him to a pharmacy, where Leaphorn was able to find out Santillanes's identity and address from a prescription number.

Maddox, Linda Betty (PD)
Colton Wolf's mother used this name when

she was living with a man named Maddox, and she gave the name when she was picked up with Buddy Shaw on a drunk-and-disorderly charge. One day Colton came home from school and found his mother and Shaw gone, along with all their belongings; he was twelve at the time and had searched for her ever since. She was a thin, blue-eyed blond woman; Colton thought if he could find her she'd tell him who his father was and tell him about his family. This character was based on a real person: see **Small, Mama** (FLG); see also **Fry, Linda Betty** and **Shaw, Linda Betty.**

Madman, Alice (DD)

Frank Bob Madman's wife died from a stroke inside their hogan. Frank had a white rancher remove her and bury her and then sealed the hogan properly so her *chindi* wouldn't bother people, but the hogan still belonged to Alice's ghost.

Madman, Frank Bob (DD)

Frank had held the allotment for the land on which the Jason's Fleece commune was grazing its sheep. While Frank was in Gallup buying salt, his wife of many years, Alice, died. After she was buried and the hogan properly sealed, Frank made a deal with Halsey for his allotment, took his wagon and his sheep, and went back to his own people, the Red Forehead Clan.

Madrid-Peña, Hilario (TG)

Santillanes used this false name while traveling from Washington, D.C., to Gallup, New Mexico. His address and telephone number were also phony.

Maestas, Antonio (Tony) (FW)

Tony, the ten-year-old nephew of Cirilio Maestas, was alone when a 600-pound black bear wandered into camp. Tony shot and killed the bear with an old .30-.30 short-barreled carbine.

Maestas, Cirilio (FW)

This old Hispanic sheepherder rode up to Cotton while he was fishing in San Antonio Creek. Maestas had his nephew with him and was very proud of him. He shared his coffee and hand-rolled cigarettes with Cotton in exchange for news of what had been happening recently. Cotton remembered him as the epitome of civility.

Man, the (GW)

The Man didn't want Jay Leonard killed by Eric Vaggan, but he did want some publicity so others would pay him what they owed. He normally paid Vaggan a 15 percent collection fee on bad debts; this time he told Vaggan he'd give him a bonus for good publicity. Vaggan wanted the entire $120,000 that Leonard owed.

Man from the Albuquerque Journal (FLG)

One of the reporters who attended the execution of George Tobias Small at the New Mexico State Penitentiary, he wondered why they had put windows in the death chamber.

Man Who Wore Moccasins (DD)

The footprints of Man Who Wore Moccasins were found in the bloody area where Ernesto Cata had been killed and also at the lake, where Leaphorn and Susanne had gone to hunt for George Bowlegs.

Many Goats, Naomi (LW)

Naomi drove her GMC pickup to Short Mountain Trading Post to pick up supplies. Leaphorn thought Theodora Adams had persuaded Naomi to take her to Hosteen Tso's hogan; Naomi, however, had refused.

Many Mules, Old Lady (CW)

An Enemy Way sing conducted for his much-loved paternal grandmother was one of Jim Chee's earliest memories. She had been happy after the sing but then died of lung cancer or tuberculosis.

Manygoats, Old Lady Daisy (TT)

She was head of a family fervently following the Jesus Road as prescribed by the tenets of Slick Nakai's sect. Her family lived near Coyote Canyon.

Manymules, Old John (SW)

Manymules told John McGinnis he had heard that an old fella got killed at his hogan, and the policeman who was there got shot right in his middle. McGinnis didn't know it was Leaphorn who had been shot.

Marchment, Robin (SC)

The weather forecaster at station KRQE assured everyone that the snowstorm hitting Utah would remain to the north. It was November, and Chee had been listening to the weather forecast before venturing out with Sergeant Blizzard the next day to search for Delmar Kanitewa.

Marcy, L. G. (TT)

Director of Public Affairs at Nelson's, an art auction house in New York City, she was a "slender, stylish woman with gray hair and eyes as blue as blade steel." She looked to be in her mid-thirties, but she was more Leaphorn's age. Leaphorn told her he wanted to see the documentation on a certain Anasazi artifact; the pot had been sold, and Nelson's wouldn't normally divulge the name of the buyer without a court order. After Leaphorn and Ms. Marcy discussed Ellie Friedman-Bernal, her work, and her disappearance, the woman obtained the name of the buyer and gave it to Leaphorn; she wanted Leaphorn to call her when the police found Ellie.

Maria (PD)

Maria was the elderly Pueblo woman who was the maid at the Vineses' home. She was Acoma and spoke the Keresan language; she warned Chee to be careful—in Spanish.

Markham, Theodore F. (LW)

One of the Boy Scouts held hostage by the Buffalo Society, he was thirteen years old, five feet two inches tall, weighed 100 pounds, and had blond hair, blue eyes, and a pale complexion.

Martin (PD)

The young FBI man who visited Chee at the Bernalillo County Medical Center was dressed in a brown suit with vest and had a trim mustache and haircut. Martin wanted to go over the details of Tomas Charley's death and the description of the blond man; he wanted Chee to look at the FBI collection of mug shots.

Martin, Robert M. (FLG)

Robert Martin was a newlywed from Cleveland, Ohio, married for only two days, on his way to California with his new wife on a honeymoon trip. He stopped to help Toby Small with his stalled truck and Small killed him by beating him on the head with a jack handle, because Martin resisted Small's attempts to rob him.

Martin, Mrs. Robert M. (FLG)

Mrs. Martin was the pretty young newlywed killed on the Fourth of July by Toby Small in New Mexico; she and her new husband were on their honeymoon trip from Ohio to California. The police found her in a field forty yards from the highway, beaten to death.

Martinez (CW)

Prospective juror for the Ashie Pinto trial in Albuquerque, Martinez was an elderly Hispanic.

Martinez, Paddy (SC)

Martinez was a Navajo prospector who found a vein of radioactive pitchblende near the Little Haystack Mountain and opened the great Ambrosia Lake uranium mining district.

Matthiessen, Officer (FW)

Unit 17 was ordered to pick up this capital city police officer at the eastern entrance of the federal building.

McDaniels, Merrill (Mac) (FW)

When he entered the pressroom, *Capitol-Press* reporter McDaniels appeared rumpled and drunk; he threw his notebook down on his desk and told Cotton he had been celebrating because he had "a hell of a story," one that would rock the statehouse and make heads roll. He died shortly after leaving the pressroom, when he apparently fell or jumped over the railing of the fourth floor of the statehouse rotunda.

McDaniels had always wanted to be a political writer and win a Pulitzer for breaking a big story; Hall said he was a pro, a good digger. Cotton decided he'd been a highly competent reporter. McDaniels had sat on a story about the highway bonding to protect a bigger story he was working on. McDaniels had confirmed a tip from a letter writer about a $150 million highway bond package and earned favor from the governor's office at the same time. He had known about the highway proposal a week before anyone else did.

McDaniels was fat and wore glasses; he was married and didn't cheat on his wife.

McDermott, John (TG)

Attorney with Dalman, MacArthur, White and Hertzog, this former professor of law at the University of Arizona was "Janet Pete's mentor, faculty advisor, boss, lover, father figure. The man she'd quit her job with the Navajo Tribe to follow to Washington. Ambitious, successful John." Janet Pete didn't believe John wanted her to take Henry Highhawk's case to demonstrate the firm's social consciousness. One of the firm's clients was the Sunbelt Corporation, who wanted to get the right-of-way across a piece of land that belonged to Tano Pueblo; John was the firm's Southwestern expert.

McDonald, Ashie (DW)

McDonald had reportedly beaten up his cousin. When Chee visited their camp, his mother-in-law told Chee that McDonald had gone to Gallup and she didn't know anything about it.

McDonald, Nelson (SW)

When Chee came into the Shiprock police station one night, officer McDonald was sitting in a chair with the two top buttons of his uniform shirt open, reading the sports section of the *Farmington Times*. Chee considered him a friend.

McGaffin, Tom (FW)

McGaffin worked in the Insurance Department Office of the Corporations Commission. He remembered that McDaniels had asked to see the Mid-central Surety files. Midcentral seemed to be writing the performance bonds for six of the state's big high-way builders, including Reevis-Smith.

McGee, Carl (TT)

Member of Utah State Police, Criminal Investigation Division, Detective McGee was a tall man, middle-aged, with a thin bony face and acne scars on his cheeks and forehead; he wore a blue windbreaker and a billed cap. He had the business card on which Harrison Houk had written Leaphorn a message about Ellie Friedman-Bernal; when he questioned Leaphorn, Leaphorn felt he was being treated like a murder suspect.

McGill, Theresa (GW)

Theresa was a friend of Mary Landon. She married a man who had just finished his training to become a priest, and they had a daughter. Theresa realized her husband was unhappy because he could no longer work as a priest.

McGinnis, John (Shorty) (LW) (SW) (CW)

In *Listening Woman*, McGinnis owned the Short Mountain Trading Post; he was a "one-man radar station/listening post/gossip collector." When Leaphorn had been working in that area regularly, he had thought it wouldn't have been very hard to have caught McGinnis doing something illegal enough to have resulted in a ten-year jail sentence. McGinnis had bought the trading post, which was in an extremely isolated area, from a Mormon with two wives in the 1930s. He had quickly realized his error and put up a FOR SALE sign, which had been hanging on the front of the store for forty years. According to local lore, it was the only time McGinnis had ever been out-smarted. McGinnis's asking price was grotesquely high—he didn't really want to leave. He knew all the people and all the news for miles around.

McGinnis was a stumpy, stooped, white-haired old man with a shrunken, lined face and watery, pale old eyes; he didn't fill out the new, oversized blue overalls he wore. He enjoyed drinking Jack Daniels from a Coca-Cola glass, but his doctor had told him he should quit drinking because it was affecting his eardrums.

Hosteen Tso had asked McGinnis to write a letter to his grandson Ben for him, but McGinnis couldn't help him because Tso didn't have any address for Ben; McGinnis was miffed when he found out someone else had written Tso's letter for him. McGinnis told Leaphorn it was strange he hadn't heard any more news about the Tso-Atcitty killings, and for that reason he didn't think the killer was a Navajo; no Navajo (except a witch) would plan a murder. Word about the helicopter being sighted had been passed from a woman herding sheep to a veterinarian to a school bus driver to McGinnis; by the time McGinnis told Tomas Charley about the sighting, nine months had elapsed.

In *Skinwalkers* we learn that the previous owner, a Mormon, had established the trading post because he thought there would be an oil boom in the area; he had sold it to McGinnis and moved to Mexico when his church ruled against polygamy. McGinnis had no family and endured anyway. He wore wire-rimmed bifocals and his usual blue-and-white-striped overalls with a blue work shirt. He had gray stubble on his chin and appeared smaller, his former sturdiness missing. His blue eyes looked faded and his face was not round anymore. He walked with a limp, stooped more, and repeated himself. He still drank his bourbon from a Coca-Cola glass and remembered that Leaphorn didn't drink.

Leaphorn had talked to McGinnis for over twenty years; McGinnis was interested in everything, and Leaphorn considered him sort of a friend. McGinnis didn't recognize Emma's Chevy sedan that Leaphorn was driving. He had heard from Old John Manymules that a policeman had been shot, but hadn't known it was Leaphorn. He had known Wilson Sam since he was a buck and knew all about Wilson Sam's comings and goings. He thought it odd that Sam had received a letter in the middle of the month from the Office of Social Services.

In *Coyote Waits*, John McGinnis is described as a good man, "honorable in his way but notoriously grouchy, pessimistic, perverse, quick with insults and overflowing with windy stories and gossip," a bent, white-haired old man in faded blue overalls, his face deeply lined and creased, drinking coffee he'd reheated all day.

There was a sense of winding down in the store; the stock and the pawn were both down from what they used to be. He appreciated the letter Professor Bourebonette had sent him, thanking him for his help. He knew she and Joe Leaphorn had come to talk to him about Ashie Pinto; he had written a letter for Pinto to Professor Tagert. Pinto had agreed to work for Tagert again.

McKee, Bergen Leroy (Berg) (BW)

Tenured Professor of Anthropology at the University of New Mexico, ex-husband of Sara McKee, and good friend of Jeremy Canfield and Joe and Emma Leaphorn, Bergen was a bulky, big-boned, tired-faced man who looked powerful and clumsy; he enjoyed smoking cigarettes and drinking martinis. He had an apartment on the tenth floor of a building in Albuquerque and drove a pickup truck. He had two crooked fingers on his left hand, both injured while he was playing baseball; Bergen had wanted to be a professional ballplayer but could never learn how to field properly.

Bergen grew up in Nebraska and served in the army in the 1st Cavalry in Korea. He had met Joe Leaphorn when they were both undergraduates at Arizona State University, and they had remained life-long friends. Bergen started his research on Navajos when he was twenty-seven, acquiring fluency in the Navajo language as he studied. He was particularly interested in Navajo Wolves and witchcraft and had written a book, *Social and Psychotherapeutic Utility of Navajo Wolf and Frenzy Superstitions*. His theory was that "the Wolf superstition was a simple scapegoat procedure, giving a primitive people a necessary outlet for blame in times of trouble and frustration." He thought Navajo Wolves were harmless—until he met one armed with a .38 pistol.

McKee, Sara (BW)

Sara was Bergen McKee's ex-wife. She left him a note one day saying she was going to meet Scotty in Las Vegas and wouldn't contest a divorce.

McKibbon, Father (FLG)

A prison chaplain who counseled Toby Small and supported him spiritually until he was executed, Father McKibbon talked to Small every morning, mainly, Small said, about Jesus; he didn't talk about sin and hell as much as the chaplain had at Logan. Small didn't think McKibbon would lie to him and wanted to know how McKibbon could be so sure about what he believed.

McNair, George (GW)

George McNair owned an import-export business, McNair Factoring, on the San Pedro docks. Along with the normal trade he exported stolen cars and imported cocaine. McNair had a heavy rawboned face, pale skin marked with liver spots, green eyes, bristling gray eyebrows, and even white teeth. He and his family lived on an estate in the Flinthills district; in his study there was a map of Scotland on the wall, photos of British royalty, a bagpipe, and a claymore. Because of Kenneth Upchurch he had been indicted on eleven counts by the grand jury, and there were witnesses; McNair said he'd never go to jail. He hired Eric Vaggan to kill Margaret Sosi, then wanted to know how Vaggan was going to do it; he wanted to know what Vaggan's favorite method of killing was.

McRae (PD)

Colton Wolf used the name McRae when he rented a car at the Albuquerque airport; McRae was supposed to be from Indiana.

Mills, Jake (FW)

Mills was a member of the Broadcast Information Network, one of the TV people who used the capitol pressroom but weren't included in its camaraderie.

Milovich, Justin (CW)

An old professor from the University of Utah who worked with Ashie Pinto gathering data about the Navajos, Dr. Milovich was interested in linguistics and spoke Navajo fairly well but hadn't worked with Pinto for a very long time.

Minton, Charles (PD)

Another alias used by Colton Wolf, it was on the driver's license (and credit card) he used to rent a car from Hertz in Albuquerque, with a Dallas P.O. box number.

Mitchell, Frank (SW)

Frank Sam Nakai told Chee that Mitchell, the famous Navajo Singer, had started when he was young.

Monroney, Lieutenant (GW)

Monroney was watch commander at the Kingman police station. Chee described Margaret Sosi to Monroney and asked him to pick her up and keep her safe.

Montoya, Mrs. (SC)

Acting assistant director of Saint Bonaventure Indian Mission, she was clearly a Pueblo Indian, perhaps a Zuñi. She had plump shoulders and plump fingers and said she gossiped too much, that you shouldn't gossip about the dead. Her son Allen was in Eric Dorsey's class and had been making a koshare.

She'd thought a lot about who would have wanted to kill Eric Dorsey and couldn't come up with a suspect. She was sure no woman was involved. She thought Eric had told Father Haines he was gay. She didn't think Eric had a boyfriend, though, because everyone in Thoreau would have known about it.

Montoya, Allen (SC)

Son of the acting assistant director of Saint Bonaventure Indian Mission, Allen was making a koshare in Eric Dorsey's class and was hoping to sell it.

Moon (DF)

Zuñi. The Moon is sometimes referred to as the Moon Mother; she is not the sexual partner of the Sun Father but shares in the cult dedicated to him.

Morgan, Howard (PD) (SW) (TT) (TG) (CW)

Chee watched Morgan, a weather forecaster, on Channel 7, KOAT-TV, in Albuquerque; Chee thought Morgan was often correct in his predictions. In *People of Darkness, A Thief of Time,* and *Talking God* he'd predicted wintry weather.

Morris, Frank (LW)
One of many aliases of **Jimmy Tso**, aka **Frank Hoski**.

Mother Earth (DF)
Zuñi. Mother Earth is the sexual partner of the Sun Father and is associated with fertility. All life was conceived in the deepest fourth womb of Mother Earth.

Mucho, Ganado (LW) (TG)
Standing Medicine stayed behind with Chief Narbona and Ganado Mucho to fight Kit Carson and the army in 1864. In *Talking God*, Henry Highhawk claimed to be the grandson of the granddaughter of Ganado Mucho.
Ganado Mucho was present at the signing of the treaty with the Americans in 1868 and, with Barboncito and Narbona, led the Navajos back to their home in Dinetah. It is said that when they reached the pass between the Sandia and Manzonas mountains on July 4, 1868, they saw Tsoodzil's ragged blue shape and cried for joy.[4]

Mudheads (DF)
Zuñi. Mudheads were members of the brotherhood of clowns, the Koyemshi. Old Uncle had once been a Koyemshi. See **Koyemshi; Old Uncle.**

Musket, Hosteen (WI)
Musket had seen the witch. He had seen a man walk into a grove of cottonwoods, and then an owl flew out. See **Kicks-Her-Horse**.

Musket, Fannie Tsossie (DW)

4. See *Hillerman Country*, text by Tony Hillerman (New York: HarperCollins, 1991), p. 32.

Mother of Joseph Musket and wife of Simon Musket, she and Simon lived on the southern edge of Black Mesa plateau and drove a pickup. She was born to the Standing Rock Clan and born for the Mud Clan. Besides Joseph, she had married daughters. She knew her son didn't steal the pawn from the Burnt Water Trading Post because he had a lot of money when he came home from prison. Fannie told Chee her son was afraid to talk to the police because he had been in prison twice already. She asked him to tell her son to come home if Chee found him.

Musket, Irene (TT)

A handsome middle-aged Navajo woman who kept house and cooked for Harrison Houk, she was born to the Towering House People and born for the Paiute Dineh. She had been a great friend of Houk's wife and had stayed on after Alice died. She mourned the death of Harrison Houk; she said he was good to good people and mean to mean people. She had found Houk's body in the barn when she came to work in the morning and had called the sheriff. She told Leaphorn she had helped Houk get his kayak to the river and had picked him up later in the truck on several occasions. She helped Leaphorn put the kayak in the water and warned him to be careful—but she wasn't referring to the river.

Musket, Joseph (Ironfingers) (DW)

Son of Fannie and Simon Musket, Joseph was in his early thirties, clean-shaven, with a thin mustache, high straight forehead, and a look of intelligence. He had been born near Mexican Water and attended the Teec Nos Pos boarding school. As a boy he had always been good with the sheep, especially shearing and castration. He had been thrown from a horse once and his fingers had been smashed; his fingers had been in metal splints for a long time. He became friends with Thomas West when he attended the high school at Cottonwood; Tom was the only white man Joseph trusted.

His criminal activities started when he was arrested on a drunk-and-disorderly charge when he was eighteen; next he was arrested for grand theft (dismissed), then burglary (suspended sentence), and then another burglary in El Paso, for which he received one to three years in Huntsville. His next escapade was an armed robbery of a 7-Eleven store in Las Cruces with Tom West; he had not been indicted because he was outside the store at the time. The last time he was arrested, he and Tom were found with 800 pounds of marijuana in their pickup, and he was sentenced to three to five years in the New Mexico State Penitentiary. He had no visitors or mail while he was in prison.

When he was paroled from prison he hired a Singer to perform an Enemy Way for him. He had intended to work all summer at the Burnt Water Trading Post, buy his own herd of sheep, and find a young woman to marry whose family had grazing rights. According to Jake West, Joseph disappeared from the Burnt Water Trading Post on July 28 along with the pawn items. (This character is an expanded version of **Taylor Yazzie** in "The Witch, Yazzie, and the Nine of Clubs.")

Musket, Ramona (PD)

Windy Tsossie's sister-in-law, she lived between Thoreau and Crownpoint. Ramona was a "gray-haired, sturdy woman [who] wore a red-and-green mackinaw over the voluminous velveteen blouse and skirt of traditional Navajo womanhood." She had grandchildren and attended the Peyote Church. Chee thought Ramona lied when she told him Tsossie had died of corpse sickness in her sister's hogan and that a white man put him in a hole in a cliff and covered his body with rocks. He realized later she had been using peyote and was nervous.

Musket, Simon (DW)
Simon was the father of Joseph Musket and husband of Fannie Tsossie. He and his sons-in-law herded the sheep.

Mustache, Old Woman (SC)
Old Woman Mustache sat beside Hosteen Barbone outside Gracie Cayodito's hogan. She looked older than Barbone and had a very old but surprisingly clear voice. Chee had heard she was the wise person of the Streams Come Together Clan. After the others had spoken, she said only maternal clans matter in determining kin relationships, an opinion that encouraged Chee's interest in Janet Pete.

Myers, Mrs. (PD)
Chief nurse on the middle shift on the cancer ward at the University of New Mexico Hospital, she had come to know Colton Wolf because he had been calling to check on Emerson Charley's condition over a two-month period and thanking her for her kindness.

Nails, Joe B. (TT)
Nails lived in Aztec and had worked for Wellserve, Inc., until August; he had been arrested once, for driving while intoxicated. Nails rented a truck with dual rear wheels and a power winch from the Farmington U-Haul; Largo's men wanted to bring him in for questioning because they thought he might be the Backhoe Bandit. Chee

found him shot to death inside the cab of the stolen backhoe at a site where he had been digging up Anasazi pots; Nails was thirty-one when he died.

Nakai, Eddie (SC)

A Navajo Tribal Policeman who operated out of Many Farms, Sergeant Nakai had sold Roger Applebee a very old silver pollen flask. Chee had met him.

Nakai, Hosteen Frank Sam
(PD) (DW) (GW) (TT) (CW) (SC)

In *People of Darkness*, Hosteen Frank Sam Nakai is introduced as Chee's uncle, brother of Chee's mother; he had chosen Chee's war name. Nakai is a well-known Singer and sometimes teaches ceremonialism at the Navajo Community College at Rough Rock. He refused to teach Chee to be a Singer until Chee understood the white man's ways, and then Chee could choose either to follow the Navajo Way or the white man's way.

In *The Dark Wind*, Chee's maternal uncle is known as possibly the greatest Singer along the New Mexico-Arizona border. Nakai had taught Chee how to read and follow tracks, and he had taught him that "All is order. Look for the pattern."

In *The Ghostway*, Nakai is the older brother of Chee's mother who had taught Chee never to speak the name of the dead; he has been Chee's teacher, his friend ever since boyhood, his key clan uncle. Nakai lives near Tah Chee Wash in an octagonal log hogan; the mother of his late wife and his daughter live in a square plank building not far from the hogan. Nakai tells Chee the tribe needs him because there are so few *yataalii*.

In *A Thief of Time*, Chee states that Nakai was full of aphorisms; one of them was that things will even out.

In *Coyote Waits*, Nakai knows the Blessing Way, Mountain Top Chant, and others, but doesn't know the Ghostway. Chee will have to learn the Ghostway from someone else.

In *Sacred Clowns*, Chee refers to Nakai as his "Little Father." Chee knows that, as a *hataalii*, Nakai would not reveal the final secret of the ceremonial he was teaching until he knew his student was worthy. Nakai is very traditional; he doesn't like the modern way of splitting a ceremony over two weekends; he thinks it does more harm than good.

Nakai's sheep camp is in the Chuska Mountains forty miles west of Chaco Mesa. Chee finds him sitting on a log and watching his goats, sheep, and dogs. He is rolling his own cigarettes, using Bull Durham tobacco, and listening to KNDN on a portable radio. For the first time Chee notices his uncle is aging. He asks his uncle to spread word among the other medicine men about the driver who hit the old man and left him to die. Nakai feels that finding the driver won't help the man much if it means putting him in jail—the man needs healing, not punishment. He tells Chee the evil outside both the good men who died has caused their deaths, and that Delmar Kanitewa's grandmother probably knows where Delmar is because she had stopped calling the police about him. He promises to let Chee know what he finds out about the Hunger People as quickly as possible, since a young lady is involved.

Nakai, Mrs. Frank Sam (Little Mother, Blue Woman) (GW)

To Chee, Nakai's second wife was always Little Mother; to her friends she was Blue Woman, because of her spectacular turquoise jewelry.

Nakai, Old Lady (LW)

Old Lady Nakai was a Navajo born to the Mud

Clan. One of her girls drove Margaret Cigaret's truck for her to the Kinaalda for the Endischee girl. The truck had passed the Short Mountain Trading Post, so John McGinnis knew Margaret Cigaret wasn't home when Leaphorn came looking for her.

Nakai, Rosemary (WY)

Rosemary's daughter had seen a big dog bothering her horses; when she shot at it, it changed into a Navajo Wolf and ran away. The same story about the big dog bothering the horses is told in "Chee's Witch"; see **Nashibitti, Rosemary.**

Nakai, Shelton (BW)

According to Old Woman Gray Rocks, Shelton may have had trouble with the Navajo Wolf around his hogan.

Nakai, Reverend Slick (TT)

In Ellie Friedman-Bernal's room, Leaphorn noticed that Nakai's name was written in the margin of an auction catalog from Nelson's. Leaphorn had met Nakai once or twice. Nakai was a fundamentalist Christian evangelist; he traveled around the reservation in an old Cadillac sedan, pulling a four-wheel trailer in which he carried his tent, portable electric organ, and sound system. Wherever he went he tacked up fliers telling where his next revival meeting would be held.

Nakai was a "short man, sturdily built, neat and tidy, with small, round hands, small feet in neat cowboy boots, a round, intelligent face." He was small and agile and walked gracefully, an ugly little man with poor people's teeth. Leaphorn thought he was a smart man but also a dreamer.

Nakai didn't recognize Leaphorn when he

walked up to him at the revival. He told Leaphorn he had known Ellie Friedman-Bernal for three to four years, but not very well. Ellie had bought an occasional pot from him; sometimes people gave them to him for his services. He didn't know Ellie was missing. Leaphorn noticed the thin Navajo playing the guitar at the revival was the same one he'd seen helping Maxie Davis at the dig.

Naranjo, Cipriano (Orange) (DD)

A McKinley County, New Mexico, deputy sheriff, Orange Naranjo's job was to cover the non-Navajo periphery of the Zuñi reservation, talking to anyone who might have noticed something unusual, like a low-flying plane. He was an older man with black eyes and a wrinkled face who "would do his work honestly and faithfully with full awareness that . . . the sheriff . . . was seeking reelection." Orange wore a straw hat even in cold weather.

Narbona, Chief (LW) (CW)

In *Coyote Waits* it is said that this honorable and peaceable Navajo was killed by Colonel John Macrae Washington. In *Listening Woman*, Standing Medicine stayed behind with Chief Narbona and Ganado Mucho to fight Kit Carson and the army in 1864.

According to Stephen Trimble's calendar ("The People: Indians of the American Southwest"), Narbona was murdered by Washington on August 31, 1849, so he was probably the same man who signed a peace treaty with the Americans on November 22, 1846. He was a renowned chief, a man of great wisdom and foresight. On June 1, 1868, another peace treaty between the Navajos and the Americans was signed by twelve Navajo chiefs, including Barboncito, Narbona, Ganado

Mucho, and Manuelito. The Narbona of 1868 was possibly a son of the earlier chief.[5]

Nashibitti, Hosteen (DD)

Leaphorn's maternal grandfather, he was a great Singer and so wise he was called Hosteen when he was less than thirty years old. His family had chosen to stay and fight Kit Carson in 1864, and Nashibitti's mother had been dying when she delivered him in a remote canyon. Nashibitti's secret war name was He Who Asks Questions. Leaphorn knew him when he was quite old and fondly remembered him as One Who Answers. He taught Leaphorn the Blessing Way, songs from the Night Way, and many other ceremonies and legends, as well as instructing him in the Navajo Way. He stressed the interdependency of nature and the natural order of the universe.

Nashibitti, Rosemary (WI)

Her daughter had seen a big dog bothering her horses; when she shot at the dog, it turned into a man wearing a wolfskin and he had left, half running, half flying. The same character occurs in "The Witch, Yazzie, and the Nine of Clubs" as **Rosemary Nakai.**

Natonabah, Mary Joe (DW)

Chee went to see her about her complaint that someone else was grazing their sheep on her land. She lived near the Utah border.

Natonabah, Taylor (GW)

Natonabah was a Navajo Tribal Policeman attending a Monday morning meeting in Largo's

---

5. See *Indians of the American Southwest* by Bertha P. Dutton (Englewood Cliffs, N.J.: Prentice-Hall, 1975), pp. 82, 84.

office. He had a grim look because Largo had disapproved of his behavior in performing his duties.

Navajo people (DF)

Zuñi. The A'shiwi knew the Navajo and the Apache were their younger brothers. The Navajo and the Apache arrived in the region after the A'shiwi were firmly established, and the Navajo learned certain skills from the A'shiwi.

Navajo Wolf (Witch) (BW)

According to legend, the Navajo Wolf comes out mainly on nights when there is a full moon. He maims or kills people's livestock, tries to throw corpse powder on people (sometimes down the stovepipe or smokehole of their hogan while they are asleep), and may maim or kill people. When he is discovered, he turns into a man and runs away. The man is seen wearing a wolfskin draped over his head and shoulders. He is usually seen by a boy who can't identify him accurately because of the darkness. The Navajo Wolf can fly when necessary and can turn into a coyote, bear, fox, owl, or crow. The Navajo carry medicine pouches with pollen and gallstones to fend off Navajo Wolves. The ultimate fate of a Navajo Wolf is death, either at the hands of the people he has bothered or as a result of a Prostitution Way or an Enemy Way. In *The Blessing Way*, the Navajo Wolf killed and maimed livestock and also killed people by suffocating them in sand.

Neal (TG)

One of the men at Joliet who raped and beat Leroy Fleck was named Neal.

Newton, W. L. (FW)

Newton was governor when the Highway

Department scandal occurred; he worked with Flowers to cover it up.

Nez (GW)

Chee was ordered to pick up Nez because he'd beaten his brother-in-law with a hammer at their sheep camp above Mexican Water.

Nez, Hosteen (DW)

Hosteen Nez jokingly speculated that a Yazzie boy had pulled down the windmill on the Joint Use Reservation.

Nez, Billy Horseman (BW)

Member of the Red Forehead Clan, son of Annie Horseman, and brother of Luis Horseman. When Billy went to live with his uncle, he changed his last name from Horseman to Nez; he helped his uncle raise sheep over on Cottonwood Flats near Chinle. This sixteen-year-old was typically seen wearing a red-checked shirt, blue jeans, a red baseball cap, and rubber-soled sneakers. Like many of his people, he smoked cigarettes and carried a medicine pouch containing a gallstone to ward off witches.

Billy knew where Luis was hiding and took food to him. When he heard that the Mexican had not died, he decided to tell Luis to come in and talk to the police, but Luis was killed before Billy could reach him. Billy thought the Navajo Wolf had killed his brother, and he was determined to find and kill the Navajo Wolf. Even though he hadn't had an Enemy Way sung over him, Billy was able to persuade his grandfather to let him steal the scalp from the Navajo Wolf for the Enemy Way sing for his uncle; the "scalp" he stole was a big black Stetson hat. (This character is another version of **Big Hat** in "The Witch, Yazzie, and the Nine of Clubs.")

Nez, Charley (BW)

Charley Nez was another name for Charley Tsosie, Billy Nez's uncle. A Navajo may use more than one given name; a person's given name is not as important as his war name, which is kept secret. Charley had to have an Enemy Way done because he had been bothered by a Navajo Wolf who was a stranger; see **Nez, Emerson.**

Nez, Delbert (CW)

Delbert Nez was a stocky man who was trying to grow a mustache. Joe Leaphorn remembered him as a small, quiet, neat young officer who worked out of Window Rock. Nez told Jim Chee he should do his own clan checks on the chicks, because his wife would be mad at him if she found out he was doing it. Delbert Nez and his wife lived between Birdsprings Trading Post and Jadito Wash.

Nez was fascinated that someone would put paint on an area where skinwalkers were supposed to gather; he wanted to know what the painter's purpose was. He had been laughing when he radioed Chee; he thought he was going to catch the phantom painter. Nez had been shot high in the chest by a .38 revolver at close range and his patrol car set on fire. He'd been alive but unconscious when the fire suffocated him; he died close to Witchery Rock. The police found an expensive .38 Ruger pistol on Ashie Pinto, picked up by Chee a short distance from the patrol car.

Nez, Emerson (WY)

The Navajos were having an Enemy Way ceremony at the home of Emerson Nez; Chee hoped to get a lead on Taylor Yazzie there. It was said that Emerson had become sick because he was witched by a foreigner, so an Enemy Way had been prescribed to heal him. The Listener thought it was the same witch that killed John Doe. This character was also used in *The Blessing Way*; see **Nez, Charley.**

Nez, Gray Woman (SW)
Born to Bitter Water People, Gray Woman Nez was the mother of Bent Woman. Bent Woman was introduced to Jim Chee by Iron Woman Ginsberg at the Badwater Wash Trading Post when Chee visited to question Iron Woman about the Endocheeney murder.

Nez, Old Grandmother (SW)
Chee successfully performed a Blessing Way sing for Old Grandmother's niece. Chee was distantly related to her family.

Nez, Old Woman (PD)
Old Woman Nez was Henry Becenti's mother-in-law. When she came to visit her daughter, Henry vacated the area as required by Navajo tradition.

Nez, Ronald (TT)
Major Nez was more or less Leaphorn's boss at police headquarters in Window Rock. Leaphorn noticed he was getting fat; his stomach sagged over his belt, and he'd always been barrel-shaped. Nez wanted to know if Leaphorn wanted to take back his resignation.

Nezzie, Edna (DW)
A twenty-three-year-old woman from the Graywoman Nezzie camp, she had pawned a squash-blossom necklace at Mexican Water from the Burnt Water Trading Post robbery. She said Joseph Musket had given it to her after they had sexual intercourse, and she hadn't seen him again.

Nezzie, Graywoman (DW)
When Chee called the Teec Nos Pos trading post, one of Graywoman's sons-in-law told him that Graywoman was born to Standing Rock Clan and born for Bitter Water Clan and that her husband was Water Runs Together and Many Poles.

Niece of Old Grandmother Nez (SW)
Chee did his first Blessing Way sing for this young lady, who had the "malaise of being sixteen." She was the daughter of a first cousin to Chee on her mother's side of the family.

Noni, Jackie (LW)
Member of the Buffalo Society, he told John McGinnis he was a Seminole. Noni came into the Short Mountain Trading Post and said that he and a bunch of Indians had a government loan and wanted to buy the trading post. McGinnis didn't like his looks, thought maybe Noni was thinking about stealing from him. Noni was actually a "young part-Potawatomi with a brief violent police record"; he had apparently driven the car that blocked the Wells Fargo armored truck in Santa Fe so it could be robbed and was one of the kidnappers of the Boy Scout group.

Novitski, Albert (PD)
One of the crew killed in the explosion of the oil rig in 1948, his age and address were unknown.

O'Malley, John (DD) (LW)
In *Dance Hall of the Dead*, O'Malley was the FBI agent Leaphorn met in the Zuñi police department office. He was a handsome man, square-jawed, long-faced, with tanned skin and sunburned light hair; he had dimples in his cheeks and light blue eyes. O'Malley and Leaphorn were not particularly fond of

each other; Leaphorn thought John was a typical FBI man: "trimmed, scrubbed, tidy, able to work untroubled by any special measure of intelligence."

O'Malley felt Leaphorn should have left the investigation of the death at the Bowlegs hogan to the FBI, and he pressured Leaphorn to find George Bowlegs for him. Leaphorn found it interesting that O'Malley had introduced Baker as just another agent and then made an "uncasual remark about low-flying planes." O'Malley finally showed Leaphorn surveillance photos of Halsey and others and a mug shot of Otis, revealing the FBI's angle on the case.

In *Listening Woman* it is told that Leaphorn and FBI agent O'Malley had worked poorly together on the Cata case, which still remained open and unsolved as far as the FBI was concerned. Leaphorn read a transcript of O'Malley's interrogation of John Tull regarding his participation in the Santa Fe robbery; O'Malley had tried unsuccessfully to persuade Tull that he was taking the fall for the robbery and that his friend would never get him out on bail.

Old Uncle (DF)

Zuñi. Old Uncle lived in the house of the boy and girl who had shared their corn cake with the Corn Maidens. He had once been a Koyemshi but was now the oldest man in Ha'wi-k'uh, "too weak to wear the mud mask and do the hard work of the brotherhood of clowns." He hobbled around slowly and was afraid he would be left behind when the people made the trip to the Hopi, so he left early. The villagers had been angry with him when he told them playing with foodstuffs was not the way of the A'shiwi and they should feed the old beggar women; he said the A'shiwi had caused their own problems.

After the A'shiwi had been in the land of the

Hopi for a while, Old Uncle came back to the house to retrieve a loom he had left there and was overjoyed to find the children still alive and well. After four days they spoke to him, and he realized they had been blessed by the gods. The boy told him he was to carry a live corn plant to the people and lead them back to Ha'wi-k'uh. Because of his kindness and concern, the boy made Old Uncle his chief warrior-priest and put him in charge of the harvest.

Old Woman (DF)

Zuñi. The Old Woman lived alone in a fallendown house at the bottom of the village of Ha'wi-k'uh; every morning she had to clean up the trash that people threw on her house. "Because of years of misfortune she couldn't share in the plenty of the people": her brothers had all been killed in wars, her husband had died of a disease, and her sons had gone to live with their wives' families and had forgotten her. There was no one to help her plant corn or to water her plants, no men to bring her deer hides, and no way for her to get cotton, so she wore rags. She was very poor, and people didn't like having her around.

When she saw the two Corn Maidens she thought they were old hungry women like herself, and she invited them in to rest and to share what she had to eat. When one of the old ladies brought out a beaded pouch containing food, and a mist smelling like spring flowers came from the pollen she sprinkled, the Old Woman knew the old ladies must be two of the Beloved Ones, and she was afraid. Then the old ladies became young maidens with black glossy hair, perfect silver on their wrists, and happy faces, and they invited her to eat with them; the Old Woman forgot her loneliness and remembered how it had been when her children had been around her.

The Corn Maidens left a magic cape for her so she would have enough food for the winter; she was so happy she cried. When the drought came to the village she offered to share her food with the villagers, but they thought the Old Woman was a sorceress and were afraid to accept, so the Old Woman lived by herself in the village, sharing her food with the birds and animals, unaware of the children who had been left behind; when the Council of the Gods decided to help the children, the Corn Maidens asked the Old Woman to care for them for a while. When the villagers returned, the Old Woman was held in high esteem and became known as the mother of her people.

Oliver, Mrs. (TG)

Leroy Fleck's mother tripped this resident of Eldercare Manor, and she fell. Mrs. Oliver had told the people at Eldercare that Fleck's mother was stealing the tableware.

Oliveras, Rosemary Rita (LW)

A twenty-eight-year-old divorced immigrant from Puerto Rico, she met Frank Hoski at a laundromat in Washington, D.C., and went for a three-hour walk with him. Hoski spent most of his free time with her after the robbery of the Wells Fargo truck. Rosemary was distraught when Hoski disappeared without telling her; Hoski seemed to have fallen in love with her.

Onesalt, Alice and Homer (SW)

Alice and Homer were Irma Onesalt's parents.

Onesalt, Irma (Welfare Woman) (SW)

Born to the Bitter Water Clan, born for the Towering House People, this thirty-one-year-old unmarried Navajo woman, agent of the Navajo

Office of Social Services, was "tough as saddle leather, mean as a snake." People had a hard time finding anything good to say about her; Dilly Streib described her as "a full-time world-saver." Irma was unusually arrogant, rough-talking, an obnoxious jerk and a troublemaker; she was a busybody, a militant, angry young woman. She didn't like policemen, especially Navajo Tribal ones; when Chee brought her the wrong Begay, she cussed him out.

She went to extraordinary lengths to protect the Navajos who were her clients; she would consult other agencies about matters not directly related to her job in the interest of her clients. She asked Dr. Jenks to furnish her with the dates of death for people on a list she had but wouldn't tell him why she wanted this information. She told him she thought some people were getting bad advice from Singers. The boyfriend she lived with was teaching math the day she was found dead, shot by a .30-.06 rifle, in her overturned Datsun.

Oslander, Gene (FW)

Oslander, a wholesale grocery broker, was a state representative. Janey Janoski joked that if peanut butter was being mixed into the roadbed, Oslander would probably have been subcontracting it.

Otis (Oats) (DD)

When Leaphorn saw him at the Jason's Fleece commune, Otis was lying on a rug in the corner of the room suffering from the effects of some drug. He was a young man with a shaved head, and what he said didn't make any sense. A short time later Susanne told Leaphorn that Halsey had taken Otis to Gallup and put him on a bus and that Otis was not much better than he had been.

Ozzie, Darcy (TT)

The only person at home at the hogan of Old Lady Daisy Manygoats, this young man gave Leaphorn a schedule of Nakai's revivals for the next few weeks.

Pa'u-ti-wa (DF)

Zuñi. Because the boy and his sister had followed the instructions of the Council of the Gods, Pa'u-ti-wa, the chief god of the kachinas and god of all dance gods, told the Cornstalk Insect the gods would shape rain clouds above the mesa and runners would plant the flatlands with seed for the boy and his sister.

Palanzer, Richard (Dick) (DW)

Palanzer was a "known associate of the narcotics traffic"; he had been indicted two years before in Los Angeles County for conspiracy and narcotics. The DEA thought he had driven off with the drugs in his car after the plane crash. Chee found him dead in the back seat of a dark-green carryall that had been rented in Phoenix by Jansen; he'd been shot and there were no drugs in the car. Palanzer was a smallish white man in his middle forties, with iron-gray hair, close-set eyes, and a narrow, bony face; he was wearing a gray nylon jacket, a white shirt, and cowboy boots. By the time Cowboy Dashee found the car, Palanzer's body had disappeared.

Parker, Theodore (LW)

Jimmy Tso, calling himself Frank Hoski, used the name Theodore Parker while working for Safety Systems, a security company in Washington, D.C. Rosemary Oliveras probably also knew him by that name.

Pasquaanti, Ed (DD)

Chief of the Zuñi Police, his allegiance was

first to the Zuñi laws and then to the white man's. He wanted it clearly understood that the Zuñi police would be in charge of the investigation on the Zuñi reservation, but otherwise he didn't tell the Navajos and others how to do their jobs. Ed had cropped gray hair and wore rubber-heeled boots or shoes; he looked old to Leaphorn. Leaphorn told Ed about the fake Salamobia mask and alerted Ed that George Bowlegs would probably appear at the Shalako ceremony looking for the person wearing that mask. Ed had some sort of ceremonial role in the Shalako ceremony and had members of the tribe watching for the fake mask. According to the Zuñi laws, wearing such a mask was sacrilege, a crime punishable by death.

Paterson, Mrs. (TG)

Mrs. Perry was temporarily replacing Mrs. Paterson at the Smithsonian. Mrs. Paterson had always wanted her mail placed on her desk and left unopened by Mrs. Bailey.

Pauling, Gail (DW)

Robert Pauling's sister, she accompanied Ben Gaines to the crash site; she knew her brother was too good a pilot to die the way he did. She was a small woman in her fifties, with short dark hair that curved around an oval face. Gail was five years older than her brother and loved him dearly; when they were young her mother left them, and Gail took care of Robert until her father remarried. She wanted to see Robert's killer punished.

She told Chee she had only known Gaines for three days and was surprised to find out that Robert had an attorney. She and Gaines were staying at the Hopi Cultural Center motel. She became alarmed when Gaines had been gone more than twenty-four hours and told Chee. She listened in on a call for

Gaines from Richard Palanzer and learned that Palanzer wanted money for the missing drugs.

Pauling, Robert (DW)
Pilot of the Cessna flying over Balakai Mesa, he was going from Chihuahua, Mexico, to Wepo Wash, flying low to avoid the radar at Albuquerque, Salt Lake, and Phoenix; he was carrying one passenger in addition to his cargo. He regularly flew for big outfits; he'd had to quit flying for Eastern because of a bad reading on his heart. Before he flew for Eastern he had been in the Tactical Air Force and had learned to land planes in the dark. He had chosen this route himself and had practiced landing in Wepo Wash before the flight. He and his passenger were killed when someone moved his landing lights and he crashed into an outcropping of rock.

Pearce, Tommy (LW)
One of the Boy Scouts held hostage by the Buffalo Society, he was thirteen years old, five feet tall, weighed about ninety pounds, and had brown hair and eyes.

Pedwell, T. J. (TT)
Employed by the Navajo Cultural Preservation Office, Dr. Pedwell handled applications for digging on reserved Anasazi sites on the reservation. He told Chee that Randall Elliot had applied to dig at the north end of Many Ruins Canyon, but Ellie Friedman-Bernal had not. Elliot had also requested permission to dig at the site of the oil well pump where Jimmy Etcitty and Joe Nails had been killed; both requests had been denied.

Pekwin (DF)
Zuñi. In *The Boy Who Made Dragonfly* the

Pekwin, priest of the Sun Father, urged the people to come out of their houses and follow the Hopi guides to their land, where the Hopis would feed them and help them. In the Emergence Myth the Pekwin was an old man chosen by the twin gods to become the Sun Priest, the spiritual leader of the people.

The Pekwin is the most powerful of the Zuñi priests. The keeper of the calendar, it is his job to determine the dates of the winter and summer solstices. He does this by standing in a cornfield east of town and observing the time when the sun rises over a certain part of Corn Mountain. He controls the Corn Dance held each fourth summer, as well as various other ceremonies and rituals. He is chief of all the priests: he officiates at meetings and at the council of priests, he installs new priests, and he sanctions the impersonators of the kachina spirits.

Penitewa, Bert (SC)

Tano. Penitewa was a short, heavy-bodied man in his late seventies. His belly hung over the belt of his jeans, but his hair was still thick and black, his face hardly lined, and his back straight like that of a younger man. He had a daughter, Della. Penitewa was in favor of the toxic-waste-disposal dump and was up for reelection as governor of the Tano in January. Applebee figured the number of Pueblo people who didn't want the dump on Pueblo land could defeat Penitewa.

The governor was the keeper of the Lincoln cane, a sort of sacred trust. (In 1863 each of the nineteen New Mexico Indian pueblos had been sent an inscribed silver and ebony cane by President Lincoln in recognition of tribal authority and as an inducement to remain neutral during the Civil War.) Penitewa could remember that the cane had hung on the wall when his great-grandfather had been governor. It would be the highest insult to accuse the governor of being willing to sell the cane.

He told Leaphorn he thought at first the cane in the clown wagon was the real one, and he had come back home to check that it was still on the wall. One of his nephews, who was a clown helping with the wagon, said Francis Sayesva had directed Henry Agoyo to put the cane in the wagon. Penitewa wondered where the replica had come from. He told Leaphorn that it hurt when an old friend like Francis Sayesva died thinking he was a traitor.

Penitewa, Della (SC)

Tano. Governor Penitewa's middle-aged daughter, she met Leaphorn at the door of his home and invited him in. She had her shawl and jacket on and was going to a neighbor's. Her father was sorry she had left because she made much better coffee than he did.

People of Darkness (PD)

A group of Navajos who belonged to the branch of the Native American Church founded by Dillon Charley, they used peyote to get visions. When Henry Becenti tried to find and arrest them for using peyote, the church went underground, took to wearing the mole amulet, and called themselves the People of Darkness. Chee first heard of them from Mrs. Vines.

Perez (TG)

Conductor on the Amtrak train from Washington, D.C., to Chicago and Los Angeles, formerly chapter chairman for the Brotherhood of Railroad Trainmen, Perez said he liked to speak

Spanish with some of the passengers; he had checked on Santillanes after the unscheduled train stop and saw a very small man with short, curly red hair in the compartment, but not Santillanes. When they arrived at the regular stop, the only thing in the compartment was the passenger's belongings.

Perry, Catherine Morris (TG)

Mrs. Perry was a lawyer who worked for the Smithsonian as "Temporary Assistant Counsel, Public Affairs, on loan from the Department of the Interior." Her office was decorated with artifacts amid pastels; she was unhappy because her secretary, Markie Bailey, had left an unopened, ugly brown box on her antique desk. She was extremely upset when she found the artifacts in the box were her ancestors' bones.

Pete, Mr. and Mrs. (SC)

Janet Pete's father was Navajo and her mother's people were Scots. Her father's people had been relocated to Chicago in the 1940s when he was a small boy. Mr. Pete's father had died before they moved, so he had no information about his father's clans. He had heard his mother say her clan was the Hunger People (Dichin Dine'e). The clan name of Janet Pete's mother's people was MacDougal, and the MacDougals were certainly not related to anyone named Chee.

Pete, Janet (Silk Shirt) (SW) (TT) (TG) (CW) (SC)

Janet is a lawyer from the Shiprock (later, the Window Rock) Office of the Dinebeiina Nahiilna be Agaditahe (DNA), "People Who Talk Fast and Help the People Out," the Navajo equivalent of the Legal Aid Society or public defender organization. In *Skinwalkers*, Chee wonders who had asked her to be Roosevelt Bistie's lawyer, since Bistie had been uninterested in obtaining one; Janet had been very serious about defending Bistie's constitutional rights. Leaphorn had had a run-in with her the year before over a drunk she had accused them of roughing up.

Janet is a small, skinny young Navajo woman, with short black hair and large angry black eyes; her skin is smooth and glossy and she moves gracefully. She dresses professionally in silk shirts and tweed skirts. Chee notices her small narrow hands, her long slender fingernails with clear nail polish, and her very nice slim legs.

Janet is quite upset when Chee tells her that Roosevelt Bistie has been killed. As she talks with Chee at the Turquoise Café she realizes that someone may have used her to get Bistie out of jail so they could kill him before he talked; she feels responsible for his death.

In *A Thief of Time*, Janet and Jim Chee have developed a friendship. While Janet is in Phoenix she wants Chee to test-drive a Buick she wants to buy; Chee is suspicious when she tells him the dealer has offered her $1,000 for her old Datsun, and he decides to take the car to Bernie Tso to examine. When Bernie asks him if Janet is his girlfriend, Chee says that Janet is tougher than nails and not his type—unless he needs a lawyer.

While Chee is test-driving the Buick for Janet, he spots the Backhoe Bandit and gives chase; because the steering is bad, Chee wrecks the car. When Janet sees the Buick, the first thing she wants to know is if Chee is hurt; when she hears about the condition of the car from Bernie, she calls the dealer and tells him where to pick up his car, saying he might be hearing from Chee's lawyer because of tampering with the odometer and other defects. She is angry because she doesn't feel the car dealer would have tried that ploy on a man.

She understands Chee's problem with Mary Landon. She has had a similar problem with her former law professor, John McDermott, now chief legal counsel of a multinational conglomerate, who wants her to marry him and practice law with his firm in Europe. She thinks that one of the things he wants is an Indian maiden helpmate, and she is miserable because she doesn't know what she really wants to do.

In *Talking God*, Chee tells Cowboy Dashee that Janet isn't his girlfriend, that he is just her confidant and friend. Chee thinks, however, that Janet has a kind of strong, clean-cut dignity and pride; that she is classy.

Janet is working for John McDermott. She calls Chee from Washington to tell him about Henry Highhawk and Rudolfo Gomez; she is frightened because a small red-haired man is following her around. McDermott has asked her to take Highhawk's case, and she knows Highhawk won't compromise; she feels maybe she is being used by McDermott or Highhawk for publicity purposes. She thinks McDermott might have hired Highhawk to make a copy of the Tano War God to give to Eldon Tamana. In Washington Janet calls Chee after seeing him on television at the Smithsonian with the Talking God mask, then personally takes him to the D.C. airport to return to Farmington. Chee gives her the Tano War God mask to give to McDermott, but she decides to take the mask home to the Tano Pueblo Indians.

In *Coyote Waits*, Janet is back from Washington, D.C., and has broken off with John McDermott; Chee is delighted. Janet is working for the Department of Justice, with the Federal Public Defender in Albuquerque, as a court-appointed attorney. She tells Chee that Ashie Pinto won't tell her anything.

313

In this book Janet is described as having sleek dark hair and very nice legs, an intelligent face, and skin as smooth as silk. She drives a little Toyota two-door. Janet wasn't raised on the reservation in the Navajo Way; her parents had wanted her to speak perfect English, so they wouldn't speak Navajo very much around her. She had attended Stanford University. In Window Rock she stays overnight with Emily, in the apartment they had formerly shared.

When she goes out to Witchery Rock with Chee he discovers that she hates snakes, that they scare her. During Chee's questioning of Redd she interrupts, which irritates Chee, but he knows she isn't attuned to Navajo etiquette.

In *Sacred Clowns*, Janet and Jim Chee are good friends, but both of them are beginning to think about a serious relationship. Chee does his best to impress Janet but can't seem to get her alone. When they go to the Tano ceremonial, Cowboy Dashee and Asher Davis accompany them; when they go to see the movie *Cheyenne Autumn*, Harold Blizzard tags along.

Chee notices every little detail about Janet, including the expensive watch she may have received from her lawyer boyfriend in Washington. She and Chee and Harold go to the Gallup drive-in movie in her Ford Escort. Janet feels out of place on the reservation and has armored herself with expensive clothing, education, wit, and humor. Chee feels he should have recognized her loneliness since he feels the same way in Anglo society.

Chee is happy when Janet shows signs of understanding what it means to be one of the Dineh by carefully listening. He enjoys telling her about the Navajos in the movie *Cheyenne Autumn* and the culture of the Tanos, although he realizes he doesn't entirely understand their culture either.

She remarks that anytime she is representing someone in a case Chee is involved in, he always pushes her to the edge of violating professional ethics. She decides that Leaphorn is a kind, smart person who thinks the same of Jim Chee. She feels that Chee should have been promoted to sergeant long ago.

Janet had started liking Chee because he was kind to people. She has heard rumors that he has a girl at every chapter house and tells him she doesn't want to be just another one of his girlfriends. She wants to know the status of his relationship with Mary Landon, and she tells Chee she doesn't know how she could have been so naive and stupid in her relationship with John McDermott.

Although city-raised and only half Navajo (her mother is a Scot), she has decided she wants to live as a Navajo. She also wants to marry Jim Chee but doesn't think he's the marrying kind. She is angry when he decides to check out her clan status before asking her to marry him. Leaphorn encourages the match.

Pete, Ozzie (GW)

Ozzie Pete was a middle-aged Navajo who managed the 7-Eleven store at the junction of Navajo Route 1 and U.S. 666; he sold tickets for Greyhound and Continental, as his store served as the depot for both bus lines. Ozzie told Chee he hadn't sold any tickets to a girl fitting the description of Margaret Sosi.

Peters, Arthur L. (FW)

Accounting clerk in the Bureau's Tobacco Tax Division, he was described by Janey Janoski as a tall, shy, skinny man who took the records to committee meetings on the cigarette tax bills. Peters resigned a month after a half-million cigarette tax stamps disappeared from the bureau; his signature had been on the invoice for receiving the stamps. He had said he had no idea what happened to the stamps and had gone to work for Bradbury-Legg, an accounting firm. Janey Janoski didn't believe Peters was a crook; she believed this whole affair was an example of how reporters hurt innocent people.

Petresky, David (TG)

Eddy Elkins had asked Leroy Fleck to kill Petresky while Leroy was still in Joliet prison; it was a test to see if Leroy could murder someone and not get caught. When Leroy succeeded, Elkins promised him regular employment.

Pew, Elliot (SC)

Desmond Clark told Leaphorn that Pew was an honest and reputable art dealer in Tucson.

Pfaff, Dick (TG)

Leroy Fleck called himself Dick Pfaff when he checked Mama into the Fat Man's rest home.

Pino, Miss (GW)

Young Miss Pino was a close friend of Margaret Sosi at Saint Catherine's. She told Captain Largo that Margaret had received a letter from her grandfather telling her it was too dangerous for her to come to Shiprock and to stay away from Gorman.

Pino, Alice Frank (LW)

Navajo born to the Mud Clan, she attended the Kinaalda for Eileen Endischee.

Pinto, Anna (WY)

This elderly woman was Walker Pinto's mother.

Pinto, Hosteen Ashie (CW)

Ashie Pinto was Mary Keeyani's mother's brother, accused of murdering Delbert Nez. His clans were Turning Mountain and Bitter Water, although Odell Redd said he was Mud Clan. Pinto had never married and lived alone about a mile from Mary Keeyani's family place; in his house he had a tape recorder on which he made recordings for various people. He was very neat and kept all the letters he had ever received in a round tin box. Pinto had a great sense of humor and a great memory. When he was young he had been a Crystal Gazer; he still worked at it occasionally. He had an old truck that had not been driven in a long time; the battery was missing and the body was filled with debris.

Pinto was eighty years old, thin and frail, with skin almost transparent in its thinness; one of his black eyes was clouded by a cataract. He was around five feet eight inches tall and wore his gray hair tied back in a bun. He spoke hardly any English. He used to be a drinker; he liked cheap wine and anything sweet, so his relatives called him Sugarman. He had quit drinking after his doctor told him the next drink could kill him.

When Pinto was young and wild he had killed a man in a fight; he was drunk at the time. He had served a prison term and then returned to the reservation. When he drank he was a mean drunk, cranky, but no meaner than most. Mary Keeyani didn't want him working for Professor Tagert, because Tagert gave him whiskey. Pinto didn't want to work for Tagert either, but he needed money; he'd left his silver concha belt with John McGinnis, the last item he'd pawn when he was running low on money.

Chee found Pinto walking out on the highway two hundred miles from home, drunk, with an empty whiskey bottle in his right hand and a pistol stuck in the back of his trousers. He carried a pocketknife, coins, and a worn wallet with two fifty-dollar bills in it. Three of the six cartridges in the pistol had been recently fired. When Chee picked him up and handcuffed him, he told Chee he was ashamed and then would not say anything else. Pinto was taken to the county jail in Aztec and booked for assault until the FBI could get there and charge him with the murder of Delbert Nez. He was later transferred to Albuquerque for his federal court trial.

Pinto, Walker (WY)

Son of Anna Pinto, he was, according to his mother, skinny, bony-faced, and sort of ugly-looking. Walker had married a woman in the Poles Together Clan and gone over to Rough Rock to live with her; she had been no good, so he had come back to live at his mother's place.

Cowboy had heard that one of the Pintos had found the freshly killed Navajo on Piute Mesa and had seen that the skin had been flayed from the dead man's hands. Walker told Chee that while he and his son were up on Piute Mesa seeing to his mother's horses, he heard a truck nearby hit something. He went to investigate and found the body; he didn't see the truck but knew it had to have been damaged.

Place Where Summer Stays (Land of Everlasting Summer) (DF)

Zuñi. The Corn Maidens lived here; it was south of Ha'wi-k'uh.

Plaid Coat (TG)

An elderly man who attended the Yeibichai ceremony for Agnes Tsosie, he told Highhawk to wait to speak to her until after the ceremony. (In

The Ghostway, a character named Lerner had also been referred to as Plaid Coat.)

Platero (SC)

Platero drove a bus for the school Delmar Kanitewa attended in Crownpoint. He lived less than a mile from the school and knew Delmar's best friend, who attended Thoreau. He often gave Delmar's friend, Felix Bluehorse, a ride home after school.

Poher, Eddie (BW)

George Jackson's partner, Eddie was a tall young man with a pale face, blue eyes, and blond eyebrows; he had a soft voice with a midatlantic accent. His wearing apparel included a navy blue vest with black buttons, a light blue straw hat, and a shoulder holster with a semiautomatic pistol in it. George and Eddie were using a room in the Anasazi cliff dwelling ruins for a hideout; their actions were being directed by a larger group from Los Angeles. Eddie had Mafia connections and had been arrested once on suspicion of conspiracy to commit a bank robbery, but he had not been convicted. Eddie tried to force Bergen McKee to write a letter stating that he and Jeremy Canfield had moved their research operations to another area; before he could accomplish this, Eddie died from a fall into a deep crevasse.

Pointed Shoes (TG)

An aristocratic-looking corpse was found by the railroad tracks east of Gallup, wearing a worn but custom-tailored suit and handmade pointed-toe shoes; it was later identified as Santillanes.

Pots (DD)

Pots was a member of the Jason's Fleece commune.

Prayer Meal (DF)
For the Zuñi, sacred cornmeal serves a pur-pose similar to that of Holy Water for the Catholic religion. Cornmeal symbolizes all blessings. According to Hillerman, cornmeal is found today in the sacred font at the entrance to the Catholic church at Zuñi. Prayer meal was also sometimes mixed with ground white seashells and ground-up turquoise; sacred cornmeal was sprinkled on vari-ous objects, not eaten.

Prayer Plumes (or bundles) (DF)
Zuñi. The boy was instructed to tie feathers from the eagle and duck to six different willow sticks with brightly colored yarn; the sticks were to be painted yellow, blue or green, red, white, speck-led, and black. They were to be inserted in the ground and prayers said over them at planting time to bring good fortune to the fields of growing grain. The Prayer Plumes were to be tied into bun-dles. See **Six Sacred Directions.**

Putnam, R. J. (FW)
Construction Division manager at Reevis-Smith, he had no idea what Cotton was talking about and passed him on to Gary Kelly.

Rain God of the South (DF)
Zuñi. The winter following the food battle at Ha'wi-k'uh was dry; no water blessings came to the fields from the Rain God of the South.

Rainey, Robert (LW)
Thirty-two-year-old former activist with Students for a Democratic Society and former member of the American Indian Movement, he'd been arrested three times. Rainey met Frank Hoski in a bar in Washington, D.C., to relay instructions.

Raven, Amos (or Big Raven) (BW)

George Jackson, the Big Navajo, used these aliases.

Redd, William Odell (CW)

A doctoral student in linguistics at the University of New Mexico, Redd had studied Western history at the University of Texas at El Paso and decided to change to linguistics because he'd have a better chance of getting a job. He did the translation of the Ashie Pinto tapes for Professor Tagert but left out certain parts concerning the location of the cave where Butch Cassidy died. Chee noticed that Redd had been listening to the Pinto tapes at the university library and had checked out tapes for four consecutive days before Delbert Nez's murder.

Redd was a tall man with an athlete's shoulders, red hair, red mustache, and a long, narrow face sprinkled with freckles. Jean Jacobs was a friend, a nice lady; she'd known him a long time. Jean said Redd collected rare pennies and sold them to dealers to pay his way through school. Redd lived in an apartment that had formerly been a double garage, behind a stucco bungalow in Albuquerque's student ghetto. His apartment was filled with books and coins.

Redd drove a dented, rusted, dark-green Ford Bronco with vanity plates that read REDDNEK. Chee and Janet Pete saw it parked near Witchery Rock. When Chee asked Redd what he was doing out there, he told Chee he had wondered what Pinto was doing two hundred miles from home. He theorized that Pinto had told Tagert where he could find Butch Cassidy's body, so he went out to take a look.

Redd died from a rattlesnake bite on his neck.

Redhair, Bennie (SC)

The secretary and gofer for the Chief, Leaphorn's

superior, at Window Rock, he was nervous because Tribal Councilman Jimmy Chester was in the Chief's office, and Chester wasn't happy.

Regis, J. D. (SC)

Regis was named as an honest art dealer in Albuquerque by Desmond Clark.

Reynolds, Chester (DD)

A well-known anthropologist, Dr. Reynolds had written *Paleo-Indian Cultures in North America*, an accepted standard college text. He wanted to prove that Folsom Man had adapted rather than died out, based on modifications of his arrow points; he called it his modification theory. When he presented his paper at a professional scientific meeting, his colleagues walked out; he was deeply stung and determined to show his colleagues he was right. He found sites where Folsom hunters had probably camped, gave these sites to his doctoral students to develop, and found funding for them. In return he demanded scientific perfection. Unlike some professionals, he allowed his students to present their papers under their own names and gave them the credit for their work. Many students had been helped professionally by Reynolds.

Reynolds was a medium-sized man, perhaps fifty, with brown hair turning gray in spots, and had a round cheerful face with a leathery complexion; his sharp unblinking blue eyes were recessed under a heavy brow ridge. He didn't want anyone else around the site where Ted Isaacs was excavating and was outraged when he caught George Bowlegs and Ernesto Cata in his truck; later, however, he denied that anything had been taken, which Leaphorn found strange. Reynolds mysteriously disappeared at the Shalako ceremony.

CHARACTERS IN TONY HILLERMAN'S FICTION

Riccobeni (TG)
At Eldercare Manor, Mama Fleck had pulled out some of Mr. Riccobeni's hair.

Rickner, Thomas J. (Tom) (FW)
Longtime city government reporter for the *Tribune*, Rickner had been pulled off the urban renewal stuff he was working on and sent to the capital to sub for Cotton while Cotton was evading the Organization; he was to do Cotton's legwork for him. He called Cotton with more details about the involvement of Herman Gay and H. L. Singer.

Roanhorse (TG)
Roanhorse was having a Yeibichai ceremony performed at the Navajo Nation Fair at Window Rock. Leaphorn wondered how the note in Santillanes's pocket and Roanhorse's ceremony were connected.

Roanhorse, Bertha (SC)
Roanhorse, a Councilwoman on the Tribal Council Budget Committee and Delmar Kanitewa's Navajo grandmother, was concerned when Delmar ran off because he had been part of an intertribal dance group scheduled to perform soon in Durango. She had been working on Delmar's costume and said he was all excited about it. Leaphorn said she was the kind of person who would get the Tribal Police to find Delmar rather than go look for him herself. Somewhat later, Sergeant Blizzard questioned her about Delmar's whereabouts and received a lecture from her on how the police weren't doing their job. She didn't deny that she knew where to find Delmar. She did ask how she knew he'd be safe if they found him.

Roanhorse, Dick (BW)
A young Navajo police officer just out of

323

recruit school, he was left to stand guard over Luis Horseman's body.

Roanhorse, Eldon (CW)

Leaphorn remembered this skinny tribal policeman from some incident in the past. Officer Roanhorse was investigating the Ji homicide; he intended to take Taka Ji to the house of a friend, the son of one of the other teachers, after Taka's father's death. Instead, Ji went to Albuquerque to stay with his relatives.

Roanhorse, Mildred (TT)

Mildred was Jimmy Etcitty's mother-in-law.

Roark, Paul (FW)

Cotton stated in his political column for the *Tribune* that Governor Roark would probably try to win the nomination as the Democratic candidate for the U.S. Senate against incumbent Eugene Clark. Roark was a dedicated Jeffersonian: he was City Commission chairman at twenty-nine, he straightened out the Police Department and got rid of the shakedown artists, and on the State Board of Finance he had forced the holding banks to pay interest on state general-fund deposits. Roark was a young, trim, handsome man who moved with a natural grace. It was rumored his marriage was on the rocks and he had a mistress.

Robbins, William (Whitey) (FW)

A political reporter for the *Gazette*, Whitey was tall, lanky, and blond, like Cotton. The *Gazette* wanted some information from him about Health Department funding, so he borrowed Cotton's car and went back to the capitol to get it. A man driving a stolen semi swerved in front of him on a narrow bridge, forcing him through the railing and into the river; the truck did not stop and Whitey was killed. Cotton called Whitey's wife, to soften the blow if he could.

Rodney, P. J. (TG)

Leaphorn and Rodney had become friends when they were both misfits attending the FBI Academy. Rodney had left the Duluth Police Department and joined the D.C. police force; he had been working there when Leaphorn wrote to him about Emma's death the previous year. Rodney was a tall, bulky black man in bifocals, with a white-toothed grin in a craggy, coffee-colored face and kinky gray hair cropped close to the skull; the gray felt hat he wore matched his raincoat. Captain Rodney was married and near retirement age.

Rodriguez, Arsenio (FW)

While shining Cotton's shoes on the plaza in Santa Fe, this boy told Cotton about some of the changes that had occurred after Cotton left town.

Roff, Theo (PD)

A twenty-year-old employee of Petrolab, the company that supplied the nitroglycerin charge for the oil well, he was killed in the explosion in 1948.

Roser, Cadet Captain (GW)

When Eric Vaggan was at West Point, he hit Roser in the head with a softball bat; he was trying to kill Roser before Roser could report that Vaggan had cheated.

Rostik, Theodore (CW)

FBI agent, newcomer to the area, investigating officer on the Delbert Nez and Ji homicides, Rostik was young, smart, and well-trained, but he didn't know enough about Navajo culture to realize the significance of the gun, the Scotch whisky bottle, and Ashie Pinto's character. He wore a dark gray suit and felt hat, which marked him as either an FBI agent or a Mormon missionary. (Rostik probably was stationed at the Farmington office of the FBI, although he was described in another place as assigned to the office at Gallup.)

Rounder (DD)
The Zuñi roommate of Joe Leaphorn's at Arizona State had a round bland moon face. He and Joe had drunk beer and talked for hours, comparing Navajo and Zuñi ways. Joe suffered from an irrational inferiority complex from being around him, because Rounder always said Zuñis were better than Navajos.

Running, Old Woman (DD)
Mother of Shorty Bowlegs, she had several other sons.

Saiz family (FW)
The youngest daughter in this family had once been the object of Cotton's affection when he was a boy in Santa Fe; he walked past their former home.

Sakani, Robert (SC)
Tano. Robert, a cousin of Delmar Kanitewa, was supposed to drive him back to school after the ceremonial at Tano Pueblo.

Sam, Austin (SC)
Dilly Streib drank from a cup that advertised on its side AUSTIN SAM FOR TRIBAL COUNCIL, NEW LANDS CHAPTER.

Sam, Joseph (PD)
One of the Navajos who did not report for

work the day the oil rig exploded in 1948, he was of the Mud Clan and married into the Salt Clan. He died of leukemia.

Sam, Roscoe (PD)

Another Navajo who heeded Dillon Charley's warning and did not go to work at the oil rig the day of the explosion, he later died at the Bureau of Indian Affairs hospital in Tuba City from a malignancy affecting his liver and other vital organs.

Sam, Wilson (SW)

Born to the One Walks Around Clan and born for the Turning Mountain People, he married into the Yazzies. Wilson Sam was fifty-seven years old and was a sheepherder who sometimes worked on Arizona Highway Department grader crews as a flagman. He could read and write and was not a drunk or a thief. Having cut his hand the previous winter, he had gone to the Badwater Clinic, had the cut sewn up, and received a tetanus shot. His name was on the list Irma Onesalt had, and he had received a letter from her. He was killed when hit on the back of his neck with a shovel; his body was dragged to the rim of Chilchinbito Canyon and thrown over the edge. He died about the same time as Dugai Endocheeney.

Sanchez (TT)

Sanchez worked for Flight Contractors at the Farmington airport. Flight Contractors had been renting helicopters to Randall Elliot for two or three years. When Chee tried to rent a helicopter and have it billed to the Navajo Tribal Police, Sanchez insisted that Chee use his own MasterCard.

Sanchez, Felix (CW)

A good, solid, hardworking Hispanic policeman with the Federal Defender's Office, he had formerly been with the El Paso Police Department and knew how to collect information.

Sanchez, Thomas (FW)
Thomas Sanchez lived in the house of Cotton's boyhood friend Eloy Sisneros.

Sandoval (BW) (TG)
In *The Blessing Way*, Sandoval was the eighty-two-year-old Singer who was conducting the Enemy Way for Charley Tsosie. He had learned his craft from his father; he thought the People were losing too many of the old ways. In *Talking God* a noted Navajo *hataalii* of the same name was asked by Dr. Hartman to examine the accuracy of the mask exhibit at the Smithsonian and make sure the exhibit was not sacrilegious.

Santero, Miguel (Bad Hands) (TG)
Santero was the name by which Leroy Fleck knew Rudolfo Gomez; Fleck was to locate Santero for Stone. Stone's group didn't know where Santero had gone when he left Washington, D.C., and that worried them.

Santillanes y Jimenez, Elogio (Pointed Shoes) (TG)
The body of this exiled leader of the left-wing opposition to the Pinochet regime in Chile was found beside the Amtrak rails. There was no identification; even his false teeth had been removed. There was no apparent medical reason why all his teeth should have been pulled. He was finally identified almost a month later.

Santillanes, Mrs. (or Miss) (TG)
This woman was middle-aged and slender, with a thin face, glasses, and black hair pulled

severely back. When Leaphorn came to the door he sensed she was expecting to hear that her husband (or brother) had been killed. No one knew that Leroy Fleck had hidden a sound-activated recorder in the ceiling of the apartment where she lived with other Chileans.

Sawkatewa, Taylor (DW)

Hopi. Member of the Fog Clan, he lived in the nearly abandoned village of Piutki. Sawkatewa was elderly, extremely traditional, sort of crazy, and perhaps a *powaqa* (Hopi sorcerer). Cowboy Dashee had heard Sawkatewa was a member of the Ya Ya Society, which initiated people who wanted to become sorcerers. Sawkatewa had a round head with a broad fine nose, a long toothless jaw, and wrinkled cheeks and chin around a sunken mouth; his skin and eyes looked ageless and his hair, cut in the traditional Hopi bangs, was still mostly black.

Sawkatewa didn't speak English and Chee knew only a few Hopi words, so it was necessary for Dashee to translate. Sawkatewa said there was a higher law than the white man's, and for a Navajo or Hopi to become involved in the affairs of white men was not good. Sawkatewa had been near the windmill and had seen the airplane crash.

Sayatasha (DF)

Zuñi. Sayatasha, the Rain God of the North, had a single long horn on his head and a misty rain cloud surrounding his horn. In the Sacred Lake he addressed the Cornstalk Insect as "our Grandfather" and explained how to teach the boy to make prayer plumes to offer to the gods, so the Council of the Gods could bring its blessings on the children. He told He'hea-kwe to take corn grains to Ha'wi-k'uh, where the Cornstalk Insect could easily find them to give to the children.

Sayesva, Francis (SC)

Tano. Brother of Teddy Sayesva and maternal uncle of Delmar Kanitewa, he was a plump man, the leader of the Tano koshare society. He was clubbed to death about forty yards from where Chee was sitting at the Tano Pueblo ceremonial. Francis had been a certified public accountant and worked for a savings and loan company in Phoenix that had gone belly up. He lived in Albuquerque and as usual had used his brother Teddy's home as his base while preparing for the ceremonial. Both his office in Albuquerque and his brother's home in Tano had telephones, so Delmar could have called his uncle if necessary.

Teddy said Francis had seemed preoccupied, perhaps because he had to testify the next week before a federal grand jury about an auditing technicality in a banking case. Francis was the type of man who did his duty. He was well-liked and respected, a good man, and he didn't do foolish things. Francis and Governor Bert Penitewa had been friends for a long time. The governor described him as loving to argue but a valuable man. The Lincoln cane in the clown wagon implied that the governor would sell out his people, and the governor couldn't understand this. After the ceremony, Francis had removed the cane from the wagon and been killed. Francis's wife and family reclaimed his body following the autopsy in Albuquerque to prevent the authorities from embalming him.

Sayesva, Teddy (SC)

Tano. Teddy, brother of Francis Sayesva and uncle of Delmar Kanitewa, wasn't much in the mood to repeat his story for a fifth time but followed his culture's rules of hospitality and prepared coffee for Leaphorn. Teddy was a small, thin man, tired-looking, with a lined face. He had a burr haircut and wore wire-rimmed glasses. His kitchen reflected the fact that he lived alone.

The last time Teddy had talked to his brother was the afternoon preceding the day of the murder, and the last time he had seen him, Francis was sleeping in the bed they had shared as boys. He hadn't seen his nephew arrive and didn't know at the time what Delmar had been carrying. After the murder he had searched his house and hadn't found anything unusual there. He couldn't believe his brother had ordered a replica made of the Lincoln cane and then sent Delmar to pick it up. Teddy didn't think Francis would insult the governor because they were friends, but Francis had insisted that the cane be placed in the clown wagon.

Scotty (BW)

Sara McKee ran off with Scotty because he was more exciting and witty than Bergen, and because she wanted to enjoy Scotty's world of money, executive jets, and vacations in the Caribbean.

Sena, Lawrence (Gordo) (PD)

As sheriff of Valencia County, his jurisdiction was the Valencia County area around the Checkerboard reservation; he had an office in the County Office Building in Grants. Sena was hard, smart, and abrasive, like Rosemary Vines. He had power because his family had money; uranium had been found beneath the family ranch lands. He felt his nickname was demeaning and tried unsuccessfully to get rid of it. He was a bulky but agile man with heavy black eyebrows and black eyes in a round face.

Sena was obsessed with finding out who had

caused the explosion on the oil rig that killed his brother, and he hated Dillon Charley and B. J. Vines. Rosemary Vines said he was dishonest; B. J. Vines said Sena had killed his own brother in order to inherit the family ranch and mineral rights. Sena told Chee how he and Henry Becenti had problems over jurisdiction after the oil-rig explosion and warned Chee twice not to interfere in his jurisdiction.

Sena, Robert (PD)

Robert, the older brother of Sheriff Lawrence Sena, was killed when a nitroglycerin charge prematurely exploded on an oil rig in July 1948. Robert had been valedictorian of his Grants High School class and was offered a college scholarship. His father had severe heart problems, and Robert stayed home, worked, and took care of the younger children. When his father died, he went to the university and studied engineering. Robert was everybody's favorite, especially his mother's; he was only twenty-four when he was killed, and his mother went out to the site frequently and hunted for his bones. His brother Lawrence was still intent on finding out who had caused the explosion thirty or so years later.

Sena family (SC)

Tano. The Sena family, neighbors who lived three houses down from Mrs. Kanitewa, had a telephone where the police could leave messages for her.

Shalako Messenger Birds (DF)

Zuñi. The Shalako are messengers from the Dance Hall of the Dead. They are represented by six gigantic masked figures denoting the six sacred directions. Each impersonator carries a ten-foot pole that holds up the costume and the facial mask on top; the huge heads have crests of eagle feathers and clapping beaks, which they use to rouse those who have dozed off during the dancing. The impersonators peer out from holes in the blankets that cover the bottom part of the masked figures.

The Shalako bring blessings of fertility and long life, and their arrival is eagerly awaited. They are preceded by Singers and Koyemshi and rise out of a riverbed on the south shore of the Zuñi River quite suddenly in the middle of the night, then proceed into the town, where they spend the night dancing. The Shalako festival is celebrated for fourteen days in late November or early December.

Sharkey, Agent (GW) (TT)

In *The Ghostway*, Sharkey was the FBI's investigating officer for the Lerner killing, directing the approach to Ashie Begay's hogan to capture Albert Gorman. He was a small, hard-looking man, about forty-five, with short-cropped curly blond hair. He was unfamiliar with Navajo death rituals. He was reintroduced in *A Thief of Time* as an FBI agent Leaphorn had worked with in the past. Leaphorn persuaded him to call Nelson's auction house and ask them to cooperate with him. Sharkey hadn't wanted to make the call, but Leaphorn talked him into it; when the ploy didn't work, Leaphorn knew Sharkey would be angry and hard to deal with.

Shaw, E. W. (Buddy) (PD)

Shaw had lived in San Francisco and worked at the Mayflower Van Lines warehouse in Bakersfield; he worked there for eleven months before being fired for drunkenness. He'd been arrested three times: drunk and disorderly, aggravated assault, and assault with a deadly weapon. He lived with Colton Wolf's mother when Colton was eleven. He was a burly man and used to beat Colton when he was drunk.

Shaw, Linda Betty (PD)

Colton Wolf thought his mother might have used the last name of Shaw while living with Buddy. See **Fry, Linda Betty; Maddox, Linda Betty;** and **Small, Mama.**

Shaw, Willie (Shortman) (GW)

Sergeant Shaw, a Los Angeles arson squad detective nearing retirement and Detective Wells's partner, was a "short man, middle-aged, with a stocky, disciplined body and a round, pink face"; he was a tough man with three commendations from the department. He wore a gun in a shoulder holster under his seersucker coat. Shaw was an expert on Albert Gorman and wanted to know why Chee wanted to find him; he had seen the FBI report on the killing of Lerner by Gorman. Before he would give Chee any information, he checked Chee's credentials by a call to headquarters. When Chee said he was working on the case in his spare time, Wells told Chee he was a vigilante like Shaw. Shaw was sure Gorman's bunch had caused the death of Kenneth Upchurch, but he couldn't prove it.

Shi-wa-ni (DF)

Zuñi. Cornstalk Insect told the boy that Shi-wa-ni had instructed him both as a man and as a priest. Shi-wa-ni was one of the two superhuman beings instructed by A'wonawil'ona to create the starry skies, the earth, and the living creatures in the fourth underworld of the earth.

Shi-wa-no-kia (DF)

Zuñi. Shi-wa-no-kia was the other superhuman who was ordered to create the starry skies, the earth, and the living creatures in the fourth underworld by A'wonawil'ona.

Shoemaker, Old Man (BW)

This elderly man owned and operated Shoemaker's Trading Post and had an endless number of stories he liked to tell.

Shorty, Officer (TT)

Officer Shorty from the Shiprock substation took the report from Delbert Tsosie about the stolen backhoe.

Shulawitsi (DD) (DF)

Zuñi. In *The Boy Who Made Dragonfly*, Shulawitsi, the Little Fire God, noticed the Cornstalk Insect had entered the Dance Hall of the Dead and brought it to the attention of the Council of the Gods. Shulawitsi was pleased with the prayer plumes the boy had made and told the Cornstalk Insect the gods had heard the boy's prayers and the boy would be a great man among his people.

In *Dance Hall of the Dead*, Ernesto Cata was training to portray Shulawitsi in the upcoming Shalako ceremony at Zuñi.

Silver, Milton Richard (LW)

One of the Boy Scouts held hostage by the Buffalo Society, his description reminded Leaphorn of his nephew in Flagstaff.

Simons, Judy (LW)

Theodora Adams tried to get Leaphorn to believe her name was Judy Simons; he quashed that quickly by making her produce her driver's license.

Singer, Harold L. (FW)

The initials of Singer, State Highway Department

project engineer, were on scores of change-order sheets, increasing the high-profit items and decreasing the low-profit items of Reevis-Smith, low bidder on the contracts. A month after Flowers became chairman of the Highway Commission, Singer was hired in the Construction Division to supervise a "Quality Experiment" on certain secondary highways; Reevis-Smith was awarded all the Quality Experiment projects.

Less than a year earlier, Singer had been implicated in a case involving kickbacks in Chicago construction projects. Cotton called Singer to confirm the details of his story and give Singer a chance to contradict or deny it; Singer started to say he hadn't falsified anything, then refused to comment. Cotton felt sorry for Singer because Singer had a daughter in high school, and the scandal would hurt her.

Sisneros, Eloy (FW)

In Santa Fe, Cotton walked past the old house of this boyhood friend.

Six Sacred Directions (DF)

Zuñi celebrations, ceremonies, and dances follow the directions of the compass, starting with north and going counterclockwise. Each kiva is associated with one of the compass directions, and each direction has associated with it a specific color and part of the environment: North is yellow and air; West is blue or green and water; South is red and fire; East is white and earth; the Zenith is multicolored and sky; the Nadir is black and the underworld. Each direction also has its own beast god, or animal of prey: for North it is the mountain lion; West is the bear, the most powerful of all; South is the badger; East is the wolf; the Zenith is the eagle; and the Nadir is the mole. Specific game animals are also associated with each direction: mule deer for North, mountain sheep for West, antelope for South, whitetail deer for East, jackrabbit for the Zenith, and cottontail for the Nadir.

Skeet, Leonard (Lenny) (SW)

Assigned to work out of the Piñon Chapter House, Skeet also used the subagency police station, a double-width mobile home, as his house. He was a member of the Sleep Rock Dinee, born to the Ears Sticking Up Clan, and was married to Aileen Beno. Leaphorn had worked with him at Tuba City. Skeet was reliable if you weren't in a hurry. He drove Leaphorn out to Goldtooth's place (because Leaphorn's arm was in a cast) and proved to be a skillful driver on the slick back roads.

Small, George Tobias (Toby; G. T.) (FLG)

Small was executed in the gas chamber of the New Mexico State Penitentiary at Santa Fe for the murder of Robert Martin and his wife during an attempted robbery.

Small was a white man, 188 pounds and six feet four inches tall; he walked with a noticeable stoop and carried his right shoulder higher than his left. He had brown eyes and a ruddy complexion and would smile shyly; there was a deep scar on his left upper lip and MOTHER was tattooed inside a heart on his left inner forearm. The two upper joints of his left ring finger were missing, which he said was caused by a rock falling on his finger when he was a little boy. Around thirty-eight years old, he had been under twenty-one when he started serving the first of three prison terms.

Small wanted reporters Hardin and Thompson to help him find his mother, so she could bury him with his family; he didn't know his mother's current last name, where her original home was, or who his relatives were. He remembered living with her in San Diego, in Oregon, and in Salt Lake City. In Salt Lake City he had attended school and lived in a trailer with his mother and her man. One day they had both been drinking, and the man beat him and ran him off; he stayed for a while in the garage of a school friend. On his twelfth birthday he returned to the trailer, hoping things would be better, but Mama, the man, and the trailer were gone; they hadn't even left a note. Small thought Mama might have gone to Los Angeles, so he stole a car and tried to follow her. The police arrested him for car theft and put him in the Utah State Reformatory on July 28, 1941, the start of a long prison record. Whenever he wasn't in prison he would hunt for his mother.

When Thompson asked Small how he felt the day before his execution, Small said he wasn't afraid of being hurt because he'd been hurt before; he was afraid of what he would find when he came out of the gas chamber. He didn't want to be alone; he wanted to believe someone would be waiting for him.

Hillerman wrote that Small was a real person—with a different name—who was executed in the New Mexico State Prison when Hillerman worked for the United Press. He reincarnated Small as Colton Wolf in *People of Darkness* and said he felt Small would have been another Colton Wolf had he been allowed to "live a few murders more."

Small, Mama (FLG)

Mama Small moved around from town to town, living with one man after another. She was an alcoholic. When Small came home on his twelfth birthday, Mama and her man had left without a word. Small thought Mama might have moved to Los Angeles because the man she was living with wanted to go to the West Coast. Mama was the model for Colton Wolf's mother in *People of Darkness*.

Sosi, Emma Begay (GW)
     Emma was the (deceased) mother of Margaret Billy Sosi.

Sosi, Franklin (GW)
     Franklin was the father of Margaret Billy Sosi. Her school had no address where he could be reached.

Sosi, Margaret Billy (GW)
     Margaret, Ashie Begay's seventeen-year-old granddaughter, was small and appeared to be about fifteen. She ran away from Saint Catherine's Indian School in Santa Fe because she had received a letter and was worried about her grandfather; she was not the type to run away. At the school they listed Franklin Sosi as her father (no known address), mother Emma Begay Sosi (deceased), and grandfather Ashie Begay (contact in emergency).
     Chee found her inside Begay's abandoned hogan; she'd "borrowed" a horse to get there. Margaret wasn't afraid to go inside because her grandfather was a holy man and would leave no *chindi*. Her grandfather had taught her the Navajo Way and the death rituals. She hoped her grandfather was still alive; she had no other relatives on the reservation. She ran away from Chee before he could question her.
     She found a man named Grayson, asked him where her grandfather was, and told him she was going to find an old woman. Chee followed her to Los Angeles, where she had found one of her great-aunts (Bentwoman's Daughter) and her great-grandmother (Bentwoman Tsossie). She was an

extremely sensible, practical young lady who didn't scare easily.

St. Germain, Bernard (TG)

St. Germain is a real person written into the story by Hillerman, as a brakeman-conductor with the Atchison, Topeka, and Santa Fe Railroad. Leaphorn called him to find out if it was possible for a passenger to stop an Amtrak train; St. Germain found out the train had stopped close to where the body was found, but nobody had pulled the emergency stop lever; there had been an air brake malfunction.

Standing Medicine (LW)

Famous great-grandfather of Hosteen Tso from the time before the Long Walk, he wouldn't surrender when Kit Carson came through. He was a big medicine man; he knew the entire seven days of the Blessing Way, the Mountain Way, and several other sings. He had been headman of the Bitter Water Dinee and was noted for his wisdom. He decided the Sun Way was the most important ceremonial, which was to be used with the Calling Back Chant to start the Fifth World; he was afraid it would be forgotten or destroyed, so he hid the ceremonial sand paintings and told only his oldest son about their significance and where they were. This information was to be passed down to the oldest son of each generation. After the bitter starvation winter of 1864, his group surrendered and was taken to Bosque Redondo, where he died in 1865.

Steiner, Alexander (LW)

Dr. Steiner, John Tull's psychiatrist in prison, established an odd sort of rapport with Tull; Tull told Steiner he got a new face every time he was reborn. Steiner smoked Pall Mall cigarettes.

Stone (the Client) (TG)

Stone was a phony name used by the man in charge of security for the Chilean Embassy. He told Leroy Fleck that if there was no identification of Santillanes's body and no publicity for a month, Leroy would get the balance of the $12,000 they owed him. Stone wanted Leroy to kill Santero the same way he'd killed Santillanes. He didn't know Leroy had photographed him when he went to the public telephone booth and that Leroy would get his money or get even.

Streib, David W. (Dilly) (SC)

Special Agent Streib worked out of the Farmington office of the FBI and was responsible for investigating the murder of Eric Dorsey. He accompanied Leaphorn and Ed Toddy to Saint Bonaventure Indian Mission to examine Dorsey's woodshop and discovered the forms for sand-casting silver objects. He set things up for Leaphorn to go to Tano but wouldn't go with him because he didn't feel like solving problems for the FBI's Albuquerque office.

He was a bureau old-timer, a laid-back, contented man with many friends in Indian country. His whimsical sense of humor had earned him the nickname Dilly and had not endeared him to Hoover's group, so he had been banished to the Southwest. He was getting close to retirement and planned to build a greenhouse behind his home when he quit.

Dilly was an old friend who knew about Leaphorn's proposed trip to Asia with Professor Louisa Bourebonette, although Leaphorn didn't recall ever having discussed it with anyone. He asked Leaphorn why he didn't just stay in the United States and pursue her. Leaphorn explained he had become interested in finding his roots. Dilly said his German ancestors came from Alsace and he'd never particularly wanted to go see the area. He told Leaphorn he thought it would be a good idea for him to become involved with Louisa; he'd been alone long enough.

See **Streib, Delbert L.,** the same character with a slightly different name.

Streib, Delbert L. (Dilly) (SW)

FBI agent from Gallup in charge of investigating the murders of Dugai Endocheeney and Irma Onesalt, Dilly had been with the FBI for twenty years. He smoked a pipe and wore the FBI summer uniform: a dark blue suit, white shirt, and tie; the suit looked like he slept in it. Leaphorn thought he was smarter than most and had been exiled to Indian country because he didn't fit in with J. Edgar Hoover's elite circle. Dilly knew that bone beads in wounds signified skinwalkers. Leaphorn knew it would be hard to persuade Dilly to file a complaint so the Navajos could pick up Roosevelt Bistie again for questioning; he knew the FBI wouldn't like losing their case against Bistie.

See **Streib, David W.,** the same character with a slightly different name.

Sun Father (DF)

Zuñi. The Sun Father leaves the sky and returns to his sacred place each day; he has a lodge behind the Eastern Mountains and a home in the west.

Sun-i-a-shi'wa-ni (DF)

Zuñi. The Ice God is the god of winter. The children would know the Corn Maidens were coming because they would smell the scent of flowers and springtime and a mist would melt away the frost of Sun-i-a-shi'wa-ni's breath.

Supergrandson (PD)

Supergrandson, the twelve-year-old grandson of Ramona Musket, told Chee where Ramona was and drew him a map to where a Peyote Way service was being held. Supergrandson wore a Superman T-shirt.

Susanne (Susie) (DD)

Member of the Jason's Fleece commune and friend of Ted Isaacs, Ernesto Cata, and George Bowlegs, Susie was a sympathetic person who cared deeply about other people. She had left school in the tenth grade and couldn't go back home because her father didn't want her; she had a fourteen-year-old sister at home whom she wanted to take to a safe place somewhere, and she had a grandmother she didn't know who lived in the East. She lived at the commune because she didn't have anywhere else to go; she washed and cooked and slept with Halsey in order to be allowed to stay there.

Susanne was in her late teens but looked very thin, tired, and nervous; her small hands were grimy and she had broken fingernails. Her face was oval and freckled and surrounded by blond hair, and she spoke with a slight stammer. The long sleeves of her clothing covered scars shaped like old cigarette burns. In spite of her own problems, Susanne continued to help others; Leaphorn reasoned that Susanne wasn't a loser.

Susanne spent part of her time at the dig helping Ted Isaacs until Dr. Reynolds put a stop to it; she and Ted had formed a deep friendship and she hoped that one day Ted would marry her, after he had obtained his degree and become established in a good position. Ted said he cared for her, but when Susanne had no money and no place to stay, he chose not to help her because it would jeopardize his position with Reynolds. Leaphorn took Susanne with him, to help him contact George, since George was more apt to respond to Susanne than to him. (Susanne had been George's friend and had tried to teach him to play the guitar.) Her information about George's deer-hunting skill was helpful to Leaphorn in locating him. When Leaphorn was shot with the tranquilizer dart, Susanne protected him until the effects wore off. Since Ted had rejected her, she had no reason to stay in the area, so she left.

Symons (LW)

Symons was one of the Boy Scout leaders held hostage by the Buffalo Society. Three adults and eleven children were captured because three Kiowa adults and eleven children had been killed by the whites in the Olds Prairie murders, one of the historic crimes to be avenged.

T. L. (FW)

The person who received John Cotton's political article by teletype in the *Tribune* office had the initials T. L.

Ta'a'shi-wani (DF)

Zuñi. The Corn Priests were first created by the little boy (now a great priest) when he named his counselors. They directed the people in the harvest of the gods, one eighth of which was reserved for them.

Tafoya, Reverend (TT)

An Apache who worked with Slim Nakai at his revivals, he told the crowd he had a skin cancer that had been cured at a revival in Dulce. (In one version of *The Thief of Time*, Slick Nakai told Leaphorn Tafoya was Mescalero; in another version he was identified as Jicarella.)

Tagert, Christopher (CW)

A history professor from the University of New Mexico, Dr. Tagert's specialty was Law and Order in the Old West, and he wanted to be regarded as *the* authority in this area. When Chee was on campus, he'd been told to avoid Tagert's classes. Tagert was Chairman of Jean Jacobs's dissertation committee. In his office he had a high-volume telephone because he was hard of hearing. He had two cars: a white 1990 Oldsmobile Cutlass four-door sedan and a sexy red 1982 Corvette coupe, which he drove to impress the female freshmen students, or so his wife said; he was separated from his wife. When Chee went out to his house to see if he was there, he noticed that both cars were in the garage.

Tagert had been missing for several weeks; he had not come to his assigned classes. The notation on his desk calendar indicated he had intended to contact Odell Redd to see what he wanted, pick up Ashie Pinto, do his research, and then be back in time for the beginning of fall semester classes. It had been a year since he had worked with Pinto; Mary Keeyani had torn up his letters to Pinto because she didn't want Pinto working with him. Pinto was an alcoholic who had quit drinking, and Tagert would give him whiskey, to get him to tell things he wouldn't say when he was sober. Pinto said Tagert was a coyote but he paid well. Tagert believed Butch Cassidy had returned to the United States in 1909, robbed a bank and a train, and died at the hands of the Navajos; he believed Cassidy's body was somewhere on the Navajo reservation, and he wanted Pinto to lead him to it so he could destroy the theory of his rival, Henderson.

Tagert, Mrs. Christopher (CW)

Dr. Tagert's wife had separated from her husband. When Jean Jacobs called about her husband's whereabouts, she told Jacobs she didn't know, didn't want to know, and if they found him please not to tell her.

Takes, Sam George (BW)

A law and order sergeant in the Chinle subagency, he was a round-faced, barrel-chested young man who thought Billy Nez might be out visiting his girlfriend. Sam lent Leaphorn his horse and trailer.

Talking God (Yeibichai) (TG)

The Night Chant or Yeibichai was named for Talking God; he is the maternal grandfather of all the spirits.

Tamana, Eldon (TG)

A youngish Tano Pueblo man who wanted to get elected to the Tribal Council, Tamana was in favor of granting the right-of-way to the Sunbelt Corporation. He wanted the Smithsonian to return the Tano War God so he could walk into the Tribal Council and present the fetish to them, to show them he was a young man who could get things done. He had known John McDermott at the University of Arizona and asked his advice about how to obtain the Tano War God.

Thatcher, L. D. (TT)

Thatcher was with the Bureau of Land Management law enforcement; one of his jobs was to license tour boatmen on the San Juan River. He admitted to having some prejudices of his own: he thought women with hyphenated last names must be rich and hard to work with, and he couldn't understand what kind of fool would pay thousands of dollars for an ancient pot. He had a warrant to search Ellie Friedman-Bernal's room and belongings, because the bureau had received an anonymous tip that Ellie had violated the Antiquities Preservation Protection Act. He asked Leaphorn to accompany him because he wanted to divert Leaphorn from his grief over Emma's death, and he wanted to persuade Leaphorn not to quit his job. Later he accompanied Leaphorn to Harrison Houk's home because it was out of Leaphorn's jurisdiction.

Thief of Time (TT)

The term is applied to the pot hunter who tries to get rich selling pots or other artifacts and obtains finds illegally, digging up graves and destroying archaeological evidence.

Thomas, George (BW)

George Jackson, the Big Navajo, used George Thomas as one of his aliases.

Thompson (FLG)

One of the reporters covering Toby Small's execution at the New Mexico State Penitentiary, Thompson said the death chamber looked like a big incinerator or an old wood stove with the chimney out of the top. He had asked Small what he remembered about his mother and how he felt about his impending execution. (Hillerman has written that the Thompson of the story was the late John Curtis of the Associated Press.)

Thompson, Shirley (CW)

Clerk at the Red Rock Trading Post, she was Towering House Dinee, single, and giggled a lot. Shirley had large brown eyes, long lashes, and perfect skin; she thought whoever painted the mountain white was crazy.

THE TONY HILLERMAN COMPANION

Thoreau (SC)

Thoreau was a railroad engineer; the village of Thoreau (pronounced "threw") was named after him. The Saint Bonaventure Indian Mission School was located in Thoreau.

Tobias, T. J. (FW)

The Capitol pressroom's senior citizen, he had written for the *Evening News* since the first Roosevelt administration. Tobias remembered too much, drank too much, and coasted into retirement on nostalgic news articles.

Todachene, Victor (SC)

An old man who lived near Crystal, he was the pedestrian victim of a hit-and-run homicide. The driver had sideswiped him, backed up to see what had happened, and then driven away. During the next two hours Todachene had lain there and bled to death.

There were no witnesses and no clues as to the identity of the driver. Leaphorn thought the Chief would agree that Chee should receive his sergeant's stripes if he could solve the mystery.

Toddy, Ed (SC)

Lieutenant Toddy was in charge of the Crownpoint police station, and Eric Dorsey had died in his jurisdiction. He told Leaphorn some Anglo man had called and reported that a box of things taken from Dorsey's shop was under Eugene Ahkeah's mobile home. Toddy had investigated and found the box. He later accompanied Leaphorn and Dilly Streib to Saint Bonaventure Indian Mission to examine Dorsey's shop and opened Dorsey's trailer so Leaphorn could search it again.

Todman, John (CW)

Todman was looking at "Golightly mining camp photographs" at the University of New Mexico library while Chee listened to the Ashie Pinto tapes.

Toledo, Virginia (Virgie) (SC)

Administrative Assistant at Window Rock Tribal Police Station, she had worked for twenty-three years for the Navajo Department of Public Safety and was the workaday nerve center for the police station. She knew how to deal with everyone in the building but had not decided what her relationship would be with Jim Chee. She didn't like his abrupt questioning, and she had heard he was something of a screwup. She suspected maybe he had been around white men too long but then decided he was just young and excited.

Virginia told Chee that the police should lock their doors and desks. She had once had her purse and jacket stolen, and she had no idea who had laid the manila envelope on his desk. Virginia was a true friend to Leaphorn, which he didn't realize until he was suspended; she was angry about it and defended him. She had no kind comments about Councilman Chester.

Tom, Hosteen (BW)

Hosteen Tom had several sons. One son had tried to enlist in the Marine Corps but was now mining coal because he had not been able to fill out the Marine Corps forms correctly.

Tom, Jefferson (GW)

Father of Bentwoman's Daughter, he belonged to the Salt Dinee.

Tom Bob (DD)

When Tom Bob, Blackie Bisti, and Joe Leaphorn

THE TONY HILLERMAN COMPANION

were attending Arizona State University, they went to a meeting of the Native American Church and sampled peyote.

Tonale, Lizzie (SW)

A Mud Clan Navajo who married Isaac Ginsberg, she was the mother of Iron Woman. She converted to Judaism after marrying Ginsberg and persuaded Ginsberg to build his trading post as far away as possible from her relatives. She always closed the trading post on the Sabbath and ran it for twenty years by herself before her death.

Topaka, Shirley (DW)

Dispatcher at Tuba City substation, she was two years out of Tuba City High School, where she'd been a cheerleader. Shirley had pretty eyes, very white teeth, perfect skin, and a plump figure; she had a tendency to flirt with any available male. She received a tip from the Arizona State Highway Patrol about Priscilla Bisti, which she passed on to Chee.

Truck Driver (FW)

Organization man who drove the semi stolen from Reevis-Smith, he was twenty-five to forty years old, wore large sunglasses and gloves, and had blond hair and a bushy mustache; he was a big, bulky-looking man. After he ran Whitey Robbins off the bridge, he abandoned the truck near the railroad yards in the capital's industrial district.

Tso, Hosteen (LW)

Hosteen Tso, the father of Ford Tso and grandfather of Jimmy and Benjamin Tso, was physically ill and sick at heart and asked Margaret Cigaret what was wrong with him. Margaret was frustrated because Old Man Tso wouldn't tell her

350

everything she needed to know to prescribe the appropriate ceremonial. Tso told her he'd dreamed of his dead son and a painted cave. Also, some sand paintings had been disturbed and he'd killed a frog. He had been where his great-grandfather's ghost might be, and he might have been around some witches. Tso wanted to stay alive until he could pass on a family secret to his grandson Ben. Before Margaret could prescribe a ceremony for him, someone hit Tso on the head and killed him.

Tso, Father Benjamin (LW)
      Grandson of Hosteen Tso and younger brother of Jimmy Tso, Ben was a largish young man, perhaps six feet tall, with narrow hips and a heavy muscular torso; he had black hair and a Navajo face, longish rather than bony, shrewdly intelligent. He was a Roman Catholic priest and had just returned from Rome, where he had been completing his studies at the Vatican's American College and the Franciscan seminary. He had lived with his grandfather briefly when he was young and then went to Saint Anthony's boarding school; he didn't know much about his grandfather because he hadn't seen him since he was eleven or twelve.
      He'd met Theodora Adams in Rome and was considering breaking his vows and marrying her; when he received the letter from his grandfather, he decided to come home and think about what he really wanted to do. His grandfather had died and was buried before Ben arrived; Theodora followed him and they were both taken hostage with the Boy Scout group.

Tso, Bernie (TT)
      Chee took the Buick that Janet Pete wanted to buy to Bernie Tso, the auto repairman in Shiprock. Bernie examined the car and figured the car dealer

had turned back the odometer; the tire treads were worn, the universal joint rattled, and the steering was slack. He told Chee the car was a junker. He had repaired the transmission on the car of the Backhoe Bandit and gave Chee the man's description.

Tso, Emerson (SW)

The principal of the Kinlichee Boarding School complained to Leaphorn that Emerson Tso was selling bootleg liquor to his students again, and he wanted Tso locked up forever. Leaphorn promised to take care of him immediately; he had no use for bootleggers.

Tso, Emma (Old Woman) (WI)

Old Woman Tso used the word "anti'l" to describe murder and mutilation, the worst kind of witchcraft. Her son-in-law had been out looking for some sheep and had found the body of a man killed by a witch; the skin was cut off the palms and fingers of his hands.

Tso, Ford (LW)

Only child and son of Hosteen Tso, Ford married a girl of the Salt Cedar Clan at Teec Nos Pos and moved with her near her family. John McGinnis said Ford was no good, "got to drinking and whoring around Farmington until her folks run him off . . . always fighting and raising hell." Ford's wife was also a drunkard. Ford had died many years ago in Gallup, from a beating he received from the police. One of their younger sons, Ben, stayed briefly with Hosteen Tso and then went to boarding school at Saint Anthony's.

Tso, James (Jimmy) (LW)

Jimmy was the grandson of Hosteen Tso, older son of Ford Tso, brother of Ben Tso, and friend of

John Tull. He looked just like Ben except that he wore gold-rimmed glasses; he was a year older than Ben. Jimmy had lived with his father and watched as the police beat his father to death; he was fourteen at the time. Ben said Jimmy was never the same after that. Jimmy hated the fact that Ben had prostrated himself before the whites when he became a priest, and he was angry that Ben had broken his vows because of a woman, especially one he considered a slut. Hosteen Tso wanted Ben to come home because Jimmy was acting "like a damned white man" and because Tso wanted to tell Ben the family secret before he died. Jimmy needed Ben on the reservation for his plans to work. Jimmy used the aliases Frank Hoski, Colton Hoski, Frank Morris, Theodore Parker, and Van Black. See also **Hoski, Frank**.

Tso, Jimmy (SW)
A Navajo Tribal Policeman, officer Tso handled the liaison with the Gallup police department. Leaphorn wanted him to check the suppliers for jewelry makers and others to learn how an Indian jewelry maker might obtain bone beads.

Tso, Lilly (BW)
Lilly was a member of the Many Goats Clan, mother of Elsie (Agnes) Tso. She and the other in-laws despised Luis Horseman and would have turned him over to the police if Luis had tried to hide in their area.

Tso, Minnie (BW)
Luis Horseman married into Minnie Tso's family; they were Many Goats Clan.

Tso, Tom (SC)
A student at Saint Bonaventure Indian Mission, he wanted to know after Eric Dorsey's death when he

could pick up the silver concha belt he had been making.

Tsosie, Agnes (BW)

Charley Tsosie's wife, she was the mother of their two sons. An uncle took her place in one of the ceremonies of the Enemy Way for Charley.

Tsosie, Agnes (Old Woman) (TG)

Agnes Tsosie, a thin, gray-haired lady dying of liver cancer, was matriarch of the Bitter Water Dinee. Agnes had twice served on the Navajo Tribal Council representing the Lower Greasewood Chapter; she had worked to get water wells drilled and water supplies for every chapter house. Her picture had been used in an article by *National Geographic*, which is where Henry Highhawk saw it. She remembered her mother's aunt had gone to boarding school and never returned; she thought Highhawk might be a relative, so she invited him to her Yeibichai ceremony. Agnes had decided to come home to her husband, daughter, and son-in-law and be buried the Navajo way.

Tsosie, Billy (SC)

Chee asked one of the workers at the Navajo Agricultural Industries produce warehouse if the man with the bent-brim cap was Billy Tsosie. The man told him the man was Clement Hoski and he carpooled to work with people from the Navajo Agricultural Industries housing.

Tsosie, Charley (BW)

Charley Tsosie was Billy Nez's uncle. It was confirmed by the Hand Trembler that Charley had been witched by the Navajo Wolf, so Charley and his family hired a Singer, Sandoval, to perform an Enemy Way for them.

Tsosie, Delbert (TT)

Delbert worked at the Texaco service station directly across the road from the Navajo Tribal Police motor pool in Shiprock. He watched someone drive a truck with a flatbed trailer into the motor pool and leave with the backhoe. He figured it was one of the tribal employees and didn't report it. He told Chee there were two men, and he didn't recognize either of them. One was a tall, skinny Navajo wearing a cowboy hat; he drove the truck. The other was a white man driving a dark blue Plymouth two-door sedan; he was short and stocky with freckles and a sunburn and wore a baseball cap.

Tsossie, Bentwoman (GW)

Bentwoman Tsossie, Ashie Begay's grandmother, was born to the Turkey Clan. She was in a wheelchair; she was blind and partially deaf, her voice was slow and faint, and she fell asleep periodically. She wanted Margaret Sosi to go back to Dinetah; she had told her Ashie Begay was dead, but Margaret wouldn't believe her. Bentwoman said Ashie followed the Navajo Way and would have removed Albert Gorman from his hogan before he died; she thought a white man killed and buried Albert and then broke the hogan wall.

Tsossie, Mustache (LW)

Grandson of Standing Medicine, born to the Mud Clan and married into the Salt Cedar Clan, he was an oldest son, and *his* oldest son was Hosteen Tso.

Tsossie, Windy (PD)

Windy was one of the Navajo crew who did not show up for work at the oil rig the day it exploded in 1948. He was of the Mud Clan and his wife was of the Standing Rock Clan. After they moved to Bisti country, his wife died. His kinsmen thought he was a witch. Chee followed up on Fannie Kinlicheenie's story and knew he had found Tsossie's skeleton because Tsossie had a finger missing. Tsossie had died of bone cancer.

Tsossie family (LW) (WI)

In *Listening Woman* the Tsossies were the family that lived in the area of the Short Mountain Trading Post. The Tsossies or the Begays would have been most likely to have found the downed helicopter and would have taken anything of value in to John McGinnis for trade. In the short story "Chee's Witch," the Tsossie family had a hogan north of Teec Nos Pos; they had a sick child and a water well that had gone alkaline, and they blamed it on a skinwalker, the City Navajo.

Tull, John (LW)

Tull worked with Frank Hoski and stressed he did not work for Henry Kelongy. Tull had the usual police record, heavy on crimes of violence; he had been in jail several times, for armed robbery and attempted homicide. Tull's mother, a Seminole, was a drunkard who had lived with a series of men; John didn't know who his father was. At some point he went to live with an uncle; when he was thirteen, while he was at his uncle's, he was kicked in the head by a mule. He survived but was blinded in his left eye, and his face was terribly disfigured.

Tull had psychotic symptoms of schizophrenic paranoia, with delusions and hallucinations. He believed he was immortal and had died and been reborn two or three times; he walked right up to the gun barrel of a guard once in a robbery, because he had no fear of dying. He liked Hoski because he thought Hoski was immortal too and

CHARACTERS IN TONY HILLERMAN'S FICTION

mesa and its desecrated shrines were visible proof, right beside New Mexico Highway 44, that the old religion had lost its power in the modern world.

Whether or not that young Navajo converted his audience to the fundamentalist version of Christianity, one could hardly miss the other lesson his presence taught. If Indians are to preserve their traditional way of worshiping their Creator, their sacred places must be protected from such desecration.

It is relatively easy to protect the shrines of European and Asian faiths. Despite their political differences with Islam, the Israelis would never erect television towers atop the Dome of the Rock, from which Muhammad ascended into heaven. When Muslims controlled Jerusalem, they left the Wailing Wall undefiled. Nor would Islamic Jordanians destroy Christian shrines in the territory they control. If a winery bought real estate at Lourdes to erect a warehouse at that Roman Catholic shrine, the French would never permit it.

Protection of tribal shrines presents a unique problem. Most are natural landmarks: mountains, lakes, springs, salt deposits, eagle nests high in mesa walls. They are never buildings. And the land where most of them are found is controlled by a dominant culture that hardly knows they exist.

One of the rare victories for Indian religions came when Taos Pueblo regained control of Blue Lake. The government had taken possession of that Taos Mountain territory in 1906 and made it part of the Carson National Forest (named for Indian-killer Kit Carson). It wasn't until 1970, after years of struggle and a wealth of legal and lobbying fees, that the Pueblo regained its land. Even that victory was based on the wrong reason. Taos Pueblo regained its land not because the little lake is its most sacred place but because it proved exclusive use and occupancy.

The nature of most shrines, and the nature of the tribal religion, makes such proof difficult for most sacred places. Mount Taylor, for example, is not only one of the four Holy Mountains of the Navajo people, it is also sacred to the Acomas, the Lagunas, and some of the Rio Grande Pueblos. The same is true of the San Francisco Peaks in Arizona, the gateway between the worlds for the Hopi kachinas and also holy to the Navajos.

While exclusive rights might not be provable, sacred places could be protected from desecration in other ways. Many of them are on land under federal control. Department of Interior agencies could be required to work with tribal religious leaders, listing holy places and giving them legal status. Those on private property could, through public condemnation proceedings, be given the same sort of protection offered to historical and cultural landmarks. In places where it is appropriate (for example, Huerfano Mesa and the San Francisco Peaks), roadside signs could inform the ignorant of their religious significance.

There are ways to grant full First Amendment rights of religious freedom to all Americans. We only lack the will.

Taos Restores the Spirit

The last time I was in Taos, the Oakland A's were playing the Yankees on the hotel room TV. A manager-pitcher-catcher-shortstop discussion was under way, and the cameraman passed the time by showing us the moon—yellow as a lemon—over the Bronx. Through my window I could see the same moon. But over Taos, two thousand miles west of Yankee Stadium, it hung in the sky like a scarred white rock. The moonlight, too, was robbed of color. It turned the infinity of sage into stark, dark silver.

A little earlier Richard Vaughn, one of the numerous artists of Taos, had talked to me of just such things. He had come here from England, and when I asked him what had drawn him to this odd place, he gave me a thoughtful answer.

"First, it's the elemental beauty," Vaughn said. "And then it's an interesting place to be."

That sums up well enough what made Taos an art colony, and what draws an estimated half-million visitors a year to a dinky, dusty little town 130 miles from the nearest place a jetliner can land and half that far from the nearest interstate highway. It *is* an interesting place. And even after decades of looking at Taos, I still am awed by its beauty.

Taos and neighboring Taos Pueblo sit literally in the shadow of the Sangre de Cristo Mountains on the Taos Plateau. Just to the east the mountains rise to more than 13,000 feet, and to the west the Rio Grande roars through its spectacular gorge. Town and pueblo are built in an oasis of lush green meadows. An artist couldn't ask for more.

Part of that elemental beauty is a matter of light. Taos is seven thousand feet above sea level. Air contains less oxygen and carbon dioxide here than at lower altitudes—and relatively more hydrogen. Also absent are humidity and those smoggy pollutants that prosperity brings. Thus the moon is whiter, and, when it's down, the night sky is a-dazzle with a billion stars lowlanders never see. Sun produces a sharper contrast of light and shadow, the blue of the sky is implausibly dark, and San Antonio Mountain, 50 miles away by road on the Colorado border, looks near enough to touch. Artists have been commenting on all this for generations.

Frederick Remington, the famous painter of cowboys and the frontier, came to Taos in 1882, riding in from the east.

"I trotted all day over the dry tableland and yet the great blue wall of the Sangre de Cristo Range seemed as near and as far as it had in the morning. It was as though we could not get near it. . . .

"At the edge of a slight drop in the mesa we saw the blue evening smoke of two villages—the Indian Pueblo of Taos and the Mexican town of the same name. . . .

"They looked hopelessly small and forgotten."

They still look hopelessly small and forgotten. Taos Pueblo was five hundred years old when Remington saw it, and the additional century has hardly affected it. It still makes the same blue evening smoke. Although the tribe recently installed electricity and telephones, the Taos Indians still use wood for fuel. They decided against gas and indoor plumbing.

Taos town has grown a bit since 1882 to a summer population of perhaps 6,000 and has added traffic lights and a traffic jam. But it remains an adobe village of crooked buildings on narrow crooked streets.

Here the antiquity is genuine. The town was founded on its present site in 1615, after the Taos Indians asked Spanish settlers to move a bit farther from the pueblo. And archaeologists believe the two great mud-and-straw structures that form the pueblo itself were built much earlier, about 1300. Yet Taos Pueblo is as lively as it was when Spanish explorer Francisco Vásquez de Coronado saw it in 1540. Few places today offer such a giant step backward in time.

I like to visit as early as the pueblo will allow—currently 8 A.M.—because slanting morning sunlight gives a molding of shadow to these remarkable buildings. It's a pleasant two-and-a-half mile trip from town. The road enters the pueblo through a narrow passageway between the chalky white wall of the Church of San Geronimo and an adobe gatehouse. There a tribesman will collect a three-dollar charge for parking and a camera fee.

Even if you've paid the camera fee, it's the worst of bad manners to photograph Pueblo Indians without personal permission. They believe that photographing a person diminishes his power. Youngsters often won't mind. Older Indians, and especially those wearing the traditional braids and blankets, probably will.

The earthen courtyard of the plaza into which the tribe admits its visitors is walled off to the north and west by the massive five-story shape of North House. Across Rio Pueblo de Taos, a clear, cold trout stream that bubbles through the court, stands South House, almost equal in size. Both complexes were designed as fortresses in which the Indians could defend themselves against raids. But they have a distinct natural beauty, as if they had grown from the Mother Earth the pueblo honors.

The plaza is the pueblo's ceremonial dance

ground, considered to be the center of the universe. Off-limits signs restrict visitors principally to the plaza and to shops in the North and South houses, where residents sell bread baked in the outdoor earthen ovens around the plaza or fried to a delicious but stomach-wrenching crunchiness. Other made-in-the-pueblo items for sale include drums of rawhide stretched over hollow cottonwood, moccasins, beadwork, jewelry, local pottery, and toy bows and arrows.

Strictly off limits—not only to non-Indians but also to tribe members not properly initiated—are the six kivas of the pueblo's religious societies. Four cluster at the east end of North House; the others are across the river. They are easy to identify because they can be entered only from the roof, and their access ladders jut skyward.

In the Taos kivas, revolutions have been planned. Twice they restored control of this part of America to the Indians. The first time was in 1680. From here runners moved along the river and across the desert to deliver knotted cords to the other Pueblo tribes. One knot was to be untied each day, and, when the last one was undone, the Indians struck—killing the Spanish who occupied their villages and driving the survivors down the Rio Grande. For twelve years a consortium of Indian tribes ruled the territory, until Don Diego de Vargas recaptured Santa Fe in 1692.

The second revolt challenged the United States, which had taken New Mexico in the Mexican War. The following year, in 1847, the Taos Indians, joined by Mexicans unhappy with American occupation, killed Territorial Governor Charles Bent and other officials in Taos and then marched on Santa Fe. Defeated by U.S. Army troops, they took shelter at the Taos Pueblo in the original Church of San Geronimo. The army bombarded the church, pointed a howitzer through a hole cut in the wall, and fired point-blank into the building. The tribe never rebuilt the desecrated church, and you pass its ruins as you enter the pueblo.

The "new" church is worth a visit, even though it can't compare in antiquity with many other Franciscan mission churches in northern New Mexico. Most of the pueblo residents are Roman Catholics—which doesn't interfere with their maintaining their original religion. The Indians simply added Catholicism to their existing theology and kept the old ways intact.

It was the exoticism, more than natural beauty, that first attracted painters. Ernest Blumenschein, one of the greatest of the Taos artists, recalled that he and his contemporaries were bored with more traditional material. "We felt the need of a stimulating subject," he wrote, and they found it in the Indian and Spanish colonial cultures of Taos.

The story of the art colony begins in September 1898. Blumenschein and Bert Phillips—on a sketching trip in the Rockies—impulsively decided to follow the sun down to Mexico. They headed south from Denver but broke a buggy wheel in the San Luis Valley. Blumenschein rode to the nearest settlement for repairs. It was Taos. Three years earlier a young New York painter, Joseph Sharp, had regaled the two young artists with enthusiastic accounts of the Taos Indians and of the beauty of the place. By the time Blumenschein returned with the wheel, he too was converted. He and Phillips ended their odyssey then and there—and quickly attracted others. By 1915 the work of the Taos Society of Artists was well known, with some one hundred painters and sculptors at work.

Today? Who knows. Although artists are notoriously hard to identify and count, finding them here is easy enough. Among other places, the town displays their talents on its trash cans. Taos displays artwork—painting, watercolor, sculpture, jewelry, leatherwork, woodwork, among others—in more than fifty galleries.

In the years I've been visiting Taos as a tourist, I've developed a personal Very Best Way of Doing It. I drive from Albuquerque—as most visitors will, since that's as near as the national airlines will bring you—via New Mexico Route 14, instead of taking Interstate 25 direct to Santa Fe. This old back road offers long views of ranching country and takes you through the semi-ghost towns of Golden, Madrid, and Cerrillos—all located in a mining district that has produced turquoise, gold, silver, and coal. North of Santa Fe, I detour again on the ancient "high road" to Taos. It leads through a string of eighteenth-century Spanish colonial mountain villages, right past the famous San José de Gracia Church, which the villagers of Las Trampas finished in the late 1700s. Beyond Las Trampas I wind back to the Rio Grande and New Mexico 68. The highway wriggles out of the river canyon, tops a ridge, and suddenly the entire Taos plateau spreads before you.

Though I've seen this view innumerable times, it still thrills me. The Sangre de Cristo Mountains rise on the northeastern horizon, an immense tableland of silver-gray sage stretches away to the north and west, and the Rio Grande Gorge forms a crooked black chasm all the way to the Colorado border and beyond. The panorama is so vast, grand, and empty that all humanity seems small. This is the setting of Taos, but I have a final stop to make before I get there.

The stop is at Ranchos de Taos, the town's seventeenth-century suburb. The highway passes just behind the buttressed rear of the Church of San Francisco de Asis, gem of Spanish colonial mission architecture. Artists have found this building irresistible for a century. The Impressionists and Romantics who made up the first Taos Society of Artists painted and sketched it. So did the Cubists, Dadaists, Neo-Realists, and all the rest who followed. It has been the focus of the giants of photography: Edward Weston, Ansel Adams, Alfred Stieglitz, and a dozen others. Georgia O'Keeffe painted it. Everybody paints it. And when the majordomos of the parish (the four couples chosen annually to be responsible for maintenance of the church) decided to replace the traditional mud-and-straw plaster with more durable concrete, it created an uproar among lovers of Art and Beauty. The concrete leaked and was removed, and the traditional mud coating is now back in place.

Two blocks after I leave the church, I turn left onto Ranchitos Road, which meanders through the farms and fields outside town and avoids the commercial clutter lining the main highway. Then I check into a central hotel, which means either La Fonda—colorful if a bit threadbare—or the Taos Inn, a newly remodeled national historic site.

Wherever you stay (Taos offers fifteen hundred hotel or motel rooms, if you count those serving the nearby Taos Ski Basin), for a one-dollar fee the desk clerk at La Fonda will open the hotel office, and you can inspect at your leisure the paintings of D. H. Lawrence. The internationally famous author of *Lady Chatterley's Lover*, *Sons and Lovers*, and other classic novels was lured to Taos by Mabel Dodge Luhan, the town's eccentric collector of celebrities. He left the pictures behind. They reveal how the author saw himself—naked, plump, pink, and zany—entangled with equally pink friends. I've invested about eight dollars, reminding myself again and again that such a good writer could be such an awful painter.

The best of many pleasant features of the Taos Inn is its curbside patio, where one can sit in shady comfort and observe the Taos traffic jam edging by. Another possibility for lodging is Las Palomas de Taos, the fabulous home of the fabulous La Luhan. It's now owned by an educational foundation and advertises bed and breakfast for visitors. Your bedroom probably will have sheltered such luminaries of arts and letters as Willa Cather, Georgia O'Keeffe, Robinson Jeffers, Thomas Wolfe, and Aldous Huxley. Mabel was hostess to enough poets, painters, and photographers to staff a university.

The walled courtyard of the house features multistoried dovecotes, raised atop poles to discourage raiding cats. The long porch roof is lined with porcelain chickens. My own favorite feature is a glass-walled room on the second story: the late owner's bathroom, built so she could watch the world while bathing. House guest Lawrence, troubled by this display, painted garish designs on the glass, thereby protecting the modesty of all concerned. It's a curious reaction from the man whose novels preached sexual liberation.

Touring Taos involves walking. A stroll down Kit Carson and North Pueblo roads, Ledoux and Bent, and around the plaza exposes one to dozens of galleries housing a dazzling variety of art. Nonrepresentational work is solidly established. So is landscape, Western, and representational art, as well as just about any school extant anywhere. You can look at, and buy, bronze, marble, or steel sculpture; quilts; wood carvings of the *santeros*; kachina dolls; Indian pottery, beadwork, featherwork, leatherwork, basketry; stone fetishes; Navajo sandcast jewelry; weaving from Two Grey Hills, Chimayo, or Guatemala; custom goldwork; inlaid wood; Cochiti "storyteller" figures; even pawn silver from Navajo trading posts. Taos is, above all, an art town—and the items for sale range from simple souvenir stuff to items worth far more than the building in which they are displayed.

Taos is also a history buff's town. Most popular is Kit Carson's home, where the West's most famous scout, frontiersman, and Indian fighter raised his eight children. The house was built in 1825, about the time Carson hit town as a sixteen-year-old runaway. Today it is a museum. A short walk away on Bent Street is the Governor Bent House Museum, where New Mexico's first territorial governor was scalped in the uprising of 1848. Mrs. Bent had warned her husband not to open the door to the mob, but the governor replied, "It's all right. They're my friends." New Mexico politicians tend to overestimate their popularity.

My favorite among historic houses is the Don Antonio Severino Martínez Hacienda, two and a half miles west of the plaza on Lower Ranchitos Road. Don Antonio moved into the house in 1804, and it provides an authentic look at how life was lived on the Western frontier.

Five miles north of the plaza but well worth the drive is the Millicent Rogers Museum, which houses a superb collection of Spanish colonial and Indian art, jewelry, and costumes. Back in town there's the Harwood Foundation two blocks southwest of the plaza. Here you can see a fine collection of paintings by those who founded the Taos art colony.

Taos also serves as a base for one of the West's most striking mountain drives, a half-day circle that climbs by means of U.S. Route 64 over Palo Flechado Pass (around 9,100 feet) and drops into the beautiful Moreno Valley, then takes another dizzying dive off 9,852-foot Red River Pass into the Red River Valley on New Mexico 38. The route winds back to Taos on Route 3. Bona fide D. H. Lawrence fans will want to take a seven-mile side trip to the ranch and shrine where Lawrence's ashes are kept, but except for a tacky crypt there's not much to see there. I recommend instead an eight-mile detour westward on U.S. 64, which takes you over the sagebrush flats until, almost without warning, you seem to be abruptly airborne—rolling across the Rio Grande Gorge Bridge with the river six hundred feet below you. The bridge, second only to the Royal Gorge among American high bridges, is designed to allow you to park and look and offers a breathtaking view.

What calls me back to Taos, though, is something less dramatic—smaller, more vague, harder to define. A poet named Victor knows what I mean, I think. I met him last summer, as he sat on a bench beside the door of the Harwood Foundation with a sign on a clipboard beside his briefcase. It read:

ENJOY
POETRY
CHEAP

Victor told me he'd come from Santa Fe and was en route to California. Santa Fe considers itself America's most relaxed city, but there Victor found himself engulfed in tension, pressure, and high-level nervousness, with "everybody into nonsense sayings and the tourists fleeing in panic." In California he expected earthquakes and general craziness. So he was biding awhile in Taos. "The air is better here," he said. "People have time to listen to my song." He smiled out at weeds and hollyhocks along a sunny adobe wall. "Taos," said Victor, "restores the spirit."

Taos has been restoring my spirit for thirty years.

A Day in the Life of Chapter Two

Driving to the university in the morning, reconsidering what needs to be accomplished. To wit: (a) Introducing the protagonist, Navajo Tribal Policeman named Leaphorn, with some slight first steps toward developing his character, and (b) giving the reader his/her first look at Gruesome George, and (c) beginning the story line by having Leaphorn stop G.G. for speeding, and (d) having G.G. attempt to kill Leaphorn and flee scene. While pondering how to make (d) seem plausible, make left turn from wrong lane and am honked at by indignant motorist.[1]

At faculty office put Chapter Two aside to go over lecture notes: 9 A.M.–10 A.M. lecture on Social Effects of Mass Communications. At 10 A.M., in Arts and Sciences College curriculum committee meeting, decide on setting. Leaphorn will be heading home after fruitless hunt for escapee from Tuba City jail. Place will be between Cow Springs and Castle Butte on U.S. 160. Combine memory of that part of the Navajo Reservation with imagination to create garish red afterglow, slight breeze from south, smells of a desert summer, silence. Lights of a car roaring toward us on empty 160. Committee

---

1. Author's note: This was written years ago to Professor of Journalism William Rivers, in response to a request from him for about a page of stuff about writing for something he was editing, and left unpurged and forgotten in my computer. The dog, incidentally, became crucial to the plot.

meeting adjourns with nothing accomplished except I have augmented my reputation for being a good listener in committee meetings. Go into afternoon lab, itching to get to word processor. Decide on Leaphorn's internal monologue thoughts while driving home. Honked at for not moving when light turns green.

Home. Turn on Leading Edge computer. Call Chapter One to screen to refresh memory about mood I had tried for. Open Chapter Two. Write rapidly, mostly simply describing sights, sounds, thoughts from my memory. Four hundred words into it, become aware of dragginess. Internal monologue stilted. Stop for supper. Wife senses "lost in chapter" condition and leaves today's problems for later. Back at word processor, change scene. Monologue becomes dialogue by putting Tuba City jail escapee, now handcuffed, in front seat. The two chat, some kidding, some banter. Find self liking this uninvited character. Decide to try to work him into plot. Writing goes fast now. Speeder is stopped. So am I. Go into living room. Lie on couch, daydreaming into red twilight. Two cars beside empty highway. Sky. Wind. Temperature. Insect sounds. Sound of Leaphorn's shoes on gravel. The red light of his cop car flasher blinking off the windshield. Through the reflecting glass, the face of the driver.

Back to the computer, transcribing from imagined scene. Get to exactly what he sees through windshield. Remember that Gruesome George will be nameless until deep in book. Will need label. Add gold-rimmed glasses. Will tag character "Goldrims."

Papers to grade and feeling weary and whimsical. In said mood, add line having Leaphorn see second pair of eyes through windshield, in the back seat. Turn off computer. Grade papers.

Who would be sitting in the back seat with only driver in front? Make it a dog. A big dog. Huge. Tomorrow I will write in the dog. If I can't use a dog, he goes out on the delete button.

To bed, yawning. (Dog proves crucial to plot!)

Dear Bill:

The attached is based upon a presumption that you meant "a page" literally. If it's not what you want, let me know and I will take another crack at it. If it is close to what you are after, feel free to trip, tinker, edit, improve.

My purpose, as you can probably see, is to demonstrate that one can write outside the isolation booth surrounded by the real world and that good things happen to those of us incapable of outlining or otherwise planning ahead.

By the way, I used to use your book on Washington reporting in one of my classes and while I was chairman of the dept. had a notion of trying to hire you. Never had enough money to mention it without being insulting. However, I did bag John Hightower, who won the Pulitzer while covering Moscow for AP, and Stuart Novins, who had about eight Overseas Press Club prizes.

Have now quit the teaching business, so the page is based on a book previously written (*Listening Woman*).

Regards,
Tony

Dancing Gods

THOUGHTS ON THE REPUBLICATION OF A CLASSIC
FIFTY YEARS LATER

One of the first books I bought, when fate and
United Press brought me permanently to New
Mexico in 1952, was a used copy of the original
Alfred A. Knopf edition of *Dancing Gods* by Erna
Fergusson. It was twenty-one years old, out of date
in a place or two, and already bringing a premium
price as an item worth collecting for libraries of
Southwestern Americana. In 1957, the University of
New Mexico Press republished the book with six-
teen illustrations by the painters who'd given Santa
Fe and Taos their enduring reputations as art
colonies. By then the book had become a bit more
timeworn. But UNM Press called it a classic, and it
deserved the title. It still does.

Age increases this book's value in an odd way.
Those interested in the evolution of the dances of
the Rio Grande Pueblos, and of the Hopis, the
Zuñis, and the quite different ceremonials of the
Navajos, can witness in the striking scenes
Fergusson gives us just how much, and how
remarkably little, a half century has changed rituals which are as old as time. But that's a special
dividend and not the reason the book deserves the
"classic" label the UNM press put upon it in 1951. It
is a classic because of the remarkable woman who
wrote it.

Erna Fergusson was born in 1888, a daughter
of the rich, influential, and cultured Franz Huning
family of Albuquerque. Being native-born, she

spent her childhood among the cultures she would write about, understanding them with that special intimacy I think only the innocence of childhood makes possible. She went east for her education, studying the cultures of Latin America at Columbia University and receiving a Master's degree. She spent two years working for the Red Cross in rural northern New Mexico. Then her talent for writing brought her home to Albuquerque and a position on the *Albuquerque Tribune*.

Dancing Gods seems to have grown directly from all of this—and directly from Erna Fergusson's subsequent career as what she called the world's first female dude wrangler. She established Koshare Tours, named for one of the Pueblo clown fraternities, to give Eastern visitors an up-close and personal look at what her advertisements called an area "still unspoiled by civilization." She bought the first of what would become a caravan of Franklin touring cars and began signing up customers to see—among other things—the ceremonials she would soon be writing about in her book.

"For the price of a good dinner for a half dozen people we will give you enough conversational food for a dozen dinners in any company," her brochure promised. "It is one thing to see a place. It is another to see it knowingly." And this was the strength both of Koshare Tours and of *Dancing Gods*. Erna Fergusson knew the Pueblo people, and to some extent the Navajos. More important for the book, she had a delightfully clear and uncluttered writing style and a talent for the details that will set the scene and bring the participants to life.

Fergusson operated Koshare Tours only five years (before selling out to the Santa Fe Railroad), and even then it was a part-time occupation—done while holding her society desk job on the *Tribune*. Her fees seem incredibly low by today's standards (twenty dollars for a guided tour of Acoma Country, for example, included meals as well as transportation). Anyone familiar with the love for the high desert country and its cultures expressed in her subsequent books will suspect she did it as much to show Easterners the land and people she cared about as to make money. There was a sense of urgency in the ads she wrote to attract visitors to "the most foreign land in the United States." Civilization has not yet spoiled it, she said, but it will. "In a few years, its primitiveness will be gone forever."

I think wordsmith Erna Fergusson must have chosen that noun "primitiveness" very carefully. Those few years have passed. The Dancing Gods still form their swaying lines on the Hopi mesas, on the packed earth of the plazas of the Rio Grande Pueblos, and in the winter firelight at Navajo Yeibichai ceremonials. Changes have indeed taken place. And the most notable of them have something to do with that fragile sense of the primitive. It is not just that the wagons are replaced by pickups, that English is mostly the language heard, that some bits and pieces of the dancers' costumes look Korean-made, that the background lighting when evening comes is produced by electricity. It is a sense that the skeptical modern religion of materialism is crowding in on all sides of the plazas.

And yet nothing important has changed at all. Sometimes I think it has. I see a group of teenagers practicing basketball while the Council of the Gods makes its dramatic entrance down Greasy Hill into Zuñi Village, and I think of faith lost. The next day I see the same teenagers reverently sprinkling pollen on a passing procession accompanying Sayatasha, the Rain God of the North, and I understand endurance of the faith has little to do with endurance of the primitive.

Among the Navajos, some of the arsenal of curing ceremonials Fergusson must have seen have been lost to time. Among the Pueblos, some adjustments have been made to cope with encroaching strangers. But the essentials have not changed since 1921, and will not have changed when the new edition of *Dancing Gods* is old.

Those who intend to compare Erna Fergusson's view of Indian ceremonialism of the 1920s with today's liturgical events should be warned that the rising flood of tourism has had some effects on the Pueblo people's traditions of hospitality. It endures, outsiders are still welcome at most events, but some rules that were only implied by the dictates of good manners are now enforced.

For example, never photograph, sketch, or tape ceremonials without first making sure of the rules. Many Pueblos either ban cameras or recording equipment or charge fees. Some ban cameras from some events and allow photography at others. Rules tend to change, so ask.

Do not go into, or snoop or hang around, a kiva. They are sacred places.

You are likely to see scores of local people watching dances from rooftops and other vantage points. Do not try to join them. And don't occupy a chair unless you brought it yourself. It may be empty when you see it but it's somebody's property brought out specifically for someone else to sit in.

If invited to join a Pueblo family for a meal, accept if possible. It was a sincere offer of hospitality, and if you can't stay, take time to explain your reason

At some ceremonials visitors run some risk of becoming the butt of ridicule by koshares or members of another of the clown fraternities. If it happens, accept it with good nature. If you want to make sure it doesn't happen, hang back a bit.

Remember that both Pueblo and Navajo people are far more physically modest than mainstream America, some Pueblos more than others. To show up at a Hopi ceremonial in shorts and a halter top is downright insulting—about like appearing in church or synagogue naked from the waist down. My Hopi friends tell me that nothing strains tribal tolerance more than the immodest dress of visitors.

Stay away from shrines. Your presence may be a desecration. It may even be unhealthy. If you notice feathers tied to a chamisa, an unnatural-looking rock pile, a feather-decorated prayerstick stuck in the ground, leave it alone.

More modern insights into some of the ceremonials can be had in Jill D. Sweet's *Dances of the Tewa Pueblo Indians*, published in 1985 by the School of American Research. Many other excellent publications are available for those wishing a broader knowledge. My own favorites include Frank Waters's *Masked Gods* and *Book of the Hopi*, Ruth Underhill's *The Navajos*, a collection of papers entitled *Southwestern Indian Ritual Drama* edited by Charlotte Frisbie, the selected writings about the Zuñi by Frank Hamilton Cushing in *Zuñi*, and Hamilton A. Tyler's *Pueblo Gods and Myths*.

There are many others. But none of them except *Dancing Gods* lets you tag along with Erna Fergusson on a Koshare Tour before fifty years of tourists made it just a little different.

Skinwalkers

The driver was young and shaken by what he'd seen. He leaned against his truck in the cold moonlight, stuttering while he described it. He was hauling oil field equipment from Texas to a well near Bluff Creek in southern Utah. It was his first time out here. He'd missed his turn at Red Mesa and was halfway to Kayenta before he knew it. Someone there told him to circle back to Bluff through Monument Valley and Mexican Hat. He had covered about thirty-five of those fifty empty miles when he saw it.

"I noticed motion and glanced out the window. There he was. A man running beside the truck, motioning me to stop. Looked like he had on a fur coat, but the head was still on it. Like a dog's head. Or a coyote's. I was geared down for that long slope there and I looked at the speedometer. I was doing thirty-six but he stayed right with me. With the load and the grade I couldn't get it past forty, and he stayed with me for at least three miles until I finally got it over the ridge. I was doing over seventy downhill when I finally lost him."

The driver telling this at the Mexican Hat service station had encountered a skinwalker. The Navajo name is *mai tso* (wolf man), or *yenaldlooshi*, which translates roughly into "he who trots on all fours with it." The "it" is the power to fly, to run supernaturally fast, to take animal form, and to cause sickness, death, despair, and other evil. The skinwalker is the Navajo version of the witch.

In my years around Navajo country, reading Navajo lore and exchanging yarns with Navajos, I have encountered a score of stories of skinwalkers trying to stop drivers. The other usual skinwalker incidents involve finding the witch bothering the family's cattle or hearing him (rarely her) on the roof at night.

"The first time I saw a skinwalker," a Navajo friend once told me, "I was eleven and helping my grandmother get in the sheep because they were going to dip them the next day. It was twilight and I saw it walking along the ridge against the sunset. Just a dark shape. Two legs like a man, but bent way forward. And a head like a dog. I said, 'Grandma! Look!' and she said, 'Dennis, run and get the gun.'" Dennis, now a college student, said he had shot at the witch and it "sort of flew away."

More commonly such encounters involve hearing the sounds of panic among the livestock at night, running outside to find a large dog attacking the animals, shooting, seeing the dog convert itself into human form and run away. It often happens that later it is learned that a neighbor has suffered a gunshot wound.

Most common of all are the "witch on the roof" accounts, which often seem to be remembered from childhood and which I will summarize and generalize like this:

The family is sleeping in its hogan (a one-room structure usually round or octagonal, with a single door facing east, a floor of packed earth, and a fire pit in the center under a smoke hole). Usually the father is away. One of the children is awakened by the sound of the wolfman on the roof, trying to drop corpse powder down the smoke hole. Usually four (the Navajo magic number) attempts are made, and usually the witch is shot or driven away.

A Navajo friend once told me that the only

fault he finds with my Navajo Tribal Police novels is that one key character, Joe Leaphorn, doesn't believe in witches. He said he's never known a Navajo who didn't. I have known a few who didn't, but not many. Belief in the reality of evil, and people who deliberately cause it, seems to thrive in every corner of Navajo country. In fact, in most versions of Dine Bahana, the Navajos' account of their origin, three of the key spirits in Navajo metaphysics, First Man, First Woman, and Coyote, were witches.

According to general tribal tradition one can become a witch by violating the most sacred tribal taboos—murdering a relative, committing incest, handling a corpse, or perhaps all three. Other witches conduct grisly initiation ceremonies, usually in a cave, in which Navajo moral rules are obscenely violated. This gives the new initiate the power to reverse the evolution into humanity and become a beast. Accounts of the ritual usually involve cannibalism and mutilation of a corpse for the preparation of the corpse powder or the "bone beans" that skinwalkers shoot into victims to produce fatal illness.

As in Anglo-American culture, witches serve Navajos as scapegoats, blamed when people get sick, cattle die, or accidents happen. (Some years ago, a Navajo father shot four other Navajos to death. He testified at his trial that they were skinwalkers who had caused the death of his daughter.) And as in the Anglo-American witchcraft culture, the Navajos have defenses against skinwalkers.

Shamans who perform curing ceremonials use at least two specific treatments for those who have been witched. In one, the medicine man sucks the witch's bone bead from the breast of the victim. In another, some item intimate to the suspected witch (his hat, a lock of hair) is attached in a "turning around" rite that cures the victim and kills the witch.

Navajo witchcraft represents a reversal of Navajo values. The Navajo's first priority is caring for the family. The witch kills relatives and commits incest. The Navajo prizes harmony, balance, the golden mean. The witch causes disharmony, glories in the ugly and in excesses. The Navajo sees no good in accumulating possessions; one who does so must be neglecting his first priority—caring for his relatives. Witches are heavy with jewelry, greedy for riches.

The Navajo account of the tribe's genesis included this incident. Witchcraft has caused a flood to destroy the Fourth World. First Man and the other spirits escaped to this Fifth World through a hollow reed. But First Man had left behind his witchcraft bundle and asked Heron to retrieve it. Not wanting the other spirits to know it contained witchcraft, he called it "the way to make money."

That says a lot about the Navajo attitude toward materialism.

But if you happen to be driving through Navajo country in the deep of night, and you see an owl flash past in your headlights, forget about the philosophy. Remember instead that you may soon see a man beside the road with a fur cloak over his shoulders. And he'll be motioning for you to stop.

Chaco Canyon

In October 1988, just one hundred years after two white cowboys discovered the ruins there, the United Nations proclaimed Chaco Canyon a World Heritage Site. Thus the stone towns abandoned at Chaco by the people we call the Anasazis joined the great pyramids of Egypt, the Taj Majal, the temples at Angor Wat, and the majestic Mayan ruins at Copán on the list of sites to be forever preserved for the wonderment of mankind.

Visitors to this strange place must wonder at first sight why it received this international distinction. From the potholed road that wanders across the prairie of northwestern New Mexico to reach Chaco, they see only a broad, grassy valley and a scattering of broken stone walls. It takes a closer look to see how a civilization arose, against amazing odds, on this dry and barren plateau—and how it abruptly vanished, leaving its great houses empty to the wind.

I have come to Chaco Canyon for years, usually in the winter when the tourists are gone and I can be alone. I like to wander through the silent corridors of the apartment house called Pueblo Bonito. I like to sit in an empty room, my back against the stones, and let the place remind me of its mysteries. Why did the people who built this massive structure abandon it to its ghosts? Why did they never return? Why did such small people (the bones found in their burials tell us they averaged not much over five feet tall) build the ceilings so unreasonably high? Why build the doorways requiring a high step up to enter them? Why did they leave behind so few skeletons?

Pueblo Bonito ("Beautiful Town" in English) is believed to be the largest prehistoric structure in the American Southwest. We know almost everything about its construction and almost nothing about why it is here. Its construction began about A.D. 1030, and the last timber used in its final addition wasn't cut until almost fifty years later. Its sandstone walls rose five stories, enclosing more than six hundred rooms and thirty-three of the round, sunken kivas used for religious ceremonies. At its peak occupancy, anthropologists believe as many as a thousand Anasazis lived in this building, with another five thousand occupying the twelve other "towns" in the canyon area.

If you climb the old staircase pathway to the top of Chaco Mesa, a look across the canyon raises a larger question. How could this treeless, arid place provide food, water, and fuel for so many people? Why did it become the ceremonial center of the Anasazi civilization? Instead of answers there are simply more parts to the puzzle.

There were better places to build a capital, and the Anasazis certainly knew it. Four thousand years before the time of Christ their forefathers were hunting and gathering seeds and roots in this corner of the Colorado Plateau. By A.D. 500 they were occupying tiny extended-family communities of pit houses in its canyons. They knew exactly where the rivers flowed, where the land was fertile, where fruits and nuts could be picked, where wood was easy to get. In fact, just a long day's walk north of Chaco, the ruins of a little Anasazi town still stand beside the San Juan River. A few miles beyond, the Anasazis formed another little settlement in the valley of the Animas River. Both places offer the bounty of deep, fertile soil, a dependable water supply, and plentiful wood for fuel and construction.

When I stand at the rim of Chaco Mesa and look across the roofless ruins of Pueblo Bonito, I can see for some fifty miles in every direction, with no sign of river or fertile farmland. I see high desert tundra—a plateau colored silver-gray and tan by dry country grass and sagebrush. The only trees in sight are a few cottonwoods and Russian olives growing along the bottom of Chaco Wash, and both species arrived with European settlers centuries after the Anasazis had vanished. And yet up and down the broad valley below I can see the broken walls of nine communities. Four more ruined structures stand on the mesas that protect the valley. As the Anasazis built them, those structures required huge timbers for roof beams. Where did the Anasazis get these beams?

Far to the south, the blue hump of Mount Taylor rises on the horizon, looming over modern Grants, New Mexico. Ponderosa pine, fir, and spruce grow there, but reaching that mountain from here means a fifty-mile walk. To the west you can see the dim line that marks the ridge of the Chuska Mountain range on the Arizona-New Mexico border between Gallup and Farmington. There, too, ponderosa grow, and a few fir, but the Chuskas are also almost fifty miles away. When I was eighteen and a grunt in the infantry, I could walk fifty miles in two days, carrying food, water, bedroll, and forty pounds of weapons. How many additional days did it take the Anasazis to cut down the huge trees they needed with axes of stone? And how many days would it take to walk back, one of a team of men carrying a massive log on their collective shoulders? Which brings us back to the original question: Why not build the towns near the trees?

When the scientists knew less about this

415

strange place than they know now, such questions either didn't arise or seemed easy to answer. They presumed that when the Anasazis built their towns at Chaco the climate was wetter. They took for granted that a thousand years ago the little valley of Chaco Wash was made green by summer rains, that ponderosas grew on the mesas, and that the wash itself—where now you must literally dig into the sand to find moisture in the dry season—ran with clear water all year long. Now we know better. Studies of pollen deposits, tree rings, and sedimentation layers have proved that the climate on this plateau a thousand years ago was much like it is today, and today's climate would not attract farmers. Rainfall at Chaco averages less than nine inches a year—not a third of what "dry land" farmers need. Worse, the heaviest rains come in late summer and autumn—too late for growing crops. And they come in brief thunderstorms that wash away irrigated fields. Temperatures are just as inhospitable. Thirty-year records show July highs at a scorching 106 degrees Fahrenheit and January lows at 24 degrees below zero. The Anasazis placed their buildings to shelter them from winds and to catch the slanting winter sunlight. Even so, it is easy to imagine how bitterly cold the rooms of Pueblo Bonito must have been on a subzero morning.

Archaeologists have found more than twenty-four hundred living sites in the thirty-two square miles marked off and called the Chaco Culture National Historical Park. Their research shows that Anasazis lived here in small numbers for at least four hundred years—not more than a few families usually, subsisting on what game they could kill with their spear throwers, what wild foods they could collect, and what corn and squash they could raise by diverting the runoff from rains into their little terraced fields along Chaco Wash. Similar settlements had developed across much of the high dry country of southern Colorado, southern Utah, Arizona, and New Mexico, which geographers call the Colorado Plateau.

Then, late in the tenth century, something happened at Chaco Canyon. The population suddenly grew at a pace far faster than the birth rate could explain. Construction began on structures much larger than the traditional pit houses. Materials imported from afar began appearing. An oddly sophisticated network of roads—seeming of little use to a people with neither wheels nor pack animals—was built, linking outlying settlements to the Chaco center. No one knows exactly what happened to touch off this so-called Classic Period at Chaco. Some anthropologists believe a religion evolved (or perhaps was brought in by missionaries from as far south as the Central American tropics) and that Chaco Canyon became its ritual center. There is evidence to support that idea. For example, the ruins called Casa Rinconada seem to have had only a ceremonial purpose, being built around the largest great kiva ever found. Was it the central cathedral, the Saint Peter's of the Anasazi world? The remarkably small number of burials suggests that many of those in Chaco were merely visitors. The odd network of roads reinforces this notion, as well as the theory that Chaco must have also become a trading center. Ceramics experts estimate that less than 20 percent of the pottery found in some of the ruins was made at Chaco. Although the nearest source of turquoise is a hundred miles away, more than sixty thousand pieces of this valued gemstone were found in the Chacoan ruins. Also found were the feathers (and the droppings) of tropical birds that must have been brought up alive from Mexican jungles.

The same 150-year period saw the little sub-surface kivas grow into massive structures—like family chapels growing into cathedrals. The one at Casa Rinconada, just across the valley from Pueblo Bonito, is more than 63 feet in diameter. A multi-storied structure attached to its great circular wall appears to have housed dressing rooms. It is connected to the underground floor of the kiva by a concealed tunnel. Why? I like to imagine priests, wearing masks representing the spirits, emerging from that walkway to the sound of drums and flutes. I will return to Chaco one winter day soon, when the weather report assures me that the dirt road I must travel to reach it will be passable. I will stand on the wall of that great kiva and wonder, as I always do, why the priests and the people went away.

The archaeologists tell us that Chaco reached its peak between 1100 and 1130. Two years later, in 1132, all building ceased. Population dwindled. Then a small influx of newcomers arrived, believed to be refugees from the cliff dwellings at Mesa Verde in Colorado. By about 1300, Chaco Canyon was as empty as it is today. Why?

No one knows. Drought was unusually severe in the period leading up to the abandonment. But the settlement had survived earlier droughts. And even in good years the valley could not have produced more than a tiny fraction of the food needed for its Classic Period population. Nor is there any evidence that the Anasazis were driven away by more warlike people. They seem to have left at their leisure, taking their belongings. Yet they abandoned what must have been to them a treasure of turquoise jewelry. They left with their great stone towns and kivas standing undamaged and unburned—not to be looted until two white cowboys found them in 1888.

Where did the Chacoans go?

The Hopis have an answer to that question. The Anasazis were their ancestors, and the ancestors of the other Pueblo tribes of the Southwest. The Anasazis had been told by God to complete a sequence of migrations and to settle, finally, at the middle place of the Universe. The Anasazis left Chaco and other ruined stone towns in the cliffs and canyons of the Colorado Plateau, the Hopis tell us, to complete that destined migration in the Hopi villages that still exist on Arizona's First, Second, and Third Mesas.

The Navajos, whose vast reservation now surrounds Chaco Canyon, are believed by anthropologists to have reached this part of America hundreds of years after the Anasazis had vanished. (Anasazi is a Navajo word meaning "fathers of our enemies.") But the Navajo tradition disagrees. The legend of the Navajo creation deals with the Chaco ruins. It reports that when the Navajos emerged from the Underworld they found the occupants of Pueblo Bonito and the other stone towns enslaved by a man called Never Loses. The Anasazis had lost everything they owned to this supernatural gambler. Then they bet their freedom and lost that too. So the Navajo spirits—Talking God, Wind Boy, Growling God, Coyote, Corn Beetle, and the rest of them—devised their own games and challenged the gambler. They won the Chacoans their freedom and sent the angry Never Loses into perpetual exile. The Navajo myth also has a short, clear explanation for what happened to the Anasazis then. "After that," the legend says, "the Anasazis went away."

Without doubt, the Anasazis went away. They left behind in Chaco Canyon a fascinating monument to humanity's rise toward civilization—and a reminder of civilization's terrible fragility.

The Budville Murders

REARDON RULES IN ACTION

On Friday, November 18, 1967, the paths of two strangers crossed near Budville in the lonely west central New Mexico Indian country where strangers are noticed and remembered. Because they were remembered—but not quite well enough—New Mexico witnessed effects of the Reardon Commission rules not generally anticipated in the free press/fair trial arguments these rules provoke. The so-called "Budville Case" showed that enforced police secrecy may not—as intended—protect the accused.

One of the strangers was a twenty-three-year-old Navy first class petty officer named Larry E. Bunten. On leave after completing an accounting course on the East Coast, Bunten was visiting relatives of his wife (an Acoma Indian) on the nearby Acoma Reservation. The other stranger, John Doe for our purposes, came to Budville on business. He had bought a "setup" on the Budville Trading Post from a source in the Albuquerque underworld and made the sixty-mile drive from the city to rob the establishment. Both men wore black trousers, black shirt, and black jacket, and—to stretch the coincidence—even an unusual type of jodhpurs with high tops and pointed toes. Doe was about Bunten's age, Bunten's height, and Bunten's weight. And—to strain coincidence further—his hair, eyebrows, and face are remarkably like those of the petty officer. Even with their police file photographs side by side, it is hard to tell which is which.

These look-alikes didn't meet. Bunten, with his wife and son and daughter, aged three and one, spent Friday night at the home of Acoma relatives. Doe spent part of Friday evening (police now believe) hunting the Budville Trading Post—which is far enough off Interstate 40 to be invisible from the highway. He then drove back to Albuquerque without finding it. Saturday afternoon, with better directions, Doe drove back to Budville.

Bunten and his family left the Budville area Saturday afternoon and drove to the duplex apartment of Mrs. Bunten's brother and sister-in-law in Albuquerque. At 7:30 P.M. Saturday, Bunten was making a home movie of his children having a pillow fight in the living room. At 7:30 P.M. Saturday, Doe was walking into the trading post operated by H. N. "Bud" Rice. He drew a 9-millimeter pistol from his belt, shot Rice to death, then turned the pistol on Miss Blanche Brown, eighty-one, and killed her with two bullets. Doe walked out with about $150 in bills and an assortment of old coins—leaving Rice's widow bound and gagged. Another woman witness hid in the bathroom and survived.

At the beginning of the Budville case, police cooperation with newsmen was good. Despite some deadline pressure the *Albuquerque Journal* managed a detailed account of the incident in its first edition for Sunday, including a description of the suspect and the information that Mrs. Rice had noticed a tattoo on his stomach. Cooperation continued Sunday as the hunt for this man developed. In the story he wrote for the Monday morning edition, Pat Lamb of the *Journal* reported police roadblocks were watching for a sedan driven by a young man accompanied by an "adult Indian female and a small child." He also reported that an Alabama parole violator sought in Louisiana for robbery and attempted murder and in Albuquerque for a loan company robbery was "wanted for questioning" in the case.

He followed this with a guarded paragraph:

"There were unconfirmed reports that Mrs. Rice, a witness to the double murders, had made positive identification of a suspect from a photo."

What Lamb knew of this at this first-edition deadline was what he picked up from monitoring the police radio—the call to arrest Doe on the strength of a photo identification. He didn't have time to confirm details before the early edition. Within the hour he couldn't confirm for another reason. The "light-colored sedan" had stopped at a roadblock not far from Budville, an arrest had been made, and, with the arrest, police were automatically operating under the secrecy strictures of the pretrial publicity rules.

Newsmen learned of the capture about midnight and contacted the manhunt headquarters set up by state police at Budville. They were told by a deputy state police chief that officers had the man they wanted, that he was being taken to Valencia County jail at Los Lunas, where he would be arraigned in court Monday morning. The manhunt, they were told, was over. Roadblocks were being called in and some fifty officers involved were released from duty to get some overdue rest. The deputy police chief provided information allowed by the guidelines—the age and identity of the suspect and the fact he was unarmed and offered no resistance to arrest.

The *Journal* had time to delete from its last edition story the reference to the Alabama parole violator—which now seemed pointless—and to insert a bulletin reporting the arrest and the end of the manhunt. Since the suspect was not yet formally charged, it withheld the name. The name was Larry E. Bunten.

Bunten had fallen victim to an odd combination of fast, competent police work, freak circumstances, and a police error. Only a few hours after the murder, police had matched the method of operation of the crime and the description of the gunman with the habits and appearance of John Doe. A photograph of Doe was shown to Mrs. Rice, who identified the man pictured as the killer of her husband. Police then used copies in attempting to pick up Doe's trail. Instead, they picked up the crossed trail of Larry Bunten. Shown the Doe photograph with the description of his size and black attire, several witnesses remembered Bunten. By Sunday afternoon roadblocks were supplied with accurate descriptions of Bunten's car and his family.

Bunten's luck was to improve later, but through Sunday it was all bad. Chance made his arrest almost inevitable, and another chain of circumstances led to a blunder which made filing of charges equally inevitable.

As it happened, a high ranking state police official who had been a personal friend of Rice for seventeen years was in the area when the murders were committed and had taken personal command of the investigation. When Bunten was arrested, this official—a nationally recognized authority on traffic control—had him driven to the Budville Trading Post. It was after midnight. The official went inside. Mrs. Rice, who had been given a sedative earlier, was roused, brought to the front window of the store, and asked to look through the window into the police car where Bunten was seated with a flashlight shining on his face. She was asked if she "saw anything familiar." Under these peculiar circumstances, Mrs. Rice identified Bunten as the gunman.

In New Mexico, the release by law enforcement officials of information after an arrest (or the filing of charges) is theoretically governed by guidelines issued by the state attorney general. These guidelines are identical in effect to the Reardon Commission rules. They specifically bar law enforcement officials from revealing information concerning character or prior criminal record of the defendant; concerning statements, admissions, alibis, or confessions attributed to him; concerning fingerprints, ballistic tests, lie detector examinations, laboratory findings, and so on, or "any evidence or arguments in the case, whether or not they might be used in trial." The guidelines were issued in the form of recommendations, and their enforcement has varied. But Monday, after ordering Bunten held without bond for trial for murder, District Judge Paul Tackett specifically ordered the secrecy ban into effect. Judge Tackett had previously sentenced a newsman who commented on a pending case to thirty days in jail for contempt of court. His orders are not lightly ignored.

The arraignment stories carried in the afternoon editions of the *Albuquerque Tribune* Monday and on Tuesday morning by the *Albuquerque Journal* reflected the effects of the ban. They reported the court's action; the naming of a court-appointed attorney to defend Bunten; Bunten's complete identification, including his service rank and marital status; the complete circumstances of his arrest, including the information that he was traveling with wife and children, was not armed, and had not resisted; and a detailed but brief recapping of the nature of the crime. Obviously this information left the reader with a key question unanswered. Why was this chief petty officer, husband, and father charged with murder?

Under the Reardon rules no answer is

allowed since it would bear on the guilt of the defendant. Reporters, however, managed a partial answer when tidbits of information leaked through the secrecy regulations. They learned that Bunten had been identified as the killer by Mrs. Rice and that he had been identified in a police lineup "by persons who saw him in the vicinity of the holdup." They were told by another officer that Bunten had declined to talk after his arrest and thus were left with the impression that he had offered no alibi. And they were told that the tattoo Mrs. Rice had reported seeing was probably not a tattoo at all but an impression left on the skin by the butt of the pistol carried under the gunman's belt. (Bunten, unlike John Doe, had no tattoo.)

The nature of these leaks is significant. Only information that indicated police had arrested the right man slipped through the guidelines. Information that might have raised doubts didn't leak. The Reardon rules did not modify the human nature of police.

Had the Reardon rules not been in effect, *Journal* and *Tribune* reporters would have learned that police—as of Monday afternoon—had no physical evidence linking Bunten to the crime. Their routine questions would have established that the charge was based on the testimony of three persons who identified him as a man who stopped in a bar near the trading post just before the crime, and on Mrs. Rice's eyewitness identification. The obvious questions about how Bunten first came to be suspected would have led them back to John Doe, to confirmation of Mrs. Rice's identification of Doe's photograph, to the information that other witnesses looked at this photograph and confused the face with Bunten's and—almost inevitably—to the highly irregular nature of Bunten's identification at Budville. Much more important, they would have learned—contrary to their leak—that Bunten had offered a detailed alibi.

As soon as he was booked into the jail at Los Lunas about 1:30 A.M. Monday, Bunten had given officers a step-by-step account of his activities on Friday, Saturday, and Sunday. His wife, questioned at the Grants jail, provided an identical account. State police made a partial check immediately. At approximately 3 A.M. Monday an officer arrived at the duplex apartment of Bunten's brother-in-law in Albuquerque. He and his wife confirmed that Mr. and Mrs. Bunten had been at the apartment when the crime was being committed in Budville. At this point state police also had testimony of two witnesses who had seen the murders and identified Bunten as the killer and of three persons who identified him as the nervous black-clad stranger who left the bar near the trading post a few minutes before the crime. In the face of this contradiction, authorities discounted the testimony of Bunten's interested relatives in favor of the accounts of disinterested witnesses.

Any experienced newsman aware of these facts would have scented the possibilities of an unusual and important story. The duplex was within a five-minute drive of both newspapers. A check would have been easy and quick. It would have shown that in addition to his wife's relatives, whose testimony might be discounted, several other persons living in the block remembered seeing either the young sailor, or his car, or both at the apartment at the time of the crime. The left rear window of the car was covered with a colorful array of tourist stickers, which people remembered. They also remembered seeing him unloading luggage. Even more persuasive, the occupants of the adjoining duplex had not only seen Bunten at the duplex but heard him—through the thin walls of the partition—chatting with his wife and in-laws at dinner, making a movie of his children, even—such is the privacy of duplexes—taking a bath.

If a clincher was needed, the movie was it. When finally developed, the film showed the apartment television set tuned to *Mannix*, a detective program aired Saturday night shortly after Rice was shot to death.

Had the *Albuquerque Tribune* reported Bunten's alibi, the wealth of evidence supporting it, and the peculiarities surrounding his identification in its Monday afternoon edition, it seems extremely likely that he would have been freed within forty-eight hours. But Bunten was being protected by the secrecy rules, which hide innocence even more effectively than guilt. Reporters believed Bunten had offered no alibi. They had not a hint of his stop in Albuquerque. Two of them who tried to find his wife were left with the impression that she was either out of contact somewhere on the Acoma Reservation or that she was en route to San Diego. Another reporter contacted Mrs. Rice and found she did not want to talk about the case. After the arraignment wrap-ups, the Budville story died of malnutrition. Larry E. Bunten sat in his cell, his innocence hidden by efforts to assure him an unprejudiced jury.

He might have sat for months. On the crowded court calendar in New Mexico (and most other states), it usually takes more than a year to bring such a case to trial. Police and prosecutors, with a fresh supply of crime daily, have no reason to hurry investigations after an arrest. Nor do court-appointed defense attorneys, who get no pay for their labors. But Bunten finally had a change in luck. The man picked to defend him was Jim Toulouse, a vigorous and highly respected young attorney. Equally important, District Attorney

Alexander Sceresse is not one of those prosecutors who rates his performance on his percentage of convictions. Sceresse was dismayed by the irregular identification. He arranged a meeting with Toulouse, explained some of the oddities of the case, and suggested they cooperate. Toulouse talked to his new client, concluded he was innocent, and agreed that he and Bunten would work with the district attorney's office. Bunten volunteered to submit to a lie detector test and to be questioned under narcosis.

On Tuesday, a warrant was issued allowing state police to search Bunten's car. They were looking for a black shirt with three white buttons missing, blood-stained black trousers, a 9-millimeter pistol, a wrist-watch with a broken crystal, or part of the loot from the trading post. They found only the Bunten family luggage, toys, and Bunten's movie camera, and they didn't know about the pillow fight film in its magazine. By Tuesday night, Albuquerque police picked up the trail of John Doe, finding he had attempted to rent an Albuquerque motel room some four hours after the Budville murders. On Wednesday a check was started with the Navy to establish Bunten's reputation and determine if he owned a pistol. (He didn't.) On Friday, Bunten took the lie detector test. It indicated he had no knowledge of the crime and that his alibi was true. Questioning under the influence of "truth serum" was equally conclusive. Early the next week Bunten was informed that authorities were convinced of his innocence. But he still faced a problem. When the real murderer was brought to trial, the blundered identification procedure would allow the defense to point to Bunten in an effort to raise "reasonable doubt" in the mind of the jurors.

Sceresse, with the all-out help of Toulouse, set about to undo this damage by accumulating what was needed to prove beyond any doubt that Bunten was innocent. On November 29, ten days after his arrest, the FBI laboratory reported that prints picked up in the trading post did not match Bunten's fingerprints. On December 5, laboratory studies of other evidence was completed with negative results. On the same day, reporters, acting on a tip from Toulouse, found Mrs. Bunten in Albuquerque. The story reporting his alibi appeared December 6. At the same time Bunten was again brought before the court. On motion of the district attorney, Judge Tackett dismissed the murder charge against him. He had faced execution in the gas chamber for eighteen days. They were, he said, the "longest weeks of my life."

In the Budville case it's obvious the Reardon rules did not accomplish their intended effect—the protection of the defendant. Indications of Bunten's guilt leaked. Evidence of his innocence did not.

They did accomplish side effects:

1) The public was comforted with the erroneous impression that a dangerous gunman was in jail when in fact he was living—still armed with his murder weapon—in an Albuquerque apartment.

2) State police were spared a modest amount of embarrassment. Reporters learned of their blunder by interviewing Bunten on his release, but the details of how it came to happen are still covered by the secrecy rules—which now in theory "protect" John Doe. They may be brought fully to public attention if Doe is tried in New Mexico for the Budville murders (and not in Louisiana or Alabama for one of the other killings with which his name is connected) and if his attorney decides to resurrect the identification of Bunten.

3) Friends and relatives of Mrs. Bunten spent eighteen days (instead of one) digesting the thought that her husband was probably a cold-blooded killer. Mrs. Bunten told newsmen just before her husband's release that "even when the truth comes out, the stories will go on."

4) An innocent man was denied his freedom substantially longer than he would have been had police-press cooperation been normal.

These unpleasant effects of secrecy occurred under near-ideal conditions—with a vigorous defense attorney on the job, the district attorney more interested in justice than in a conviction, and a police force not intentionally involved in a cover-up operation.

What happens when the situation is less ideal?

7

A SELECTION OF TONY HILLERMAN'S FICTION

Tony Hillerman has written only a small number of mystery short stories in his distinguished career, far too few for a collection. We are thus particularly pleased to present three of his best for your enjoyment.

The Witch, Yazzie, and the Nine of Clubs

All summer the witch had been at work on the Rainbow Plateau. It began—although Corporal Jimmy Chee would learn of it only now, at the very last—with the mutilation of the corpse. The rest of it fell pretty much into the pattern of witchcraft gossip one expected in this lonely corner of the Navajo Reservation. Adeline Etcitty's mare had foaled a two-headed colt. Rudolph Bisti's boys lost their best ram while driving their flocks into the high country, and when they found the body were-wolf tracks were all around it. The old woman they call Kicks-Her-Horse had actually seen the skin-walker. A man walking down Burnt Water Wash in the twilight had disappeared into a grove of cottonwoods, and when the old woman got there, he turned himself into an owl and flew away. The daughter of Rosemary Nakai had seen the witch, too. She shot her .22 rifle at a big dog bothering her horses and the dog turned into a man wearing a wolfskin and she'd run away without seeing what he did.

Corporal Chee heard of the witch now and then and remembered it as he remembered almost everything. But Chee heard less than most because Chee had been assigned to the Tuba City subagency and given the Short Mountain territory only six months ago. He came from the Chuska Mountains on the Arizona–New Mexico border three hundred miles away. His born-to clan was the Slow Talking People, and his paternal clan was the Mud Dinee. Here among the barren canyons along the Utah border, the clans were the Standing Rock People, the Many Goats, the Tangle Dinee, the Red Forehead Dinee, the Bitter Waters, and the Monster People. Here Chee was still a stranger. To a stranger, Navajos talk cautiously of witches.

Which is perhaps why Jim Chee had learned only now, at this very moment, of the mutilation. Or perhaps it was because he had a preoccupation of his own—the odd, frustrating question of where Taylor Yazzie had gone and what Yazzie had done with the loot from the Burnt Water Trading Post. Whatever the reason he was late in learning, it was the Cowboy who finally told him.

"Everybody knew there was a skinwalker working way last spring," the Cowboy said. "As soon as they found out the witch killed that guy."

Chee had been leaning against the Cowboy's pickup truck. He was looking past the Emerson Nez hogan, through the thin blue haze of piñon smoke which came from its smoke hole, watching a half-dozen Nez kinfolks stacking wood for the Girl Dance fire. He was asking himself for the thousandth time what Taylor Yazzie could have done with $40,000 worth of pawn—rings, belt buckles, bracelets, bulky silver concha belts, which must weigh, altogether, 500 pounds. And what had Taylor Yazzie done with himself—another 180 pounds or so, with the bland round face more common among Eastern Navajos than on the Rainbow Plateau, with his thin mustache, with his wire-rimmed sunglasses? Chee had seen Taylor Yazzie only once, the day before he had done the burglary, but since then he had learned him well. Yazzie's world was small, and Yazzie had vanished from it, and since he could hardly speak English there was hardly any place he could go. And just as thoroughly, the silver pawn had vanished from the lives of a hundred families who had turned it over to Ed Yost's trading post to secure their credit until they sold their wool. Through all these thoughts it took a moment for the Cowboy's message to penetrate. When it did, Corporal Chee became very attentive.

"Killed what guy?" Chee asked. Taylor Yazzie, you're dead, he thought. No more mystery.

The Cowboy was sprawled across the front seat of his truck, fishing a transistor radio out of the glove box. "You remember," he said. "Back last April. That guy you collected on Piute Mesa."

"Oh," Chee said. He remembered. It had been a miserable day's work, and the smell of death had lingered in his carryall for weeks. But that had been in May, not April, and it hadn't looked like a homicide. Just too much booze, too much high-altitude cold. An old story on the reservation. And John Doe wasn't Taylor Yazzie. The coroner had put the death two months before the body was recovered. Taylor Yazzie was alive and well and walking out of Ed Yost's trading post a lot later than that. Chee had been there and seen him. "You see that son of a bitch," Ed Yost had said. "I just fired his ass. Never comes to work, and I think he's been stealing from me." No, Yost didn't want to file a complaint. Nothing he could prove. But the next morning it had been different. Someone with a key had come in the night, and opened the saferoom where the pawn was kept, and took it. Only Yost and Yazzie had access to the keys, and Yazzie had vanished.

"Why you say a witch killed that guy?" Chee asked.

The Cowboy backed out of the pickup cab. The radio didn't work. He shook it, glancing at Chee. His expression was cautious. The bumper stickers plastering the Ford declared him a member of the NATIVE AMERICAN RODEO COWBOYS' ASSN., and proclaimed that COWBOYS MAKE BETTER LOVERS and COWGIRLS HAVE MORE FUN, and recorded the Cowboy's outdated permit to park on the Arizona State University campus. But Cowboy was still a Many Goats Dinee, and Chee had been his friend for just a few months. Uneasiness warred with modern macho.

"They said all the skin was cut off his hands," the Cowboy said. But he said it in a low voice.

"Ah," Chee said. He needed no more explanation. The ingredients of *anti'l*, the corpse powder which skinwalkers make to spread sickness, was known to every Navajo. They used the skin of their victim which bears the unique imprint of the individual human identity—the skin of palms, and finger pads, and the balls of the feet. Dried and pulverized with proper ritual, it became the dreaded reverse-negative of the pollen used for curing and blessing. Chee remembered the corpse as he had seen it. Predators and scavenger birds had left a ragged sack of bones and bits of desiccated flesh. No identification and nothing to show it was anything but routine. And that's how it had gone into the books. "Unidentified male. About forty. Probable death by exposure."

"If somebody saw his palms had been skinned, then somebody saw him a hell of a long time before anybody called us about him," Chee said. Nothing unusual in that, either.

"Somebody found him fresh," the Cowboy said. "That's what I heard. One of the Pinto outfit." Cowboy removed the battery from the radio. By trade, Cowboy was the assistant county agricultural agent. He inspected the battery, which looked exactly like all other batteries, with great care. The Cowboy did not want to talk about witch business.

"Any of the Pinto outfit here?" Chee asked.

"Sure," Cowboy said. He made a sweeping gesture, including the scores of pickups, wagons, old sedans occupying the sagebrush flats around the Nez hogans, the dozens of cooking fires smoking in the autumn twilight, the people everywhere. "All the kinfolks come to this. Everybody comes to this."

This was an Enemy Way. This particular Enemy Way had been prescribed, as Chee understood it, to cure Emerson Nez of whatever ailed him so he could walk again with beauty all around him, as Changing Woman had taught when she formed the first Navajos. Family duty would require all kinsmen, and clansmen, of Nez to be here, as Cowboy had said, to share in the curing and the blessing. Everybody would be here, especially tonight. Tonight was the sixth night of the ceremonial, when the ritual called for the Girl Dance to be held. Its original purpose was metaphysical—part of the prescribed reenactment of the deeds of the Holy People. But it was also social. Cowboy called it the Navajo substitute for the singles bar and came to see if he could connect with a new girlfriend. Anthropologists came to study primitive behavior. Whites and Utes and even haughty Hopis came out of curiosity. Bootleggers came to sell illegal whisky. Jim Chee came, in theory, to catch bootleggers. In fact, the elusive, invisible, missing Yazzie drew him. Yazzie and the loot. Sometime, somewhere, some of it would have to surface. And when it did, someone would know it. But now to hell with Yazzie and pawn jewelry. He might have an old homicide on his hands. With an unidentified victim and the whole thing six months cold, it promised to be as frustrating as the burglary. But he would find some Pinto family members and begin the process.

Cowboy's radio squawked into sudden life and produced the voice of Willie Nelson, singing of abandonment and sorrow. Cowboy turned up the volume.

"Specially everyone would come to this one," Cowboy said toward Chee's departing back. "Nez wasn't the only one bothered by that witch. One way or another it bothered just about everybody on the plateau."

Chee stopped and walked back to the pickup. "You mean Nez was witched?"

"That's what they say," Cowboy said. "Got sick. They took him to the clinic in Tuba City, and when that didn't do any good they got themselves a Listener to find out what was wrong with the old man, and he found out Nez had the corpse sickness. He said the witch got on the roof"—(Cowboy paused to point with his lips—a peculiarly Navajo gesture—toward the Nez hogan)—"and dropped *anti'l* down the smokehole."

"Same witch? Same one that did the killing?"

"That's what the Listener said," Cowboy agreed.

Cowboy was full of information tonight, Chee thought. But was it useful? The fire for the Girl Dance had been started now. It cast a red, wavering light, which reflected off windshields, faces, and the moving forms of people. The pot drums began a halting pattern of sounds, which reflected, like the firelight, off the cliffs of the great mesa which sheltered the Nez place. This was the ritual part of the evening. A shaman named Dillon Keeyani was the Singer in charge of curing Nez. Chee could see him, a tall, gaunt man standing beyond the fire, chanting the repetitive poetry of his part of the cure. Nez stood beside him, naked to the waist, his face blackened to make him invisible to the ghosts which haunt the night. Why would the Listener have prescribed an Enemy Way? It puzzled Chee. Usually a witch victim was cured with a Prostitution Way, or the proper chants from the Mountain Way were used. The Enemy Way was ordered for witch cases at times, but it was a broad-spectrum antibiotic—used for that multitude of ills caused by exposure to alien ways and alien cultures. Chee's family had held an Enemy Way for him when he returned from the University of New Mexico, and in those years when Navajos were coming home from the Vietnam War it was common every winter. But why use it to cure Emerson Nez of the corpse sickness? There was only one answer. Because the witch was an alien—a Ute, a white, a Hopi perhaps. Chee thought about how the Listener would have worked. Long conversations with Nez and those who knew him, hunting for causes of the malaise, for broken taboos, for causes of depression. And then the Listener would have found a quiet place and listened to what the silence taught him. How would the Listener have known the witch was alien? There was only one way. Chee was suddenly excited. Someone must have seen the witch. Actually seen the man—not in the doubtful moonlight, or a misty evening when a moving shape could be dog or man, but under circumstances that told the witness that the man was not a Navajo.

The Sway Dance had started now. A double line of figures circled the burning pyre, old men and young—even boys too young to have been initiated into the secrets of the Holy People. Among Chee's clans in the Chuskas, ritualism was more orthodox and these youngsters would not be allowed to dance until a Yeibichai was held for them and their eyes had seen through the masks of Black God and Talking God. The fire flared higher as a burning log collapsed with an explosion of sparks. Chee wove through the spectators, asking for Pintos. He found an elderly woman joking with two younger ones. Yes, she was Anna Pinto. Yes, her son had found the body last spring. His name was Walker Pinto. He'd be somewhere playing stick dice. He was wearing a sweatband. Red.

Chee found the game behind Ed Yost's pickup truck. A lantern on the tailgate provided the light, a saddle blanket spread on the ground was the playing surface. Ed Yost was playing with an elderly round-faced Hopi and four Navajos. Chee recognized Pinto among the watchers by the red sweatband and his mother's description. "Skinny," she'd said. "Bony-faced. Sort of ugly-looking." Although his mother hadn't said it, Walker Pinto was also drunk.

"That's right, man," Pinto said. "I found him. Up there getting the old woman's horses together, and I found him." Wine had slurred Pinto's speech and drowned whatever inhibitions he might have felt about talking of witch business to a man he didn't know. He put his hand on the pickup fender to steady himself and began—Navajo fashion—at the very beginning. He'd married a woman in the Poles Together Clan and gone over to Rough Rock to live with her, but she was no good, so this winter he'd come back to his mother's outfit, and his mother had wanted him to go up on Piute Mesa to see about her horses. Pinto described the journey up the mesa with his son, his agile hands acting out the journey. Chee watched the stick-dice game. Yost was good at it. He slammed the four painted wooden pieces down on the base stone in the center of the blanket. They bounced two feet into the air and fell in a neat pattern. He tallied the exposed colors, moved the matchsticks being used as score markers, collected the sticks, and passed them to the Hopi in maybe three seconds. Yost had been a magician once, Chee remembered. With a carnival, and his customers had called him Three Hands. "Bets," Yost said. The Hopi looked at the sticks in his hand, smiling slightly. He threw a crumpled dollar onto the blanket. A middle-aged Navajo wearing wire-rimmed glasses put a folded bill beside it. Two more bills hit the blanket. The lantern light reflected off Wire Rims's lenses and off Yost's bald head.

"About then I heard the truck, way back over the ridge," Pinto was saying. His hands created the ridge and the valley beyond it. "Then the truck it hit something, you see. Bang." Pinto's right hand slammed into his left. "You see, that truck it hit against a rock there. It was turning around in the wash, and the wash is narrow there, and it banged up against this rock." Pinto's hands re-created the accident. "I started over there, you see. I walked on over there then to see who it was."

The stick-dice players were listening now; the Hopi's face patient, waiting for the game to resume. The butane lantern made a white light that made Yost's moist eyes sparkle as he looked up at Pinto. There was a pile of bills beside Yost's hand. He took a dollar from it and put it on the blanket without taking his eyes from Pinto.

"But, you see, by the time I got up to the top of the rise, that truck it was driving away. So I went on down there, you see, to find out what had been going on." Pinto's hands reenacted the journey.

"What kind of truck was it?" Chee asked.

"Already gone," Pinto said. "Bunch of dust hanging in the air, but I didn't see the truck. But when I got down there to the wash, you see, I looked around." Pinto's hand flew here and there, looking around. "There he was, you see, right there shoved under that rabbit brush." The agile hands disposed of the body. The stick-dice game remained in recess.

The Hopi still held the sticks, but he watched Pinto.
So did the fat man who sat cross-legged beside him.
The lantern light made a point of white in the center
of Yost's black pupils. The faces of the Navajo players were rapt, but the Hopi's expression was polite
disinterest. The Two-Heart witches of his culture
did their evil with more sophistication.

Pinto described what he had seen under the
rabbit brush, his voice wavering with the wine but
telling a story often repeated. His agile hands were
surer. They showed how the flayed hands of the
corpse had lain, where the victim's hat had rolled,
how Pinto had searched for traces of the witch, how
he had studied the tracks. Behind the stick-dice
players the chanting chorus of the Sway Dancers
rose and fell. The faint night breeze moved the perfume of burning piñon and the aroma of cedar to
Chee's nostrils. The lantern light shone through the
rear window of Yost's truck, reflecting from the
barrels of the rifles in the gun rack across it. A
long-barreled .30.06 and a short saddle carbine,
Chee noticed.

"You see, that skinwalker was in a big hurry
when he got finished with that body," Pinto was saying. "He backed right over a big chamisa bush and
banged that truck all around on the brush and
rocks getting it out of there." The hands flew,
demonstrating panic.

"But you didn't actually see the truck?" Chee
asked.

"Gone," Pinto said. His hands demonstrated
the state of goneness.

"Or the witch, either?"

Pinto shook his head. His hands apologized.

On the flat beside the Nez hogan the chanting
of the Sway Dance ended with a chorus of shouting.
Now the Girl Dance began. Different songs.
Different drumbeat. Laughter, now, and shouting.

The game broke up. Wire Rims folded his blanket. Yost counted his winnings.

"Tell you what I'll do," Yost said to Wire Rims. "I'll show you how I can control your mind."

Wire Rims grinned.

"Yes, I will," Yost said. "I'll plant a thought in your mind and get you to say it."

Wire Rims's grin broadened. "Like what?"

Yost put his hand on the Navajo's shoulder. "Let your mind go blank now," he said. "Don't think about nothing." Yost let ten seconds tick away. He removed the hand. "Now," he said. "It's done. It's in there."

"What?" Wire Rims asked.

"I made you think of a certain card," Yost said. He turned to the spectators, to the Hopi, to Chee. "I always use the same card. Burn it into my mind and keep it there and always use that very same image. That way I can make a stronger impression with it on the other feller's mind." He tapped Wire Rims on the chest with a finger. "He closes his eyes, he sees that certain card."

"Bullshit," Wire Rims said.

"I'll bet you, then," Yost said. "But you got to play fair. You got to name the card you actually see. All right?"

Wire Rims shrugged. "Bullshit. I don't see nothing."

Yost waved his handful of currency. "Yes, you do," Yost insisted. "I got money that says you do. You see that one card I put in your mind. I got $108 here I'll bet you against that belt you're wearing. What's that worth?" It was a belt of heavy conchas hammered out of thick silver. Despite its age and a heavy layer of tarnish it was a beautiful piece of work. Chee guessed it would bring $100 at pawn and sell for maybe $200. But with the skyrocketing price of silver, it might be worth twice that melted down.

"Let's say it would pawn for three hundred

443

dollars," Yost said. "That gives me three-to-one odds on the money. But if I'm lying to you, there's just one chance in fifty-two that you'll lose."

"How you going to tell?" Wire Rims asked. "You tell somebody the card in advance?"

"Better than that," Yost said. "I got him here in my pocket sealed up in an envelope. I always use that same card so I keep it sealed up and ready."

"Sealed up in an envelope?" Wire Rims asked.

"That's right," Yost said. He tapped his forefinger to the chest of his khaki bush jacket.

Wire Rims unbuckled the belt and handed it to Chee. "You hold the money," he said. Yost handed Chee the currency.

"I get to refresh your memory," Yost said. He put his hand on the Navajo's shoulder. "You see a whole deck of cards face down on the table. Now, I turn this one on the end here over." Yost's right hand turned over an invisible card and slapped it emphatically on an invisible table. "You see it. You got it in your mind. Now play fair. Tell me the name of the card."

Wire Rims hesitated. "I don't see nothing," he said.

"Come on. Play fair," Yost said. "Name it."

"Nine of clubs," Wire Rims said.

"Here is an honest man," Yost said to Chee and the Hopi and the rest of them. "He named the nine of clubs." While he said it, Yost's left hand had dipped into the left pocket of the bush jacket. Now it fished out an envelope and delivered it to Chee. "Read it and weep," Yost said.

Chee handed the envelope to Wire Rims. It was a small envelope, just a bit bigger than a poker card. Wire Rims tore it open and extracted the card. It was the nine of clubs. Wire Rims looked from card to Yost, disappointment mixed with admiration. "How you do that?"

"I'm a magician," Yost said. He took the belt and the money from Chee. "Any luck on that burglary?" he asked. "You find that son of a bitch Yazzie yet?"

"Nothing," Chee said.

And then there was a hand on his arm and a pretty face looking up at him. "I've got you," the girl said. She tugged him toward the fire. "You're my partner. Come on, policeman."

"I'd sure like to catch that son of a bitch," Yost said.

The girl danced gracefully. She told Chee she was born to the Standing Rock Dinee and her father was a Bitter Water. With no clan overlap, none of the complex incest taboos of the People prevented their dancing, or whatever else might come to mind. Chee remembered having seen her working behind the registration desk at the Holiday Inn at Shiprock. She was pretty. She was friendly. She was witty. The dance was good. The pot drums tugged at him, and the voices rose in a slightly ribald song about what the old woman and the young man did on the sheepskins away from the firelight. But things nagged at Chee's memory. He wanted to think.

"You don't talk much," the girl said.

"Sorry. Thinking," Chee said.

"But not about me." She frowned at him. "You thinking about arresting somebody?"

"I'm thinking that tomorrow morning when they finish this sing-off with the Scalp Shooting ceremony, they've got to have something to use as the scalp."

The girl shrugged.

"I mean, it has to be something that belonged to the witch. How can they do that unless they know who the witch is? What could it be?"

The girl shrugged again. She was not interested in the subject or, now, in Jim Chee. "Whyn't you go and ask?" she said. "Big Hat over there is the scalp carrier."

Chee paid his ransom—handing the girl two dollars and then adding two more when the first payment drew a scornful frown. Big Hat was also paying off his partner, with the apparent intention of being immediately recaptured by a plump young woman wearing a wealth of silver necklaces who was waiting at the fringe of the dance. Chee captured him just before the woman did.

"The scalp?" Big Hat asked. "Well, I don't know what you call it. It's a strip of red plastic about this wide"—Big Hat indicated an inch with his fingers—"and maybe half that thick and a foot and a half long."

"What's that got to do with the witch?" Chee asked.

"Broke off the bumper of his truck," Big Hat said. "You know. That strip of rubbery stuff they put on to keep from denting things. It got brittle and some of it broke off."

"At the place where they found the body?"

Big Hat nodded.

"Where you keeping it?" Chee asked. "After you're finished with it tomorrow I'm going to need it." Tomorrow, at the final ritual, this scalp of the witch would be placed near the Nez hogan. There, after the proper chants were sung, Emerson Nez would attack it with a ceremonial weapon—probably the beak of a raven attached to a stick. Then it would be sprinkled with ashes and shot—probably with a rifle. If all this was properly done, if the minds of all concerned were properly free of lust, anger, avarice—then the witchcraft would be reversed. Emerson Nez would live. The witch would die.

"I got it with my stuff in the tent," Big Hat said.

He pointed past the Nez brush arbor. After the ceremony he guessed Chee could have it. Usually anything like that—things touched with witchcraft—would be buried. But he'd ask Dillon Keeyani. Keeyani was the singer. Keeyani was in charge.

And then Jim Chee walked out into the darkness, past the brush arbor and past the little blue nylon tent where Big Hat kept his bedroll and his medicine bundle and what he needed for his role in this seven-day sing. He walked beyond the corral where the Nez outfit kept its horses, out into the sagebrush and the night. He found a rock and sat on it and thought.

While he was dancing he had worked out how Ed Yost had won Wire Rims's belt. A simple matter of illusion and distraction. The easy way it had fooled him made him aware that he must be overlooking other things because of other illusions. But what?

He reviewed what Pinto had told him. Nothing there. He skipped to his own experience with the body. The smell. Checking what was left of the clothing for identification. Moving what was left into the body bag. Hearing the cloth tear. Feeling the bare bone, the rough, dried leather of the boots as he—

The boots! Chee slapped both palms against his thighs. The man had his boots on. Why would the witch, the madman, take the skin for corpse powder from the hands and leave the equally essential skin from the feet? He could not, certainly, have replaced the boots. Was the killing not a witch killing, then? But why the flayed hands? To remove the fingerprints?

Yazzie. Yazzie had a police record. One simple assault. One driving while intoxicated. Printed twice. Identification would have been immediate. But Yazzie was larger than the skinned man, and still alive when the skinned man was dead. John Doe remained John Doe. This only changed John Doe from a random victim to a man whose killer needed to conceal his identity.

The air moved against Chee's face, and with the faint breeze came the sound of the pot drums and of laughter. Much closer he heard the fluting cry of a hunting owl. He saw the owl now, a gray shape gliding in the starlight just above the sage, hunting, as Chee's mind hunted, something which eluded it. Something, Chee's instinct told him, as obvious as the nine of clubs.

But what? Chee thought of how adroitly Yost had manipulated Wire Rims into the bet and into the illusion. Overestimating the value of the man's belt. Causing them all to think of a single specific card, sealed in a single specific envelope, waiting to be specifically named. He smiled slightly, appreciating the cleverness.

The smile lingered, abruptly disappeared, reappeared and suddenly converted itself into an exultant shout of laughter. Jim Chee had found another illusion. In this one, he had been Yost's target. He'd been totally fooled. Yazzie *was* John Doe. Yost had killed him, removed the fingerprints, put the body where it would be found. Then he had performed his magic. Cleverly. Taking advantage of the circumstances—a new policeman who'd never seen Yazzie. Chee re-created the day. The note to call Yost. Yost wanting to see him, suggesting two in the afternoon. Chee had been a few minutes late. The big, round-faced Navajo stalking out of Yost's office. Yost's charade of indignant anger. Who was this ersatz "Yazzie"? The only requirement would be a Navajo from another part of the reservation, whom Chee wouldn't be likely to see again soon. Clever!

That reminded him that he had no time for

this now. He stopped at his own vehicle for his flashlight and then checked Yost's truck. Typical of trucks which live out their lives on the rocky tracks of the reservation, it was battered, scraped, and dented. The entire plastic padding strip was missing from the front bumper. From the back one, a piece was missing. About eighteen inches long. What was left fit Big Hat's description of the scalp. His deduction confirmed, Chee stood behind the truck, thinking.

Had Yost disposed of Yazzie to cover up the faked burglary? Or had Yazzie been killed for some unknown motive and the illusion of burglary created to explain his disappearance? Chee decided he preferred the first theory. For months before the crime the price of silver had been skyrocketing, moving from about five dollars an ounce to at least forty dollars. It bothered Yost to know that as soon as they sold their wool, his customers would be paying off their debts and walking away with that sudden wealth.

The Girl Dance had ended now. The drums were quiet. The fire had burned down. People were drifting past him through the darkness on their way back to their bedrolls. Tomorrow at dawn there would be the final sand painting on the floor of the Nez hogan; Nez would drink the ritual emetic and just as the sun rose would vomit out the sickness. Then the Scalp Shooting would be held. A strip of red plastic molding would be shot and a witch would, eventually, die. Would Yost stay for the finish? And how would he react when he saw the plastic molding?

A split second into that thought, it was followed by another. Yost had heard what Pinto had said. Yost would know this form of the Enemy Way required a ceremonial scalp. Yost wouldn't wait to find out what it was.

Chee snapped on the flashlight. Through the back window of Yost's pickup he saw that the rifle rack now held only the .30.06. The carbine was gone.

Chee ran as fast as the darkness allowed, dodging trucks, wagons, people, and camping paraphernalia, toward the tent of Big Hat. Just past the brush arbor he stopped. A light was visible through the taut blue nylon. It moved.

Chee walked toward the tent, quietly now, bringing his labored breathing under control. Through the opening he could see Big Hat's bedroll and the motionless outflung arm of someone wearing a flannel shirt. Chee moved directly in front of the tent door. He had his pistol cocked now. Yost was squatting against the back wall of the tent, illuminated by a battery lantern, sorting through the contents of a blue cloth zipper bag. Big Hat sprawled face down just inside the tent, his hat beside his shoulder. Yost's carbine was across his legs.

"Yost," Chee said. "Drop the carbine and—"

Yost turned on his heels, swinging the carbine.

Jim Chee, who had never shot anyone, who thought he would never shoot another human, shot Yost through the chest.

Big Hat was dead, the side of his skull dented. Yost had neither pulse nor any sign of breath. Chee fished in the pockets of his bush jacket and retrieved the concha belt. He'd return it to Wire Rims. In the pocket with it were small sealed envelopes. Thirteen of them. Chee opened the first one. The Ace of Hearts. Had Wire Rims guessed the five of hearts, Yost would have handed him the fifth envelope from his pocket. Chee's bullet had gone through the left breast pocket of Yost's jacket— puncturing diamonds and spades.

Behind him Chee could hear the sounds of shouting, of running feet, people gathering at the tent flap. Cowboy was there, staring in at him. "What happened?" Cowboy said.

And Chee said, "The witch is dead."

First Lead Gasser

John Hardin walked into the bureau, glanced at the wall clock (which told him it was 12:22 A.M.), laid his overcoat over a chair, flicked the switch on the teletype to ON, tapped on the button marked BELL, and then punched on the keys with a stiff fore-finger:

ALBUQUERQUE . . . YOU TURNED ON? . . . SANTA FE

He leaned heavily on the casing of the machine, waiting, feeling the coolness under his palms, noticing the glass panel was dusty, and hearing the words again and that high, soft voice. Then the teletype bumped tentatively and said:

SANTA FE . . . AYE AYE GO WITH IT . . . ALBU-QUERQUE

And John Hardin punched:

ALBUQUERQUE . . . WILL FILE LEAD SUBBING OUT GASSER ITEM IN MINUTE. PLEASE SEND SCHEDULE FOR 300 WORDS TO DENVER . . . SANTA FE

The teletype was silent as Hardin removed the cover from the typewriter (dropping it to the floor). Then the teletype carriage bumped twice and said:

SANTA FE . . . NO RUSH DENVER UNTHINKS GASSER WORTH FILING ON NATIONAL TRUNK DIXIE TORNA-DOES JAMMING WIRE AND HAVE DANDY HOTEL FIRE

452

AT CHICAGO FOLKS OUTJUMPING WINDOWS ETC
HOWEVER STATE OVERNIGHT FILE LUKS LIKE
HOTBED OF TRANQUILITY CAN USE LOTS OF GORY
DETAILS THERE . . . ALBUQUERQUE

Their footsteps had echoed down the long concrete tube, passed the dark barred mouths of cell blocks, and Thompson had said, "Is it always this goddam quiet?" and the warden said, "The cons are always quiet on one of these nights."

Hardin sighed and said something under his breath and punched:

ALBUQUERQUE . . . REMIND DENVER NITESIDE THAT
DENVER DAYSIDE HAS REQUEST FOR 300 WORDS TO
BE FILED FOR OHIO PM POINTS . . . S F

He turned his back on the machine, put a carbon book in the typewriter, hit the carriage return twice, and stared at the clock, which now reported the time to be 12:26. While he stared, the second hand made the laborious climb toward 12 and something clicked and the clock said it was 12:27.

Hardin started typing, rapidly:

First Lead Gasser
    Santa Fe, N.M., March 28—(UPI)—George Tobias Small, 38, slayer of a young Ohio couple who sought to befriend him, died a minute after midnight today in the gas chamber at the New Mexico State Penitentiary.

He examined the paragraph, pulled the paper from the typewriter, and dropped it. It slid from the top of the desk and planed to the floor, spilling its carbon insert. On a fresh carbon book Hardin typed:

First Lead Gasser

Santa Fe, N.M., March 28—(UPI)—George Tobias Small, 38, who clubbed to death two young Ohio newlyweds last July 4, paid for his crime with his life early today in the New Mexico State Penitentiary gas chamber.

The hulking killer smiled nervously at execution witnesses as three guards pushed three unmarked buttons, one of which dropped cyanide pills into a container of acid under the chair in which he was strapped.

Hulking? Maybe tall, stooped killer: maybe gangling. Not really nervously. Better timidly: smiled timidly. But actually it was an embarrassed smile. Shy. Stepping from the elevator into that too-bright basement room, Small had blinked against the glare and squinted at them lined by the railing—the press corps and the official creeps in the role of "official witnesses." He looked surprised and then embarrassed and looked away, then down at his feet. The warden had one hand on his arm: the two of them walking fast toward the front of the chamber, hurrying, while a guard held the steel door open. Above their heads, cell block eight was utterly silent.

Hardin hit the carriage return.

The end came quickly for Small. He appeared to hold his breath for a moment and then breathed deeply of the deadly fumes. His head fell forward and his body slumped in death.

The room had been hot. Stuffy. Smelling of cleaning fluid. But under his hand, the steel railing was cold. "Looks like a big incinerator," Thompson said. "Or like one of those old wood stoves with the chimney out the top." And the man from the *Albuquerque Journal* said, "The cons call it the space capsule. Wonder why they put windows in it. There's not much to see." And Thompson said, with a sort of laugh, that it was the world's longest view. Then it was quiet. Father McKibbon had looked at them a long time when they came in, unsmiling, studying them. Then he had stood stiffly by the open hatch, looking at the floor.

Small, who said he had come to New Mexico from Colorado in search of work, was sentenced to death last November after a district court jury at Raton found him guilty of murder in the deaths of Mr. and Mrs. Robert M. Martin of Cleveland. The couple had been married only two days earlier and was en route to California on a honeymoon trip.

You could see Father McKibbon saying something to Small—talking rapidly—and Small nodded and then nodded again, and then the warden said something and Small looked up and licked his lips. Then he stepped through the hatch. He tripped on the sill, but McKibbon caught his arm and helped him sit in the little chair, and Small looked up at the priest. And smiled. How would you describe it? Shy, maybe, or grateful. Or maybe sick. Then the guard was reaching in, doing something out of sight. Buckling the straps probably, buckling leather around a warm ankle and a warm forearm which had MOTHER tattooed on it, inside a heart.

Small had served two previous prison terms. He had compiled a police record beginning with a Utah car theft when he was fifteen.

Arresting officers testified that he confessed killing the two with a jack handle after Martin resisted Small's attempt at robbery. They said Small admitted flagging down the couple's car after raising the hood on his old-model truck to give the impression he was having trouble.

Should it be flagging down or just flagging? The wall clock inhaled electricity above Hardin's head with a brief buzzing sigh and said 12:32. How long had Small been dead now? Thirty minutes, probably, if cyanide worked as fast as they said. And how long had it been since yesterday, when he had stood outside Small's cell in death row? It was late afternoon, then. You could see the sunlight far down the corridor, slanting in and striped by the bars. Small had said, "How much time have I got left?" and Thompson looked at his watch and said, "Four-fifteen from midnight leaves seven hours and forty-five minutes," and Small's bony hands clenched and unclenched on the bars. Then he said, "Seven hours and forty-five minutes now," and Thompson said, "Well, my watch might be off a little."

Behind Hardin the teletype said *ding*, *ding*, *ding*, *dingding*.

SANTA FE . . . DENVER NOW SEZ WILL CALL IN 300 FOR OHIO PM WIRE SHORTLY. HOW BOUT LEADING SAD SLAYER SAMMY SMALL TODAY GRIMLY GULPED GAS. OR SOME SUCH???? . . . ALBUQUERQUE

The teletype lapsed into expectant silence, its electric motor purring. Outside, a car drove by with a rush of sound.

Hardin typed:

Small refuted the confession at his trial. He claimed that after Martin stopped to assist him the two men argued and that Martin struck him. He said he then "blacked out" and could remember nothing more of the incident. Small was arrested when two state policemen who happened by stopped to investigate the parked vehicles.

"The warden told me you was the two that work for the outfits that put things in the papers all over, and I thought maybe you could put something in about finding . . . about maybe . . . something about needing to know where my mother is. You know, so they can get the word to her." He walked back to his bunk, back into the darkness, and sat down and then got up again and walked back to the barred door, three steps. "It's about getting buried. I need some-place for that." And Thompson said, "What's her name?" and Small looked down at the floor. "That's part of the trouble. You see, this man she was living with when we were there in Salt Lake, well, she and him . . . "

Arresting officers and other witnesses testi-fied there was nothing mechanically wrong with Small's truck, that there was no mark on Small to indicate he had been struck by Martin, and that Martin had been slain by repeated blows on the back of his head.

Small was standing by the bars now, gripping them so that the stub showed where the end of his ring finger had been cut off. Flexing his hands, talking fast. "The warden, well, he told me they'd send me wherever I said after it's over, back home, he said. They'd pay for it. But I won't know where to tell them unless somebody can find Mama. There was a place we stayed for a long time before we went to San Diego, and I went to school there some but I don't remember the name of it, and then we moved someplace up the coast where they grow figs and like that, and then I think it was Oregon next, and then I believe it was we moved on out to Salt Lake." Small stopped talking then, and let his hands rest while he looked at them, at Thompson and him, and said, "But I bet Mama would remember where I'm supposed to go."

Mrs. Martin's body was found in a field about forty yards from the highway. Officers said the pretty bride had apparently attempted to flee, had tripped and injured an ankle, and had then been beaten to death by Small.

Subject: George Tobias Small, alias Toby Small, alias G. T. Small. White male, about 38 (birth date, place unknown); weight, 188, height, 6'4"; eyes, brown; complexion, ruddy; distinguishing characteristics: noticeable stoop, carries right shoulder higher than left. Last two joints missing from left ring finger, deep scar on left upper lip, tattoo of heart with word MOTHER on inner right forearm.

Charge: Violation Section 12-2 (3) Criminal Code.
Disposition: Guilty of Murder, Colfax County
     District Court.
Sentence: Death.

Previous Record: July 28, 1941, sentenced
    Utah State Reformatory, car theft.
April 7, 1943, returned Utah State
    Reformatory, B&E and parole violation.
February 14, 1945, B&E, resisting arrest.
    Classified juvenile incorrigible.
August 3, 1949, armed robbery, 5–7 years at . . .

Small had been in trouble with the law
since boyhood, starting his career with a car
theft at twelve and then violating reformatory
parole with a burglary. Before his twenty-first
birthday he was serving the first of three
prison terms.

Small had rested his hands on the brace
between the bars, but they wouldn't rest. The fingers twisted tirelessly among themselves. Blind
snakes, even the stub of the missing finger moving
restlessly. "Rock fell on it when I was little. Think it
was that. The warden said he sent the word around
about Mama, but I guess nobody found her yet. Put
it down that she might be living in Los Angeles.
That man with us there in Salt Lake, he wanted to
go out to the coast and maybe that's where they
went."

It was then Thompson stopped him. "Wait a
minute," Thompson said. "Where was she from, your
mother? Why not . . . "

"I don't remember that," Small said. He was
looking down at the floor.

And Thompson asked, "Didn't she tell you?"
and Small said, still not looking at us, "Sure, but I
was little."

"You don't remember the town or anything?
How little were you?" And Small sort of laughed
and said, "Just exactly twelve," and laughed again,
and said, "That's why I thought maybe I could come

home, it was my birthday. We was living in a house trailer then, and Mama's man had been drinking. Her too. When he did that, he'd whip me and run me off. So I'd been staying with a boy I knew there at school, in the garage, but his folks said I couldn't stay anymore and it was my birthday, so I thought I'd go by, maybe it would be all right."

Small had taken his hands off the bars then. He walked back to the bunk and sat down. And when he started talking again it was almost too low to hear it all.

"They was gone. The trailer was gone. The man at the office said they'd just took off in the night. Owed him rent, I guess," Small said. He was quiet again.

Thompson said, "Well," and then he cleared his throat, said, "Leave you a note or anything?"

And Small said, "No, sir. No note."

"That's when you stole the car, I guess," Thompson said. "The car theft you went to the reformatory for."

"Yes, sir," Small said. "I thought I'd go to California and find her. I thought she was going to Los Angeles, but I never knowed no place to write. You could write all the letters you wanted there at the reformatory, but I never knowed the place to send it to."

Thompson said, "Oh," and Small got up and came up to the bars and grabbed them.

"How much time have I got now?"

Small stepped through the oval hatch in the front of the gas chamber at two minutes before midnight, and the steel door was sealed behind him to prevent seepage of the deadly gas. The prison doctor said the first whiff of the cyanide fumes would render a human unconscious almost instantly.

"We believe Mr. Small's death will be almost painless," he said.

"The warden said they can keep my body a couple days but then they'll just have to go on ahead and bury me here at the pen unless somebody claims it. They don't have no place cold to keep it from spoiling on 'em. Anyway, I think a man oughta be put down around his kin if he has any. That's the way I feel about it."

And Thompson started to say something and cleared his throat and said, "How does it feel to—I mean, about tonight?" and Small's hands tightened on the bars. "Oh, I won't say I'm not scared. I never said that but they say it don't hurt but I been hurt before, cut and all, and I never been scared of that so much."

Small's words stopped coming and then they came loud, and the guard reading at the door in the corridor looked around and then back at his book. "It's the not knowing," he said, and his hands disappeared from the bars and he walked back to the dark end of the cell and sat on the bunk and got up again and walked and said, "Oh, God, it's not knowing."

Small cooperated with his executioners. While the eight witnesses required by law watched, the slayer appeared to be helping a guard attach the straps which held his legs in place in the gas chamber. He leaned back while his forearms were strapped to the chair.

The clock clicked and sighed and the minute hand pointed at the eight partly hidden behind a tear-shaped dribble of paint on the glass, and the teletype, stirred by this, said *ding, ding, ding.*

461

SANTA FE ... DENVER WILL INCALL GASSER AFTER
SPORTS ROUNDUP NOW MOVING. YOU BOUT GOT
SMALL WRAPPED UP? ... ALBUQUERQUE

Hardin pulled the carbon book from the typewriter and marked out "down" after the verb "flagging." He penciled a line through "give the
impression he was" and wrote in "simulate." He
clipped the copy to the holder above the teletype
keyboard, folding it to prevent obscuring the glass
panel, switched the key from KEYBOARD to TAPE, and
began punching. The thin yellow strip, lacy with
perforations, looped downward toward the floor
and built rapidly there into a loopy pile.

He had seen Small wiping the back of his hand
across his face. When he came back to the bars he
had looked away.

"The padre's been talking to me about it
every morning," Small had said. "That's Father
McKibbon. He told me a lot I never knew before,
mostly about Jesus, and I'd heard about that, of
course. It was back when I was in that place at
Logan, that chaplain there, he talked about Jesus
some, and I remembered some of it. But that one
there at Logan, he talked mostly about sin and
about hell and things like that, and this
McKibbon, the padre here, well, he talked different." Small's hands had been busy on the bars
again and then Small had looked directly at him,
directly into his face, and then at Thompson. He
remembered the tense heavy face, sweaty, and
the words and the voice too soft and high for the
size of the man.

"I wanted to ask you to do what you could
about finding my mama. I looked for her all the time.
When they'd turn me loose, I'd hunt for her. But

maybe you could find her. With the newspapers and all. And I want to hear what you think about it all," Small said. "About what happens to me after they take me out of that gas chamber. I wanted to see what you say about that." And then Small said into the long silence, "Well, whatever it's going to be, it won't be any worse than it's been." And he paused again, and looked back into the cell as if he expected to see someone there, and then back at us.

"But when I walk around in here and my foot hits the floor I feel it, you know, and I think that's Toby Small I'm feeling there with his foot on the cement. It's *me*. And I guess that don't sound like much, but after tonight I guess there won't be that for one thing. And I hope there's somebody there waiting for me. I hope there's not just me." And he sat down on the bunk.

"I was wondering what you thought about this Jesus and what McKibbon has been telling me." He had his head between his hands now, looking at the floor, and it made his voice muffled. "You reckon he was lying about it? I don't see any cause for it, but how can a man know all that and be sure about it?"

The clatter of the transmission box joined the chatter of the perforator. Hardin marked his place in the copy and leaned over to fish a cigarette out of his overcoat. He lit it, took it out of his mouth, and turned back to the keyboard. Above him, above the duet chatter of tape and keyboard, he heard the clock strike again, and click, and when he looked up it was 12:46.

McKibbon had his hand on Small's elbow, crushing the pressed prison jacket, talking to him, his face fierce and intent. And Small was listening, intent.

Then he nodded and nodded again and when he stepped through the hatch he bumped his head on the steel hard enough so you could hear it back at the railing, and then Hardin could see his face through the round glass and it looked numb and pained.

McKibbon had stepped back, and while the guard was working with the straps, he began reading from a book. Loud, wanting Small to hear. Maybe wanting all of them to hear.

"Have mercy on me, O Lord; for unto thee have I cried all the day, for thou, O Lord, art sweet and mild: and plenteous in mercy unto all that call upon thee. Incline thine ear, O Lord, and hear me: for I am needy and poor. Preserve my soul; for I am holy: O thou my God, save thy servant that trusteth in thee."

The pile of tape on the floor diminished and the final single loop climbed toward the stop bar and the machine was silent. Hardin looked through the dusty glass, reading the last paragraph for errors.

There was his face, there through the round window, and his brown eyes unnaturally wide, looking at something or looking for something. And then the pump made a sucking noise and the warden came over and said, "Well, I guess we can all go home now."

He switched the machine back from TAPE to KEYBOARD and punched:

SMALL'S BODY WILL BE HELD UNTIL THURSDAY, THE WARDEN SAID, IN THE EVENT THE SLAYER'S MOTHER CAN BE LOCATED TO CLAIM IT. IF NOT, IT WILL BE BURIED IN THE PRISON LOT.

He switched off the machine. And in the room the only sound was the clock, which was buzzing again and saying it was 12:49.

AUTHOR'S NOTE: Whatever the merits of "First Lead Gasser" as a short story, it is important to me. The incident it concerns happened (with "only the names changed to protect the innocent"), and it caused me to think seriously for the first time about writing fiction. The Thompson of the short story was the late John Curtis of the Associated Press. I was Hardin, then New Mexico manager of the now defunct United Press. Toby Small, under another name but guilty of the same crime, did in fact inhale cyanide fumes at midnight in the basement gas chamber of the New Mexico State Prison. Thus "First Lead Gasser" is more or less autobiographical. That alone is scant reason to present it to a magazine whose readers have come to expect mystery short stories.

What makes it important to me, and perhaps of some interest to you, are two facts. First, my inability to deal with the "truth" of the Toby Small tragedy in the three hundred words allotted me by journalism stuck in my mind. How could one report the true meaning of that execution while sticking to objective facts? I played with it, and a sort of nonfiction short story evolved. Second, Toby Small's hands on the bars, Toby Small's shy smile through the gas chamber window, and the story Toby Small told Curtis and me became part of those memories a reporter can't shake.

Those of you who have read *People of Darkness* met Toby Small under the name of Colton Wolf, reincarnated as he might have evolved if fate had allowed him to live a few murders longer. The plot required a professional hit man. Since it seems incredible to me that anyone would kill for hire, I was finding it hard to conceive the character. Then the old memory of Small's yearning for his mother came to my rescue. I think I did a better job of communicating the tragedy of Small in the book than in the short story. A quarter century of additional practice should teach one something. But I'm still not skilled enough to do justice to that sad afternoon, listening to a damaged man wondering what he would find when he came out of the gas chamber.

Chee's Witch

Snow is so important to the Eskimos they have nine nouns to describe its variations. Corporal Jimmy Chee of the Navajo Tribal Police had heard that as an anthropology student at the University of New Mexico. He remembered it now because he was thinking of all the words you need in Navajo to account for the many forms of witchcraft. The word Old Woman Tso had used was *anti'l*, which is the ultimate sort, the absolute worst. And so, in fact, was the deed that seemed to have been done. Murder, apparently. Mutilation, certainly, if Old Woman Tso had her facts right. And then, if one believed all the mythology of witchery told among the fifty clans who comprised the People, there must also be cannibalism, incest, even necrophilia.

On the radio in Chee's pickup truck, the voice of the young Navajo reading a Gallup used-car commercial was replaced by Willie Nelson singing of trouble and a worried mind. The ballad fit Chee's mood. He was tired. He was thirsty. He was sticky with sweat. He was worried. His pickup jolted along the ruts in a windless heat, leaving a white fog of dust to mark its winding passage across the Rainbow Plateau. The truck was gray with it. So was Jimmy Chee. Since sunrise he had covered maybe 200 miles of half-graded gravel and unmarked wagon tracks of the Arizona–Utah–New Mexico border country. Routine at first—a check into a witch story at the Tsossie hogan north of Teec Nos Pos to stop trouble before it started.

Routine and logical. A bitter winter, a sandstorm spring, a summer of rainless, desiccating heat. Hopes dying, things going wrong, anger growing, and then the witch gossip. The logical. A bitter winter, a sandstorm spring, a summer awry. The trouble at the summer hogan of the Tsossies was a sick child and a water well that had turned alkaline—nothing unexpected. But you didn't expect such a specific witch. The skinwalker, the Tsossies agreed, was the City Navajo, the man who had come to live in one of the government houses at Kayenta. Why the City Navajo? Because everybody knew he was a witch. Where had they heard that, the first time? The people who came to the trading post at Mexican Water said it. And so Chee had driven westward over Tohache Wash, past Red Mesa and Rabbit Ears to Mexican Water. He had spent hours on the shady porch giving those who came to buy, and to fill their water barrels, and to visit a chance to know who he was until finally they might risk talking about witchcraft to a stranger. They were Mud Clan, and Many Goats People, and Standing Rock Clan—foreign to Chee's own Slow Talking People—but finally some of them talked a little.

A witch was at work on the Rainbow Plateau. Adeline Etcitty's mare had foaled a two-headed colt. Hosteen Musket had seen the witch. He'd seen a man walk into a grove of cottonwoods, but when he got there an owl flew away. Rudolph Bisti's boys lost three rams while driving their flocks up into the Chuska high pastures, and when they found the bodies, the huge tracks of a werewolf were all around them. The daughter of Rosemary Nashibitti had seen a big dog bothering her horses and had shot at it with her .22 and the dog had turned into a man wearing a wolfskin and had fled, half running, half flying. The old man they called Afraid of His

Horses had heard the sound of the witch on the roof of his winter hogan, and saw the dirt falling through the smoke hole as the skinwalker tried to throw in his corpse powder. The next morning the old man had followed the tracks of the Navajo Wolf for a mile, hoping to kill him. But the tracks had faded away. There was nothing very unusual in the stories, except their number and the recurring hints that City Navajo was the witch. But then came what Chee hadn't expected. The witch had killed a man.

The police dispatcher at Window Rock had been interrupting Willie Nelson with an occasional blurted message. Now she spoke directly to Chee. He acknowledged. She asked his location.

"About fifteen miles south of Dennehotso," Chee said. "Homeward bound for Tuba City. Dirty, thirsty, hungry, and tired."

"I have a message."

"Tuba City," Chee repeated, "which I hope to reach in about two hours, just in time to avoid running up a lot of overtime for which I never get paid."

"The message is FBI Agent Wells needs to contact you. Can you make a meeting at Kayenta Holiday Inn at eight P.M.?"

"What's it about?" Chee asked. The dispatcher's name was Virgie Endecheenie, and she had a very pretty voice, and the first time Chee had met her at the Window Rock headquarters of the Navajo Tribal Police he had been instantly smitten. Unfortunately, Virgie was a born-into Salt Cedar Clan, which was the clan of Chee's father, which put an instant end to that. Even thinking about it would violate the complex incest taboo of the Navajos.

"Nothing on what it's about," Virgie said, her voice strictly business. "It just says confirm meeting time and place with Chee or obtain alternate time."

"Any first name on Wells?" Chee asked. The only FBI Wells he knew was Jake Wells. He hoped it wouldn't be Jake.

"Negative on the first name," Virgie said.

"All right," Chee said. "I'll be there."

The road tilted downward now into the vast barrens of erosion that the Navajos call Beautiful Valley. Far to the west, the edge of the sun dipped behind a cloud—one of the line of thunderheads forming in the evening heat over the San Francisco Peaks and the Coconino Rim. The Hopis had been holding their Niman Kachina dances, calling the clouds to come and bless them.

Chee reached Kayenta just a little late. It was early twilight and the clouds had risen black against the sunset. The breeze brought the faint smells that rising humidity carry across desert country—the perfume of sage, creosote brush, and dust. The desk clerk said that Wells was in room 284 and the first name was Jake. Chee no longer cared. Jake Wells was abrasive, but he was also smart. He had the best record in the special FBI Academy class Chee had attended, a quick, tough intelligence. Chee could tolerate the man's personality for a while to learn what Wells could make of his witchcraft puzzle.

"It's unlocked," Wells said. "Come on in." He was propped against the padded headboard of the bed, shirt off, shoes on, glass in hand. He glanced at Chee and then back at the television set. He was as tall as Chee remembered, and the eyes were just as blue. He waved the glass at Chee without looking away from the set. "Mix yourself one," he said, nodding toward a bottle beside the sink in the dressing alcove.

"How you doing, Jake?" Chee asked.

Now the blue eyes reexamined Chee. The

question in them abruptly went away. "Yeah," Wells said. "You were the one at the Academy." He eased himself on his left elbow and extended a hand. "Jake Wells," he said.

Chee shook the hand. "Chee," he said.

Wells shifted his weight again and handed Chee his glass. "Pour me a little more while you're at it," he said, "and turn down the sound."

Chee turned down the sound.

"About thirty percent booze." Wells demonstrated the proportion with his hands. "This is your district then. You're in charge around Kayenta? Window Rock said I should talk to you. They said you were out chasing around in the desert today. What are you working on?"

"Nothing much," Chee said. He ran a glass of water, drinking it thirstily. His face in the mirror was dirty, the lines around mouth and eyes whitish with dust. The sticker on the glass reminded guests that the laws of the Navajo Tribal Council prohibited possession of alcoholic beverages on the reservation. He refilled his own glass with water and mixed Wells's drink. "As a matter of fact, I'm working on a witchcraft case."

"Witchcraft?" Wells laughed. "Really?" He took the drink from Chee and examined it. "How does it work? Spells and like that?"

"Not exactly," Chee said. "It depends. A few years ago a little girl got sick down near Burnt Water. Her dad killed three people with a shotgun. He said they blew corpse powder on his daughter and made her sick."

Wells was watching him. "The kind of crime where you have the insanity plea."

"Sometimes," Chee said. "Whatever you have, witch talk makes you nervous. It happens more when you have a bad year like this. You hear it and you try to find out what's starting it before things get worse."

"So you're not really expecting to find a witch?"

"Usually not," Chee said.

"Usually?"

"Judge for yourself," Chee said. "I'll tell you what I've picked up today. You tell me what to make of it. Have time?"

Wells shrugged. "What I really want to talk about is a guy named Simon Begay." He looked quizzically at Chee. "You heard the name?"

"Yes," Chee said.

"Well, shit," Wells said. "You shouldn't have. What do you know about him?"

"Showed up maybe three months ago. Moved into one of those U.S. Public Health Service houses over by the Kayenta clinic. Stranger. Keeps to himself. From off the reservation somewhere. I figured you federals put him here to keep him out of sight."

Wells frowned. "How long you known about him?"

"Quite a while," Chee said. He'd known about Begay within a week after his arrival.

"He's a witness," Wells said. "They broke a car-theft operation in Los Angeles. Big deal. National connections. One of those where they have hired hands picking up expensive models and they drive 'em right on the ship and off-load in South America. This Begay is one of the hired hands. Nobody much. Criminal record going all the way back to juvenile, but all nickel-and-dime stuff. I gather he saw some things that help tie some big boys into the crime, so Justice made a deal with him."

"And they hide him out here until the trial?"

Something apparently showed in the tone of the question. "If you want to hide an apple, you

471

drop it in with the other apples," Wells said. "What better place?"

Chee had been looking at Wells's shoes, which were glossy with polish. Now he examined his own boots, which were not. But he was thinking of Justice Department stupidity. The appearance of any new human in a country as empty as the Navajo Reservation provoked instant interest. If the stranger was a Navajo, there were instant questions. What was his clan? Who was his mother? What was his father's clan? Who were his relatives? The City Navajo had no answers to any of these crucial questions. He was (as Chee had been repeatedly told) unfriendly. It was quickly guessed that he was a "relocation Navajo," born to one of those hundreds of Navajo families that the federal government had tried to reestablish forty years ago in Chicago, Los Angeles, and other urban centers. He was a stranger. In a year of witches, he would certainly be suspected. Chee sat looking at his boots, wondering if that was the only basis for the charge that City Navajo was a skinwalker. Or had someone seen something? Had someone seen the murder?

"The thing about apples is they don't gossip," Chee said.

"You hear gossip about Begay?" Wells was sitting up now, his feet on the floor.

"Sure," Chee said. "I hear he's a witch."

Wells produced a pro-forma chuckle. "Tell me about it," he said.

Chee knew exactly how he wanted to tell it. Wells would have to wait a while before he came to the part about Begay. "The Eskimos have nine nouns for snow," Chee began. He told Wells about the variety of witchcraft on the reservations and its environs: about frenzy witchcraft, used for sexual

conquests, of witchery distortions, of curing ceremonials, of the exotic two-heart witchcraft of the
Hopi Fog Clan, of the Zuñi Sorcery Fraternity, of the
Navajo *chindi*, which is more like a ghost than a
witch, and finally of the Navajo Wolf, the *anti'l*
witchcraft, the werewolves who pervert every taboo
of the Navajo Way and use corpse powder to kill
their victims.

Wells rattled the ice in his glass and glanced
at his watch.

"To get to the part about your Begay," Chee
said, "about two months ago we started picking up
witch gossip. Nothing much, and you expect it during a drought. Lately it got to be more than usual."
He described some of the tales and how uneasiness
and dread had spread across the plateau. He
described what he had learned today, the Tsossies
naming City Navajo as the witch, his trip to
Mexican Water, of learning there that the witch had
killed a man.

"They said it happened in the spring—couple
of months ago. They told me the ones who knew
about it were the Tso outfit." The talk of murder,
Chee noticed, had revived Wells's interest. "I went
up there," he continued, "and found the old woman
who runs the outfit. Emma Tso. She told me her
son-in-law had been out looking for some sheep,
and smelled something, and found the body under
some chamiso brush in a dry wash. A witch had
killed him."

"How—"

Chee cut off the question. "I asked her how he
knew it was a witch killing. She said the hands
were stretched out like this." Chee extended his
hands, palms up. "They were flayed. The skin was
cut off the palms and fingers."

Wells raised his eyebrows.

"That's what the witch uses to make corpse

473

powder," Chee explained. "They take the skin that has the whorls and ridges of the individual personality—the skin from the palms and the finger pads, and the soles of the feet. They take that, and the skin from the glans of the penis, and the small bones where the neck joins the skull, and they dry it, and pulverize it, and use it as poison."

"You're going to get to Begay any minute now," Wells said. "That right?"

"We got to him," Chee said. "He's the one they think is the witch. He's the City Navajo."

"I thought you were going to say that," Wells said. He rubbed the back of his hand across one blue eye. "City Navajo. Is it that obvious?"

"Yes," Chee said. "And then he's a stranger. People suspect strangers."

"Were they coming around him? Accusing him? Any threats? Anything like that, you think?"

"It wouldn't work that way—not unless somebody had someone in their family killed. The way you deal with a witch is hire a Singer and hold a special kind of curing ceremony. That turns the witchcraft around and kills the witch."

Wells made an impatient gesture. "Whatever," he said. "I think something has made this Begay spooky." He stared into his glass, communing with the bourbon. "I don't know."

"Something unusual about the way he's acting?"

"Hell of it is I don't know how he usually acts. This wasn't my case. The agent who worked him retired or some damn thing, so I got stuck with being the delivery man." He shifted his eyes from glass to Chee. "But if it was me, and I was holed up here waiting, and the guy came along who was going to take me home again, then I'd be glad to see him. Happy to have it over with. All that."

"He wasn't?"

Wells shook his head. "Seemed edgy. Maybe

that's natural, though. He's going to make trouble for some hard people."

"I'd be nervous," Chee said.

"I guess it doesn't matter much anyway," Wells said. "He's small potatoes. The guy who's handling it now in the U.S. Attorney's Office said it must have been a toss-up whether to fool with him at all. He said the assistant who handled it decided to hide him out just to be on the safe side."

"Begay doesn't know much?"

"I guess not. That, and they've got better witnesses."

"So why worry?"

Wells laughed. "I bring this sucker back and they put him on the witness stand and he answers all the questions with 'I don't know' and it makes the U.S. DA look like a horse's ass. When a U.S. attorney looks like that, he finds an FBI agent to blame it on." He yawned. "Therefore," he said through the yawn, "I want to ask you what you think. This is your territory. You are the officer in charge. Is it your opinion that someone got to my witness?"

Chee let the question hang. He spent a fraction of a second reaching the answer, which was they could have if they wanted to try. Then he thought about the real reason Wells had kept him working late without a meal or a shower. Two sentences in Wells's report. One would note that the possibility the witness had been approached had been checked with local Navajo Police. The next would report whatever Chee said next. Wells would have followed Federal Rule One: Protect Your Ass.

Chee shrugged. "You want to hear the rest of my witchcraft business?"

Wells put his drink on the lamp table and untied his shoe. "Does it bear on this?"

"Who knows? Anyway there's not much left. I'll let you decide. The point is we had already picked up this corpse Emma Tso's son-in-law found. Somebody had reported it weeks ago. It had been collected and taken in for an autopsy. The word we got on the body was Navajo male, in his thirties probably. No identification on him."

"How was this bird killed?"

"No sign of foul play," Chee said. "By the time the body was brought in, decay and the scavengers hadn't left a lot. Mostly bone and gristle, I guess. This was a long time after Emma Tso's son-in-law saw him."

"So why do they think Begay killed him?" Wells removed his second shoe and headed for the bathroom.

Chee picked up the telephone and dialed the Kayenta clinic. He got the night supervisor and waited while the supervisor dug out the file. Wells came out of the bathroom with his toothbrush. Chee covered the mouthpiece. "I'm having them read me the autopsy report," Chee explained. Wells began brushing his teeth at the sink in the dressing alcove. The voice of the night supervisor droned into Chee's ear.

"That all?" Chee asked. "Nothing added on? No identity yet? Still no cause?"

"That's him," the voice said.

"How about shoes?" Chee asked. "He have shoes on?"

"Just a sec," the voice said. "Yep. Size ten-D. And a hat, and—"

"No mention of the neck or skull, right? I didn't miss that? No bones missing?"

Silence. "Nothing about neck or skull bones."

"Ah," Chee said. "Fine. I thank you." He felt great. He felt wonderful. Finally things had clicked into place. The witch was exorcised. "Jake," he said. "Let me tell you a little more about my witch case."

Wells was rinsing his mouth. He spit out the water and looked at Chee, amused. "I didn't think of this before," Wells said, "but you really don't have a witch problem. If you leave that corpse a death by natural causes, there's no case to work. If you decide it's a homicide, you don't have jurisdiction anyway. Homicide on an Indian reservation, FBI has jurisdiction." Wells grinned. "We'll come in and find your witch for you."

Chee looked at his boots, which were still dusty. His appetite had left him, as it usually did an hour or so after he missed a meal. He still hungered for a bath. He picked up his hat and pushed himself to his feet.

"I'll go home now," he said. "The only thing you don't know about the witch case is what I just got from the autopsy report. The corpse had his shoes on, and no bones were missing from the base of the skull."

Chee opened the door and stood in it, looking back. Wells was taking his pajamas out of his suitcase. "So what advice do you have for me? What can you tell me about my witch case?"

"To tell the absolute truth, Chee, I'm not into witches," Wells said. "Haven't been since I was a boy."

"But we don't really have a witch case now," Chee said. He spoke earnestly. "The shoes were still on, so the skin wasn't taken from the soles of his feet. No bones missing from the neck. You need those to make corpse powder."

Wells was pulling his undershirt over his head. Chee hurried.

"What we have now is another little puzzle," Chee said. "If you're not collecting stuff for corpse powder, why cut the skin off this guy's hands?"

"I'm going to take a shower," Wells said. "Got to get my Begay back to LA tomorrow."

Outside the temperature had dropped. The air moved softly from the west, carrying the smell of rain. Over the Utah border, over the Coconino Rim, over the Rainbow Plateau, lightning flickered and glowed. The storm had formed. The storm was moving. The sky was black with it. Chee stood in the darkness, listening to the mutter of thunder, inhaling the perfume, exulting in it.

He climbed into the truck and started it. How had they set it up, and why? Perhaps the FBI agent who knew Begay had been ready to retire. Perhaps an accident had been arranged. Getting rid of the assistant prosecutor who knew the witness would have been even simpler—a matter of hiring him away from the government job. That left no one who knew this minor witness was not Simon Begay. And who was he? Probably they had other Navajos from the Los Angeles community stealing cars for them. Perhaps that's what had suggested the scheme. To most white men all Navajos looked pretty much alike, just as in his first years at college all Chee had seen in white men was pink skin, freckles, and light-colored eyes. And what would the impostor say? Chee grinned. He'd say whatever was necessary to cast doubt on the prosecution, to cast the fatal "reasonable doubt," to make—as Wells had put it—the U.S. District Attorney look like a horse's ass.

Chee drove into the rain twenty miles west of Kayenta. Huge, cold drops drummed on the pickup roof and turned the highway into a ribbon of water. Tomorrow the backcountry roads would be impassable. As soon as they dried and the wash-outs had been repaired, he'd go back to the Tsossie hogan, and the Tso place, and to all the other places from which the word would quickly spread. He'd tell the people that the witch was in the custody of the FBI and was gone forever from the Rainbow Plateau.

MARTIN H. GREENBERG has written or edited more than four hundred books, including *The Tom Clancy Companion* and *The Robert Ludlum Companion*. He lives in Green Bay, Wisconsin.

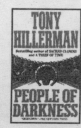

The Fly on the Wall

A dead reporter's secret notebook implicates a senatorial candidate and political figures in a million-dollar murder scam.

Skinwalkers

Three shotgun blasts in a trailer bring Officer Chee and Lt. Leaphorn together for the first time in an investigation of ritual, witchcraft, and blood.

Talking God

A grave robber and a corpse reunite Leaphorn and Chee in a dangerous arena of superstition, ancient ceremony, and livng gods.

The Ghostway

A photo sends officer Chee on an odyssey of murder and revenge that moves from an Indian hogan to a deadly healing ceremony.

Sacred Clowns

Officer Chee attempts to solve two modern murders by deciphering the sacred clown's ancient message to the people of the Tano pueblo.

Coyote Waits

When a bullet kills officer Jim Chee's good friend Del, a Navajo shaman is arrested for homicide, but the case is far from closed.